You like this, don't you?
You want me to fuck you so hard you forget you were ever his?
Turn the page and find out what it's like to be owned by me. —-
Vox Hatchett

TRIGGERS

Stalking
Dub con
Degrading
Forced Proximity
Bully
Humiliation

If you find something triggering that has not been listed please email authorsamanthabarrett@gmail.com. I do endeavor to include all triggers but what I may not find triggering others may so please be kind and reach out to me so I may include those triggers here rather than reporting to Amazon.

FILTHY FEW

DIRTY TEMPATION SERIES

BOOK I

SAMANTHA BARRETT

CHAPTER ONE

Nova

Moving to Hollow Hills wasn't something I was on board with, but I couldn't deny my mother the chance at happiness, and Thomas gave her that. He was kind enough to me, but it still felt strange being in his home and around his son, Nexus. Thomas and my mom married a couple of weeks ago, they chose to keep the ceremony small and intimate and held it in the Bahamas. I hadn't ever been on a plane until then. Nexus and I did manage to find some common ground and even got along. It made me feel less anxious about sharing a house with him and my new stepdad.

"I hope everything is to your liking?" I turn away from the window that overlooks the lavish backyard and smile at Thomas.

"This is the biggest room I have ever had, it's perfect. Thank you, Thomas," I say sincerely.

"I'm glad it is to your liking." I don't know what else to say so I just smile. Don't get me wrong, he is nice, but it's still awkward being alone with him and trying to find ways to fill the strained silence. "I had Lisa place your school uniform in the closet, Nexus will accompany you to and from school." I bite the inside of my cheek to keep from lashing out. Mom and I had planned to check out the local high schools next week and pick which one I would like to attend.

"I don't think Haven Hills is the school for me—"

"Nonsense, every Valerian goes there."

"I'm not a Valerian, I'm a Quinlin." At the mention of my last name, Thomas' eyes darken and narrow slightly for a second before he blanks his face and smiles. If I hadn't been paying such close attention, I would have missed it. He tried to convince my mother to change my last name and allow him to adopt me, but I put my foot down and so did my mom. I may not know who my father is or where the fuck he is, but I would never allow some strange man to erase a part of me without even having the chance to find out who I truly am.

"Your mother and I will be out this evening, Nexus and you will have the place to yourselves," he says before he leaves me standing here, staring after him. For the remainder of the day I try to brush off the weird encounter with Thomas but a niggling feeling in the pit of my stomach feels like it's trying to warn me that Thomas isn't a good man.

I shuck off the feeling and return to my task of unpacking and making my new room my own. It's going to take a long time to get used to having my own bathroom as well as a closet that is bigger than my last bedroom. How Thomas has managed to become this wealthy is a mystery to me. As I finish unpacking my last box, light tapping on my open bedroom door brings my attention to Nexus standing there.

His green eyes shine with mischief, and I can't help but smile at him. "Feel like causing some trouble?"

I beam up at him. "What did you have in mind?"

"I feel like being the big bad wolf and blowing some shit up, piggy." I scrunch my face and shoot him a loaded look.

"*Piggy?*"

He shrugs his shoulders, causing his black hair to flop forward onto his face. He brushes it back before smirking and shooting me a wink. "Get changed, *piggy*. We leave in half an hour," he calls out as he stalks away, then adds almost like an afterthought. "You're fresh meat, so don't let my boys fuck you." I jerk back and scoff.

As if I would let any of these preppy fools touch me!

Nexus drives us across town and I spend the drive gazing out my window, taking in my surroundings. Nexus wasn't pleased to see what I was wearing, but he doesn't get to tell me what the hell I can and can't wear. I have never been ashamed of my body, and I won't allow my new stepbrother try to make me feel differently about myself. Women are scrutinized enough as it is, we don't need some pigheaded male trying to control our wardrobe choices as well as every other aspect of our lives.

Plus, I think my outfit is cute. It may not be designer or a brand name like the clothes he wears, but I think it shows my assets. The skin-tight, dark wash jeans sit low on my hips, and the black cotton T-shirt I wear has a V-neck that exposes my ample cleavage. I have the shirt tied in the back to expose my toned stomach. I paired the outfit with Retro Jordan Ones and a black and white flannel shirt tied around my waist. My long raven hair is straight and loose. I don't really care much for makeup so I just applied some eyeliner and mascara to make my green eyes pop.

"My friends are off limits." I pull my gaze from the window to peer over at Nexus.

"What is that supposed to mean?" I ask as he parks the car, my eyebrows raising when I realize we're at the beach. I can see a bonfire in the distance and people milling about. The bass of the music and the laughter of the kids partying can be heard over the sound of the waves crashing against the shore.

Nexus reaches out and grips my chin between his thumb and index finger and draws my gaze back to him. "It means, Vox, Ezekiel, Hayze, and Archer are not making themselves at home between your legs." I reel back in disgust as I bat his hand away.

"I'm not some easy chick who spreads her legs for the fucking team." I cross my arms over my chest and slouch back in my seat, staring out the windshield. "Take me home, I'm not in the mood for this shit," I grit out.

"No can do. Either sit in here and pout or come make friends before school starts on Monday," he says as he climbs out of his fancy Audi. I ignore the asshole and watch him walk toward the party. Nexus is stopped at least five times by people wanting to say hi. I watch the girls flock to him and practically throw themselves at him. I scrunch my face in disgust. Why do girls always think portraying themselves as easy is going to get them what they want? Hey, they may get dicked at the end of the night, but that's it. They won't get a relationship or a ring.

I shake my head when I see some blonde in a gold sequin dress fake stumble into Nexus. She bats her lashes up at him and giggles. The sight of her in a pair of high heels in the sand has me scoffing and shaking my head. I step out of the car and shove my hands in my pockets as I head toward the fire. I can feel people staring at me and I know it's because most of them just saw me climb out of Nexus' car. I'm not deluded enough to think it's because they are curious about who I am or anything like that. It's clear to me that my stepbrother is some kind of king around here.

The crowd around the fire is giving off weird vibes; so I walk toward the water's edge and gaze out at the ocean, the moon is high in the sky and casting its reflection on the surface of the water, the sight brings a smile to my face. I have never been so close to the ocean before. Mom and I moved here from the city, where it was always loud and busy, but being here in Hollow Hills is a stark change. To be a short drive to the beach and able to have a bonfire without the cops turning up is not something I am used to.

"I'm assuming you're the sister that is off-limits?" I turn my head to the side to see a guy standing beside me—he's hot. His brown hair is windblown, the smile on his face is warm and his green eyes hold a kind edge to them.

"What makes you think that?" He jerks his chin to the side, and I peer over my shoulder to see Nexus standing in front of three guys. I can see he is angry from the way he is gesturing from them to me. My gaze is captured by the one standing in the middle, his hood is up and covering his face, but I can feel his gaze on me. Not wanting to be caught staring, I turn back to my new companion and snort. "He can take a tall glass of fuck off with a side of kiss my ass."

The guy chuckles and tips his bottle toward me before taking a sip. I can't help but stare at him. Unlike Nexus, who wears expensive clothes and struts around with an air of superiority, this guy doesn't. He seems laid back. His board shorts are faded, and the plain white cotton T-shirt he wears has a few blotches of paint on it.

"I'm Hayze." I nod, not offering him my name, which just brings a smirk to his full lips. He may be hot, but I'm not trying to complicate my life more than it already is.

"Catch you later, Hayze," I say as I turn to leave, but he

grabs my wrist, halting my escape. I look from his face to the hand that is on me, then back to his face with a glare.

"Don't let him push you around. He can come off as an asshole, but he's a good guy."

I frown as I yank my hand free. "I can handle Nexus and his tantrums."

Hayze shakes his head. "I wasn't talking about Nexus," he mutters, then stalks off toward where Nexus and the three guys are standing by the bonfire. I manage to catch a glimpse of the guy with the hood when he turns, the light of the fire illuminating his face, and I gasp—his blue eyes burn with such an intensity that it has my breath hitching.

"Turn away, girlfriend, he isn't worth your time, trust me." I tear my gaze from the guy and face the girl. My brows raise at the sight of her. She is fucking stunning. Her blue eyes are striking, and the black hair that frames her face only enhances their color. Unlike the other girls here, she isn't dressed to tease. Like me, she wears a pair of jeans, sneakers, and a tube top.

"I wasn't doing anything," I say in defense. She purses her lips and quirks a brow which pisses me off. "Who the hell are you anyway?" I snap.

She smiles and loops her arm through mine like we are old friends. I'm about to tear free of her hold until she starts talking. "The guy with the hood up is Vox Hatchett." *Vox.* That name suits him, he has a darkness to him, and the name fits his aura. "The guy beside him with the black hair is Archer Malik. The one on his other side with the blond hair is Ezekiel Tempest. You just met Hayze Draven, and rumor has it, you already know who the hell Nexus Valerian is." The distaste in her tone when she says my stepbrother's name draws my attention back to her.

"Not a fan of his?"

She scoffs and rolls her eyes. "I can't prove it, but I know for a fact he is nasty as fuck. There have been more than a few girls saying they have blacked out at a party only to wake up with his dick inside them and no idea how they wound up there." I jerk and scrunch my face in disgust.

"The fuck?" I grit out.

She waves her free hand. "Unless you are a Hatchett, Valerian, Malik, Draven, or Tempest, then nothing you say or do will ever touch them. They are the gods of this town and rule the school."

"How do you know this?"

She ignores my question and begins leading me toward the five guys who have a crowd of guys and girls forming around them like they really are Gods. As I look up, I falter in my steps when I feel Vox's gaze searing into me. As we draw near, I see the snarl on his lips, and the way he eyes me with disdain sends a shiver down my spine.

"You found my piggy," Nexus calls out when we stop a few feet away from them, drawing the attention of the crowd around us, who all laugh at their king's remark. I may not have seen it before, but I see it now, these five guys are royalty to their peers. Anything they say is law, and it makes me sick. I've met my fair share of assholes and know how they work. If they think I am intimidated by them because I didn't grow up with money and live in a lavish house like them, then they have another fucking thing coming.

I'll show them all that I bow to no one.

CHAPTER TWO

Vox

Vivian glares at Nex, I don't interfere, my boys know Vivi is off limits to any of our games, and if they so much as make her shed a tear, I will break their fucking necks. Everyone in this town knows she is not to be fucked with or touched by any cunt. Every guy here knows if they so much as look at her for longer than a second or utter her name in a way I don't like, they will end up with broken fucking bones. Like Chase, he is sporting a broken nose because he thought he was a tough cunt and said he wanted to ask her to Homecoming. He learned real fucking fast why everyone stays the fuck away from Vivian.

"The only pig I see here is *you*," Vi bites back. Nexus opens his mouth to argue, but Vivian turns her focus to us. "Meet my new friend..." She looks to the girl at her side waiting for her to say her name, the raven-haired girl sighs and meets our stare with a bored look.

"Nova," she says, her voice is raspy and holds an edge of

annoyance. I run my gaze over her and take note of her style. Unlike most of the girls around town, she doesn't seem to give a fuck what anyone thinks about her. She's dressed for comfort tonight, not for attention.

Nexus steps in front of me, blocking the girl from my view. "Anyone who touches my new sister, they will have me to deal with." His declaration lacks heat. I scan the crowd to see half of the guys fighting back smirks. Nexus doesn't have the balls to back up his threat like I do. He doesn't like to get his hands dirty like the rest of us. Unfortunately for him, he needs to learn how to get down and dirty real fucking fast, or we will all go down together.

"You aren't my anything, asshole!" Nova grits out as she pulls her arm free of Vi's hold and steps into Nexus. I see his shoulders tense. Hayze and Archer both shift forward discreetly, ready to intervene if they need to. "You don't own me."

Nexus chuckles, but there is no humor in it. He reaches out and grips a strand of her hair, allowing it to slip through his fingers. "Correction, piggy, I do fucking own you. You're in my world now. Look around you, little sis. They are all here for us." He opens his arms wide and everyone around us begins to whoop and holler like a herd of fucking sheep following their shepherds lead.

Nova doesn't seem deterred or even put off by the fact that Nexus has the entire school body at his back.

"You think because you have all these fools falling for your bullshit that I'll bow down and take whatever you dish out?"

"That's exactly what I *know* you will do," he clips out.

She laughs humorlessly. She eliminates the sliver of space between them until her chest brushes against his. She reaches out and rests her forearm on the top of his shoulder in a bold as fuck move that has my brows raising in intrigue.

"Oh, Nexy boy, challenge a-fucking-ccepted. You have no idea how petty I can be. We could have been friends, but now you have just made an enemy out of the wrong bitch. Game on, rich boy," she spits out as she turns and saunters away. The crowd parts for her. We all watch her walk away, but I can't help but stare at her perfect ass.

"You can find your own way home, piggy!" Nexus shouts, her only reply is shooting him the middle finger over her shoulder, which has me chuckling. This girl has balls of steel. Nexus whirls around and scowls at me. We may be *friends* but it wasn't by choice. We are stuck together until I figure out a way to get us out of this shit.

"Something fucking funny?" he snarls, his tone has my lip twitching. I take a step forward but I'm stopped when Vivi cuts in the middle, giving Nex her back as she stares up at me with a pleading look.

"Vox, please." I grind my teeth in irritation, knowing exactly what she is asking. I want to finish what I started with Nexus, but I know it will ruin everything if I smash his smug fucking face in.

"Let's go," I grit out as I snag her hand and drag her toward my car. I can tell the guys are following behind me. I don't need to look back to know Nexus is staying where he is. Without me, Ez, Hayze, and Archer at the party, he'll have every piece of pussy at his beck and call. I pull my keys from my pocket and click the beeper. My Dodge Hellcat's lights flash as the locks disengage. I release Vivi's hand so she can climb in as I get behind the wheel, Hayze, Ez, and Archer climb in the back.

They never question my reasons or motives, these guys are my brothers, and we have proven that time and again that we are loyal. When one of us fights we all fight, no questions asked. We never leave a brother behind, it's always been our code even before we were inducted.

I start the engine and smirk at the sound of the 6.2L Hemi SRT Demon V8 engine—the Hellcat and my Challenger Demon are my most favorite cars. The Demon is faster, but I only bring that bad bitch out on nights I want to fuck shit up. I spin the back tires as I plant my foot, making sure that I have everyone's attention as we peel out of the lot just to fuck with Nexus.

"Okay, Vin Diesel, calm the hell down and look for Nova." I say nothing in reply to Vi. The only reason I am leaving the party is because Vivian never makes friends or even wants to. She's afraid people are only using her to get closer to me and the guys, so the fact she cares enough to go after this girl means something to her, which is why I am now pulling over near where Nova is leaning against the bus stop with her phone in her hand. She snaps her head up when I roll to a stop beside her. Vi leans over me and pushes the button to slide the window down. I keep my gaze ahead not wanting to look at the little troublemaker.

"Get in, loser, you're coming with us." I see Nova shake her head out of the corner of my eye, then feel Vivian sag in disappointment. I grit my teeth and turn to the girl, her eyes dart to mine instantly.

"Get in the fucking car," I growl, causing her brows to raise.

"Say please, and I'll think about it." My nostrils flare in anger.

"Please get in the car, we'll take you home," Vi says in a placating tone. I watch the witch's shoulders sag as she nods. She moves to the back door, and the instant she pulls it open, Hayze doesn't give her a chance to back out. He grips her waist and hoists her inside the car, ignoring her protests as he sits her on his lap while he yanks the door closed. She reaches for the handle to get out, so I push Vi back in her seat and plant my foot.

"I will break your fucking nose if you don't get your hands off me!" she shouts. I flick my gaze to the rearview mirror, watching as Hayze lifts his hands as if surrendering. Ezekiel doesn't look comfortable sitting in the middle, but doesn't complain, he never does. Archer just looks like he's trying not to laugh at this situation.

"Calm down, sugar, we aren't going to hurt you," Hayze says.

"Oh, right, so kidnapping is normal in this fucking town?" she bites back.

"I'm sorry, this was my idea. I didn't want you walking home alone," Vivi says as she peers back at Nova. I white knuckle the steering wheel, hating the sound of uncertainty in her voice.

I hear the witch sigh in the backseat, the hard edges of her face begin to smooth out when she looks at Vi. "Thank you, that was... nice of you." I can tell she doesn't mean a word she says and is saying that to be nice for Vivian's sake.

"I swear we aren't assholes like Nexus." I shoot her a look, telling her without words to keep her mouth shut, she knows no one can know who we are, and outing Nexus means outing the rest of us. "Anyway, Nova meet Archer, Ezekiel and Hayze." Nova looks at each of them but doesn't so much as crack a smile. "This big angry asshole here," Vi says, patting my arm, "is my twin brother, Vox." Her brows raise in surprise.

"You're twins?" She sounds surprised.

"Yeah, but obvs I am the better looking twin," my sister says, earning a glare from me. The guys snicker in the back seat which has a smile spreading across Nova's face.

"Of course," the witch says, making my boys laugh. I growl and take the next turn hard so she slams into the door. "Dick." I hear her mutter as she rights herself on Hayze's lap, the sight of him placing his hands on her hips has me gripping the wheel tighter.

"So, I'm guessing you will be attending Haven Prep?" Vi asks her, the hopeful lilt in her tone has guilt swirling inside me.

"I guess so." Nova sounds bitter about it.

"Hey, don't worry you can hang out with us—"

"No offense but I'll pass." I'm about to rip the bitch a new one when Vi's face falls, but she pushes on. "I don't want to hang out anywhere near my new asshole stepbrother but if you want to kick it somewhere else, I'm down," she says with a shrug, making my sister's face light up.

"Totally, having you at school is going to be so much fun, I can tell already."

"What makes you say that?" Nova asks Vi.

"Call it intuition. I can tell you are going to shake things up around here, Nova, and I am totally fucking here for it!"

CHAPTER THREE

NOVA

To my utter shock Vox parks in the driveway next to my new house and kills the engine as Vi announces that this is their house. I don't comment as I climb off Hayze's lap and out of the car. I call out my thanks for the ride and try to escape back to my house, but I'm yanked backward by my arm. I spin around ready to fight but when I slam into Vox's chest I'm rendered immobile, his blue eyes pierce me and hold me captive. Vivian's plea for him to let me go falls on deaf ears when I see Archer wrap an arm around her waist to hold her back.

"You can fuck with Nexus all you want but you don't fuck with my sister or use her." His voice sends shivers down my spine, my body is flushed with heat from being this close to him. His eyes blaze with anger but I can't stop myself from drinking in his features, his cupid bow or the hard set of his jaw. I flick my gaze to see his hair for the first time now that his hood is off. It's long enough to be tucked behind his ears and is black as night.

"Your sister is the one who came after me, dickwad," I manage to grit out.

His eyes narrow. "Don't fuck with Vivian or you will have me to deal with."

My brows raise, I drape my free arm on his shoulder and press up onto my tiptoes. Rather than giving me the satisfaction of pulling back he remains still, I ghost my lips over his and hold his gaze as I speak.

"Don't threaten me or you won't like the raging bitch I become, Voxy." His eyes darken. Before he can say or do anything, I place a chaste kiss to his lips, shocking not only him, but myself. I then tear free of his hold and dart across the lawn back to my house with his friend's laughter following after me.

"Game on for real, witch!" Vox calls after me as I step through the front door. I slam it closed and lock it. His words have a pit of dread settling in my gut, I think I have just made an enemy of the wrong guy and I don't know why the hell that thought sends a thrill through me. I race up the stairs to my room and lock the door in case Nexus thinks to come in when he gets home. I strip off my clothes, leaving me in nothing but my panties as I rummage through my drawers and pull out one of Waylen's old shirts and tug it on.

Sadness sours my mood. God, I miss him so fucking much.

I'm woken on Monday morning to the sound of my phone ringing. I'm not a morning person and it pisses me the fuck off when people smile and are happy first thing when they wake up. No one is fucking happy at the ass crack of dawn. I reach for my phone blindly and bring it to my ear without checking who it is.

"Someone better be fucking dead!" I grit out.

"Baby, that is no way to greet your man." At the sound of his voice, I smile and pop my eyes open. I stretch out on my plush bed and change the call to Facetime. The second his handsome face graces the screen I smile wide. "There's my girl."

"Fuck, I miss you!" I whine.

Sadness clouds his eyes at my words. "I know, same here babe, same here."

I change the subject, trying to bring the conversation back to a lighter tone. "What's been happening back home?" Waylen begins telling me everything that I have missed since the whirlwind wedding and moving across the country. Truth is, I don't care about anything that has happened since I've been gone, I just like listening to the sound of his voice.

"You ready for your first day of your rich school?" His brown eyes are alight with mischief. I groan and turn my face into the pillow. "Bring that beautiful face back here!" I turn back to the screen and glare playfully at him, Waylen is my best friend and my rock. I don't know if I would have survived middle school or even high school without him—he has been by my side through everything. He was there three years ago when mom first got diagnosed with breast cancer. She beat that fucker, thank God, but it was a hard time for me.

"I don't want to go." I pout at the screen, causing him to laugh and shake his head.

"Too bad, get that sexy ass out of bed and get ready for your first day."

"I wish you were coming with me."

A whoosh of air escapes him. "I know, me too. But, you are not going to sulk in bed and skip school. Get your ass up, go shower, then you can tell me all about your weekend." I do as he demands. When I enter the bathroom, I switch the camera off and start the shower as I tell him about the bonfire Friday night and how I spent the rest of the weekend holed up in my room, except for meal times—there I ignored Nexus and his attempts to try and speak to me. I tell him about what happened with Vox and how I kissed him as I dry myself. A look of hurt flashes through his eyes for a second before he quickly masks it. I turn my camera back on when I have my towel wrapped around me.

"What's wrong?"

He shakes his head. "Nothing." I don't call him on his bull-shit. "This Vivian sounds like our kind of girl."

I smirk as I begin doing my hair. "She is definitely not what I expected, that's for sure." It's true, I could actually see myself being friends with Vivian, she seems like a chick who doesn't beat around the bush and can't be fucked with drama.

"What are you planning on doing with your new harem?" I snort and shoot him a dirty look.

"Absolutely fucking nothing, but my harem doesn't exist. I just need to get through the remainder of the year, then you and I can fulfill our plans of traveling to Rome and touring the world." It's a pipe dream for sure but ever since we were little, Waylen and I made a pact that when we graduated we would say fuck it to college for a year and travel the world and we'd start our journey in Rome.

"I guess we should start saving for this trip, huh?" I laugh and nod as I start to get dressed. Waylen turns away from the camera and that is just another thing I love about him. I remain on the phone while I finish getting dressed and make my way downstairs. My mom kisses me goodbye and wishes me good luck, then chats with Waylen for a minute before saying bye and shooing me out the door. I expect to be making my way to the bus stop down the street but the sight of Vox leaning against his car with his arms crossed over his chest in my driveway has me slamming to a stop. I can't see his eyes, thanks to the sunglasses he wears. I run my gaze over him in appreciation, the uniform fits him perfectly—the white shirt is taut across his chest, and the navy-blue slacks hug his thick thighs. When he drops his hands back to his sides, it's then I notice that he has tattoos on the tops of his hands. I dart my gaze back to his face and my jaw unhinges at the sight of the ink on his neck. How the fuck did I miss that on Friday?

"Babe?" Vox frowns and then suddenly I remember Waylen, I tear my gaze from him and look down at my phone. Waylen's brows are bunched and he looks worried, I open my mouth to answer him but suddenly my phone is snatched out of my hand.

"Give that back, you asshole!" I scream as I jump for my phone when he holds it above his head. He turns the screen to him and I see Way's eyes widen at the sight of Vox.

"The witch is busy," he says, then ends the call... *My* fucking call, and pockets my phone. When I dart forward to grab it, he stops me with a hand around my throat. I still immediately and stare up at him. "Don't fucking push me, I promised my sister I would get your ass to school so get the fuck in the car, witch, *now*." I just stare at him, I have never had some guy lay their hands on me like this before, it's shocking and slightly... exhilarating.

He releases me, turns, and doesn't bother to look back to see if I'm following. When Nexus comes out the front door and beeps the key fob for his car, I decide to say fuck it and throw caution to the wind. I dash after Vox, feeling Nexus' glare on the back of my head the whole way as I slip inside the car. Once inside, I meet his gaze through the windshield and flip him the bird. Vox says nothing as he starts the car and reverses out, it's only when I look in the back I notice that we are not alone. Ezekiel, Archer, and Hayze are all sitting in the back, looking like they would rather be anywhere but in this car with me.

"Morning, sugar." Despite the look on Hayze's face, his tone is easy and kind. I shoot him a tight-lipped smile and turn back to stare out the windshield, suddenly feeling all kinds of out of place. Friday night proved these guys are gods among the living. Pulling up to my new school with them isn't going to make me popular, if anything it is going to put me in the firing range of every single female. I huff and cross my arms over my chest as I slide down in my seat.

"Sit the fuck up," Ezekiel snaps. I scoff but don't bother responding.

Fuck them!

"You have three seconds to do as he says, or I'll make you." I turn my head and glare at Vox.

"Fuck. You. Voxy." The last word has barely left my mouth before he yanks the wheel to the side. Gravel spits up from the side of the road when he slams on the brakes. I don't have any fucking time to prepare or defend myself before one of his hands is around my throat and the other is tangled in my hair. He uses his hold on me to yank me up. A whimper escapes me when I feel some of my hair rip out of my scalp. I try to bat his hands away but all it does is force him to tighten his grip on me so I can't take a full breath. "Get the fuck off me!" I grit out.

"You need to learn who the fuck is in charge here because it isn't you, witch. You survive for as long as I deem fit. You say anything to my sister and I will make you wish that you never survived coming out of your mommy's washed-up snatch." At the mention of my mom, I see red. I strike out and slap him across his face, keeping my shock from splaying across my face and school my features.

"Don't you ever speak about my mom!" I feel angry tears prick the backs of my eyes and force them to remain at bay. I will never give this bastard the satisfaction of seeing me cry.

CHAPTER FOUR

Vox

My cheek stings. I flick my gaze between the guys to see the three of them are just as shocked as I am that the bitch dared to touch me. I slowly turn back to face her and find nothing but defiance and hatred in her green eyes as she glowers at me. I yank her head back, she cries out as I push forward over the console and get right in her face. Her breaths are labored. Try as she might to hide her fear, I can see it in the depths of her gaze that she is terrified and I fucking love it.

"You ever touch me again, I will destroy you," I grit out through clenched teeth.

"Keep your fucking hands off me and never, ever mention my mom," she fires back.

"Shit, Vox, we need to move, Nexus is behind us." I look out the back window and mutter a curse at the sight of his emerald-green Audi drawing closer. I release her with a shove and smirk when her head bounces off the window. I slam my car into drive and plant my foot on the gas.

Me and the guys spent the weekend digging through the archives to figure out what the fuck is going on, we may be bonded but that doesn't mean shit in the grand scheme of things. Nexus isn't one of us and I will find a way out of this. I won't have mine or my sister's name tied to his or his fucking crook of a father. When we came up with nothing, we formed a new plan. A plan I know Nexus is going to hate. Before we became who we are now, we were once someone else and it's been far too long since we let our demons out to play. And, we plan to play with his new stepsister.

She is our way out. I have no idea how much she knows, but she is the only leverage we have and I plan to use the bitch and ruin any plan Nexus has for her. To the outside world, the five of us are tight, like brothers, but behind closed doors, Nexus is the odd man out. We don't condone any of his actions. He has always looked down on us since we were kids. This is the life our fathers chose and their fathers before them but unlike them, I lost my dad and I refuse to live my life like he did. I won't allow my sister to claim my place or our father's heir, I want her out of this life and I will do whatever I have to keep that promise.

I won't leave my mom or Vivian.

Archer, Ez and Hayze are the only ones I trust aside from my sister. They know why I want out and why I will never fulfill my oath to The Brotherhood. I gave my boys a choice to fall in line and follow the rules, or help me find our way to get our freedom from the life we have been forced into.

I pull into my usual spot and kill the engine. She reaches for the handle but I click the locks, keeping her where she is. She whirls around and sneers at me.

"Let me out of the fucking car, you asshole," she spits.

"You breathe a fucking word about—"

She cuts me off before I can finish. "I won't say shit, now let me the fuck out!" she yells. The second I click the locks, she shoves her door open and leaps out of the car, then slams my fucking door! I glare at her retreating back, she is going to pay for that fucking stunt.

"We going old school?" Ez asks. I meet his gaze in the rearview mirror and nod.

"I want her out of her mind and looking over her shoulder at every turn. We force her to ask the favor," I answer.

"How are we going to do that?" Archer asks with a hint of annoyance in his tone.

"When shit gets too much, my sister will tell her how to end her torment. The second she asks the favor of the *Filthy Few* she is in our debt. She will never know that she signed the contract with her tormentors. We will break her to get to him and she will be our ticket out of here."

"Let the games begin, brother," Hayze says with excitement in his tone.

As the lunch bell rings, Hayze, Ezekiel, Nexus, Archer and I all walk into the cafeteria—here we are united and a unit. No one can see the cracks in our foundation, we are master bullshitters. It's a trait I loathe but one I own without remorse. We all may wear the same uniform but none of us are the same. A hush falls over the room at the sight of us. My eyes immediately scan the room, hunting for the raven-haired bitch. My eyes twitch when I see her sitting with my sister, laughing at something Vi has said.

The second her laughter dies off, a frown builds on her face as she looks around the room, noticing for the first time the shift in the atmosphere. When she spots the five of us, her eyes burn with hatred. I smirk at the sight of the tiny orbs of fire in those big eyes. The five of us move toward the lunch line, everyone jumps to get the fuck out of our way. We get through unobscured by the others, then trays in hand, we head toward our normal table.

The moment the five of us drop our trays onto the table, Nova's gaze snaps up to meet mine. "What the fuck do you think you are doing?" she grits out through clenched teeth. I ignore her and claim my seat opposite the little shit.

"Don't make a scene, little piggy," Nexus warns before we are joined by the football team and cheerleaders. I can see Nicole and the other cheer bitches glaring at Nova who stares right back at them without backing down. I keep the intrigue from splaying across my face. I know it won't take long before Nicole and Megan snap, they can't stand not being on top. These girls are only good for a quick nut, they have let the five of us take turns on them and somehow think it makes them important or better than anyone else in this school. We know they want to wear the title of *girlfriend* but neither of them ever will—I've never had a girlfriend and have no plans to change that.

"Who is the gutter trash with you, Vivian?" Nicole asks in her annoying high pitched voice. Unlike my boys, I don't find the redhead attractive, every time I have slipped my dick in her snatch I've made her hold a pillow over her face as the sight of her plastic face makes me sick. My sister scowls up at the bitch. I may protect my twin from every male in this place but the females are up to her to control. If I step in, it makes her look weak and we can't have that.

Vi opens her mouth to answer but Nova beats her to it. She plasters the most fakest smile I have ever seen across her face and bats her lashes like a fucking idiot playing the part of a ditsy bimbo.

"Well, as of last night, I got promoted from trash to step-mom." Hayze and Archer both stare at Nova in surprise.

"Eww, so you're a whore," Pamela chirps in defense of her cheer captain.

Nova doesn't take her eyes off Nicole as she answers. "Nope, not a whore unless you count me fucking your daddy and becoming your step mommy?" The football team, Nexus, Hayze and Archer all lose it. Their laughter draws the attention of everyone in the room. I flick my gaze to Nicole to see she has turned a shade of red. Vi nudges Nova's shoulder in triumph, the sight of victory in the bitches eyes has me grinding my teeth.

"So you're just a homewrecker?" Ez cuts in, silencing everyone's laughter. Nexus shoots him a warning look to keep his mouth shut. Unlike Hayze and Archer, maybe even myself, Ezekiel Tempest doesn't conform to anyone's rules, he doesn't give a fuck about The Brotherhood. The only reason he answered the call is because we did. The bonus of being paid doesn't hurt since his father was murdered and left his mom alone to pay the bills. At least this way he can cover all the medical bills and keep a roof over their heads.

Nova snaps her head toward him. I expect her to fire back and shout and scream like most bitches would but instead she just stares at him as if trying to... see through him. Ez doesn't falter or shift his gaze from hers. I dart my gaze between them, ignoring the snickers and snide remarks of the cheer sluts. The pair seem like they are lost in their own world and it's annoying the fuck out of me—I hate not knowing shit. Vivi catches my attention, call it a twin thing or whatever the fuck you want, but I can tell what she is asking without words.

Are they having a moment? she asks. I shake my head,

denying her question. I can feel Ez's anger wafting off him from his seat beside me. He isn't someone who is easily ruffled. The fact Nova is just looking at him without saying a word and worming her way under his skin—. The moment is shattered when her phone begins to ring on the table, she tears her gaze from Ezekiel and looks down at the screen smiling.

"I'll meet you after chem," she says to Vivian as she snatches her phone off the table and snags her bag from the floor, then she stands and stalks out of the room without a backward glance. Her pleated skirt is short, a gust of wind would give anyone a view of her panties. The blazer she wears doesn't stretch across her ample chest so it's been left unbuttoned. I may want to destroy the little cunt but even I can admit that she is fucking hot and my dick wants inside that pussy.

"Can you try to tone down being a dick?" Vi snaps as she pushes back from the table and stands. Archer stares up at her but she ignores him as she shoots me an angry look, then races out after her new friend. I grip the edge of the table in a vice-like hold. Archer, Hayze, Ezekiel and I all share a loaded look.

The torture begins today.

I make my way to my next class with a smirk, the second I enter the classroom I spot her in the back scrolling through her phone. She doesn't even look up when a hush falls over the room as I make my way toward her. I stand before her bathing her in my shadow. She slowly lifts her gaze, running it up my body until she meets my eyes.

"Is this the part where you become my lab partner and warn me about how you and your little clique of friends are going to ruin my life and bully me every single day until I quit or move away?" Her assumption floors me for a moment but I don't let it show, it appears being her tormentors at school isn't the right approach, so I guess there is no warm up for her then. I shoot her a cocky smirk and claim the seat next her. She leans as far from me as she can while I pull my phone from my pocket and fire off a text to the group chat I share with my boys–the one without Nexus in it.

ME

We begin tonight.

EZ

No build up?

ARCH

I'm down.

HAYZE

Fuck yes!

ME

No, she doesn't get a warm up. I want pitch black, she needs to know who the fuck runs shit and it's time she learns.

I don't care if they agree with my call or not, Nova Quinlin is a means to an end. The fact Nexus is trying to hide his motives and play the part of bully, but not allowing shit to go further than he should, is the reason this needs to happen. She is a pawn in this game and it's time she learned how to be used.

CHAPTER FIVE

Nova

"Thanks for driving me home," I say to Vivian as she pulls into her driveway. She shuts the engine off and turns to me with a genuine smile.

"It's the least I could do after my brother and the guys were a dick to you at lunch. Was Vox nice in chem?" I debate telling her that he was a prick and constantly kept stabbing the side of my thigh with his fucking pencil but I choose to keep my mouth shut. I don't know what it is about her but I actually like this girl and I don't want my hatred of her dick-face brother to ruin our budding friendship. I can see her being one of those long-term friends, like lifelong.

"He was tolerable."

She purses her lips but doesn't comment. As I open the door to step out she stops me with her words. "Homecoming is in a couple of weeks, should we go shopping for a dress?"

I cringe, I hate school dances. "I don't go to—"

"We can go together if that helps?" The pleading tone of her voice has me slouching into the lush leather of her car seat.

"I've never gone to a school dance, normally Waylen and I blow them off." Her face lights up at the mention of Waylen.

"Is that the guy who called today?" I can't help the smile that crests on my lips as I nod. "Oh my God!" she screeches.

"What?"

"You have a boyfriend?" I open my mouth to deny her claim but don't get a chance when my door is yanked open and I'm tugged out of the car by my arm. I shove the fucker but his hold doesn't ease. Vivian rounds the car and smacks her brothers arm repeatedly until he lets me go. Vox keeps his glare on me. "What the hell are you doing?" she shouts at her brother.

"Get in the house, Vi," he snarls, I narrow my eyes at the bastard.

"Vox, I am not—"

"Get in the fucking house, Vivian, now!" he snarls. She jerks in fear and that shit pisses me off.

"Don't fucking speak to her like that, asshole!" I growl, his eyes narrow in rage and I relish in the sight of it. Vivian whirls around and faces me with a pleading look. I sigh and roll my eyes, it pains me to walk away from a fight but I do it for her, not wanting to make shit hard for her at home. "Fine, text me later," I say as I cross the lawn and head toward my new house. Don't get me wrong, it's beautiful and huge but it's just not me or Mom. We never needed lavish things. Thomas has a cook, pool boy, gardener and maid. I freaked out when I found the maid cleaning my bathroom on the weekend. I told my mom I didn't like it but she just said I would get used to it.

I can see she loves Thomas and I don't want to do anything to fuck things up for her but I can't be sure he feels the same way about her. I've barely made it two steps inside before I hear my mom calling my name and summoning me into the dining room. Yes, there is even a formal dining room here that is used for entertaining only, not family dinners.

Thomas sits at the end of the table with his laptop open, a frown tugging at the lines of his forehead. I look to my mom on his left who is sipping on a fancy looking drink with a little umbrella. I hate that I can see the look of uncertainty in her eyes. Thomas won't allow her to work because he says she needs to relax and let him take care of her, but she hates not being able to contribute.

"How was your day, Nunu?" I fight the eye roll at her nickname for me, wanting to unload all my problems of the day on her but I don't. I know she would take it upon herself to help me fix the mess I have made and that would take time away from her being with Thomas.

"It was good, I made a new friend."

Mom's eyes light up. "Tell me!"

"Her name is Vivian Hatchett–" When Thomas snaps his gaze up, I clamp my mouth shut, sensing a change in his mood. Mom follows my gaze and when he sees her looking at him, he softens his features and plasters a smile on his face. I can see through the fake mask but say nothing. Something is going on with Thomas and it's unsettling to say the least. I never got these vibes off him when he first started dating my mom but since we moved here, he has changed and not for the better in my opinion.

"They live next door, her brother is friends with your son." I fight not to cringe at him referring to Nexus as my brother.

"Who am I friends with?"

Speak of the devil and he shall appear.

Thomas smiles at his son as he saunters into the room, looking like a rotten brat as he smiles fondly at my mom even though I can see it pains him to do so. "Vox," Thomas answers.

"Ah, yeah, he's one of my boys," Nexus says.

"Nova was just telling us how she made friends with his sister," Mom says happily.

"I have a lot of homework to do," I say, ending the conversation. I choose to ignore the hurt look on my mom's face as I turn and flee from the room. The second I close my bedroom door behind me, I lock it, then lean my head against it. Today has been a fucking lot and I am mentally wrung out. I just want to crawl into bed and avoid everyone but given the fact I need to play catch up on my school work, I am left with little choice.

I've been combing over the text for my history class when a knock sounds at my door. I flick my gaze to the window and curse beneath my breath, I hadn't realized how much time has passed, it's dark out. I jump up from my bed and open the door, thinking it's my mom coming to tell me its dinner time but to my dismay it's Nexus and he's holding a tray with what looks like my dinner on it.

"Piggy, I have been instructed to deliver this to you and make sure you are okay." I reach for the tray but he shifts, then barges his way into my room while I glare at the back of his head. He places the tray on the edge of my bed, then peers at all the textbooks that cover the space. When he goes for my laptop, I dart forward and push him back. His laughter grates on my nerves. "That wasn't very nice," he scolds mockingly.

"I don't give a shit. Get the hell out of my room, Nexus, and stay away from me. Oh, and tell your stupid friends to stay away as well." At the mention of his friends his brows slant.

"What have they been doing?" I can't tell if the concern in his voice is genuine or not but I answer regardless.

"Being assholes. I have chem with Vox, gym with Ezekiel, math with Archer and English with Hayze. The bastards, tell them to stay away from me and quit being dicks, I don't need or want their bullshit in my life. As soon as this year is over, I will be out of here and out of the five of your lives!"

"You aren't going anywhere, piggy," he vows before storming out of my room and slamming the door closed behind himself. I stomp my foot and groan in anger, then check the time on my phone and groan. I guess Waylen is showering with me again tonight. He always calls at nine sharp on a Monday, no idea why but it has become our thing. I scarf down my dinner, then smile as my phone begins to ring at nine on the dot. I chat with Waylen as I lock my bedroom door and head into the bathroom. I flick the camera off as I undress and fill him in about the remainder of my day while I wash the bad juju from it away.

"What are you going to do?" he asks as I condition my hair.

"Ignore the fuckers and hope they forget I am the shiny new toy in town," I answer. I wait for him to respond but after a minute when he still doesn't, I push the glass door open and grit my teeth.

Fucking Nexus!

My phone isn't on the counter where I left it propped up. I dart my head back under the water to rinse the conditioner out so I can go after that asshole but the lights shut off. I'm not afraid of the dark but given the fact my stepbrother is clearly unhinged and has a death wish, I am worried about how much blood will be spilled tonight.

"I'm gonna make you wish your mother had swallowed you, you little rat!" I call out as I shut off the water and push the glass open. I reach blindly for my towel but grasp at air. A chill runs down my spine, if he managed to get in here to steal my towel then he definitely saw me naked and that doesn't sit well with me. I wring out my hair as best as I can with my hands and take a deep breath holding my head high as I step out of the shower and squint my eyes to see better in the dark. The chill in the air has my nipples hardening and goose flesh dotting my skin but I don't acknowledge it, I would rather freeze than give him that satisfaction.

An eerie feeling overcomes me as I step into my bedroom, I feel eyes on me. "Nexus, give me my phone and towel now or I will put my foot through your fucking windshield." I step further into the room and my senses become heightened as fear begins to worm its way through me. I stop next to my bed and I brush my thigh against the comforter to better orient myself with the room. I slowly scan the room and try to see clearly but the fucker closed my blinds blocking out any light from the moon.

I inhale through my nose and slowly creep toward my wardrobe across the room, taking it slow so I don't bang into anything. I feel the frame of the closet and exhale. Once inside, I reach blindly for a shirt or something, I refuse to turn any lights on to give the fucker a better view of my nakedness. As I reach out I still at the sound of the door clicking shut behind me. I feel him at my back and tense, my breaths turning ragged. I have two options, reach for the clothing or turn to face him head on.

My pride wins out, I drop my hand to my side and turn to face the fucker ready to tear him a new one but something is off. Nexus smells like fancy cologne and has an aura of arrogance that clings to him. The person before me smells like pine, cedarwood and... mint. I may not be able to make out any features but the dark shadow before me is definitely taller than my stepbrother. Dread pools in my belly, I am locked inside this tiny closet with a stranger. Fear urges me to curl into a ball and scream but my stupid fucking pride refuses to allow me to do either of those things.

"A favor is a debt owed." His voice is low and distorted, I can tell he is using a machine of some sort so I won't be able to recognize his voice. Still I begin to tremble with fear and to my utter disgust my body begins to heat. I have next to no sexual experience except Waylen. We both wanted to get rid of our V cards and decided to help each other out. It was awkward and we only did it a couple of times until we realized it wasn't worth risking our friendship over. "The *Filthy Few* will grant you one favor."

"I don't need anything from you, asshole. Get the fuck out of my room and house now before I scream." The last word has barely left my mouth before a large hand is wrapping around my throat. I claw at the fuckers forearm when he squeezes, not cutting off my air supply but restricting it. He leans in and I tremble when I feel the rough texture of a... mask. I can't make out what it is made of but his voice has dropped when he speaks against my ear.

"We are the *Filthy Few* and will be *forever filthy*. A favor is granted to those who ask, should you need it all you must do is ask." The bastard releases me with a hard shove. I stumble back and trip over my own feet, falling to my ass. I bat my hair out of my eyes as I gasp for air, the closet door is open and the bedroom light is on. My nakedness forgotten, I jump to my feet and race into my room, seeing the balcony doors are open and my room is empty.

He's gone.

I spot my phone on the bedside table and rush to retrieve it, but what lays under it catches my eye. I gingerly pick up the post card looking thing—it's matte black with the green writing.

Where they rest for eternal life is where a favor is asked.

The stone with the head is where you will be led.

*Be certain of the favor you ask, no second is
offered.
The debt will be collected when the favor is
complete.
A favor asked is a debt owed.*

A chill runs through me as I reread the words, I have no idea who the fuck that was but I am damn sure never asking anything of that creepy fuck. I toss the card into the drawer of my bedside table and force myself to forget about it as I lock my balcony doors and quickly get changed. There is no fucking way I am sleeping tonight. I'm tempted to call for my mom and force her to sleep with me but I won't put her in danger if that fucker comes back. Instead, I facetime Waylen and make him stay on the phone with me until one of us falls asleep.

CHAPTER SIX

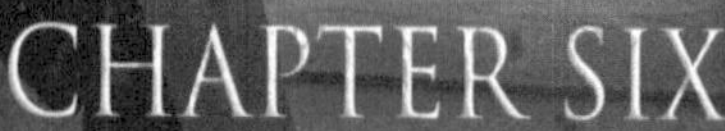

Vox

The instant the witch steps foot outside her front door and she sees my car idling in her driveway I smirk. Her upper lip pulls back in a snarl, then she squares her shoulders as if she is ready to go into battle. She takes a few steps toward the car but pauses when Nexus brushes past her, causing her brows to draw in at the sight of her stepbrother. He spins around and walks backward toward us as he shouts.

"Catch the bus, *Piggy*, we got shit to do." She doesn't answer him with words, instead she flips him the bird and marches back inside the house, something tells me she is about to fuck shit up for Nexus. He climbs in the back beside Hayze who sits between Nexus and Archer. Ez is riding shotgun with me. "Why the fucking rush man?" he asks as I peel out of his driveway and plant my foot.

"We've all been summoned," I say in response as I head across town, not even Nex seems happy about being summoned by The Brotherhood. We all try to avoid attending any of these things as much as we can—well, except for Nexus. He loves attending the galas and all the parties they throw at the surf and golf club. Unlike the four of us, he loves the limelight and being paraded around by his daddy. The music playing through the speakers becomes white noise as I get lost in my head. Since being inducted at eighteen, we have had no choice but to adhere to all the rules and make sure the school we attend conforms to the rules we set.

Never draw any attention to The Brotherhood.

All those inducted must remain in high standing with the community.

All school aged persons maintain an A average.

Only Ivy League colleges must be attended.

When the age of twenty-five is met, all must be called to serve.

None of us really know what we are expected to do once we reach twenty-five but all we know for sure is that The Brotherhood owns this place and most of the people in it. Politicians are a part of The Brotherhood and as decreed twenty years ago by Ezekiel's father, the next leader to be chosen for our generation would be a woman. As the Lord of The Brotherhood at the time, he wasn't able to be overruled.

Ez's dad was killed a couple of years after he was born, at the time we thought it was just a car accident but when my dad died in a similar situation, we began digging into everything our father's did and that is how we found out about The Brotherhood and the law Ez's dad passed. We made sure we did everything to get inducted. From the inside we plan to find a way to find out who killed our fathers and change the law so my sister doesn't ever have to be a part of this scum-infested society.

Every person has a part to play. We all have to pull together to ensure the survival of The Brotherhood and keep money rolling in to line the pockets of those before us. With mine and Ez's dad out of the picture, Thomas is now the Lord of the Haven Saints, aka The Brotherhood. I know for a fact Thomas has been trying to get Vivian and Nexus together for years, even when we were all kids he would say and hint at them being cute together. No woman knows about The Brotherhood. Vivian is the only female in our family line and therefore the oldest so she will be called to serve when she is twenty-five. The past four lords, sans Thomas, have been murdered. I will not allow my sister to suffer the same fate. Being a woman she will become a target, every money hungry, power wanting bastard will come for her. Not only that, if the Haven Saints have a job for you, any job, and you are assigned it, you must complete it. If you disobey a direct order from the elders or the lord, the punishment is your life.

I put the car in park in front of the town hall. To the outside world it looks like a normal hall, one that can be hired out for functions and host kids birthday parties, but beneath the building is where everything takes place. The five of us make our way inside and head toward the back. Archer pulls the side door open for us and we continue down the hallway until we reach the last door on the left. Nexus pulls the key from his pocket and unlocks both locks. Before opening it, he looks around and makes sure no one is following before heading inside and going down the stairs.

For a pack of rich schmucks, they should have just sprung for a new location. At the bottom of the stairs everything changes. Gone is the peeling wallpaper from the hallways and in its place is freshly painted walls and wooden flooring with chandeliers that light your pathway. Pictures of members line the walls as you make your way toward the grand room. I never look at them because I hate seeing mine and my dad's faces up there.

Hayze pushes the double wooden doors open and we all walk in—all eyes turn to us. The room is set up like a panel, a long table that spans the back of the room, each elder sits behind that table with Thomas Valerian sitting in the middle. He looks pissed off and annoyed about something when Nexus shifts so he is in the middle and standing a foot in front of us when we stop before them. I don't protest.

"We have a problem," Thomas spits out, the frown lines that mar his forehead tell me whatever this problem is he isn't happy about it.

"What is it?' Nexus asks, taking another step forward as if to show he stands on his own rather than with us. I refrain from shaking my head, this fucker went from being one of us to a suit-wearing fucking pussy as soon as his daddy took over as the Lord of Haven Saints.

"Someone has been blacklisting us and canceling our permits. We have the Governor's election coming up and our candidate is being stonewalled at every fucking turn."

"How is that possible?" Hayze mutters, drawing Thomas' attention to him.

"Find out! That's why the five of you are here. Figure out who the fuck is trying to sabotage us and take the fucker out with whatever means necessary." What Thomas means is kill the fucker. The five of us aren't the first to deliver this type of punishment and we won't be the last if this lot has anything to say about it. Unlike Nexus, the four of us are trying to find a way to shut The Brotherhood down or find a replacement for Vivian. The last time I put the idea of a replacement to Thomas, I was made to stand in the pit while the elders delivered their brand of punishment.

"Consider it taken care of," Nexus says cockily. With a bow of his head, he turns ready to flee but I see an opportunity I can't ignore.

"If this person is targeting our weak spots, then I request access to the Haven Saints records." Thomas' eyes blaze, he does a shit job of hiding his hatred for me. A lord is to be unbiased and fair to all his brothers but this cunt isn't. He hates that I best his son in everything and does his fucking best to make my life a living hell. He'll find a way to keep his precious son's hands clean of the killing of whoever the fuck is behind this.

"You have no need for those records—"

"Whoever is behind this clearly has knowledge of The Brotherhood and combing through those records may help us narrow down our search and be able to put this mess behind us faster, *Lord*." Ezekiel spits the last word like it burned his tongue. Before Thomas can answer, Elder Jamie speaks—his right hand man.

"Access granted, no book may leave the archives and no photos are to be taken." I nod my head and charge out of the room before Thomas can find some bullshit ass excuse as to why we can't access those records. He has been cagey about them for months and always finds an excuse to not grant us permission. The fact Jamie has allowed us entry means this problem The Brotherhood is facing is bigger than Thomas let on.

Once inside the car, Nexus turns to me with a sour look on his face. "I am not scouring through those dusty ass fucking books for hours, hoping to find a needle in a hay stack!" he snarls.

"Well, lucky for you, no one asked you to."

"Stay the fuck out of this, Archer," Nexus grits out.

"Fuck you, go find some poor innocent girl to date rape, you cock head," Archer claps back.

"Suck my nut sack, you cunt, take me back to my car, now!" I don't argue with the little bitch. The second I reach his driveway, he leaps from the car and marches toward the garage to get his Audi. I wait for Ezekiel to climb into the front seat before I back out and head to school.

"When do we start?" Hayze asks.

"Tonight. I need to find a way out for my sister. I won't let them blood her into this fucking bullshit." A shudder rolls through me at the thought of Vivi having to be blooded into The Brotherhood.

"They won't touch her," Archer says, trying to reassure me.

"Damn fucking right, because we are going to find a way to take them down and get rid of Thomas-fucking-Valerian once and for all," I vow.

CHAPTER SEVEN

Nova

I thought the day was off to a shit start when I saw Vox's car in the driveway, but turns out he was there for Nexus not me. Vivian gave me a ride in her luxurious Range Rover. I have no idea what it is with these kids and all their expensive cars but I saw an opportunity for a selfie and took it. I snapped a pic of me by Vivi's car and sent it to Waylen. Much like me, he didn't see the point of wasting money on a lavish car, we would rather save and put that money toward our trip. The day went amazing, I didn't have to endure Hayze or Archer's presence in math and English. I make my way to the gym feeling good about the day. I stop by my locker to drop my books off and grab my gym bag but when I open it, a letter floats toward the ground. I look around the crowded hallway but don't catch anyone watching me.

I pick up the black envelope and inhale sharply, praying it wasn't from my unwanted guest last night. With shaky hands I turn it over to see it is sealed with an old school seal, it has a T in the middle of the gold stamp. I open it and find a note inside, I unfold the piece of faded parchment and read the contents.

Nova-Scotia

Trust no one, they are hunting me, so I can't come to your aid yet.

Find a way to keep your head down. Your mother made a grave error marrying the slimy bastard. Never let your guard down around him or his vile son.

I will come to you when it is safe, I won't risk putting you in danger.

I reread the contents of the letter, trying to decipher if this is some riddle like the fucking postcard from that asshole last night but something inside me is telling me this is different. The warning about Thomas and Nexus sends a shiver through me. I scan the hallways again trying to catch a glimpse of someone or anything really. The sound of the bell ringing pulls me from my thoughts, so I return the letter to the envelope, stash it back in my locker and hurry to my gym class. I change quickly and rush outside to the track where everyone is gathered. My eyes narrow at the sight of Ezekiel, though unlike the other three, he doesn't stare at me or shoot me a dirty look in warning he just... ignores me.

The teacher begins explaining what is happening in this class but I can't focus on a word he is saying, between my visitor last night, the letter today and having Ezekiel in this class it is throwing me off.

"Hey." I shake my head and look to my left to see a boy with rugged brown hair and kind brown eyes looking at me.

"Hi," I say lamely.

His smile broadens. "I'm Lenny."

I return his smile, grateful not every guy here is dick. "Nova."

He nods. "I know, I'm pretty sure everyone around here knows who you are."

I draw back and frown. "Why is that?"

He shrugs as if it's no big deal. "Coming to school with Vox, Ezekiel, Hayze and Archer wasn't the best way to go if you wanted to fly under the radar. Every girl here hates you."

"What the fuck for?" I hiss trying to keep my voice low so we don't get in trouble.

"For being in the position they have all dreamed of being in." My spine stiffens as I slowly turn my head to my other side, I didn't even fucking hear Ezekiel make his way over here let alone know he was standing behind me.

I keep my features schooled. "Well, they can have it because I sure as fuck don't want it or anything to do with the four of you and Nexus," I grit out.

"You may not want it but you have it. When you want it, you won't have it." I stare up at him utterly fucking confused.

"You know that makes no sense, right?" I bite back.

"Quinlin?" I snap my gaze toward the front and smile sheepishly at the teacher who is glaring at the three of us.

"Yeah?" I wheeze out, trying to not sound guilty.

"Three laps, go!" My jaw unhinges at the fucker.

"It was my fault—" Lenny is cut off by the teacher.

"You can join her, Mr. Connelle." Lenny curses beneath his breath but doesn't answer back as we make our way toward the track and begin jogging. I don't hate running but I don't exactly love it either. When we are halfway around the track, I spot the football team training and can't help but stare when I see Vox and Hayze amongst the team.

"That's Haven Preps dream boy right there." I tear my gaze

from Vox's back as I look over at Lenny who looks almost angry at the sight of them.

"Who?" He pins me with a dry stare.

"Vox Hatchett is the guy every male wants to be and every girl wants to be under. He and his friends are the golden boys, no teacher here will do anything against them. They own the fucking school and the rest of us have no choice but to exist in their world."

I flick my gaze back to Vox and quickly turn away when I see him looking right at me. "I don't want to be under any of them," I mutter.

"Tell me that in two weeks when you see them all in suits for Homecoming." I ignore Lenny's taunt as I finish my laps. I would be lying if I said I wasn't picturing Vox Hatchett in a suit with all his ink on display, the thought of him dressed up and looking like a bad decision has my mouth watering and my panties soaking.

Fuck my life!

Rather than repeating the incident in the cafeteria, I texted Vivi that I was going to eat outside with Lenny, and to my surprise, she joined us. Lenny introduced me to a couple of his buddies, Ben, Tyson and Parker. The six of us are sitting on the grass in the quad, enjoying the sun and talking shit when a shadow suddenly falls over me. The conversation the guys were having stops, Ben and Tyson pale at the sight of the shadow behind me. I choose to ignore him and grind my teeth, ignoring them is going to be my new thing. The five of them think they can bully and intimidate me but they are fucking wrong.

I bow to no fucking man.

"So, do we have any classes together?" I ask my new friends, ignoring the presence behind me.

"They're about to have broken jaws if you don't get your ass up right now." I spy Vivian, out of the corner of my eye, climb to her feet and face her brother.

"Vox, cut it out. These are my friends and you are being a real dick, stop it." I appreciate her sticking up for me but even I know that her plea is falling on deaf ears. I want to drag this out and see what he will do next, but I also don't want Vivian arguing with her brother because of me. I shoot the guys a smile hoping to reassure my new buddies as I climb to my feet, I dust my skirt off and take my time straightening my shirt, feeling Vox's gaze on me the entire time.

I turn around and lift my gaze to his making sure he can see my inner bitch. "My ass is up, Voxy. What the hell can I do for the four of you assholes?" A gasp comes from our left, drawing my attention toward Nicole and her pack of bitches. Each of them standing there with their phones out like this is going to be the video to send them viral and finally give them the fame they all crave so desperately.

Vox pushes forward until his chest brushes up against me. I know he wants me to step back and cower beneath his angry glare but he has another thing coming, I'm not that bitch that will bow and suck a dick just to please some guy on a power trip. Instead, I crane my neck and smile up at him. Ez and Archer press forward, coming to stand on either side of him. I fight not to snort, it's not like he needs any back up.

I wait for him to berate me and cuss me out or whatever the fuck it is he is here to do but what I don't see coming is him reaching out to grip my hip in his large hand. I fight to keep the shock from splaying on my face as he leans down until his lips brush against my ear, sending a shiver down my spine that I know he didn't miss.

"Stay the fuck away from my sister, witch," he whispers, his voice is low but his words are filled with warning. Not one to go down without a fight, I throw my arms around his neck loving how he stiffens, I brush my lips against the shell of his ear as I answer.

"Scared your sister likes me more than you, Voxy, or are you just worried she will enjoy playing on the dark side with me?" His other hand grips the back of my head tangling in my hair, I bite down on my bottom lip to keep from hissing out in pain when he tugs on the strands. To everyone else we look like a loved up couple not two people at fucking war. My mouth parts in a silent gasp when he brushes his lips against the side of my neck.

"You just made this ten times worse for yourself, witch. You will be the one tapping out. Don't say I didn't warn you." He releases me without another word and stalks off, his three shadows all shoot me sinister smirks before following after their leader. Before I can stare after them and wrap my head around what the fuck just happened, Nexus is in front of me gripping my arms and shaking me.

"What the fuck was that?" he hisses low enough for only us to hear. I try to break free of his hold but the bastard just tightens his grip

"Get your fucking hands off me," I grit out.

Nexus darts his gaze around the quad, his features smooth as he takes in the crowd Vox and I gathered. He releases me and places his hands on my shoulders as if he is massaging the wrinkles out of my shirts.

"Stay the hell away from my friends, piggy," he warns.

"Fuck off, Nexus," Vivi grits out, then snags my hand and drags me away from my stepbrother. The cheer bitches don't shift out of our way. "Move!"

Nicole pays Vivian no attention, she looks directly at me

with a look of disgust plastered over her plastic face. "Stay the hell away from Vox—"

I cut her off before she can finish. "Bitch, please, you want him? Take him because he is the last guy I want on me or inside me." Vivian makes a show of gagging. I smirk at Nicole. "Here's a tip, you want Voxy warming your bed every night, maybe try not being a cunt to his twin sister."

"Like how you are befriending the school reject?" she claps back, without thinking I tug my hand free of Vi's and step into Nicole. Her eyes widen in surprise before she schools her features.

"The only reject I see here is you. Unlike your pack of mutts I don't have ulterior motives with my friendship with Vivian. I'd rather fuck her than her twin, that is where you and me are different." Just to be a bitch, I tap her on the nose with my finger, shoot her a wink, then shoulder past the bitch.

CHAPTER EIGHT

Vox

I have chem with the witch last period, if she thinks because that video of her sticking up for my sister is trending that I will go easy on her, she is mistaken. All she has done is painted a bigger target on her back.

"What the fuck was that?" Nexus grits out as he falls into step beside me toward last period.

"What was *what*?" I say acting dumb.

"Don't fuck with me, Vox. Your sister is off limits and so is mine." I whirl around on him and grip the front of his shirt, not giving a fuck that everyone in the crowded hallway is watching.

"Don't ever compare her to Vivian again, she isn't even your blood."

A wicked glint enters his eyes. "Maybe not mine but she is someone's blood." I release his cryptic ass with a hard shove and stalk off toward my last class. The second I enter the room I spot her in the back of the class in her usual seat. I smirk, I have to give her credit, I expected her to change seats and try to avoid me but she is proving to be a tough bitch to crack, never backing down and always rising to the challenge. I drop my books on the table, she doesn't flinch at the loud sound instead she just shifts as far away from me as she can.

I admit, I am finding it odd that she isn't throwing herself at me or my boys like every other cum guzzler here with a hole. The fight in her and the way she didn't back down today made my cock hard, I may just give her a pity fuck before I destroy her. I watch her from the corner of my eye and can see she is tense, I would even go as far as to say she seems concerned about something.

"Something on your mind, witch?" I taunt. She ignores me and continues to stare ahead, waiting for the lesson to begin. Not one to be ignored, I grab my pencil off the top of the table and stab it into the side of her thigh. When my pencil snaps, I turn to her and glare. A smirk tugs at the edge of her mouth.

"Tsk tsk, Voxy. Do you think I don't learn from my mistakes?" When she moves her hand to lift the side of her skirt up my brows raise, she has an exercise book taped to her thigh. My eyes narrow at the sight of it, two can play this game, witch. I toss my pencil on the top of the table. She smiles triumphantly until I lay my hand on the top of her thigh. She sits ramrod straight and snaps her gaze to me. "Get your hand off me," she hisses.

I cock my head to the side and lean in, brushing my nose along the column of her neck as I dip my hand between her thighs, allowing my pinky to brush against her panties. I even groan low in her ear when I brush against it again.

"I bet you would spread those creamy thighs for me if I told you too." She turns her head so her cheek brushes against mine.

"Miss Collier, Vox has his hand up my skirt!" I reel back with wide eyes, every set of eyes in the room is focused on us.

The little witch shoots me a wink before plastering on a frightened look for the benefit of the teacher.

"Mr. Hatchett, the principal's office, now!" Miss Collier snaps, I shoot Nova a look that promises pain and retribution as I stand and snatch my books off the table.

"You are going to pay for that," I grit out.

"Mmm hmm," she says as she waves me away with her fucking hand. We may get a free pass with a lot of shit at school because of who we are and what our last names are, but not even the school can overlook something like this. I won't be punished but to save face they have to act like I am going to get in shit. We're supposed to fly under the radar and not draw any unwanted attention to ourselves. I give it five minutes tops before every student's phone is blowing up with the news of what happened. Instead of going to the principal's office, I wait by my locker knowing my boys will be alerted and come looking for me.

Right on time.

Hayze and Ezekiel come around the corner a minute later, Archer comes barreling through the side door in his gym clothes with a dark look in his eyes. "She needs to be taught a fucking lesson," he growls.

I nod my agreement. "I want her in pain, scared of her own fucking shadow," I hiss.

"We bringing her down a peg or ten?" Ez asks.

"Hayze, fuck with my sister's car. Her and the witch are going to eat after school, I want her car to make it there and then as far as the woods before it breaks down." The three of them beam. Hayze rubs his hands together and starts walking backward toward the parking lot as he says, "Fuck yes, this is the shit I live for!"

"Come on, we need to get our shit but no one is to touch my sister, got it?" Archer and Ezekiel nod.

"How do you want her restrained?" Archer asks. I eye him when I hear a hint of concern in his voice, whatever he sees on my face has him adding, "Dude, where your twin is concerned you are a raging fucking dick, so I want you to spell it out for us so none of us ends up with a black eye or a broken fucking jaw like last time!"

"You shouldn't have touched her!" I snarl right in his face.

Archer throws his hands up exasperated with me but I don't give a fuck. "It was a pool party. I threw her in the fucking pool, dude. You broke my nose for that shit!" I shrug, not worrying to justify my actions as I head for my car.

"Just be grateful that's all you did to her or I would have killed you," I say without an ounce of remorse.

The four of us sit in my car across the street from the diner that a lot of the school kids go to hang out at. I drum my fingers on the steering wheel pissed off at the sight of Nova and Vivian sitting with those assholes from lunch, but the sight that has me seeing red is Ezra, Leo and James standing around their booth with a few others from the football team. I told those cunts to stay the fuck away from her and my sister.

"I'm going to break Leo's arm for touching Vivian," I force out through clenched teeth. He's touched her twice now, the first one I could let go of but the second, I won't.

"Break his fucking neck," Archer snarls from the backseat. I cut a glance to him in the rear-view mirror. He's glaring out his window at the group, his bloodlust is feeding the anger inside me and I revel in the feeling.

I don't need a shrink to tell me that I am a toxic fucker. I may hate The Brotherhood but I love the violence of it. The way they shred their enemies is something we are already accustomed to. Each of us loves getting our hands dirty but the problem we have with them is that they order it. None of us follow orders well. Even if we didn't have problems with The Brotherhood, we still would want to find a way out from under their rule.

"This is the first time I have seen Vivian smile freely like that in years," Ezekiel says—out of the three of my boys, he is the only one who dares to speak about my sister openly. I allow it because I know Ez loves her like a sister, but with Hayze and Archer I have seen them looking at her in an unbrotherly way and that shit is the reason why I broke Arch's nose.

"I know," I admit begrudgingly. Five months after we turned sixteen Vivian changed. She became depressed and withdrawn, she stopped smiling and hanging out with us, dropped off the cheer team. Her and Nicole used to be best friends and were thicker than thieves, but something happened to my sister and she still refuses to tell me what it was. She was a goddess at school, everyone wanted to be her but then suddenly she just stopped... caring.

"She is going to be pissed about what we have planned for Nova, you know that, right?" Ez asks as he turns to face me. I keep my eyes on the group as I ponder his question. I watch Nova throw her head back and laugh at something James said as I answer.

"The witch is her ticket to freedom, she'll get over it," I bite out.

"And if she doesn't?" Hayze claps back.

I white knuckle the steering wheel. "I'll deal with my sister —" The rest of my sentence dies off when I see Nexus' Audi pull into the parking lot. "What the fuck?" I mutter as I watch him park and climb out of the car. When the passenger door opens and I see Nicole climb out, I cringe in disgust when she wipes the corner of her mouth.

"Bitch can suck dick better than a hoover," Hayze says, the rest of us grunt in agreement. Nicole has had all our dicks inside her holes. She thinks as long as she rotates between the five of us that she is end game material. The bitch is delusional.

"What the fuck is he doing here?" Ez mumbles as he leans forward in his seat. We watch Nexus and Nicole stalk toward the back of the diner where Nova and the others are. When she spots her step brother, she clamps her mouth closed, crosses her arms over her tits and slouches back in the chair. The whole table seems to grow silent. I don't need to be inside to see that the tension among their little group must be high.

Nexus and Nova are clearly arguing from the way both their faces are pinched in anger. Nova's hands are cutting through the air violently. The moment Nexus grips her arm and pulls her to her feet I reach for my door handle, but Ezekiel snaps his hand out and grips the front of my shirt.

"Stay the fuck where you are, he's doing our job for us," he scolds. My chest is rising and falling in anger at the sight of him dragging her out of the diner. I watch my sister jump to her feet and attempt to go after her friend, but Leo wraps his arm around her waist holding her back.

"Fuck this, go after them and I'll get Vi home," Archer snaps as he leaps out of the car and races across the road. Nexus doesn't spot him running through the back door as he shoves Nova in the car and rounds the hood to get behind the wheel. I'm torn between going after my sister and finishing what I started, but the second Nexus reverses out of the lot, I see Archer swing a solid right hook to Leo's nose and cringe. He definitely broke that fuckers nose. He grips my sister's hand and leads her out of there. That is the only reason I go after Nexus because I know she is safe now.

CHAPTER NINE

Nova

"You ever lay your fucking hands on me again and I'll break your eye socket!" I scream at the bastard. His laughter just fuels my anger. I already have bruises forming on my arms from where he grabbed me today and the new one on my forearm is going to be on display tomorrow for all to see.

"Stop acting like a slut that the boys can run a train on and I won't manhandle your ungrateful ass."

"Fuck you!" I scream.

"I'm down." I reel back in disgust at his answer.

"You're fucking sick!" I spit out.

"You have no fucking idea, piggy, now shut the fuck up. I have a stop to make before we head home." I cross my arms over my chest and lean back in the seat, staring out the window trying to tame my anger. My phone rings in my pocket but I ignore it, knowing it's Waylen. The last thing I want to do is answer the phone and let him see the look on my face, he would know something is wrong and call me on it. "You stay the fuck in the car and don't move," Nexus grits out when we pull up in front of... the town hall!

"Why the hell are we here?" He ignores me as he climbs out of the car and stalks off toward the building. I wait till he disappears inside the hall before shoving my door open and climbing out. Fuck him if he thinks I would actually listen to what he has to say and wait for his entitled ass. I break out in a run across the parking lot and cross the road using the cover of the buildings to hide me. It's getting dark out and I know I don't want to be walking all the way home at night. I could call my mom but then she would ask questions, I'm no fucking snitch so I choose to call Vivian instead.

"Nova, are you okay?" she asks as soon as she answers.

"Yeah, hey, is there any chance you could pick me up?"

"Girl, in a heartbeat but my car is broken down on the side of the road. Archer is fixing it now."

I scrunch my face. "Archer's with you?"

She sighs. "Yeah, he showed up as Nexus was dragging you out and broke Leo's nose." For someone who was flirting with the linebacker she doesn't seem too put out about her brother's best friend breaking his nose. "I can't believe he did that to you!"

I tug the band from my hair and let it fall down my back as I continue walking home. "I'm not surprised. I think Nexus likes to think he's the boss when it's clear without him needing to even try who is the top dog." Vi snorts out a laugh.

"I should not be laughing at you calling my brother a dog," she says through her laughter. A breeze has my hair flying around my face and obscuring my view. I bat it out of my face and dart across the road, pulling my blazer tighter to shield me from the cold. Being in a skirt doesn't help but it's not like I have a fucking choice.

"Where are you?"

I look around trying to find a street sign but come up blank. "I don't know, I'm by the woods," I answer.

"Well, that narrows it down." I hear Archer mutter in the background.

"Drop me a pin to your location, Archer fixed the battery terminal."

My shoulders droop in relief. "Thank you, I'll send it now."

"See ya soon," she says, then ends the call. I do as she asked and send her my location as I wait on the side of the deserted road with my back to the creepy ass woods. A feeling of being watched sends a cold shiver down my spine, I shake out my shoulders trying not to dwell on the thought of being watched. My eyes skirt around as I wrap my arms around myself to ward off the chill that has seeped into my bones. I hear a branch snap behind me and my spine stiffens, I have seen enough horror movies to know if I turn around I will probably see something that will have me running and screaming.

"Deep breaths, it's probably just Nexus being a prick," I mutter to myself as I fake being brave and don't turn around, telling myself it's just my fear playing tricks on me. Then I hear rustling of leaves and I know for a fact that isn't my mind playing tricks on me. I peer over my shoulder and my eyes bug the fuck out of my head at the sight of two masked men standing there dressed head to toe in all black. Fear cripples me and my knees begin to shake. Both of them wear wooden, satanic looking masks. The one on the right has two horns on his mask with specks of blue through it, there is a carving in the forehead of it but I can't make it out.

When the one on the left cocks his head to the side as I look to him. Unlike the other guy, his mask only has one horn on the right and his mask has flecks of gray through it. Much like the other guy there is a carving in the center of his mask but I can't see it. Both the masks are eerie and designed to impose fear. The intricate carving of them has me intrigued but scared out of my fucking mind. I've heard of the standard Halloween masks and all that shit but these are so different, there is an aura of darkness that clings to the men and the masks—they aren't friends, they are foes.

Then it hits me, the guy with the mask in my room. I felt the rough texture of his mask scrape along my neck and cheek and I know with certainty that it was one of these creeps that broke into my house and tried to scare me. My phone begins to ring in my pocket but I'm too stunned to move to answer it.

"A favor is a debt owed," the two-horned guy says, his voice is distorted like the one from the other night.

I shake my head. "I want nothing from either of you, leave me the fuck alone!" I scream trying to fake braveness but even I can hear the quiver in my own voice.

One horn takes a step forward and I snap out of it. I step back, causing him to stop or risk me bolting like any sane fucking person would. "A favor can be granted to those invited, no favor is unanswered but the debt will be owed to the *Filthy Few*." I store that name away on the back of my mind to dissect later and look into it more.

"I don't want a favor. I don't need anything from you, now fuck off before I call the cops," I warn, the maniacal distorted laughter that comes from them both has me gritting my teeth.

"A favor is a debt owed," two-horns repeats.

"Fuck you!" I snap. When his body coils like he is about to charge at me, I make a split second decision. I turn to run but don't even make it a step when I see another masked person standing in the middle of the road, illuminated by the light of the street lamp. My jaw unhinges and I suck in a large gulp of air. This one has only one but on the left side. His mask is exactly the same as the others, except this one has flecks of green through the grooves of the wood. His relaxed stance and the way he just stands there staring at me without uttering a single word is unnerving and has my pulse thrumming through my body at a worrying rate. I look left and right trying to decide if I can make a run for it without these bastards catching me, when out of nowhere a hand wraps around me from behind plastering my back against a solid chest. Another hand comes up to grip my throat in warning, he doesn't apply pressure but he doesn't need to, the threat is clear.

"Ask the favor and it will stop until the debt is paid." I swallow audibly and close my eyes, trying to ward off my impending tears, I have never been this scared in my life. Behind my lids flashes of the faces of the two people I love most in this world can be seen—all I can think about is never seeing my mom or Waylen again, and that has a sob tearing out of me. Masked guy bends down and groans in my ear when the first tear rolls down my cheek. "Ask the favor—"

I shake my head ignoring the tears that flow down my cheeks. "No." I choke out as I blink my eyes open and see left horn and right horn standing a few feet away from me—two horns is clearly the leader of this sick fucking group! "Just let me go," I plead as I flick my eyes to the side, my brows draw in when I'm met with intense blue eyes staring back at me. His eyes don't scan my face or hold a hint of emotion, the void of everything except for retribution and malice.

"A favor is a debt owed—"

I cut him off before he can continue spewing the same fucking line again. "I know!" I scream right in his face, my fear has me in its clutches, forcing me to not listen to rational thought. "I have the fucking postcard. I have nothing to ask and I don't need any favors from you or your sick fucking friends." His hand around my waist shifts and glides along my stomach until he is cupping my pussy. My breath hitches as I jerk onto my tiptoes. I dart my gaze to his friends who stand there just watching, offering no form of help. I implore them with my eyes to help me and not watch their friend rape me. When he flicks my skirt up, I begin thrashing in his hold, swinging my arms and legs, trying to break free until his hold on my throat turns punishing and has me gasping for air.

"Ask the favor," he says loudly but then he drops his voice to a whisper so only I can hear. "They wear gloves but I don't."

My brows slam together in confusion. "I don't understand," I rasp out. He lessens his grip on my throat and I drag in lungfuls of much needed air.

"You get off on fear." I shake my head trying to deny his claim but he pushes on. "I felt how you soaked through your panties." I inhale sharply through my nose. "If the favor isn't asked soon, I will return just to play with my new toy."

"I'm not your anything," I grit out through clenched teeth. He pushes his hand under my skirt, forcing a whimper from me as he runs a single finger along my pussy. The distorted groan that comes from him has me hating my body's reactions to this situation and the fact that he is right, I can feel how soaked I am and it disgusts me.

"Ask soon or I will be forced to take what you are unwilling to give," he growls before releasing me and shoving me forward so I fall to the hard ground. I keep my head down and breathe in and out, listening to their pounding footsteps racing away from me—thank God. My blood is rushing in my ears as I try hard not to give into the black dots in the corners of my eyes and pass out. I see headlights out of the corner of my eye, then jump to my feet and dash into the middle of the road waving my arms forcing whoever it is to stop.

"Help!" I scream as the car skids to stop. Smoke clouds surround the vehicle and me from the sudden stop. Both doors open and I want to weep when Vivi rushes toward me with wide eyes filled with worry. Before she can utter a word, I throw my arms around her and hold her close, all the fight fleeing my body and I sag against her.

"Archer, help me!" she calls out, then in two seconds I'm pulled from her hold and scooped off my feet as Archer places me in the back seat. Vivian climbs in beside me and looks me over for injury. "What happened? You're pale as fuck and look like you have seen a ghost." I open my mouth to answer but clamp it shut when Archer puts the car in drive and plants his foot. I shake my head and flick my gaze toward the front hoping she understands that I don't want to say anything in front of him. She nods then reaches across and places her hand on my leg in a gesture of comfort.

I lean my head against the window and close my eyes, my heart still working overtime and I can feel the fear still lingering inside me. I have never been so afraid in all my life. I just want to go home, climb into bed beside my mom, then have her stroke my hair and tell me everything is going to be okay, it was just a bad dream.

I have a feeling those masked sicko's aren't done with me and will be back sooner than I want.

CHAPTER TEN

Vox

It's been two weeks since Nova Quinlin arrived in Hollow Hills and started Haven Prep. The guys and I have made sure to make her hate her life a little more each passing day. Archer torments her and destroys her books every math lesson. Hayze spreads rumors all throughout their English class that she has been blowing him after practice every day. I poke and prod her with my pencil in chem, yesterday I took it one step further and slid my hand between her thighs, forcing her to clench them. Given we had a test she couldn't call out for help so I had the entire lesson to tease her and brush my fingers over her pussy the whole class. By the end of it I could feel how wet she was for me. It gave me great satisfaction to watch her run out of class with her head down in shame.

Today though, Ezekiel took it a step further and loosened the top rope in the gym. I was shocked to hear that she nearly reached the top before the rope gave way and she fell. The whole school has been talking about it all morning and I haven't been able to stop myself from smiling at the thought of her screaming her head off and being in pain. She won't last much longer and soon she will be begging for the torment to end. I walk out of my math class and head toward the cafeteria to meet the guys. I head out the side door to go around the back of the building so I don't get in the throes of students, but at the sound of her voice I pause and slowly slink forward to peer around the corner, then frown at the sight of her being dragged against the side of the building by her arms as Nexus gets right in her face.

"Fuck off, Nexus," she snarls. I thought after her fall she would have been sent home but clearly I underestimated the bitch.

"Tell me which one of them did this to you?" he shouts.

"They didn't do shit—" Her words are cut off when he yanks her shirt up and I spy the purple bruise along her side and I have no doubt the rest is hidden beneath her skirt.

"I know they did this to you. Leo told me he saw Ezekiel go into the gym first thing this morning before school started and made sure you were the first to climb before anyone else!" Leo is getting more than a broken nose now, that fucker is getting nailed at training today. I'll make sure he can't finish out the season for this.

"Leo is full of shit, he just wants to get into Vivian's pants." My nostrils flare at the way this cunt is speaking about my sister. "He's lying because he wants to get back at Vox for making Vivi off limits to everyone. Easiest way for him to do that is to go for the kings' minions and cause distress from the inside. Now get the fuck off me, Nexus!" He growls right in her face then shoves her hard against the wall before stalking off. I wait till he disappears around the corner before making my presence known. She straightens her shirt and skirt, then winces as she bends down to collect her bag off the ground. When she straightens up and sees me standing there her eyes narrow and hatred wafts off her in waves. "You here to collect your blow job?" she spits.

I purse my lips and pretend to ponder her request for a second before shaking my head. "Nah, that's more of Hayze's thing." She rolls her eyes, flips me off, then starts walking toward the cafeteria. I eat the space up between us in two strides and fall into step beside her. She looks up at me in outrage, then slams to a stop. I peer down at her with a brow raised.

"What the fuck do you want, Vox?" I take in the sight of her. The dark circles under her eyes tell me she isn't sleeping well. I reach out and twirl a strand of her hair around my finger. A week ago she would have batted my hand away but she has learned that fighting back just makes shit worse for her not us.

"Why was Nexus hassling you?"

She snorts. "Because it's the little weasels M.O. Why the fuck do you care?"

I tug her hair and relish in the sight of her wincing in pain but she doesn't make a sound. "I don't, but the next time my sister's name comes out of your mouth like that, I will make sure that the rumors of you sucking my boy's cock aren't just rumors." She shoves me in the chest but I don't budge.

"Fuck you and fuck your stupid-ass friends."

"You want to fuck me?" Her nostrils flare in outrage.

"I wouldn't fuck you if you were the last person on earth!" she grits out through clenched teeth.

I lean down so my lips brush the shell of her ear. "Your pussy getting wet for me says otherwise."

"My pussy got wet for someone else the other night so don't think you're special." I pull back and stare right into those green eyes with a hint of yellow and ask.

"Got a secret admirer?" As if she has just realized her slip, she swallows and tries to act unbothered as she answers.

"No, just Waylen." She stalks off leaving me standing here wondering who the fuck this Waylen cunt is and where can I find the little bitch.

I'm sitting in the living room with Arch, Hayze and Ezekiel, waiting for Vivian to get her ass home so I can grill my sister. For the rest of the fucking day I have been trying to track down this Waylen cunt. If this little fuck thinks he can play with our toy he has another thing coming. Nova is ours to play with and torment, no one else gets to touch her.

"Nexus is starting to show his crazy," Archer says from his seat, his focus on the TV as him and Hayze battle each other in *Fortnite* like a couple of fucking twelve-years-olds.

"Why?" I ask.

He shrugs. "He's been to the hall four times since we last went. When I asked him about it he lied to my face and said he hadn't been back." I scratch my chin and lean back in my seat, mulling over his words.

"There is only one reason that little cocksucker would be lying and going back there without us." All three of them turn to me but it's Ezekiel who speaks.

"He's trying to find a way to change my father's ruling so he can take over." I nod my head somberly.

"He won't let us live if he takes over," Hayze adds.

"We need information on Nexus. I need blackmail material and there is only one person who can get that for us. I won't allow him to lead and I sure as fuck won't allow my sister to be blooded in." The three of them have angry looks on their faces at the thought of Vivian being blooded in. Unlike movies, you don't slice your palm and drip blood into a bowl then boom you're in. If it were only that simple. For the Haven Saints you have to walk the fucking line. Being a woman, they will make her strip and do that shit naked and bare for all to maim anyway they see fit. My father did it, so did Ez's dad and Thomas. Every Lord has had to walk the line and they have all wound up in the hospital for weeks after it—like fuck will I ever allow my sister to be put through that.

"You want to press Nova for information on her stepbrother?" Archer asks with his gaze now focused out the window.

"She has to know something," I bite out.

"What if she doesn't?" Hayze says.

I scrub a hand down my face. I have thought about that fact but living in the same house as Thomas and Nexus she would have to have heard something or seen something at the very least.

"We're about to find out," Archer announces. I frown at the fucker but I don't get a chance to question him, the front door opens and Vivian walks in with Nova. I smile at the sight of them both until I spot Nova's split lip and bruised cheek, her shirt is torn and covered in dirt and grass stains. Her hair is littered with leaves. I cut a glance to my boys asking them without words if one of them did this—they all shake their heads. We have fucked with her but none of us would ever go as far as to actually beat her.

"My room is the second on the right up the stairs, I'll grab some things and be up soon." Nova nods and keeps her head down, refusing to look at any of us as she follows Vivi's order. The second I hear my sister's bedroom door click shut, I leap over the arm of the sofa and dash into the kitchen after her with the guys trailing behind me.

"What the fuck happened?" I snap at her. She keeps her back to me as she rummages through the medicine cabinet.

"Stay out of it, Vox," she snarls as she retrieves the first aid kit and turns to face us with a hurt look in her eyes. "I asked you to back off and leave her alone. I told you she was my friend and now look what you've done!" she screams at me.

I reel back. "Vivian, I didn't fucking touch her!" I roar as I pound a fist against my chest.

"We've been here all afternoon since they got out of practice," Archer says, backing me up.

She shakes her head and sighs. "Yeah, sure." She brushes past us and goes toward the stairs but I dart in front of her, taking the stairs two at a time ignoring my sister's protest. I burst into her room and slam the door closed behind me, locking it. Nova whirls around with wide eyes in nothing but her bra and skirt.

"What are you doing here?" she asks dejectedly. I ignore her question, and the pounding on the door, as I take in the sight of the new bruises on her body. I saw the one on her side from earlier but the others are fresh, so are the bruises on her arms that were hidden earlier beneath her school blazer. I cross the room and stand before her. She doesn't flinch when I grip the tops of her shoulders and turn her, a hiss escaping me at the sight of boot prints on her back. I recognize the pattern, those are football cleats. I take a deep breath trying to tamper my rage as I turn her back toward me. I can see the unshed tears in her eyes and that sight has my anger spiking.

"Who. Did. This?"

She scoffs. "Don't try and act like you don't know. Message received, Vox." She pulls free of my hold and shakes her head, then snatches her shirt, blazer and bag off my sister's bed and heads for the door. She yanks it open to reveal Vivian and the guys standing there. My boys either don't register the bra or they are just too focused on the bruises that litter her tiny body. "You've all won, you got what you wanted."

Hayze jerks back. "Got what?" he slips out.

Nova scoffs. "At least have the decency to do your own dirty work next time and don't be cowards and cheap shot a girl from behind." She doesn't give them a chance to answer as she turns to my sister. "My mom and Thomas are out for the night and Nexus is away. Want to come help me at my house?" Vivian shoots me a death glare, then nods. The four of us watch the girls walk away and don't utter a single word until they are out of the house.

"I never fucking touched that girl!" Ezekiel vows.

"I would never," Archer tacks on.

"None of us did but I know who the fuck ordered her to be fucked with and who did it," I announce.

"Who?" Ez asks.

"Me and Hayze took Leo out for the season for snitching to Nexus. He is the one who would have put him and the others up to jumping Nova and pinning this on us," I answer.

"How do you know?" Arch grits out through clenched teeth.

"The bruises on her back, they are cleat prints. They would have jumped her after we left practice." I clench my fists at my side, trying to control my own anger. "They need to be repaid for what they did in our name, I want everyone who touched her out of this town."

"We can't get rid of Nexus," Hayze voices.

"No, but we can ice the cunt out. It's time he learns we aren't friends. I'm sick of saving face, it's time we show these cocksuckers that we are not theirs to order around. No more trying to find a way out for my sister. We have the knowledge of their crimes, we just need to find a way to dismantle them from the inside and blackmail each of them until they agree to our terms."

CHAPTER ELEVEN

NOVA

"Nunu, are you sure you're going to be okay on your own tonight?" I wince as I bend and retrieve my plate from the oven that my mom left me.

"Yes, Mom. You and Thomas just enjoy your night away. Nexus will be home in the morning." I hope she can't hear the loathing I feel toward that piece of shit in my tone. That fucker stood there against his car as three of the footballers beat my ass to a pulp until Vivian and Lenny showed up and saved me. I don't know how I am going to explain the bruises that cover my body and face when she gets back tomorrow.

"Well, that's the thing." The hairs on the back of my neck raise. "Nexus won't be coming back tomorrow." The tension flees my body at her declaration. "Thomas has some important business meetings and he would like us to stay here for a week." Hurt churns inside me, my mom is my rock and right now she is the only person I want but it's not like I can let her see me this way. I want her to be happy and if I have to put up with this shit for a few more months before I can leave, then so be it.

"Then stay, Mom. I'll be fine and Nexus and I can look after ourselves," I say, trying to reassure her.

"Nexus will be joining us, Nunu. Thomas wants to introduce him to these men he's meeting since he will be the one taking over for his father." Relief and anger thrums through me —that little cockroach gets to spend a week with my mom while I'm stuck in this fucking hell hole! "I left the keys to the Jeep on the hanger for you, I don't want you catching the bus anymore."

"Mom, I don't want Thomas spending that amount of money on me!" I abolish.

"I know but he insisted. He said he would feel better with you driving yourself around and not hitching rides." I snort.

"Yeah, sure." I sound bitter but I can't find it within myself to care.

"Are you mad at me?" The air whooshes out of me.

"No, Mom, I could never be mad at you," I mutter as I take the first bite of my beef casserole.

"I promise I will be back for Homecoming—"

I cut her off before she can continue. "Don't cut your trip short, I'm not going anyway."

"Nunu, you have to go!"

"Mom, you know Waylen and I never attended any dances and I don't plan to start now. Plus, he's flying in, remember?"

"Oh my goodness! I totally forgot about that." I roll my eyes. Mom and Thomas surprised me with this news last week. My new stepdaddy paid for my best friend's round trip ticket to join me next weekend. I sucked up my pride and thanked him for the gift.

"See, I won't be alone, so stay and enjoy yourself."

"Are you sure because I can come home—"

"No, stay and have fun and plus, that gives me heaps of

time with Waylen and you know I have missed him." I spend another twenty minutes talking to my mom, it feels good talking to her. Since moving in with Thomas she and I haven't had much of a chance to catch up or even hang out. When we say our goodbyes I clean up my plate and wince in pain. I take two of the pain pills Vivian left me and down them with a glass of water. Just as I am ready to leave the kitchen the power cuts out and I'm plunged into darkness. My breathing turns erratic for a minute until the power clicks back on. I sigh with relief and dash toward the front door to check it's locked, I double check the back one as well just to put my mind at ease.

I head back toward the staircase at the front of the house and pause when I see an envelope sitting in the middle of the floor that wasn't there a minute ago. Without overthinking it, I rush into the kitchen, grab the biggest knife I can find and return to the entryway. I dart my gaze around the area, keeping my wits about me as I crouch down and snag the envelope off the ground. I flip it over and frown at the sight of the *T* seal—like the one in my locker!

"Whoever you are, I am armed and dangerous!" I call out, waiting a few seconds and strain my hearing for any sound of someone being in the house, then look back to see the front door unlocked. I swallow in fear, whoever the fuck left this note behind must have snuck in when the power cut out, oh my God! I locked the doors which means I locked whoever it was inside with me. I quickly lock the door again and grit through the pain in my body as I take the stairs two at a time, rushing to my room. I slam the door closed, lock it and then shove a chair under the handle for good measure.

Sweat beads my brow and I swipe it away with the back of my hand, I turn on all the lights in my room, even my wardrobe and bathroom, checking every corner and under the bed just to make sure I am alone for real this time. I sent Waylen a quick text to tell him I will call him after my shower. I have avoided his calls all afternoon, knowing he is going to be asking questions when he sees my face and he is one person I can't lie to. He can see through my bullshit without even trying. I wish I could rid myself of the feeling of being watched but I can't, it feels like my skin is crawling and the only thing I can think to do is take a shower, wash away the day and pray that no more uninvited visitors make their presence known.

I feel somewhat better as I step out of the shower. I wrap my hair in a towel and wrap another around my body. I wipe the mirror to clear it of the steam and take a look at myself—my face looks like shit. The bruise on my cheek is more pronounced and the split on my lip looks better now but it still stings like a bitch when I move my mouth. I open my towel and inspect the bruises that mar my sides, I turn around and peer over my shoulder at the marks on my back and cringe. Not wanting to look further, I secure the towel around myself and step back into my room only to freeze at the sight of the blue-two horned masked guy standing in my bedroom like he owns the place.

"Seriously?" I shout, my anger overrides my fear and exhaustion at the sight of him. "I have had a shit fucking day and seeing you again after a week isn't making it better. I don't have a favor to ask and I don't want to be in your debt, so please... just go." I hate how defeated I sound but I'm way past caring what anyone in this fucking town thinks of me.

"A favor was granted." My brows slam together at his declaration. I take the chance of seeing him in the light to really take in the carving of his mask. In the center of its forehead is a carving of a tree and a headstone on either side of it, a shiver runs down my spine at the sight. His hands are covered by gloves and the hoodie he wears covers the skin around his neck, exposing nothing. "A debt is not owed for that favor."

I jerk back and shake my head to clear my thoughts. "What?"

He comes toward me slowly as if he is giving me the chance to flee should I wish to. I want to scoff at the thought. I have all the lights on in here and the door locked but it didn't stop him from coming in from the balcony. He keeps a sliver of space between us when he stops, my breaths turn shallow at his proximity.

I'm sick!

That is the only thing that can describe the reaction I am having to him, he has done nothing but taunt me and scare me out of my mind and yet here I am practically panting and wanting him to touch me. I've heard of women wanting a masked man to chase them through the woods just so they could be fucked against a tree like some dark romance book, but I never thought I would be one of those wanton bitches. Yet here I stand, wanting this masked devil to touch me and make me feel alive.

He reaches out and unfurls the knot in my towel, I don't stop him or even try to shield my body from his gaze as it drops to the floor. I cock my head to the side studying those blue eyes—they feel familiar yet not. I feel my body beginning to heat as he runs his gaze over me but when he grabs my waist I gasp until he turns me so he can take in the sight of my back. It's then I realize he isn't trying to check me out or fuck me but just wanting to check out the damage Leo, James and Ezra did under Nexus' order. Apparently Vox didn't like me telling him off and instructed my stepbrother to make sure I received my punishment, gutless fuck he is. He couldn't be caught because he would be kicked off the team if his coach found out.

He uses his grip on my waist to slowly turn me back to face him. A chill runs through me when I meet his gaze and see lust swirling in the depths of those blue eyes. I swallow audibly in anticipation.

"No debt is owed." His voice pulls me from my thoughts.

"What debt?" I rasp out.

"No more injuries will befall you, it has been taken care of." I dart my gaze between his trying to decipher his meaning. It takes a minute before it sinks in.

"Did you hurt Vox and his friends?" I snap as I press into him, clutching the front of his black shirt—I may hate the bastard and his goonies but that doesn't mean I want them hurt! His eyes narrow in suspicion and turn intense as he stares down at me.

"Is that the favor you ask?"

I shake my head. "No. I told you I don't want a favor and I don't want you to hurt Vox." I may not be able to see his face but I get the sense he is smiling at me. I steer the subject back to neutral ground not wanting to think about my fucked up situation with Vox. "You hurt somebody though... didn't you?" I keep my gaze on his, searching for any sight of deceit.

"Those who harmed you will no longer exist in your orbit." My features slacken as I grasp what he is saying.

"You hurt Leo, James and Ezra." It's not a question, just a statement. He doesn't justify me with an answer, he just stands there staring at me. "Why would you do that for me?"

"If an answer is what you seek, you will not be rewarded with an answer until a favor is asked."

I release my hold on him and step back but he doesn't allow me to move further, gripping the back of my neck to halt my movements. His hold isn't punishing or bruising but it's enough to keep me where he wants me, the material of his gloves scraping against my skin. I just stand here with my arms at my sides, naked and waiting like a wanton woman from one of those books that my mom reads. He takes a single step forward until his chest is flush against me, the heat from his body seeping into me. I swallow and suddenly feel like I have been zapped by an electrical socket with how wired I am. He uses his free hand to trail a finger from my throat to the center of my chest. I shiver in anticipation.

He continues his trail down my body, causing gooseflesh to erupt over my skin. My breathing turns ragged when he shifts slightly so he can watch as his finger slips through my folds, a gasp escaping me when he brushes against my clit. He uses that finger to circle my entrance—I can't find it within myself to feel shame at the wetness gathered there. Maybe he was right the other night when he said I get off on fear.

"All of this for me?" Even with that voice distorter I can hear the growl of approval when he brings his finger back to my clit and begins to circle it, forcing a moan past my lips. "An answer is owed," he snaps, then pushes that finger inside my pussy.

"Oh fuck!" I cry out at the feeling. I hear my phone ringing in the background but make no move to stop whatever this is to answer it.

"Answer!" he says loudly as his pace begins to pick up when he slides another finger inside me, scratching me to the point of feeling a slight burn but the pain mixed with the pleasure is oh so alluring and has me craving more. I grip his arms, needing the support to remain upright.

"Yes, it's for you!" Saying that aloud does make me feel ashamed. I turn my head to the side not wanting to meet his gaze.

"Good girl, you will be *forever filthy* after this night." I turn to face him and see nothing but approval in his blue eyes. A cry tears from me when he presses the pad of his thumb against my clit while still stroking that G-spot inside my greedy little cunt. My nails dig into his arms but he doesn't make a sound.

"Holy fuck."

"There is nothing *Holy* about this moment," he scolds. I press onto my tiptoes as I feel my orgasm cresting, while slamming my eyes closed, needing this release more than my next breath. I welcome the feeling and wait for it but the motherfucker pulls his fingers free. I snap my eyes open and stare up at him in shock with my mouth slightly ajar. "Remain on edge and you will be rewarded."

"Are you fucking serious?" I scream.

"Obey the command and tomorrow night you will be rewarded with the real thing." He doesn't wait for a reply as he heads toward the balcony, grips the railing and then leaps over the edge. I stare at the open doorway for a solid minute before I snap out of it, my anger rising. I don't bother closing the fucking doors because clearly there is no point, he will just find another way in. I flop on my bed and debate defying him but then I begin to wonder if he meant what he said. If I'm a good girl, he'll give me the real thing. Do I want him to fuck me?

Yes, yes, I fucking do and I know I will be dining with Lucifer when my time comes for the sin I am about to commit.

CHAPTER TWELVE

Vox

Mom and Vivian left this morning to go dress shopping for Homecoming, leaving me home alone. I'm tempted to go next door and pay the little witch a visit. I cross my room and peer out my window to see her blinds are still closed. My phone vibrates in my pocket, pulling my attention from her window. I fish it out to see it's Archer.

"Yeah?" I say as I answer.

"We're heading over. Hayze got all the files last night after we left yours."

"Sweet."

Before I can end the call he adds, "V, you aren't going to like some of this shit." My spine stiffens.

"Why?"

"You and Ezekiel's dad's murders aren't listed in the files under the death of members."

"Why the fuck not?" I snap angrily.

"We think they are trying to cover it up. I don't know man, we'll sort it out when we get there." He ends the call, leaving me standing here and reeling, then it hits me. They haven't got them listed because one of the members is the one who filled out the hit against our fathers.

I'll kill them all.

By the time the three guys walk through the front door, I have paced the length of my house at least thirty times trying to tame my anger. Ezekiel's face mirrors how I feel, he looks like he's on the verge of strangling anyone who looks at him wrong. Hayze and Archer both look pissed, unlike us, they both still have their dads. Since both mine and Ez's dads died, their fathers have pulled back from The Brotherhood, much like the four of us they were all best friends as well and have helped mine and Ez's moms raise us. I know this shit is hard, especially for Ezekiel. A year before his father died his sister drowned, she was just shy of a year younger than him and she was his world.

"I want answers today and if I don't get them I'm blowing that fucking hall up and killing all those cunts in it." Hayze, Archer and I all nod our agreement as we move to the sofas and take a seat. Hayze and Arch drop all the files on the coffee table and motion for us to start going through them, so we do.

My eyes begin to burn from reading all fucking day. I drop the file in my lap and groan as I rub my eyes and smack my cheeks to wake myself up. I look around my bedroom and cringe, when Mom and Vi got home we moved to my bedroom so Vivian wouldn't ask questions about what we are doing. Hayze and Archer are both crashed on the sofa in the corner of my room with papers scattered around and on the floor. I look to the other side of my bed to see that Ez's fallen asleep with his dinner plate, they brought us a few hours ago, still resting on his chest. I take the plate and gather the rest from around my room and go downstairs to wash up. As I'm finishing the last plate, something moving outside the window draws my attention. I place the plate in the drying rack and head out the back door, not turning the outdoor light on.

"No, I'm fine, like I said the rope in the gym broke and I fell." I creep closer to the edge of my house, all that separates Nova's backyard from mine is some waist high shrubs that Thomas has trimmed every week by his gardener. I wanted a fence but mom refused, saying it was a waste of money and now, I am inclined to agree since I have a perfect view of Nova walking around her pool in a pair of black booty shorts and an oversized T-shirt. Her long raven hair is piled on top of her head in a messy bun thing.

"Don't lie to me!" At the sound of a guys voice my eyes narrow—who the fuck is she talking to? Vivian did mention that she thought Nova had a boyfriend back home. I don't know why the thought of her being with another guy is making me so fucking furious to the point I want to break both their necks!

"I'm not!" she snaps in frustration. "I went to bed after my shower last night and forgot to call you." I smirk. "If you don't believe me, look up my school page on Instagram, the cheer bitches snapped pictures of me writhing in pain after I fell." I make a mental note to have Nicole take that shit down, only we get to fuck with Nova.

"Okay, I believe you." Her shoulders droop and she relaxes as she stops and flops down onto one of the loungers closest to me. She still hasn't realized she's being watched, stupid girl. "I can't wait to see you."

"Me too! God, I have missed you so much." Unable to stand here and listen to more of her bullshit, I stalk forward and break through the shrubs. She leaps to her feet and spins around, her eyes are wide with fright as I approach. I snatch the phone out of her hand and turn the camera to me, the guy looks just as surprised as she does at the sight of me.

"Who the hell—"

"Fuck off!" I growl as I end the call and toss her phone back to her. She fumbles a couple of times before she finally grasps it.

"What the fuck, Vox?" she snaps.

"Don't have a conversation outside then." My excuse is lame but fuck it.

Her face scrunches. "*You* came into *my* backyard, asshole."

I shrug. "Your point?"

"If I want to have a conversation out here or skinny dip I can and there isn't a fucking thing you can do to stop me—" Her retort is cut short when I wrap an arm around her waist and pull her to me, then smash my lips against hers. She gasps, giving me the opening I need to plunge my tongue inside her warm wet little mouth. She pushes against my chest but I don't budge as I flick my tongue across hers. Slowly she begins to relax as I continue to kiss her. The instant her eyes begin to close, I jerk back. She stumbles on her feet but quickly rights herself, then wipes her mouth with the back of her hand.

"You'll never be able to wipe the taste of me off you," I bite out, pissed off that she did that.

"Fucking males and thinking they have a right to touch what isn't theirs and leaving me on edge," she mutters to herself and winces when she presses a finger to the split on her lip, then pins me with a glare. "Fuck off, Vox. I have an appointment to keep and you sure as shit are not invited!" I watch her stomp her little ass back into her house and slam the door closed, just to make sure I know she is pissed, then she flips the lights off, plunging me into darkness. I smile as I make my way back to my house, but the second I step foot inside, I freeze at the sight before me. A guy in a hood stands there with a gun grasped in his hand and pointed at my head. I can't see his face so I shift to flick the light on but the cocking of his gun stops me.

"Don't touch what isn't yours, she isn't something to be played with." I narrow my eyes trying to get a better view of him but fail.

"You need to stay out of matters that don't concern you."

"She is my concern, you and your friends back off or I will be forced to intervene and not even your brotherhood will be able to save you from me." I still at the mention of the Haven Saints.

"No idea what you're talking about, asshole."

"Thomas has trained you well. Stay clear of the girl or I will take the head of the snake and yours." He keeps his gun pointed at me as he backs out of the room, leaving me standing here unable to do anything. When I hear the front door click shut, I run through the house and tear it open, darting my gaze around the street trying to catch sight of the fucker but I can't see him.

"Fuck!" I roar as I stomp back inside and slam the door closed behind me, then cringe when I remember everyone is asleep upstairs. Sure enough I hear the sound of pounding foot-steps and wait to see who it is—Archer and Hayze both come into view. I stab a hand through my hair in frustration.

"What happened?" Hayze asks, both of them darting their eyes around the darkened room.

"Some fucker was in the house," I grit out.

"Who?" Arch asks with a cold edge to his voice.

"I don't know, he had a hood on and a gun," I answer.

"The fuck, Vox?" Hayze snaps.

"He warned me to stay away from the little witch."

"Nova?" I can hear the surprise in Hayze's voice. I nod.

"I thought Nexus said it was just her and her mom, he never mentioned a guy in their lives." I nod my head, Arch is right. The little fucker never once mentioned anything about a male in their lives. I would go and question him myself but he's out of town for the week with his dad and Nova's mom.

"Looks like we have more work to do. This whole thing is becoming a cluster fuck and is doing my damn head in," I snarl. "We need to find out what Nexus and Thomas are hiding. We need more information on Nova because now I am more certain than ever that the little witch has information we need to take down her stepfather and Nexus." Both my boys nod their heads.

Game on little witch.

CHAPTER THIRTEEN

Nova

After nearly an hour of reassuring Waylen that Vox was just being a dick and wasn't a threat to me, I finally managed to get him to hang up and go to bed. I've now spent the past fifteen minutes sitting in the center of my bed, staring at the envelope from last night, debating if I should open it or not. The longer I stare at the freaking thing, the more my curiosity grows. I groan and give into temptation. I pop the seal and pull the letter out, purse my lips, then take a deep breath, bracing myself for more fucking riddles. I have no idea if the guy leaving these letters are the *Filthy Few* as two horns has been calling them or not, but the fact I have received a letter from him and two more since then, has me thinking it is likely him.

Nova-Scotia

Many would love to see you fall victim and land on the edge of their swords but,
I will not allow that to happen to my brother's daughter.

I drop the letter and scoot backward. I just stare at the fucking thing like it burned me. When I opened that letter I never expected to read that shit, I thought it would be more riddles not some declaration from my... uncle. Oh my God. I have a fucking uncle and he is the one who has been leaving me these notes! Shivers roll through me, I don't know who my father is, my mom told me he left when I was baby and didn't want anything to do with me, so why the fuck is his brother reaching out to me now?

Fuck it!

I reach for the note and take a deep breath before I continue reading.

Thomas is hiding a great secret, his idiot son wishes to lead the Haven Saints with your help.
To stop them you need to find the proof of the night your father died.
Your father made a grave mistake, he wanted all future sons to be free.
He never knew he would be graced with a daughter.
Don't hate him for making that error, find the proof.
I'm doing all I can to free you from this fate your brother suffers through.
When the time is right, I will come to you.

I don't know why in both letters he has left, he has called

me Nova-Scotia. I get that I shouldn't be so hung up on that part and more worried about the fact that he just admitted I have a fucking brother! I reread the letter a couple more times and allow his words to sink in.

I have a brother!

My father is dead.

I start to wonder what he looks like, is he like me? Is he older or younger? My mind is whirling with all these possibilities but they all come to a halt when I think of my mom. If I have a brother that means she either had another child I don't know about or my father had another child and I have a half-brother. I return the letter to its envelope and open my side drawer to hide it in there but freeze when I see the matte black postcard with green writing.

A favor is a debt owed.

I debate the idea of asking the *Filthy Few* a favor for the first time since meeting the masked man. If they can grant me the information I need about this Haven Saints thing, maybe I could use that information to find out who my brother is and who my father was. But, the letter said Thomas and Nexus have proof—I need to find that proof and figure out what part they played in my father dying. I close the drawer, flop back on my bed and try to sift through this new information.

My dad is dead.

I have a brother.

Thomas and Nexus have proof of his death, why?

What is Haven Saints?

What fate does my brother suffer?

I'm making myself crazy trying to piece everything together with sweet diddly squat to go on, but I can't seem to stop my mind from reeling.

How the hell did my life get so complicated?

Back home I never faced any issues like this. Here I am a

daily target for Vox and his friends. Nexus is a prick to me every single minute. I'm being taunted and stalked by a masked guy. I have an uncle sending me secret letters.

"Fuck me!" I growl into the empty room.

"That is the plan." I bolt upright and wince at the pain in my side, standing in the balcony doorway is my masked man. *My?* Since when the fuck is he mine? I mentally facepalm myself. I swallow trying to ease my nerves. He eats up the space between us and climbs onto my bed, kneeling beside me. I tilt my head back and stare up at him, I can feel my emotions warring within myself.

"Is this a favor?" I blurt, call me crazy but I can tell he's smiling even though I can't see his face, his blue eyes are so expressive and tell me everything his features can't.

"No." That one word seems like it pains him. He runs his hands up my legs, sending a shiver down my spine. When he reaches the bottom of my sleep shorts, he halts his movements and flicks his gaze back to mine. My chest is rising and falling in rapid succession, the anticipation of what is to come has me growing wet at the feeling of his hands on me. It's surreal to have such a reaction to him, I've never been this responsive to anyone—except for my daily tormentor but I refuse to admit that shit to anyone. "Take them off."

I nod and grip the waistband of my shorts. Just as I am about to push them down, I stop. "This stays between us... right?"

He cocks his masked head to the side studying me. "Who else did you invite to fuck you?"

My jaw unhinges and I scoff. "No one!" I shout then wince from the sting in my lip. "I mean, your buddies aren't going to show up and think this is a group thing and they can run a train or anything like that?"

His blue eyes darken as he stares down at me. "No one

touches you but *me!*" The conviction in which he says those words has me believing him. I dart my tongue out and moisten my lips, then slowly push my shorts down my legs. I toss my shorts to the floor and attempt to close my legs but he grips my knees and forces them apart. The hungry look in his eyes as he stares at my pussy has me clenching on air. "You're fucking drenched." The voice distorter doesn't hide the growl of approval in his voice. When his eyes flick back to mine I gasp at the intense look in those icy blue eyes. "After I slip my cock inside your cunt, you never let another touch you."

I mull over his words for a second and I hate that a picture of Vox flashes through my mind. I know, I am a fucking freak. Who in their right mind would be considering never being able to touch the guy who bullies her every single day, but the need growing inside me for my masked, two horn demon has me nodding and agreeing to his terms.

"Shirt off, I want to see those tits." Without hesitation I yank my shirt off. He snaps his arms out and cups my tits, when he flicks his thumbs over my nipples a moan escapes me. "You show these to no one, they belong to me now," he snarls as he pinches my nipples until I cry out in pain.

"Yes!" I scream out, he releases them instantly then cups my cheek and brushes his thumb along my bottom lip, careful not to hurt the split.

"You have my protection now, no one gets to scare you, touch you or torment you aside from me." My brows slam together at his words, but before I can utter a word he pushes on. "Turn around, bury your face in the comforter and get on your hands and knees." Rational people would fight and scream for this stranger wearing a satanic mask to get the fuck out but not me, I do exactly as he says and wait. He runs his hand down my back and suddenly without my sight everything feels heightened. His touch, the small sounds that escape. When his finger tips graze the side of my ribs, I shudder but then his hand clamps down on the back of my neck, forcing my face further into the pillow restricting my airway.

"Who the fuck is Waylen and what the fuck do the numbers mean?" he grits out.

Panic flares inside me, I begin to think I've made a huge mistake until I realize he is referring to the tattoo on my ribs.

"Waylen is my best friend, the numbers 4221 mean *forever together to love one another*," I gasp out, he keeps my face pressed there for another minute before releasing me. I turn my head to the side and suck in a full breath.

"You'll be getting rid of that shit," he vows. Before I can protest he pushes two fingers inside my wet pussy. I lurch forward but he returns his hand to the back of my neck and forces my face back into the pillow. I moan, unable to control the sounds coming from me as he finger fucks me at a ruthless pace. I reach down and rub my clit, his growl of approval has heat gathering in my belly. "Play with that clit and come on my fingers, then I'll destroy this dirty little cunt for any other man." His words are my undoing, my entire body tenses for a second before a scream so loud rips free and I come so fucking hard, soaking his fingers with my release. The instant he pulls his fingers free I feel empty. I feel him shift behind me and the sound of his zipper fills the room. Heat unfurls inside me as I prepare myself to live out every woman's fantasy. It may not be a forest and I may not have been running but having a masked man break into my room, finger my greedy little cunt until I come, then fuck me with the mask on has the fantasy coming to life inside me that I never knew existed until now.

The sound of a wrapper being torn has some tension easing inside me. He may be a stalker and want to scare me but at least he is being safe about it. When I feel the tip of his cock prod my entrance I tense in anticipation.

"Last chance, once I slip my cock inside you, no one touches what is mine." The pure dominance in his tone has me shivering.

"Okay," I say quietly. The head of his cock pushes inside me and I am powerless to stop my eyes from snapping wide and a shocked gasp from escaping me.

He is huge!

If this is just the tip and I already feel like I am about to be torn apart I can't imagine what it is going to feel like when he is fully sheathed inside me. I hear him grunt behind me as he slowly eases inside me some more. I'm panting and clutching the sheets in a vice-like hold.

"Fuck!" he roars as he slams the rest of the way inside me, unable to hold out any longer. A scream filled with raw pain rips out of me. I slam my eyes closed to fight back the tears that want to break free. In a gesture so shocking he runs a hand down my naked back trying to help me relax.

"Just... give me a second," I grit out. He says nothing but remains still, giving me a moment to adjust to his size. I thought he would be a tiny bit bigger than his fingers, you know like most normal guys, but I never expected him to have a dick the size of a fucking baby arm!

"You good?" I can hear the strain in his voice through the distorter. Unable to speak, I just nod. "Play with your clit, it will help." I do as he says and begin to rub myself. I'm still so sensitive and feel the burn begin to ease as he pulls almost all the way out then slams back inside. I cry out in pain but the more he continues to do this and I keep playing with my clit, the more the pain bleeds to pleasure and my cries turn to moans. "Fucking take this dick," he shouts as he grips my hips and pulls me back to meet him thrust for thrust.

"Fuck! I... I think I'm gonna come." I've never been able to come again so soon after already orgasming. The fact he is able to wring two orgasms from me in the space of a few minutes is mind blowing for me.

"Come on my cock like a good little witch." His words have my eyes snapping open but I can't utter a single word as my climax slams into me with such a force that I lose all function of my body and I flop forward unable to hold myself up as I scream out my release. His pace doesn't ease, if anything he picks up speed and the only sounds over our heaving breaths that can be heard is skin slapping on skin. "Fuck, Nova!" The sound of my name coming from him as he comes has me trembling and feeling... powerful that I was able to bring a man like him to such pleasure.

Most men would draw out their orgasm and thrust a couple more times but not two-horn, he pulls out of me and the sound of him zipping his jeans has me feeling cold and used. The second he is off my bed, I snatch the comforter and cover myself, turning over and giving him my back. I feel his gaze boring into the back of my head but I don't say anything.

"Don't get shy now, I know you are alone for the next week so I will be visiting you every night and you will be taking what I give."

I scoff. "Whatever." In a move I don't expect, he grips my hair and yanks my head back so I am forced to look up at his masked face. "You're hurting me," I grit out through clenched teeth.

"Good. Remember this pain because if you deny me what is mine you will be punished. You want this to stop, ask the favor."

"I won't be in your debt," I spit. My voice is gruff from screaming.

He releases me with a hard shove. "You already are. A favor is a debt owed, ask and all of this will stop." He may have offered me his protection from everyone else but clearly that doesn't apply to himself or his other masked friends.

CHAPTER FOURTEEN

Vox

I grit my teeth as a couple of bitches rush past me, carrying posters for Homecoming. Everyone at school has been acting like fucking idiots as they all hope and pray for a Homecoming proposal. I find Arch leaning against my locker with a disgusted look on his face.

"What's up?" I ask him as I open my locker and shove my shit inside.

"All this Homecoming shit, they are all worried about the dance and not the football game on Friday." I nod my head in agreement. Just as I turn around, I spot Nova, she has her books clutched against her chest and a smile on her face. My sister and a guy I have seen hanging around them are walking with her. He reaches out and wraps an arm around hers. As if she can sense my eyes on her, she flicks her gaze to me. I narrow my eyes. I see her cheeks flush with heat to find me staring at her.

She shakes her head and quickly looks back to my sister as they walk past. "Why are we leaving her alone again?"

I push off my locker and head in the same direction as Nova with Archer falling into step beside me. "Because pushing her wasn't working. Every night since the weekend I have seen her tearing her house apart looking for something. The second she stops searching means she found what she is looking for."

"Then we go after her?" I grind my teeth and try to temper the urge to slam my best friend's face into the lockers for daring to think that they could touch the witch—only I get to fuck with her.

"Yo." I turn my head to see Hayze and Ezekiel rushing toward us. "We got something," Hayze rasps out as Archer and I follow them outside to the parking lot where we climb inside Ez's car.

"What is it?" I grit out. Hayze pulls out a piece of paper from his back pocket and hands it to me. I read over it and frown. "What the fuck is it?" I snap angry that they wasted my time.

"It's from one of the files. The only person who can overthrow a ruling of a former lord is their chosen heir," Ez says.

"That's it, you can just change it—"

Ez cuts Archer off before he can continue. "It can only be overturned if I am the next lord heir. I can't overturn it, Vox, your father was the last lord not mine. Vivian is the next in line to become the *Lordess*."

"Fuck!" I roar as I punch the back of the seat.

"We need to find another way," Archer grits out, I frown when I see Ezekiel and Hayze sharing a loaded look.

"What the fuck are you two hiding?" I force out. Hayze deflates and Ezekiel sighs.

"Don't you dare fucking break my nose, okay?" Ez snaps,

shooting me a glare. I bare my teeth and nod. "The only way I would have the power to take her place and overturn the law is—"

Archer cuts in before Ez can finish. "Fuck you! She would never agree to that!" The anger that laces his tone surprises me.

"Fuck you, Archer. I'm trying to save her!" Ezekiel roars.

"Both of you shut the fuck up and finish saying what you were about to," I shout.

"The only way to save your sister is for her to be a Tempest. Ezekiel needs to marry Vivian so then the power or lordship would transfer to him so he would have the power to overturn the female law and end The Brotherhood." I stare at Hayze who is gasping for air having said all of that in a rush. The car is silent as the three of them wait to see how I will act.

Ezekiel needs to marry Vivian.

That shit keeps replaying over and over in my head. I sit back and take some deep breaths. The three of them seem to relax. Hayze smiles and nods his head like they have just solved the fucking Da Vinci Code, then I lose the battle. My restraint snaps and I am jumping forward trying to get to Ezekiel through the center. I manage to clip his cheek before he pushes his door open and falls out of the fucking car. Hayze tries to escape my wrath and manages to narrowly avoid my fist when he flops out of the car like a sack of shit.

"Both of you are fucking dead!" I roar as the two idiots are laughing their asses off on the ground. Archer even begins to laugh beside me but the second I snap my gaze to him he clamps his mouth shut and raises his hands.

"I was the one against the idea, remember that, okay?" I narrow my eyes at the bastard and shove him as I climb out of the car and kick Ezekiel in the side as I storm back toward the back of the school.

"It was a good fucking plan, asshole!" Hayze calls out

through his laughter. I flip that bastard the bird over my shoulder and ignore all their laughter. In a sense, they did find a solution to all our problems but I won't use my sister to achieve our goal. I scrub my hand down my face as I drop down on one of the benches, needing a minute before I go inside and face all those other assholes who can never see any of us as less than perfect as per the Haven Saints rules.

"You look like shit." I snap my head to the side and scowl at Nova.

"What the fuck do you want?" I clip out, her brows raise.

"I was sitting here first, dick." The fire in her eyes as she looks at me calls the darkest part of my psyche and I relish in the way she wants to burn me to ash with one look.

"Watch your mouth, you have had four days of peace, I can ruin that for you." She smirks.

"Ah, and here I was thinking that you and your goon squad had found a better toy to torture." She fake pouts. As of Monday I ordered the guys to leave her alone, to act like she didn't exist but make sure no one fucked with her. I even had Nicole remove the photos of her from Instagram.

"Nah, just letting you settle in before we strike."

She snorts and nods, fighting back a smile. "If you weren't such a dick, I would ask if you were okay but given the fact you are a dick, I am just going to say that I hope whoever put you in a mood has a fabulous day, and if I ever find out who it is I'll shake their hand." I can't stop the smirk from making its way to my face.

"Do me a favor." Her features twitch.

"If this favor means I'm in your debt, then no thanks." I fight the smile from blooming on my face and school my features.

"Don't let Nexus get to you." She reels back in surprise.

"Isn't he your best friend?" I stab a hand through my hair

and exhale, not sure why I even fucking said that shit but it's too late to take it back now.

"What you see isn't always what it seems. Nexus is a snake and will do whatever he has to so he comes out on top. Don't let him get to you."

"You gonna protect me from my big bad stepbrother?" The mocking tone of her voice isn't lost on me.

"No. Protect yourself, I have enough people relying on me—"

"Why do you do that?" she asks, cutting me off and earning a glare which she ignores.

"Do what?" I snap.

"Deflect. Your mouth says one thing but your eyes say another."

"You think you know what guys go through?" I don't give her a chance to answer. "Or is it just Waylen that you know?" Her brows draw together. Then she leaps to her feet and stares down at me with wide eyes.

"How do you know about Waylen?"

I climb to my feet and close the space between us, gripping the back of her neck. I bend down until my lips brush the shell of her ear. "Don't let me catch anyone touching you again, little witch. I would hate to break your friend Lenny's arm for touching what isn't his." When I draw back her face is pale and her eyes are wide.

"Two-horns," she breathes out.

I keep my features schooled as I reply, "Who?" then turn and walk away, leaving her standing there lost in her own inner turmoil.

CHAPTER FIFTEEN

I'm in Thomas' office rummaging through his files, the only light in the room is the small lamp beside me. Every night since I received the note from my uncle I have been turning the house upside down trying to find this proof he said I needed to find. Tonight is my last chance to find something, Waylen arrives tomorrow and I won't have a chance to look around while he is here without him asking questions.

I don't realize how much time has passed until I hear the office door creak open. I scream in fright until two-horns raises his hands. I suck a ragged breath and sag against the cabinet until I recall my conversation with Vox this afternoon.

Only two horns has seen my tattoo of Waylen's name.

Only Vox calls me witch or little witch.

Yet, both of them seem to know things the other shouldn't, which is why instead of paying him any attention I turn my back and say. "We're not fucking tonight, I'm not in the mood."

I'm proud of how strong my voice is. Every night he has come to my room and devoured me. God, the way he fucks is so unholy and shows he has the devil inside him. I continue rifling through the files but when I feel him against my back I still. He reaches out, turns the lamp off and plunges us into darkness. Gooseflesh dots my skin and I start to burn with need.

"You dare to deny me what is *mine?*" I attempt to turn around but he grips the back of my head and slams the side of my face against the cabinet. I hiss in pain. His free hand grips the waistband of my yoga pants and yanks them down to just below my ass. I squeal when he smacks my ass and lurch forward into the cabinet, forcing the things on top to clatter to the ground.

"What the fuck—" I'm cut off when he lands another hit to my other cheek. "Ahhh."

"Deny me again, I dare you," he taunts as he delivers another three whacks to my ass. As he delivers the final blow, a moans slips free and I clamp my lips closed, mortified at myself for getting off on this shit. "Good girl," he purrs as he leans down, scraping the rough edges of his mask against my face. The texture sends a shiver down my spine. His hand skates over the globes of my ass, massaging the sting away, I close my eyes and try to find the will to fight against him but the second he slips his fingers through my folds and growls, I lose the battle.

"Oh, fuck," I cry out when he slips his fingers inside me.

"This pussy belongs to me, your cum and your moans are for me only. Don't ever deny me again or you won't like the repercussions." I'm mute, I can't form a single word. All that comes out when I open my mouth is mewls and moans as he strokes that sweet spot inside that I can't even hit when I finger myself. "Who does this pussy belong to, *witch?*" At the use of the nickname from Vox, everything inside me tenses, if it was a common pet name like babe or baby it would mean nothing but *witch* is not common.

"Vox!" I call out but I'm met with silence as he continues to finger my pussy. I feel the orgasm cresting.

"Keep your face forward and don't fucking move," he snaps, then withdraws his fingers. I'm trembling and on edge as I wait to see what he will do next. I jolt when he grips my pants and pulls them off, then grips the back of my shirt and pulls it up. I expect him to take it off but instead he positions it so it's covering my head. "Leave it," he snaps when I try to remove it.

Anticipation builds as I feel him move behind me, his hands gripping my ass and parting my cheeks, drawing a gasp of surprise from me. I feel his hot breath blow against my core and I moan.

"I'm going to eat this cunt." The sound of his voice—his *real* voice has me stiffening. I know that voice! All thought flees me when he pushes his tongue inside my pussy.

"Fuck yes!" I cry out then push back against his face. His arms wrap around me, anchoring me to him as he laps at my pussy and fucks me with his mouth. Just the feeling of his mouth on my cunt has heat unfurling inside me, my orgasm building rapidly and I know without a doubt that this orgasm is going to put me on my ass. When he sucks my clit into his mouth... I shatter. "Vox!" I scream out. I don't know why I say his name but I am almost certain that the man I have been fucking for the past five days is my evil neighbor and my new best friend's twin brother. I'm shaking and my knees want to give out, his hold on me is the only thing that keeps me standing. Unlike all the other times, he brings me down gently, then just when I think I can't take it any longer, he pulls back. I remain still and don't move an inch as I feel him stand.

"Never say that name," he growls, his voice sounds different, almost like he is purposely changing it so I won't figure out his true identity. I feel the tip of his cock a second before he slams into me so hard I smash against the cabinet, shifting it forward on the wooden floor. His pace is punishing but fucking euphoric. He fucks me like a savage and uses my body to get off. I love that he takes what he wants from me without apology. He's sure with every thrust and touch. He knows me better than I do and I have had years to study my own wants and needs, yet none of those things compare to how he can make me feel.

"Fuck me just like that," I cry out. A hand clamps down on my throat and I hate that I can't see his face as he pulls me back, flush against his chest. His move to choke me is strategic, this way he can make sure my shirt doesn't slip and my vision remains obscured. His grip on my neck tightens and my breaths become labored as he restricts my airway. Just as black dots dance in the edges of my eyes an orgasm so strong barrels through me with such a force that I try to push away from him, but he keeps me in place with his hold. His grip on my throat loosens and I gasp as I ride out the aftershocks of my climax with him continuing to plough into me with brutality.

I feel his cock swelling inside me and I know he is about to come. I brace myself to hear the sound of his voice as he calls my name but to my surprise, he bends down and bites my shoulder, silencing himself. I cry out in pain for a moment. The pain bleeds into pleasure just as quickly, my eyes widening in horror when I feel him pull out and I know he didn't use a condom when his cum starts to leak out of me.

"Get on your knees," he growls in that weird voice. Without thought, I do as he says and quickly pushes my shirt down and look up at him hoping to catch a glimpse of his face but disappointment burns through me when I see his mask is back in place. "Clean my cock." My head reels back.

"How–" My reply is cut short when he pushes his wet cock

into my mouth then tangles his fingers in my hair to hold me in place as I gag around him.

"Fuck, yes, tomorrow I'm coming down your throat," he declares, then pulls free. I gasp and slump forward on my hands dragging some much needed air into my lungs. I see him out of the corner of my eye turning to leave but my words have him freezing.

"My friend is coming over tomorrow and will be staying for the weekend." I lift my head when he turns to face me.

"Better learn to be quiet then."

My jaw unhinges. "No–"

"I'm coming back for what is mine. Deny me my right and see what happens to your friend." He leaves with his ominous words hanging in the air. I should be angry or scared but instead, I'm turned on at the fact he doesn't give a fuck about Waylen being here. Nothing is going to stop him from getting to me and the feeling inside me tells me I am getting addicted to this masked stranger and that is a bad thing.

A really bad thing!

CHAPTER SIXTEEN

Vox

My mood is sour as I storm out of chem. I hear Ez calling out to me but I ignore him as I take off in search of my sister. I find her at her locker with that fucking geek Lenny. At the sight of me storming toward them his eyes widen, and he takes a step back when I stand behind my twin.

"Fuck off!" I snap. Without a single word or a glance at my sister, he scurries off.

Vivi turns on me and places her hands on her hips with a scowl on her face.

"Vox, that was rude—"

"I don't care. Where the fuck is Nova?" Her brows slant and she cocks her head to the side studying me for a minute.

"Why?" The accusation in her tone is clear, I get her hesitation. It's not like I have been her biggest fan and the fact I am asking about her must seem weird but I don't care, I need to know where she is.

"Just answer my question!" I snarl.

She pulls her phone out of her pocket, unlocks it and scrolls for a second before turning it toward me. My nostrils flare in anger at the picture Nova sent her. It's a picture of her and a guy who has his fucking arm around her waist but it's the quote below it that has my blood boiling.

My lover is finally here!

I snatch the phone from her and ignore her threats of kicking my ass as I send Nova's contact information to myself. I toss my sister her phone and stalk off. I pull out my phone and bring up my message thread and shoot the little witch a text.

ME

You want me to break your 'lovers' fucking jaw?

LITTLE WITCH

Who the fuck is this?

ME

The guy who is going to break that cunts jaw!

I see three dots appear and then disappear a few times. I lean against the wall ignoring all the students as they breeze past me. I can feel them eyeing me but I pay them no mind as I wait for her reply.

LITTLE WITCH

Vox?

ME

The one and only, witch.

LITTLE WITCH

How the fuck did you get my number?

ME

Not important. Where the fuck are you?

LITTLE WITCH

None of your business, asshole, now be gone. I got shit to do!

ME

Answer me!

I wait for her reply but I see no dots so I fire off another text.

ME

You have three seconds

3...

2...

1...

Game on witch!

LITTLE WITCH

Bring it on, dick bag!

Her reply has a smile stretching across my face. I pocket my phone and head for the locker room to warm up for our game tonight. It's our last one for a few weeks and I know coach is still pissed that James, Ezra and Leo are out for the season and he's had to put their backups in, but I don't give a fuck. We have the W in the bag. St Bernard's is taking the L tonight and there isn't a fucking thing anyone can do about that.

"I want you ladies to get your asses out there and make sure you keep them out of the end zone. You did good and now it's time you do great and keep them at zero! I don't want to see a single point for them on that score board, am I clear?" The entire team roars and starts banging on the lockers as we set out for the second half of the game. We are already up 32-0, they would need a million fucking Hail Mary's in order to beat us but the challenge coach has set has us all wanting to please him.

Unlike everyone else in this town or fucking school, coach doesn't care what your last name is or how much money is in your bank account. All he cares about is your skills and what you can bring to the table. He sacked Archer and Ezekiel from the team last season when he did a random drug test and both of theirs came back positive. Hayze and I tried to vouch for them and find a way to get them back on the team but Coach wasn't hearing any of it.

As I exit the tunnel, I look up at the crowd smiling, with my helmet in the air until my eyes land on *her*. She stands there between my sister and the dead cunt from the picture with a smile on her face. When she looks down and spots me glaring up at her the little witch smirks, winks and blows me a kiss.

Fire burns in my veins when the guy leans in, places his hand on her waist and says something in her ear. She nods and pats him on the shoulder as he shuffles past her and my sister.

"Get your fucking head in the game, Hatchett!" Coach roars. I shake my head and shoot Nova one last glare before putting my helmet on and jogging out onto the field. My thirst for blood is amplified by the sight of her and that cunt. Hayze stops in front of me and smacks his helmet against mine.

"What the fuck are you doing, bro?" he shouts. I shove him back and shake my head.

"Fuck off and get ready," I snarl as I get into position and try to get my head back in the game. If I cost the team this win, then coach will have my ass and so will my boys.

The game goes off without a hitch, I don't let my focus drift to the grand stands. I do as I have been trained to do and throw the ball with presession. Johnson catches every ball without a single fumble. The clock runs down the time and before I know it, we did what coach wanted. We kept them at zero and won the fucking game. The team roars along with the crowd. I want to join in with their celebration but I'm too fucking pissed off to celebrate, so I head straight for the locker room.

It's empty when I enter so I strip off and grab my shit from my locker and head for the showers. Homecoming is tomorrow so there is no after party tonight. I wouldn't have gone anyway. We only go to parties when there is nothing else to do. Ezekiel, Hayze, Archer and I are the ones who make the party—Nexus does by default but only because everyone thinks he is one of us. I'm not looking forward to him coming back on Sunday.

After my shower, I pull on a pair of jeans and drape my towel over my shoulder as I head back to my locker, I slam to a halt at the sight of Nova standing there with an angry look on her face. I keep my expression neutral and step past her to grab my shirt and letterman jacket. I feel her gaze on me the entire time and relish in the knowledge that the little witch likes what she sees. I take my time dressing, the sound of her growl of annoyance bringing a smirk to my face. I wipe it off quickly as I turn to face her, crossing my arms over my chest.

"Little witch, you must be lost," I say huskily. She tries to act unaffected but I can see through her tough girl act.

"Is Virgil Hatchett your father?" At the sound of my father's name tumbling from her lips I see red. I snap my arm out and wrap it around her throat, slamming her against the lockers as I get right in her face. She claws at my forearm, trying to get free but it's futile.

"Say his name again and I'll snap your fucking neck, am I clear?" Her face is turning red and her mouth is open as she tries to gasp for air. She gives me a shaky nod, I release her with a shove, her head banging against the lockers but I don't care.

"Your family has no right to ever speak his fucking name!" I roar as I turn away and tug on the strands of my hair, trying to calm the beast rearing to life inside me.

"Fuck you, Vox!" I hear the watery tone of her voice and feel a slight twinge of guilt but don't acknowledge her as she runs out of the locker room, leaving me alone.

"Fuck!" I roar as I slam my fist into the nearest locker denting it.

How the fuck does she know about my father?

My eyes widen as a thought hits me, she knows about my dad because she found something. I need that information!

CHAPTER SEVENTEEN

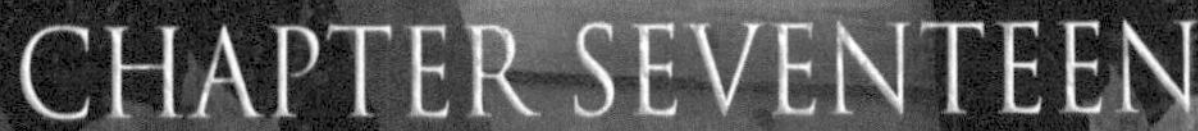

Nova

My throat feels like it's been fucked by Sasquatch!

After I ran out of the locker room to find Waylen, he took one look at me and ushered us out of there without even giving me a chance to say bye to Vivian. I shot her a text on the way home spewing some bullshit about not feeling well and I would see her tomorrow. Waylen has been shooting me worried glances ever since we got home but I don't say anything. How the fuck do I tell my best friend that I think I have moved into a town that is ruled by a secret society that is run by my fucking stepfather!

"You look like shit." I snort. Waylen shoots me a smile but it doesn't reach his murky brown eyes, his curly hair drops forward onto his forehead so I reach out and brush it back.

"You say the sweetest things," I coo.

He fans himself and bats his lashes. "Oh darling, only to you, my love." Both of us burst out laughing, he is the one person I can rely on to always bring me out of a sour mood and cheer me up without even trying. He props his head on his hand and looks down at me. I sigh knowing he isn't going to let this go, so I reach over to my side drawer and pull out the two letters from my uncle and the postcard thing from two-horns. "What's this?" he asks as I hand them to him.

"Just read them and then I'll explain." I watch a range of emotions splay across his face as he reads the letters. His jaw hangs out as he finishes and looks at me.

"You have a brother." I nod. "You have an uncle." I humph and nod again. "Who is this one from?" he asks, waving the postcard. I push my bottom lip to the side and debate how to explain that one to him.

"Uh, that one is..." I debate over my words for a second trying to think of the best way to explain. "Well, you see there is a bit of a story but it's kind of a long one and I am super tired—"

"Good try, you little shit, start explaining it to me now." I roll onto my back and stare up at the ceiling, huffing my displeasure but Waylen ignores my pouting and waits for me to tell him who the hell the *Filthy Few* is. The real question though... how much do I tell him?

I flick my eyes to him as I say, "Don't get mad though, okay?"

I can see he wants to argue but instead just says, "Okay."

"Okay, I guess in order for you to understand I have to tell you what happened from when I arrived here." And so I do, I tell him everything from the night of the bonfire and how Vox and his friends have been assholes, the masked men, my uncle leaving me notes. I tell him everything except for the fact that I am fucking two-horns. That is something he just doesn't need to know and something I am not comfortable sharing, that is my darkest fantasy that I am living out and I won't have him judge me for that.

"Jesus Christ, Nova!" He leaps from the bed and begins pacing my room while I sit up, clutching a pillow to my chest and watch him, hoping he will calm down. He stops his pacing every few seconds to look at me, then shakes his head and continues his pacing while muttering to himself.

"Waylen, I need you to stop pacing and just use your words!" He freezes and pins me with an ice-cold glare that has me sitting up ramrod straight on the bed.

"What the fuck do I say?" I flinch at the harsh tone of his voice. "You have been lying to me for weeks. We agreed that we would never hide shit from each other and here you are keeping the biggest secret of them all and keeping me in the dark." Guilt churns inside me and I drop my gaze from his, unable to stand the look of hurt in his eyes.

"I didn't mean to lie, I swear I just—"

He cuts in before I can finish. "I'm not angry at you. I'm just pissed that you have been dealing with shit alone and wouldn't let me help. How am I supposed to leave you now?" I snap my head up and stare at him in surprise.

"What?"

His features soften as he moves toward the bed and drops down onto the edge of it. "I can't just go back home and leave you alone with your crazy-ass stepbrother and this crew of masked assholes chasing your tail."

I scrunch my face. "No one says *chasing tail*." He chuckles and shrugs.

"Quit calling me out, I'm still reeling after learning all of this shit so I get a free pass." I soften and smile at my best friend, unloading all of this shit, and being able to finally tell him the truth feels freeing. "What do you plan to do about all of this?"

A sigh escapes me as I contemplate how to answer him. I wish I could sit here and say that I know exactly what my next move is but that's bullshit. "I don't know, Way-way. I'm so confused. Ever since I found that file in Thomas' office I feel like I am in some sort of thriller movie."

"What exactly did that file say?"

"Virgil Hatchett's death wasn't an accident. The coroner's report proves that and it also listed Edmund Tempest's death which wasn't an accident either," I whisper, feeling sick to my stomach about this information.

"Jesus, so your new stepfather is a murderer?"

I groan and flop back against the pillows. "It appears that way," I mutter.

"Okay. So, no one knows what he did and everyone thinks their deaths were accidents." I nod. "If that's the case then why the hell are those assholes picking on you at school and why are three masked guys coming after you and who the fuck is this secret uncle?"

"When you say it all out loud like that it sounds..."

"Crazy as fuck like a horror movie?" he supplies. I lull my head to the side and pin him with a deadpan look that has him smiling. "We need to find someone who can help us..." He clamps his mouth closed and stares down at me with wide eyes.

I sit upright and stare at my friend with worry. "What's wrong?"

He reaches out and grips my arms in a haste. "I know how we find out the truth about all of this but you aren't going to like how we do it."

I search his eyes trying to decipher what he's thinking, but I see nothing but resolution. "What are you thinking?" I ask softly, slightly terrified of what his answer might be. With how in tuned we are with each other, I know he is thinking the same thing I have been.

"We need to ask the *Filthy Few* for a favor." His ominous words hang between us for a tense moment, until I tear free of his hold, jump from the bed and begin pacing the room. He has no idea what he is asking. It's not his fault because I refused to admit that I have been fucking one of them. I can't explain but I feel a connection to two horns, it's like I know him. "Nova?" I wave my hand ignoring him as I continue pacing my room trying to think of another way but I'm running out of time. Thomas, Mom and Nexus get back on Sunday and I don't know if I will be able to stay under the same roof as him without knowing the truth.

"What if we call the police?" I hedge.

Waylen pins me with a dumbfounded look. "You are the poor girl whose mother married a rich ass real estate tycoon, who do you think they are going to believe? Plus, if what this masked crew says is true, then they would be the ones to help us find out who the fuck Thomas really is and what this Haven Saints thing is."

I chew on my bottom lip as I contemplate everything and weigh up my options. "If we do this, then we have to go after Homecoming."

"Skip the fucking dance—"

"If I skip the dance Vivian will never forgive me and if I don't show I can't guarantee that Vox and the other's won't snitch to Nexus that I never showed. If we are wrong about all of this, I can't let Thomas catch on to the fact I think he killed my friends' fathers."

"Friends?" I cringe and shoot him a sheepish smile.

"I know what I have told you sounds bad but they aren't... terrible?"

He rolls his eyes. "Are you asking me or telling me, babe?"

"Both?" Waylen and I spend the next few hours making a plan for tomorrow. I realize he is right, my only hope of finding out the truth is to ask the fucking favor and be in their debt! Waylen is fast asleep beside me while I lay here staring up at the ceiling with worry churning inside me, a favor this big is going to cost me and I'm scared to know what the price is going to be.

I startle awake to the feeling of a gloved hand over my mouth. My eyes are wide in fear but when the soft glow of the moons lighting allows me to see the mask, I relax at the sight of his two horns. He doesn't say anything when he clamps his other hand around my throat and drags me out of my bed. I bite my tongue to keep from lashing out at him as he drags me across the room to my bathroom. He closes the door and locks it. I reach for the light switch but he just smacks my hand away and releases me, not taking a step back, leaving me trapped between him and the wall.

Call me crazy but I can feel the anger wafting off him in waves and the slight hint of fear I feel inside me has me feeling light headed and intoxicated by the prospect of what he will do to me.

"You want him to die?" he says, keeping his voice low. His words snap me out of my lust-filled haze.

"Don't you fucking touch him!" I snap.

His hand wraps around my throat, his thumb stroking the underside of my jaw as he tilts my head up to meet his dark gaze. I may not be able to see his eyes clearly but I can feel the heat in his gaze when he runs it over me.

"You thought this was a good idea?" Even with the voice distorter I can hear the anger that laces his tone.

"What idea?" I rasp out.

His free hand grips my hip, the leather of his glove chaffs against my bare skin sending a shiver down my spine. "Wearing this and allowing him to sleep next to what is mine."

My eyes widen at the dominance and jealousy I feel wafting off him. I look down and take in the sight of my crop top and sleep shorts. He's never seemed to mind my sleeping attire before so I am concluding that the fact Waylen is seeing me in this is what he doesn't like.

"We're not—" My reply is cut off when he cups my pussy, drawing a gasp from me.

"Did he touch this?" he asks as his hold on my throat tightens and he leans down scraping his mask against my cheek. The roughness of his mask against my skin feels unholy and taboo, the fact I have no idea who he is only adds to the appeal. In a move so bold and risky I reach up and lock my arms around his neck. I feel him stiffen but he doesn't pull away which just fuels me to push on.

"I wore this for *you*, not him or anyone else." My words seem to ease some of the tension radiating off of him. He releases his hold on my throat, only to grip the back of my neck. He tugs me forward until my face is pressed against his mouth, I dart my tongue out needing to taste him only to be disappointed when I taste the mask and not him. Call me deluded or fucked in the head but I don't think I ever want to know who the man is beneath the mask. I love being able to indulge in my dark fantasy without being judged. Being hunted by him and at his mercy every night is something I never thought would be something I would ever get the pleasure to experience.

"On your knees, *witch*." There it is again! That fucking name is starting to haunt me and a part of me is now terrified that my masked fuck buddy is someone who knows me from school. I know it isn't Vox or his stupid friends because they have all made their feelings clear to me, none of them would touch me. Not that I would want them too, well maybe I do want one of them to touch me but I would rather chew razor blades than admit I want to be touched by Vox Hatchett. I mean, Vox did kiss me the other night and I can't seem to get that fucking kiss or the feeling of his hands on me out of my head. "You think of no one but me!" Two horns snaps angrily as he shoves me to my knees. I whimper when I hit the tiled floor.

"I wasn't thinking about anyone—"

"Your eyes told me you were."

"How the hell would you know?" I bite back as he begins to unfasten his pants. I hate that I am pissed off at him but my mouth is watering at the prospect of being able to suck his cock.

"Was it the fucker in your bed?" he growls as he grips his cock in his hand, stroking it, the sight alone has me clenching my thighs together to try and dull the ache. "Answer me."

"No!" I admit.

"Who then?" he asks as he rubs the head of his cock against my lips, smearing his pre-cum. I'm powerless to stop my tongue from darting out and tasting him. He groans when I taste the head of his cock. I moan at the taste of him, sweet and salty.

"My asshole neighbor," I admit as I grip the backs of his thighs and flick my gaze to him as I open my mouth waiting for him to fill it.

For a moment he does nothing aside from stare down at me, the pressure of his gaze has me fighting not to squirm. This whole moment has me on edge—hiding in the bathroom with my secret stranger while my best friend is asleep in my bed in the next room.

"Vox isn't yours to fuck. I am." My eyes widen. I choke on my own gasp when he thrusts his cock into my mouth. I choke on him but he doesn't allow me to back up. He tangles his fingers in my hair and holds me in place. I rap on the backs of his thighs, telling him I can't breathe but he still doesn't allow me to move. "You want air? Breath through your fucking nose because you are going to take all of me as punishment for allowing that cunt into your bed." It shocks me more that he is pissed about Waylen in my bed rather than me admitting to thinking about Vox. My mind is spiraling when I piece together that I said neighbor, *not* Vox, but he knew exactly who I was referring to!

When he finally pulls out I gasp so loud I fear the sound may wake Waylen. I barely have enough time to drag in a full breath before he is thrusting forward again, making me gag. Tears leak from my eyes, spit drips down my chin coating my throat and chest.

"Swirl your tongue, I want you to taste every fucking inch of me so you know who the fuck you belong to!" His words shouldn't turn me on but they do. I know I am fucked in the head for getting off on this shit but I can't deny my body's reaction to him or the way he uses me and demands his pleasure that I am giving him.

I give up on rational thought, my grip on his thighs tightening as I press up higher on my knees and begin to take over. When he realizes what I'm doing his hold on my hair loosens, allowing me more freedom to bob up and down on his cock. Heady moans begin to tumble from my lips as I find my rhythm and suck his dick like a starving addict desperate for their next hit.

CHAPTER EIGHTEEN

Two Horns

The feeling of her plump lips wrapped around my cock has my eyes wanting to roll back into my head. When she swirls her tongue around the tip of my cock and presses it into the slit of my dick I groan, not giving a fuck that the sound was loud enough to wake that cocksucker next door. I want him to wake up and hear her screaming my name as she comes all over my cock, he needs to know that Nova Quinlin belongs to me.

She is mine!

My brothers and I never fuck in the masks, they are our armor to hide who we are so we can do the dirty work no one else has the balls to do. We have killed for a favor, ruined lives, torn families apart and never once batted an eye. We are a team but I fucked that up when I chose to take her. She should be ours to torment, to play with but I made excuses to free her from their brand of punishment because I want her for myself, she is mine.

"Take it," I snarl as I thrust my hips, wanting to impale my dick down her throat. Her wet warm mouth feels like a fucking sanctuary. She has me crossing lines that I never would have, she is blurring everything and the only way I can think straight or stop myself from tearing her fucking world apart is to be buried inside her pretty little cunt.

"Hmmmm." The vibration from her moan sends a shiver down my spine and has my balls tightening. Tonight she was supposed to just suck my cock and I was going to leave but the need to feel her tight, wet pussy strangling my cock as she comes has me changing plans. I pull free of her mouth and use my grip on her hair to pull her to her feet. She cries out in pain but I ignore it as I shove her forward and bend her over the counter in the bathroom.

"You watch everything," I declare. She snaps her head up and meets my gaze in the mirror, the sight of her tears and the disheveled look on her face has my cock twitching. I yank her shorts down her legs and fight back my groan at the sight of her thong resting perfectly between her plump ass cheeks. I've never been more jealous of a piece of material in my life. Fuck what I wouldn't give to rest between those cheeks all day long. Rather than peeling it down her legs I tear the fucking thing at the side, relishing in the gasp that escapes her.

I take my time, slowly peeling it out of her ass, if I didn't have my mask on I would be inhaling her fucking scent. Rather than discarding the destroyed material to the side, I push it into my pocket, wanting to keep something of hers. I know she is close to asking the favor, the second she does she is no longer mine. I won't be able to hide her anymore, she will be all of ours to destroy until the debt is paid. And destroy we will, no one has ever been able or allowed to repay the debt, we can't leave witnesses behind.

"Please," she whimpers, drawing me out of my head. I meet

her gaze again and growl as I line my cock up with her entrance. She whimpers when I slide inside her slowly. She moans loudly, leaving me no choice but to cover her mouth with my hand. I slam the rest of the way inside her, loving how her back arches and she screams into my hand, which doesn't do much to muffle the sound of her cries.

"Your pussy was made for my cock," I praise as I thrust in and out of her. She grips the edge of the counter and holds my gaze in the mirror, the crazed look in her eyes sends the monster inside me haywire. I've never felt a need to consume someone or own every inch of them until I saw Nova, she is consuming my every thought and forcing me to stumble in my role as our leader.

"Ahhhh," she cries into my hand when I stroke that sweet spot inside her. I can feel her pussy quivering already, she responds so fucking well to my touch.

"Take it," I grit out as I slam into her ruthlessly, my anger peaking, forcing me to take my anger out on her body. It's better this way, it saves me from killing her. I feel my balls tightening as her cunt clamps down on my dick. I reach around and pinch her nipple between my fingers, setting off her orgasm.

Fuck!

Seeing her reflection and how sexy she looks when she comes apart on my cock has my own climax tearing through me. I bite down on my lip to stop myself from roaring out my release. I spill everything I have inside her and freeze when I realize I didn't use a fucking condom again! This girl has me making mistakes that I would never have made with anyone else. The *Filthy Few* never fuck up but I did, twice.

I release my hold on her and pull out. She flops forward gasping and shaking with the remnants of her orgasm still thrumming through her. I tuck myself back into my pants, then look down at her once more, needing to ingrain the memory of what she looks like in my brain but I falter when I find her gaze already on me. Gone is the blissed-out look and now she stands there staring at me with contempt.

"If I ask the favor... What is the debt?"

I harden my resolve and force all my emotions to take a backseat. I have a vow to uphold and lives to free from being made to wear chains and being shackled to this life.

"Your life."

I watch her face for a reaction but when I see nothing except understanding I narrow my eyes. "I figured as much."

"A favor is a debt owed, remember that, witch."

"Like you would let me forget," she mutters bitterly. "If I ask this favor, do I still get... this?"

Her question stumps me for a moment until I recover. "You want me to continue to fuck you senseless?"

Her mouth parts on a silent gasp. "Y-yes."

"Ask the favor and you shall see," I say before I leave her standing there. I scoff at the sight of the cunt in her bed still fast asleep. I make my way to the balcony and jump over the side, landing in a crouch. I don't bother to look back up, knowing she would still be in the bathroom and not tracking my movements. As I round the side of the house I slam to a stop at the sight in front of me.

Fuck!

"What are you doing here?" I grit out and clench my fists at my sides. He pushes off the side of the house and takes a hit from his blunt as he runs his gaze over me and shakes his head.

"I was going to ask you the same question." The anger is clear in his tone and eyes.

"My job."

"Is that what she is? A job?" he pushes.

"Yes," I grit out through clenched teeth. I pull my mask off and meet his angry glare with one of my own. "Why the fuck are you spying on me?"

"Because we had a meeting to attend tonight, you didn't show and I took a gamble, turns out I was right."

My nostrils flare in indignation. "So what?"

"She is a job!" he seethes. "We force the favor and she pays the debt. Your feelings mean nothing when the majority votes. I want the answers she has and that is all there is to it. I don't give a fuck what your cock wants, this is about all of us—"

"I know!" I roar, then cringe and quickly peer over my shoulder to make sure she didn't hear that and come to investigate.

"Do you?" he snarls as he closes the space between us and gets right up in my face.

"Don't fucking push me," I snarl as I shoulder past him.

"The hunt is back on, she is fair game," he calls after me. I say nothing, knowing if I do I will show my cards. He may be my brother but that doesn't mean he won't kill her just to teach me a lesson. "She has three days to ask or we're taking it from her." I still mid step and take a deep breath, everything he says is right. She is the first chance we have of finally getting the upper hand. With her information we could finally stop all of this and end the *Filthy Few*. There would be no more need to lurk in the shadows and hide who we are.

"Be ready, she will ask the favor tomorrow and pay the price like all the others." I can hear the bitterness in my own tone and I hate it, feelings aren't something I am accustomed to and I don't fucking like them.

CHAPTER NINETEEN

Nova

Waylen whistles and claps as I descend the stairs in my dress. He looks handsome with his curly hair tamed with product and his face clean shaven. I stole a tux from Nexus' closet for him and he fills it out better than that snake ever could. I found a black dress when I went with Vivian, it's a simple black silk gown with an open back and crisscross straps in the back, exposing a lot more skin than I normally do. The front has a plunging neckline, exposing the sides of my ample chest.

"You look fucking beautiful, babe," Waylen says as he meets me at the base of the steps and places a kiss to my cheek. I smile up at my best friend and my heart swells, I wouldn't be where I am today without him or Mom. Waylen is my rock and my partner in crime. He smirks and pushes my long raven hair over my shoulder. I chose to wear it straight and left it loose tonight. My makeup is simple and just enough to add some color to my cheeks and a bit of mascara to make my eyes pop but nothing too serious.

"You don't clean up too bad yourself." He laughs and steps back, turning a circle for me to take him in. It's true, he looks fucking beautiful. Waylen isn't like most guys who know they look hot. He really doesn't see his own beauty and that just adds to his sexiness. Unfortunately for me, I may be able to appreciate his beauty but it doesn't get my libido ticking.

He offers me his arm and I take it as he leads us out the front door to my car. Unlike all the other kids who I'm sure will be arriving in a limo, I chose to drive us. Mom did offer to spring for a limo saying Thomas wouldn't mind but I declined, taking anything from him feels... wrong right now. I'm anxious for her to get home tomorrow, I just need her close so if this shit does go wrong at least she is close and safe.

As we cross the drive I come to a halt at the sound of Vivian calling out my name. I turn around and smile at the beauty rushing toward me in her yellow gown. She looks fucking radiant. Her long train trails behind her, her black hair is done up in some fancy updo with a few curls loose that frame her face. Her blue eyes are alight with happiness when she comes to a stop before us. She looks us both over, smiling her approval.

"You both look edible!" Waylen and I both laugh.

"You look gorgeous," Way says kindly.

"And you look like you're going to need a new set of fucking teeth." I dart my gaze over Vivi's shoulder to see Vox, Ezekiel, Hayze and Archer standing there, glaring at my best friend. Vivian steps to the side and instantly Vox's gaze cuts to me. I fight the urge to fidget under the pressure of his perusal of me. I watch him swallow and immediately heat internally when his gaze meets mine and I see lust in the depths of his blue eyes. Vox in his daily clothes is hot but Vox Hatchett in a tux with his tattoos peeking out of the collar and his inked hands on display is a fucking weapon.

"Calm down, man, it was a compliment," Waylen says, breaking the spell I was under. Vox shakes his head and masks his emotions as he turns his focus back to Waylen. He opens his mouth to say something but snaps it closed when two women dart in front of them and come toward us. I know one of them is Vox and Vivian's mom, Jane, but I have no idea who the other woman is. She is clutching Mrs. Hatchett's arm like it's a life line, her eyes are filled with tears. I look to either side of me to find both my friends look just as confused as me. Vox and the other's creep forward as the women come to a halt before me.

"Are you okay?" I ask the woman, she sniffs and smiles nodding her head.

"I'm Olivia... Tempest." My brows furrow. I cut a glance to Ezekiel who is standing stoically behind the woman, looking uneasy. I turn back to the woman and smile.

"I'm Nova and this is my friend Waylen." The woman nods but doesn't take her eyes off me.

"It's so nice to meet you, Nova," she whispers as more tears cloud her eyes. I cock my head to the side feeling awkward.

"Are you sure you're okay?" I ask.

She nods and quickly wipes her eyes, she tries to hide her tears but fails. "You must take some photos," she says, trying to sound cheerful.

"Mom, she has her own family to do that shit with, why—"

Olivia cuts Ezekiel off. "Enough! Nova and her friend will take photos, won't you?" I shoot Ez a look imploring him to help me but the asshole just huffs and looks away, leaving me no choice but to smile and agree to the woman's terms. Waylen is a good sport and doesn't complain as we cross the lawn to stand in front of Vox's house. Their mothers position us how they want us but when they step back and ready their phones, Jane calls for Waylen to switch with Vox. I nearly choke on my own spit when Vox shoulders Waylen from behind and claims his place. I shoot my best friend an apologetic look, as he stands beside Vox.

My breath hitches when Vox wraps an arm around my front and pulls me back until I am flush against his chest. I gasp just as they begin snapping photos. The moms tell us which way to look and turn but the whole time Vox never takes his hands off me. I'm starting to feel overwhelmed and the need to get the fuck out of here is strong. Just as I'm about to say we have to go, Olivia speaks up.

"Ezekiel, I want a picture of you and Nova." Both Ez and I snap our heads toward his mother utterly at a loss for words.

"Why?" he grits out.

His mother narrows her eyes. "Do as you're told," she scolds, then looks at me with a smile. "You don't mind, do you?" I open my mouth to refuse her but to my horror no words come out and I just nod. I shift to free myself of Vox's hold but he doesn't release me. I look up at him over my shoulder only to find him glaring at his best friend.

"I'm gonna need you to let go now, Voxy." He keeps his glare pointed at Ezekiel as he reluctantly releases me. I force myself not to read too much into whatever the fuck that was as I walk toward Ezekiel stiffly. Out of the four of them, he is the one I genuinely fear as there is a darkness that clings to him. I stand beside him, keeping a body space between us. To his defense he looks just as awkward as I do. His mother purses her lips and looks disapprovingly at us.

"Come on, you can do better than that." Both of us sigh and take a step closer to the other but there is still space which his mother clearly doesn't like. "Ezekiel, wrap your arm around her." My eyes widen in horror, I can feel Vox glaring at the both of us and it takes everything inside me not to turn on him and tell him that none of this is my fault.

"Fuck," Ez grits out, then closes the space between us. When his arm comes around my back, I tense and hold my breath.

"Smile," Olivia calls out.

"Take the freaking photo, Mom!" Ezekiel snaps. She doesn't argue as she snaps a few pics. The second she lowers her camera, I tear free of his hold and rush to Waylen, grabbing his hand and dragging him to my car as I call out my goodbyes. The second we are inside the car I still don't relax, until we are out of the driveway and halfway down the street.

"What the fuck was that?"

I shake my head. "I have no idea," I answer truthfully.

"Why the fuck did his mom want a picture of just the two of you?"

I shoot Waylen a perplexed look that has his face softening. "I have no idea. I have never met her before and it's not like me and Ezekiel are even friends."

"Does she know your mom?" I shake my head again. "Maybe try calling your mom and ask her."

"I tried calling her last night, this morning and while I was getting ready but she hasn't called me since Friday morning," I admit bitterly. I know I said I was fine with Mom being away and everything but I never thought she wouldn't call. This is my first dance and I guess a part of me had hoped she would come home and surprise me.

"Oh, that's not like her." I nod my agreement. Waylen knows my mom is a helicopter mom and is always there and wanting to know everything and to make sure I am okay. I've never gone this long without speaking to her. Waylen reaches over and places his hand on top of mine. "Hey, let her have this time to enjoy herself."

I force a smile to my face and nod but I can't shake this feeling that something is wrong. It's not like her to not call or even text. She always checks in and makes sure I have eaten. It's stupid, I'm turning eighteen soon and I shouldn't need my mom to check in on me but... I do.

"Come on, get out of your head. We have a couple of hours of fun before the doom and gloom looms over us." I can't help the laughter that bursts out of me. "What?" I can hear the mirth in his tone.

"Doom, gloom and loom, seriously?" Waylen's boisterous laughter sounds out and I can't help but join him, he always knows how to get me out of a funk and make me smile without even trying.

"Babe, we have the rest of the night to be angry and scared out of our minds but for right now, let's have this moment of teenage fun and enjoy this stupid dance. If I have to feel like a penguin for a few hours the least you can do is smile and enjoy my torment with me."

"Deal!" I concede. He's right. The least I can do is try to have fun before we go in search of the *Filthy Few* and ask the favor that will cost me my freedom.

CHAPTER TWENTY

Vox

I stand with my back against the wall and watch my sister, Nova and that bitch boy dancing. They are all laughing and look like they are having the time of their lives. It must be nice not having a fucking care in the world. My phone vibrating in my pocket has me snapping out of it and pulling it out. The sight of the name on the screen has me gritting my teeth, I answer and bring it to my ear.

"Couldn't this wait until you get back tomorrow?" I snarl.

"When you are fucking summoned, you appear. It isn't a request, Vox, it is mandatory for all members to be present. You are not exempt from that rule!" I grind my teeth side to side, praying that I can control the anger thrumming through me.

"Yeah, well, I had shit to do," I clip out.

"Want to walk the line as punishment, boy?" My nostrils flare.

"Why don't we stop fucking around and speak the truth,

Thomas. You want me out and my sister in so you can try and manipulate her into doing your bidding." My words could have me killed but I am past the point of caring, Haven Saints is nothing like what it once was. It's all politics now and helps greedy cunts line their pockets instead of hunting down fuckers who harm our town.

"You want to repeat that?" he asks in a deathly calm tone. The sight of Archer and Hayze walking toward me pull me from my downward spiral when I remember it's not just my life I am fucking with here. If I step out of line they will pay the price for my crime.

"I'll be at the next summons," I force out through clenched teeth.

"That's what I thought. Have you located the bastard fucking with us yet?" I scrub a hand down my face.

"No. We haven't found a trace of him." The truth is, we haven't even been looking for the fucker trying take down the Saints, he's doing a us favor without even knowing it.

"You find that fucking cunt!" he roars, then ends the call just as Archer and Hayze come to a halt before me.

"What's up with you and Ez?" Hayze asks.

I fight not to roll my eyes. "Nothing, he's just being a bitch."

"Is that so?" I lull my head to the side to see Ezekiel glaring at me, great, it's a family reunion.

"Fuck off, I don't have it in me to deal with your shit," I mutter as I turn back to watch Nova and the others and take a pull from my hip flask. Nicole and her cheer bitches are standing across the room trying to garner our attention but none of us are in the mood for their *look at me* bullshit tonight.

"We have a plan and you are ruining it, Vox," Archer says in a firm tone that surprises me.

"How am I doing that?" I ask as I step into him, bringing us chest to chest.

"Hey," I look over Archer's shoulder to see Nova standing there looking uncomfortable as fuck but what pisses me off more is the fact she is talking to Ezekiel.

"What do you want?" Ez snaps.

"To know what the hell your mom was up to before?" she claps back.

Ez shrugs. "Fuck if I know," he says dismissively.

"Well, nice to see you are still a dick." She shoots him a filthy look before turning and heading back to the dance floor where my sister is dancing with Waylen.

"You gonna stop that shit or should I?" Archer hisses. My moment of hesitation costs me, within a second Hayze and Archer are both storming toward my sister and make a show of shouldering past Nova who stumbles in her heels. Waylen releases my sister and rushes to Nova's side and that's when I see it.

"Looks like you aren't the only one pining after the bitch," Ezekiel says from beside me. I clench my fists at my sides and slowly turn to face my best friend.

"Seems to me your mother was pining after her as well. Maybe you should check in with Mommy and see why she was crying at the sight of the *bitch*." I leave him there to stew on my words as I head for Nova. I shove my flask into my pocket and choose to ignore the sight of Vivian dancing with Hayze and Archer. I'll let it slide because they saved me from breaking bitch boy's nose for touching her.

"I'm okay," Nova says to her friend just as I arrive. She jerks her gaze to me and frowns. "Vox?" She sounds shocked and slightly worried.

"Come on," is all I say, then grab her hand and pull her away from that punk. She doesn't protest or fight when I whirl around and wrap my arms around her waist, holding her close. Her hands rest flat on my chest as she stares up at me, I can see the wheels turning in her head wondering what my game is.

"What are you doing?" she asks as she darts her gaze around the room, no doubt seeing all eyes are on us.

"Dancing," I reply dryly.

"I know, dumbass, but why are you dancing with me and not your cheer squad?"

I snort. "Because thirsty bitches don't get my dick hard."

"And I do?" she volleys back.

"Your lips wrapped around my cock would." Her mouth parts on a gasp and red tinges her cheeks. She drops her gaze from mine and I smirk.

"That's not going to happen," I hear her mumble. Having too much fun embarrassing her I push on.

"And why is that?"

She flicks her eyes back to mine and I can see the shock in her features. "Seriously?"

"Yeah."

"Uh, maybe because you have been a dick to me since I arrived here and made sure that I know I am nothing but a *little witch* to you and your friends."

"You're a witch to me, not them."

She searches my gaze for a second, trying to decipher my meaning but she won't find what she is looking for.

"Well, I'm kind of... seeing someone anyway." I roll my lips over my teeth and nod. Her eyes narrow. "I'm serious!" she defends.

"Never said you weren't."

"Well, I am so you and me, we will never happen."

"I wouldn't be so sure about that, little witch."

"Nova, we have to go." I dart my head to the side and scowl at her friend, the cunt looks me dead in the eyes and doesn't back down.

"Okay," she whispers and tries to step back but I refuse to let her go. "Vox, I have to go."

I peer down at her and shake my head. "Nexus is a cunt but he isn't worth it." Her brows draw in and her forehead crinkles.

"What?" she breathes out.

"Release her, now." At the sound of Ezekiel's voice, I am left with no choice, I drop my hold and step back. She eyes me for a moment, trying to get a read on me but she won't, I'm already walling off my emotions and preparing. She looks from me to Ez a couple of times, then sighs and turns to her friend, who leads her outside with the palm of his hand on her lower back.

I'm gonna break that fucking hand.

"It's done, you can't stop it." I ignore Ez as I nod to Hayze and Archer, letting them know it's time. Archer grabs my sister's hand and follows after me as I lead us out the other exit. Our limo is idling at the curb. I wait for the others to climb in and just as I'm about to follow after them I spot Nova and Waylen across the lot, she is plucking a black envelope from beneath her windshield wiper. Waylen and her share a loaded look before her gaze cuts to me.

For a second I just stand there, lost in the depths of her eyes but the trance is broken when fuck boy cuts her from my view.

Tonight is the night the real carnage begins and years' worth of planning is finally put into motion.

CHAPTER TWENTY-ONE

Nova

I break the seal with shaky hands, slide the letter out and take a deep breath before I begin reading it aloud.

Nova-Scotia,
You need to run.
He knows I am after him and he has your mother!
You are not safe, my dear, and need to flee before he returns. I will come to you as soon as I can and explain everything.
Forgive me for not protecting her, I had a choice to make.
She forced me to make it. When all is revealed you will know who you are.
Run, my sweet girl.

"My mom," I choke out as I flick my gaze to Waylen. I unlock the car and climb inside, finding my phone in the console and immediately dial my mom. It rings so many times I fear she won't pick up until she does.

"Oh my God, Mom. I have been so worried—."

"Your mother isn't in right now, Nova." I sit ramrod straight in my chair at the sound of Thomas' voice. It doesn't hold that kind edge to it anymore, he sounds almost sinister. Waylen lays his hand on top of my shoulder offering me his silent support. He shoots me a look, encouraging me to play along and not make a scene.

"O-oh, hi, Thomas."

"Hello, dear. Your mother is occupied at the moment. I shall endeavor to get her to return your call when she can."

I take a deep breath. "What time do you and Mom get in tomorrow?"

"Oh, she didn't tell you? She hasn't been feeling like herself lately and has chosen to spend a few extra days here relaxing. I am leaving shortly to head home." I open my mouth to protest but he pushes on. "You and I shall have a chat when I return home, I don't like people snooping through my things, Nova, and I definitely don't like unwanted guests visiting my home in the middle of the night." My blood turns to ice in my veins, but before anything more can be said he ends the call. I turn to Waylen with wide, fear-filled eyes.

"He knows."

"What?"

I reach out and grip his arms. "Waylen, he knows about my finding the file and searching the house. He knows about my masked man."

"Your masked man?"

I ignore his questions. I start the car and take off toward the cemetery. I hope my hunch is right about where I find the *Filthy Few* because now more than ever I need their help and it just turns out that two horns is in as much shit as I am. Thomas must have cameras in the house. My stomach churns at the knowledge that he has seen me naked and being fucked. I want to hurl but I force myself to swallow the bile and drive faster, I know my mom is in danger. I felt it earlier but brushed off the feeling, thinking I was being a baby but it turns out, my gut was right all along.

The moment I park the car in the empty lot and we step out, I get the eerie sense we are being watched. A shudder rolls through me as I spin around and take in my surroundings. When I see nothing, I reach into the side of my door and pull the card out. Waylen comes to my side and turns on his phone's torch so I can read the inscription on the note two horns left me the first night he broke into my room.

Where they rest for eternal life is where a favor is asked.
The stone with the head is where you will be led.
Be certain of the favor you ask, we will not offer a second.
The debt will be collected when the favor is complete.
A favor asked is a debt owed.

"The stone with the head," I mutter as I look around trying to find said stone.

"Ah, Nova." I look to Waylen to see his gaze is focused across to the other side of the cemetery. I see four little lanterns that are clearly lighting a path. I swallow audibly and nod, toss the card back in the car and interlace my fingers with Waylen's as we cross the lot.

I can hear a freaking owl hooting in the trees and it only adds to my escalating fear. I don't like being here at night but something tells me if I came during the day I wouldn't find who I was looking for. Waylen's hold on my hand tightens as we near the first lantern, I can feel how clammy my hand is in his but he says nothing. I look around at the headstones and sadness washes over me at the sight of them, they are covered in moss and look weathered. Clearly their loved ones have forgotten about them and left them in their past.

When we reach the third lantern my heart begins to pound inside my chest, I can see the fourth lantern in the distance but it stands alone. As we draw near I dart my gaze around looking for any sign of life. Waylen pulls me to a stop and angles his body slightly in front of mine to shield me from something *or* someone. I peer around his shoulder, standing at the edge of the woods are four masked men not three like I expected. The newcomer's mask is brown and unlike the others who have horns on their masks this one doesn't, but it doesn't diminish the vicious look he exudes.

My attention is pulled to two horns when he shifts, taking a single step forward, showing he's the ringleader of this crew. I run my gaze over him and I can tell from the way he is standing with his fists clenched at his sides that he doesn't like how Waylen is hiding me from him, so I shift forward and stand beside him.

"The path has been followed, your favor may be asked," the

guy with the right horn says as he comes to stand beside two horns. I dart my gaze between the two of them, something doesn't feel right. I can't explain what it is but something in the pit of my stomach is telling me that if I do this, my life is going to change forever and I don't know if that is a good thing or a bad thing.

"Before anything happens I want assurances—"

Two horns speaks cutting Waylen off. "You do not speak!" he roars. I reel back in fright. Waylen wraps his arm around my shoulders and draws me into his side, the move sparks something inside two horns. He stalks toward us but before he can get to us, the other three hold him back.

"Enough!" no horns shouts, silencing everyone. My heart is thudding in my chest and I'm struggling to control myself. Part of me wants to run but the other part, the dark sinister part of me wants to run to two horns and promise that Waylen and I are just friends and this isn't what it looks like. I can tell that his friends have no idea that he and I have been fucking and it's easy to see that if they knew, this little meeting wouldn't be happening. "A favor asked is a debt owed."

"I know," I whisper.

"The debt must be paid in full," Left horn emphasizes.

I nod then exhale. "I understand."

"The favor is granted no matter the sacrifice. When the favor is complete you will pay the debt," no horns says, eyeing me with disdain.

"What is the debt?" Waylen asks. All four of them turn their attention to my best friend, a sudden urge to protect him spurs me into action. I dart in front of him and look directly at two horns, imploring him with my eyes to believe me.

"I will pay the price and repay the debt in full when my favor is complete but no harm is to come to my friend, okay?" The four of them share a look. Three of them grunt their agreement but two horns doesn't move or even says a word. Resigned to my fate and knowing I have no other choice, I need to find my mom and figure out who the fuck I am and what Thomas is up to.

"Ask your favor," two horns demands.

I dart my tongue out to moisten my lips and try to word this as best as I can because what I have to ask is more than a single favor. I decide to be honest and pray that they can help me, if not, I am royally fucked. The thought of not being able to get my mom back scares me beyond belief. If anything was to happen to her... I don't know what I would do. I know without needing it to be confirmed that my mom is in danger because of me, it's not a coincidence that from the moment I moved here that I have been getting letters from a long lost relative and these masked men have been hunting me

"Can you guarantee that what I am about to ask is going to be something you can achieve?" The four of them shake their heads and in unison they come toward us, leaving a foot of space between us and them. I feel so small and insignificant in front of these guys. To Waylen's credit, he doesn't back down or cower away.

"No favor asked is too much," right horn answers.

"A favor asked is a debt owed," no horns adds.

"We don't play by the normal rules others do, your favor will be granted in full," left horn says, even with the voice distorters I can feel the conviction in each of their vows.

"Ask your favor," Two horns grits out.

"I need you to help me find my mom and take down Thomas Valerian." For a moment no one speaks, not a sound is made except for the wildlife in the wood. I begin to gnaw on my bottom lip, worried that they are going to deny me.

"What is the reason for this favor?" right horn asks.

"Is that a requirement that you must know the reason?"

Waylen volleys back. When two horns attempts to step forward, I place my hand flat against his chest, halting his movements. I can feel the gazes of his three friends on us but ignore them as I focus on him. I lift my head and meet his angry gaze, the blue of his eyes is shrouded in darkness.

"Thomas has taken my mother out of town. He called me earlier and said she wasn't coming home with him and Nexus." He cocks his head to the side, not picking up what I'm putting down so I push on. "He knows I have been snooping through the house and he also knows... I have a guest every night." At my declaration I see his eyes narrow into slits.

"Why were you snooping through his house?" no horns asks.

I keep my gaze on two horns as I answer. "I've been getting letters from a relative I didn't know existed. I found proof that Thomas is a part of something called Haven Saints and I think... I think he covered up the deaths of my friend's parents."

Everything happens so fast I don't have time to prepare for what is happening, one second we are standing there and in the next two of the masked guys rush Waylen and tackle him to the ground, then two horns has a hand around my throat and I'm slammed against the tombstone hard enough to knock the air out of my lungs as he and right horn get in my face. I'm trying to drag in air but failing thanks to the grip he has on me. I spy Waylen out of the corner of my eye struggling to fight off the two who are pinning him to the ground. I scream out as no horns punches him in the face knocking him out.

"Stop!" I scream.

"Shut the fuck up, witch, and answer me!" I shake my head and stare back at two horns with tears trailing down my cheeks. Through the haze of everything I must have missed his question so he asks again, "What proof do you have?"

My fighter instincts kick in replacing the fear I felt. "Tell me something, *lover*, why would you care so much about the deaths of Virgil Hatchett and Edmund Tempest?" I don't wait for a response, I strike out and smack the mask from his face and instantly a sob tears free of me at the sight before me. Betrayal stings like a bitch, a part of me I guess always knew deep down but seeing it and knowing my suspicions were real are different.

CHAPTER TWENTY-TWO

Vox

Tears cascade down her cheeks as she stares up at me with an empty look in her eyes. The fact she figured it out has me respecting her a little but it changes nothing now that she knows the truth.

"Was this all a game?" she screams. My hold on her loosens slightly, she turns to Ezekiel and wills him without words to remove his mask. The instant he does she shakes her head. "I guess those two are Hayze and Archer?" I look over my shoulder to see both of them staring at her but neither of them remove the masks to confirm her suspicion.

"Where is the proof?" Ez grits out.

She snaps her gaze back to him, fire swirls in her eyes as she glares at my best friend. "Fuck you."

Ez smiles cruelly. "He already fucked you enough for the four of us." She sucks in a ragged breath at his words, I hear Arch and Hayze snickering behind us but they don't comment.

"Answer my question, Nova, I'm not fucking with you," he roars, she doesn't cower instead she just turns emotionless and voids her face of every emotion.

"What are you going to do, kill me?" She flicks her gaze to me as she says, "Fuck me until I plead for you to stop? Get me on my knees in front of your friends so they can watch me suck your cock just the way you like?" My nostrils flare as I grind my teeth. "You wanted me here to ask this fucking stupid favor, why? Was this the whole reason, so you could laugh in my face as I admitted I needed help? Was it all a fucking game to you?" she screams right in my face then shoves me back. I release her and allow her to shoulder past me as she makes her way toward her friend. "Get the fuck off him now!" The guys look at me and I nod. Both of them climb to their feet and step back, allowing her to kneel down beside Waylen. She strokes his cheek tenderly. "I'm so sorry I got you involved in this," she whispers.

When she tries to pull him up, he begins to stir. I turn to Ezekiel, waiting to see what the fuck we are going to do next now that she knows who the fuck we are. Just as the fucker starts opening his eyes both of us place our masks back on, her knowing is one thing but having two witnesses is another thing. Getting rid of one body is easy but when two people go missing that is harder to explain.

"Nova?" he groans out as he sits up. She throws her arms around him and holds him close. The sight has me wanting to knock his fucking teeth down his throat but I refrain.

"Come on, let's get out of here," she says as she helps him to his feet. Before they take a single step I motion for Hayze and Archer to block them. Nova spins around and glares at me. "Enough! You are going to let us go, right now."

"No!" Ez grits out, and before she can announce who the fuck we are, I step in.

"Send the punk to the car." Her eyes widen.

"I'm not leaving her!" the fucker snaps.

"Want to get knocked out again?" Archer counters. Nova darts her gaze between the four of us and knows she is out matched. When her shoulders sag, I know we have her.

"Way, I'll be right behind you—"

"No, Nova. I'm not leaving you," he rebukes.

"Please, trust me they won't do shit. Just go to the car and I'll be there in a minute." He looks down at her, I can see he wants to argue so I add.

"You don't fuck off right now, I'm taking her with us." Her jaw unhinges but she says nothing. It takes her another minute to get rid of him but the moment the weak bitch is gone, I pounce on her getting right in her face. "How the fuck did you know it was us?"

"*Us* or *You?*" she counters.

"Same difference," I snarl.

"The prom photos, you held me that same way the other night. You called me *witch* and that was my first clue but tonight, that's what sealed the deal."

"How?" I snap.

She reaches out and grips my hands, lifting them between us. "The lion and the lamb gave you away, dick bag." I look down and that's when I realize my error.

I'm not wearing gloves.

"You knowing changes nothing, you asked the favor and owe us a debt, Nova Quinlin. If you think the shit we did before was bad, you just wait until you see what we have in store for you next."

She drops her hold on my hands and turns to face Ez. "You threatening to kill me, Ezekiel?" He steps forward until his chest brushes against her, forcing her to crane her head back to meet his gaze.

"You knew the rules—"

"The *Filthy Few* is nothing but a pack of bored boys playing a man's game." Ez snaps his hand out and grips the back of her neck, forcing her onto her tiptoes then bends down getting in her face but she turns at the last minute, her eyes collide with mine and I see nothing but loathing and hatred.

"Your favor will be granted and we will collect our debt. I want that evidence you have on the murders. Hand it over and we'll take that cunt and his son down for good. And maybe, if you're a good girl, we'll even help you get your mommy back." He releases her with a hard shove. She stumbles back into Archer, who grips her waist on instinct to steady her. I force myself to remain where I am and not intervene.

She tears out of Arch's hold and steps back, putting space between her and us. She looks between my three boys but ignores me completely. "Fuck you all, I'll deal with this shit myself and find my mom without your fucking help, you assholes." She spins on her heel and storms off as we stand here watching her run to her car. I don't move until her car is out of sight as she speeds away. When I turn back to my boys I'm met with a jab to the gut. I cough and hunch forward.

"The fuck, Hayze?" I snap through the pain.

"You were fucking her the whole time?" he roars.

I straighten and look at the three of them. "Yes."

"You stupid fuck! Thanks to you she knows who we are!" Archer snarls as he yanks his mask off, the rest of us follow his lead.

"She won't say anything."

"How the fuck can you know that shit, Vox? If she blabs her mouth, then people are going to start piecing together that we were behind the disappearances of the other members." I shake my head, this wasn't our first favor. We have forced members' children and friends to ask a favor, in return we have eliminated those members and disposed of the person, making sure none of it could be traced back to us. We are no saints, but we needed intel and the only way to get that shit was to torture some of them.

None of them gave up what we needed.

"She won't because she would have to admit to liking *me*, she told me more than once she was seeing someone only for it to be me she was fucking. She is too proud to admit to anyone that she has been fucking the guy that has made her life hell." The three of them eye me with disdain. I ignore their disapproving looks and head back through the woods to where we parked. We all change out of our clothes and slip the tuxes back on before climbing inside the car and heading home. It's a Saturday night, so that means these three will be crashing at my house, so I head there. When we pull into the driveway, I see Vivian's bedroom light is still on. I can't stop myself from looking next door, Nova's car sits in the driveway but no lights are on in the house.

"I want that proof, Vox. If I have to hurt the bitch to get it, then I will," Ez declares. I scrub a hand down my face and nod.

"We'll do what we have to, we won't let Thomas get away with this shit," I say.

"Even with the proof, we need more than that to stop the Haven Saints. The laws clearly state that the new lord has to be a female! Unless one of you fuckers has another idea then all of this is for fucking nothing!" Archer snaps as he shoves his door open and storms off toward the house.

"He's right, killing Thomas won't change the fact that the next in line is Vivian, Vox." I bare my teeth at Hayze. "Dude, I don't want her in this shit, I never have. Vivi is too good for this bullshit and way too good for this place. All I am saying is we need to figure something out and get her out of this place or find another way." Hayze climbs out and follows after Archer, leaving me and Ez alone in the car.

"She means nothing to me," I say after a few minutes of tense silence.

"Then prove it and destroy her, Vox, or make her give up the proof she has. I need to know what the fuck happened to my father… I have to know. Get me that information and I will let this shit go, but if I am forced to do it myself there will be nothing left of her. She is nothing to me and I won't have any issue slitting her throat and tossing her off the canyon like the others."

"We'll get the proof, take down Thomas, get rid of… the little witch then we deal with the Haven Saints."

"He gets back tomorrow."

"I know. We need to press Nexus when they get back about why they were gone and what the fuck they were doing," I say.

"If they really did do something to her mom, then we need to find out why she is so important and who the fuck this relative is that has been sending her letters."

It hits me then and I turn to Ezekiel.

"He was the fucker that was in my house!" I snap as I shove my door open and race around the back of Nova's house ready to kick her back door in, but to my surprise I find her sitting on one of the loungers with a photo clasped between her hands and tears trailing down her cheeks. I hear Ezekiel come up behind me and the both of us share a look before I step forward. The second she stiffens I halt and wait for her to say something.

"The whole house is bugged, he has cameras everywhere and knows what I did. He knows what *we* did in his house." I move forward and sit on the edge of the lounger beside her and drape my hands over the tops of my thighs.

"How do you know that, little witch?" I ask. She grabs her phone beside her and unlocks it then tosses it to me.

"Congratulations, asshole, you're famous and just ruined my life." I press play on the video and my stomach sinks, it's a video of me fucking Nova against the filing cabinet in Thomas' office. It doesn't show the full video but at the end of the thirty second clip a message appears.

> **NEXUS**
>
> Now you're mine to do with as I please, piggy, or this goes on Pornhub with your name attached to it.

I look back over my shoulder at Ezekiel who looks murderous. My own anger is rearing inside me. Yes, I fucked her and made her do things without knowing who I was, but she was consenting to that shit. Nexus and Thomas did this without her consent and that fucking bullshit won't fly. You may not be able to tell it's me thanks to my mask but you can see Nova's face clear as day.

"Nova—"

She cuts me off. "Read the message from Thomas." I purse my lips and do as she says, when the message thread from Thomas appears on the screen my mouth hangs open and my eyes widen.

> **THOMAS**
>
> Time to learn how things work, be a good girl and mommy stays safe. Be a naughty girl and mommy pays the price.

The image attached is of her mother in a plain green gown strapped to a bed with a doctor injecting her with something. Before either of us can say a word she stands and snatches her phone out of my grasp. I stare up at her and flinch at the sight of hatred and disgust in her green eyes when she looks down at me.

"You want the proof and your identity to remain a secret?"

"Yes," I say without hesitation.

"Help me find my mom, take down Thomas and his cunt of a son and I will pay whatever fucking debt you want," she says with such conviction I know she means every word.

"He's going to come after you," Ez says.

She shrugs. "I live with the bastards. I have no choice but to take what they give until I get my mom back. Don't worry, there are no cameras out here," she adds the last part as an afterthought.

"Who is the relative helping you, Nova?" Ezekiel pushes.

She shakes her head. "I have no idea. I don't even know who my father is but my long lost uncle told me he's dead. Help me and I will help you," she says, then turns on her heel and heads toward the house but as she grips the handle she pauses and looks back over her shoulder meeting my gaze. "Don't ever come to me again, Vox. You stay the fuck away from me." She darts her gaze to Ezekiel. "He comes anywhere near me. I'll burn the evidence I have about both your fathers. Oh, and if any of you ever touch Waylen again, the deal is off!" Both Ez and I suck in a ragged breath at her threat.

CHAPTER TWENTY-THREE

Nova

I forced Waylen to catch a red eye flight back home last night. He tried to fight me but I refused to bend. With Thomas and Nexus returning home today, I needed to make sure my best friend was away from here and safe, they already have my mom, the last thing I need is for them to get their filthy hands on him. I couldn't sleep at all last night, every creak in the house had me bolting upright and my breath hitching. The one thing Waylen did help me with before he left was checking my room for bugs.

We found six!

I burst into tears, they may not have had microphones and been able to hear anything that was said but the fact that two of the cameras were in my bathroom, had me emptying the contents of my stomach in the toilet. They have seen everything. I am so angry and feel violated but there isn't a fucking thing I can do about it without risking my mom. I need to find her and get her somewhere safe, away from these crazy bastards.

I feel so alone, not having my mom here or knowing where she is right now is killing me. Having to send Waylen home and not having him by my side hurts like a bitch. Waylen has been blowing up my phone since he landed but I've ignored his calls and messages. I told him to get as far away from me as he can but in true Waylen fashion he refused.

My phone pings with a text and the sight of Nexus' name on the screen has my stomach dropping. I gingerly reach for it and open the message. There's no text, just an image, me on my knees in my bathroom with Vox's cock down my throat. Bile rushes up my throat but I swallow it down when Nexus begins calling me. I take a second to gather myself before I answer.

"Yes?"

"Oh, piggy, is that anyway to greet your big brother?" I grind my teeth and fist the comforter in my free hand.

"What do you want?" I force out.

"Do you think you could suck my dick as good as you sucked your Jason wannabes?" My brows draw in as I mull over his words.

"My friend?" I hedge.

"Well, that fucking mask wearing pussy isn't a friend of mine." I swallow my gasp and play along.

"He isn't my friend."

"So you just fuck anyone with a cock, is that it?"

I brush off his question with one of my own. "What's the point of this call?"

"I'll be home tonight. Dad is staying in the city and will join us tomorrow."

"Okay..."

"Be ready to play when I get home, piggy." His ominous threat sends a shiver of dread down my spine. When he disconnects the call I sit here and stare at the wall in front of me that holds all the pictures of my happiest memories.

They don't know it was Vox in the mask.

I debate whether or not I should call but only having *his* number doesn't leave me with much of a choice—if I had one of the others I would have called them. I take a deep breath and hit call on his number, it rings three times before he answers.

"What?" I look at the clock on my wall and cringe but then remember I don't give a fuck about Vox or the fact I woke him up at six in the morning.

"Nexus called, he's coming tonight."

"Yeah?"

"Look, asshole, he doesn't know it's *you* in the videos only me."

"*Videos?*" A whoosh of air escapes me.

"Yeah, he sent me a still shot of me... it doesn't matter. He doesn't know it's you and that's my point."

"And what is your point exactly, witch?" I slam my eyes closed, hearing that name before sent a thrill through me but now I know that it was him the whole time it just fills me with disgust, knowing I allowed him to play me for a fool and let him fuck me however he wanted without protest.

"I hate you," I breathe out as I fight back tears of shame.

"Yes, we have established that but what's your point?" I can hear the anger that laces his words.

"Be his friend, let him think you guys are buddies and maybe he will open up to—"

"Nova, we are the *Filthy Few* and we have ways to take down—"

"If that were true then you wouldn't have needed me to find this proof, Vox!" I shout.

"If you don't admit that it was me in those videos with you, he is going to destroy you until you give him a name." It almost sounds like he regrets that I am the one who is going to bear the brunt of the punishment for our crime.

"So what? I don't care. Use your friendship with him to get me what I want and I will never tell him it was you."

"You know what that means, right?" I sigh and nod even though he can't see me.

"You and your band of bitches go back to making my life hell, well, good luck with that one, Voxy boy, because this time I'm fighting back and I'll make sure I fucking leave a mark on all of you."

"Game on, witch."

I scoff. "Show me what ya got, dick bag."

I'm sitting at the breakfast bench, spinning my phone round and round on the counter as I wait for Nexus. I haven't left the house all day. I know they are watching me and I'm scared to step a single foot out of line in case they take it out on my mom. Just thinking of her and the image of her strapped to that bed has tears springing to my eyes.

I'll make this right, Mom, I vow to her silently.

I won't let these assholes take her from me, I just need to buy myself some time to figure out what it is that they want from me. The instant I hear his car pull into the driveway, I force myself to remain calm and appear relaxed as I start scrolling through my phone. I know they can check the cameras but I'm doing this more for my satisfaction than his. When the front door opens, I brace myself and wait for the dreaded encounter.

"Aww, what a good piggy, waiting to greet me." I grit my teeth and don't acknowledge him until I feel him stand behind me. I stop scrolling and wait for the bastard to make his next move. I shudder in revulsion when he brushes my back, exposing the side of my neck. He rests his chin on my shoulder and wraps his arms around my waist. My breaths are coming in rapid pants, it may be irrational but I feel fear surging inside me and my flight or fight instincts are kicking in. "You want to get off, piggy, you find me hot not that mask-wearing bitch." I jerk out of his hold and climb to my feet facing him, the sinister look in his eyes and the cruel smile sends dread pooling inside me.

"I may not be able to do anything to you—"

"That's right, you are mine to do with as I please. You fuck up and all it would take to end that bitch is a single phone call." My bottom lip begins to tremble but I refuse to allow him to see me cry. "When I call, you come. When I tell you to kneel, you fucking kneel!"

I stare at him in disgust, I knew he was a bastard but I never thought him or Thomas would be cold-blooded killers. I feel tears burning the backs of my eyes as the weight of the whole situation crashes down on me—I'm living with killers and they have my mom as a hostage!

"Ahhhh, now you're starting to get it," he coos smugly.

"Get what?" I force out.

"That you are nothing, you are worthless and nothing more than a toy I get to play with until Dad calls you into action. Two more months, Nova, and then you will be mine to do with as I please. In my world your pussy makes you weak. You will learn to live beneath me and under me." Bile rushes up my throat at his insinuation.

"What happens in two months?"

"Well, your birthday of course, piggy!"

"I'm not a toy!" I scream at him. I tense when he stalks toward me, smiling. I grind my teeth when he grips the back of my neck and pulls me in close.

"You have no idea who the fuck you are and by the time you figure it out, it will be too late." Before either of us can say more, the front door opens and I hear footfalls enter the kitchen behind us. The second the hairs on the back of my neck prickle with awareness I know exactly who it is. Nexus flicks his gaze over my head and I see his upper lip twitch in a snarl before he quickly masks his features and plasters a smile on his face, then spins me around so my back is to his chest. Vox, Ezekiel, Hayze and Archer all stand there staring at us with masks of indifference in place. "What's up guys?"

Try as he might, Vox can't hide his loathing for my step-brother. I never noticed it before but I see it now in the way his eyes darken as he stares at Nexus.

"Nothing, bro, just saw your car and thought we'd come say what's up and see how your trip went?" Hayze says easily as he strolls into the kitchen and helps himself to the fruit bowl on the counter like nothing is amiss. Archer and Ezekiel follow his lead but Vox doesn't budge from his spot or take his eyes off me and Nexus.

Worried he will give us away and destroy my only chance of getting my mom back, I play along. "I'll leave you idiots to it then, I have shit to catch up on," I say in a bored tone. As I attempt to free myself from Nexus' hold, he places a kiss to the side of my head that sends disgust surging inside me.

"I'll see you soon, piggy," he says as I snatch my phone off the counter and brush past Vox without sparing him a second glance. Once I'm safely inside the confines of my room I finally breathe a little easier, until I see the black envelope on my bed. My heart pounds in my chest as I grab it and turn it over to see the same seal with a T in gold. I sigh and pull the letter out hoping that it will offer some form of help, if not this long lost uncle is as useless as tits on a bull.

Nova-Scotia,
You should have run!
Bring the masked men and meet at the same spot you met them.
I will be there at the stroke of midnight on Saturday night.
Conform to their rules, Thomas is hunting me so I can't get to you sooner.
Be strong, do whatever it takes to survive.
Trust no one!

Well, that letter doesn't help me with shit but I guess at least I will finally be able to put a face to my secret letter writer. But something that doesn't sit right with me is the fact he knows about the *Filthy Few*... How?

CHAPTER TWENTY-FOUR

Vox

Spending Sunday with Nexus wasn't my idea. Archer and Hayze knew he would be trying to push his weight around with her and in their weird attempt to try and help her, we kept him occupied all day. The fucker is so full of himself and has even planned a beach party on Saturday night for his welcome home celebration. All I want to do is break his teeth, seeing him standing there with Nova had me fighting with everything inside me not to snap his neck. I saw it in her eyes. She is terrified but has no other choice but to take what he and Thomas give.

I want to go to her and just see she is okay with my own eyes, but with the cameras inside the house I can't risk it. Vivian texted her this morning and offered her a ride to school but she refused, saying she was riding with Nexus, which we all know was his idea not hers. Ez, Hayze, Arch, Vivi and I are standing beside my Challenger Demon, it's been a hot minute since I have taken this vicious bitch out for a drive and I decided today was the day. Students mill around us, trying to spark a conversation. Vivian doesn't acknowledge any of them, instead she shrinks between Archer and Ezekiel and uses them as shields. Both my boys shift subtly to keep her from the view of everyone else. Every guy here wants her but it's the girls she hates most because they hate they can't be her.

"Yo, it's Nexus and Nova." I follow Tim's line of sight and sure enough Nexus' Audi pulls up beside us, forcing everyone to move out of their way. I look past him to Nova to see her staring straight ahead but it's the hard set of her jaw that has me frowning. Nexus climbs out smiling and shakes hands with a few of the guys before disappearing around the car. A second later my brows raise and white hot fury surges inside me at the sight of him leading Nova around the car by a lead. She has a studded leather collar around her neck and it isn't the fancy kind, it is literally a dog collar!

She keeps her head down, using her long raven hair to shield her face from everyone. I shift toward them only for Ez and Hayze to block me against my car.

"She has a part to play and so do we," Ezekiel warns. I grit my teeth and glare down at them.

"You son of a bitch!" At the sound of my sister's angry shout I spin around to see her storming toward Nexus. Archer reaches for her but she sidesteps him and gets right in Nexus' face.

"Ah, Vivian, what an unpleasant surprise," he snarks back.

"Fucking watch it," I warn. Nexus rolls his eyes, brushing off my warning as he looks down at my sister who now has Archer plastered against her back.

"You needle dick bastard, get that shit off her!" Vivi screams as she reaches for Nova. Nexus raises his hand to push her away but Archer is faster, he has Nexus' wrist gripped in his hand, then Ez is rushing toward them, pushing both Archer and Vivian back, sandwiching my sister between their bodies.

"You can fuck around with your sister but not Vox's. You know the rules," Ez snarls in a tone that has everyone bowing their heads. Nexus plays off Ez's words with a laugh and shakes his head trying to play the part.

"It's all cool, my man." He turns to Nova and unclips the lead then pats her on the head. "Off you go to class, piggy." Without lifting her head or saying a word she turns and heads toward the front doors. Nicole and her cheer bitches have their phones out snapping pictures and videos, teasing Nova who still won't say anything or even look up.

"You are a fucking piece of shit, Nexus!" Vivian snaps before running after her friend. I shoot Archer a look telling him without words to follow my sister. He taps Ezekiel on the shoulder and the both of them go after the girls. Hayze and I grab our shit and head toward the gym but Nexus calls out, stopping us in our tracks.

"Don't be late to lunch, you won't want to miss the new tricks I've taught my piggy." Everyone laughs, I say nothing and continue on to my first class.

"The shit we did to her wasn't even this bad. He had her beaten, Vox, and now this. What's he going to do to her next?" Hayze asks. I can hear the concern in his voice and that shit worries me more because he doesn't care about many people.

"The favor she asked is one we can't grant without the proof she holds," I admit bitterly.

"We've never not been able to deliver."

"I know. We need to find her mom, get her back and then she will hand over the proof. Once we have that we can take down the Haven Saints and Thomas and his little cunt of a kid," I snap as we enter the gym and head for the locker room.

We're the only ones here but I don't give a shit I needed to get away from Nexus.

"Okay, I'll make a call to Tyler and have him start tracking their movements and see if we can locate her mom—" Hayze clamps his mouth closed as we enter the locker room and see Nova standing there.

"What are you doing here?" I bite out. She says nothing as she stalks toward us and slaps a black envelope against my chest and pushes between us to escape, but I snap my arm out and grip hers, stopping her escape.

She glares up at me. "Stay away from me, Vox, I mean it." I hear the plea in her tone but the look in her eyes begs me to ignore her order.

"What's he doing to you?" I find myself asking.

She yanks her arm free of my hold. "Nothing you didn't do yourself, you just never put a leash on me." Her words knock the air out of me. She flees the locker room, leaving us standing here staring after her.

"I think you just met your match." I shoot Hayze a scowl before bending down and collecting the envelope off the ground. I flip over and immediately my breath hitches. "Dude..." Hayze breathes out. I flick my gaze to his and see the same look of shock on him that I feel inside at the sight of the *Tempest* seal.

"Edmund," I mutter. When we hear voices approaching I pocket the letter and move to my locker.

"We need to tell Ezekiel," Hayze says as he opens his locker. I nod my agreement and end the conversation as the rest of the team comes barreling in. I shoot Archer a text to keep an eye on Nova in math class, I have chem with her next and Hayze has English with her this afternoon. Archer's reply comes almost instantly, it's a picture of Nova sitting in the back of the class with Nicole right in her face.

ARCHER

Bitch is dogging your girl, bro.

ME

Not my girl, asshole, get rid of the mutt and watch her.

I get out of the solo chat with Archer and bring up our group message.

ME

Something's come up, meet us after first period.

EZ

What is it?

HAYZE

Your past has come back.

EZ

The fuck does that mean?

ME

Don't worry, just meet us after first period.

ARCHER

Oh shit! Your girl just showed her claws.

video

I hit play and instantly my brows raise at the sight of Nova shoving her chair back and getting right in Nicole's face.

"You think you're better than me," Nova snaps.

"Oh, I know I am," Nicole says as she flips her hair over her shoulder. "You think they notice you? Girl, please. I am the only one they have *all* slept with." Her three friends all nod and smile to pump up their queen but Nova's laughter is loud and mocking, silencing them all.

"Have at them, girl. Go slam that pussy of yours on their

cocks and let them destroy your self-worth some more because *none* of those fuckers are worth it. But hey, if desperate is what they are into, then you are sure to be their first pick."

> HAYZE
>
> She just shat all over Vox with that line.

I shoot the fucker a glare but he just shrugs and purses his lips.

> EZ
>
> She is never fucking you again.
>
> HAYZE
>
> So...
>
> Is she free game?

I toss my phone in my locker and shoulder the cunt as I stalk out of the locker room, his taunting laughter follows me but I ignore the bitch. I need to nail some fuckers on the field and get rid of this pent up anger before I do something stupid like go and prove to Nova I'm not someone she can forget.

I stalk into chem and spot Nova instantly in her usual spot. I slam my books down on the table but she doesn't even react, she just keeps doodling in her book and ignoring me completely. I'm on edge and need an outlet. I couldn't meet up with the guys because practice ran over and Hayze made sure to keep fucking with me and taunting me with how he would ask Nova to come out later.

I know what he is doing, he's trying to get me to admit that she means something to me. I'm more on edge because of the fucking letter that is burning a hole in my pocket than anything else.

"Desperate, huh?" I grit out. She keeps her head down and continues to draw as she answers.

"If that's what turns you on, go for it." Her answer just fuels my rage.

"Some might say you dropping to your knees for a stranger is desperate." The only indication that I have that my words are effecting her is the slight hunch of her shoulders.

"Yeah, well, unlike your pussy squad out there, I don't make the same mistake twice. You know, fool me once and all that shit."

"If I recall it was a lot more than twice," I say in a husky tone that has her finally turning her gaze to me but I did not expect her to look up at me with tears in her eyes—anger yes but not fucking tears.

"Yeah, it was a lot more but unlike you, I wasn't hiding or pretending, it was real for me!" I open my mouth to try to defend myself but she pushes on. "I'm paying for the mistakes I made, unlike you. I'm living in hell until the guy who fucked me over with his friends helps me. So, tell me, Vox, how did I wrong you again?" I open and close my mouth but no words come out. She scoffs and returns her attention back to her book and continues to scribble. I peer over her shoulder and grit my teeth when I read what she wrote.

Vox Hatchett is a bitch.
Die Ezekiel.
Hayze is a pussy.
Archer needs to be shot with an arrow.
They are filthy, disgusting and make me sick, especially two horns!

Before I realize it, the bell rings and I heard nothing from the professor. I was too lost in my own head repeating what she wrote over and over again. She tears the page from her books and tosses it to me as she stands and stalks out of the room. Students snicker and taunt her thanks to the collar and the show Nexus put on this morning. I look down at the sheet and crumple it, not wanting to read her hatred of me again.

I exit the classroom and head toward the cafeteria as my phone pings with a text.

THOMAS

Nine sharp, be there!

Son of a bitch!

I pocket my phone and round the corner, spotting Ez and Archer leaning against my locker. They shoot me a look but when I spot Nexus and Hayze coming toward us, I give them a subtle shake of my head. The letter is going to have to wait until after lunch at this fucking rate.

"Come on, boys, I have a surprise for you!" Nexus shouts, drawing the attention of everyone. I say nothing as I follow after him and the others. I dart my gaze around and don't see anything, but then my gaze lands on Nova standing at the edge of our usual table holding a tray. Nexus laughs loudly and rubs his hands together as he approaches her.

Disgust rolls through me at the sight of her standing there with her head down looking utterly powerless.

"This is how we should be greeted!" Nexus calls out. Everyone turns toward the five of us but when they spot Nova, all their phones are pulled and they begin recording her shame. I harden my features making sure not to give anything away, we can't help her or we risk fucking up the plan—I risk fucking up the plan. "Put my tray down." She does as he says and places it on the table.

"Good, piggy, now... *kneel.*" It takes everything inside me not to display my shock. I watch her inhale sharply then slowly lower to her knees. Laughter and cheers sound out around the room at the sight of her on her knees before Nexus. He pats the top of her head. "Good, piggy! Come on boys, let's eat."

I'm the first to take my seat but I don't spare Nova a glance, not even when every fucker comes over to snap pics of her and taunt her. Hayze and Archer look like they want to smash Nexus' skull in but refrain. I look around the table but don't see Ezekiel. Nexus is still there smiling and talking to a few of the guys as he eats.

"Get the fuck away from her!" I snap my head to the side to see my sister shouldering every motherfucker out of her way so she can get to Nova. My eyes narrow when I see Ezekiel standing behind her carrying something, Vivian turns around and snatches the bucket out of his grasp and then tips it on Nexus, He shoves back from the table but slips over in the... crimson liquid.

"You fucking bitch!" he roars. It takes a split second for me and the two beside me to be on our feet.

"You want to be a big boy, then let's play Carrie!" Vivi snaps as she grabs Nova's arm and hauls her to her feet.

"Oh shit, it's pig's blood!" someone calls out and then everyone is laughing and filming Nexus who is covered head to toe in pig blood. I look to Ezekiel to find his gaze already on me but it's the dark look in his eyes that gives me pause.

"I'm done playing, I don't like her but I won't watch Vivian suffer because her friend is hurting," is all he says before he turns and goes after my sister and Nova.

CHAPTER TWENTY-FIVE

Nova

I try pulling free of her hold but she won't let me go. "Vivian, stop!" I call out as she drags me through the parking lot toward Vox's car. Just as she reaches his car I manage to get free only to stumble back into someone, I whirl around to see Ezekiel standing there with a furious look on his face. I swallow audibly as I stare up at him. He takes a step forward and I take one back, causing him to narrow his eyes. When he lifts his hand I flinch and his eyes widen in anger, forcing me to remain still as he reaches around my neck and unclasps the collar.

"Don't ever let anyone do this shit to you," he snarls, then tosses the collar onto the hood of Nexus' car. When I dart forward to try and grab it, he hauls me back with an arm around my waist.

"Get the fuck off me!" I scream. He shoves me back against Vox's car, then gets right in my face.

"You want to fight, then fight him, don't fucking bow down," he grits out, anger lacing each of his words.

"I can't," I whisper, hating how defeated I sound. "Thomas gets home tonight and I need to obey everything he says or you know what he will do," I admit.

"What's going on here?" The sound of Vivian's voice breaks us apart. Ez stabs a hand through his hair and tugs on the strands in agitation.

"Nothing," I mutter.

"Oh, so is this the part where I play dumb and act like I have no idea about what you all have been up to?" Ezekiel snaps his head toward Vivian in shock. She meets his gaze with a quirked brow and a hand on her hip. "Vox may shelter me as best he can but I'm not stupid, Ez. I know a lot more than I let you all think."

"Vi, you have no idea—"

She cuts him off. "About the Haven Saints? Or is it about the *Filthy Few?*" she mock whispers their crew name. Ezekiel's mouth pops open at the same time mine does. I stare at my friend in astonishment, it never once occurred to me to reach out to her and ask for help.

"Vivian!" The moment is shattered by the sound of Vox's voice. He, Hayze and Archer all storm toward us, looking like a dark cloud of angry energy. He wraps his arm around her shoulder and then looks at me with concern and pity in his blue eyes. I scoff and turn away from him, crossing my arms over my chest.

"I know, I shouldn't have done that but can we save the lecture for later?" she pleads with her brother. My phone begins to ring, silencing everyone. I pull it out and frown at the unknown number but answer it anyway.

"Hello?"

"Miss Quinlin?"

My brows draw in. "Yeah?"

"My name is Hannah and I am one of the nurses caring for your mother." My stomach bottoms out.

"Where is she?" I shout, in an instant I feel Vox come up behind me but I ignore him and the others surrounding me.

"She has had to be sedated again—"

I cut the bitch off. "Where is she, please just tell me where she is?" I sob out. Vox wraps his arm around my waist, drawing me back into him. I allow it because right now his hold is the only thing keeping me from falling to my knees.

"That information is private, all I can tell you is she is now resting and will remain that way. Take care, Miss Quinlin."

"No!" I scream out. As the call disconnects, a strangled sound tears out of me. Vox spins me around and I bury my face in his chest as I allow the tears to fall. His hold on me is strong and protective—and as much as I know I need to pull away from him and not let myself fall into the trap he is setting, I can't find the strength to do it. I give myself another minute to break apart before I pull away from Vox. I turn my back to them as I wipe away my tears and compose myself.

I straighten and take a few deep breaths then steel my spine as I turn to face them all. Each of them stand there, looking worried and guilty—good they should feel guilty.

"Nova—"

I shake my head silencing Vivian, bless her and everything but now is not the time. I can't step out of line or allow them to help me. Nexus just showed me that he isn't bluffing. When I move forward the guys let me past but the growl that comes from Ezekiel when I grab the collar has me turning to face them. They all look pissed off at the sight of the collar in my hand but this is how it has to be. I focus my attention on Vivian knowing she is going to be the hardest to convince.

"I need you to stay away from me," I plead.

Her face falls. "Nova, we can help you."

I shake my head and smile sadly. "I appreciate that. I've never had a friend stick up for me aside from Waylen. What you did will always mean a lot to me, Vivian, but I can't allow my mom to be hurt because of me." I look to Vox next, he looks like the devil crawled inside him and is using his skin as a suit. "You need to read the letter, we have a week. Stay away from me, Vox, all of you need to pretend like I don't exist."

"What if I can't?" His question shocks the fuck out of me. It seems it has shocked the others as well because they are staring at him with wide eyes.

"It isn't your choice to make. You wanted me destroyed, wanted information from me and you used my body to get it. Every part of my house may be monitored but not my bedroom. I used your entry and exit point to sneak out and stash the files in your garden shed last night. You have your proof, Vox, now leave me alone."

"Wait, how does Vox know how to get into your room?" Vox flinches at his sister's question but unlike him I won't lie or hide shit from her.

"Vivi, you know how I mentioned I was seeing someone?" I feel like a dick saying that out loud but she nods. "Turns out the guy that was fucking me into a coma was your brother. I'm sorry I didn't tell you because truth is, I never knew it was him either or I wouldn't have let it happen." Her mouth is ajar. The guys snicker while Vox stands there working his jaw side to side. I don't stick around for a reply, I have a role to play and a stepbrother to appease, so I secure the collar around my neck and hold my head high as I stroll through the front doors of the school and ignore all the looks from everyone as I pass them, heading to my locker.

Just as I'm pulling the last of my text books out, the locker door is slammed shut. I just manage to shift my hand at the last second so it doesn't get squashed. I turn my head to the side to see Nexus standing there, covered in blood and a vindictive look in his eyes.

"Did you enjoy that phone call?"

My nostrils flare at his taunt. "I had nothing to do with what happened," I grit out.

"Seems my so called *friends* don't agree with my punishment for you." I choose to remain silent rather than instigating his wrath. He darts his gaze over my shoulder and I know without a doubt that Vox and the others just entered the hallway. "Be good or mommy gets it," he sneers, then grips the back of my head and yanks me forward, slamming his mouth against mine. I shake my head trying to break free but the look in his soulless green eyes warns me not to reject him or my mom will pay the price. His hand grips my waist in a move to show possession to everyone watching. He breaks the kiss and shoots me a wink as I drop my gaze to the floor feeling disgusted and ashamed.

"Seems we know why the toy was declared off limits," Vox says casually like I'm not standing right here. I steel my resolve. This is what I asked of him and the others to pretend they don't know me.

"A bit of taboo never hurt anyone, right?" Nexus says cockily. I feel bile rise in my throat but swallow it down and push off the lockers to head to my next class. Nexus is planning something for revenge against Vivian, there is no doubt about that in my mind, we just need to keep her and my mom safe for the rest of the week and then we can get rid of him and his father.

When the final bell sounds, I make my way out to the parking lot but come to a stop when I don't see Nexus' car in the lot. Vox and the others stand by his car, the sight of Nicole smiling up at Vox has my stomach churning. I scan the lot once more before deciding the cunt left me behind. I sigh and lower my head as I start my long walk home.

"Look everyone! There goes the piggy," Nicole calls out. I don't react to her or everyone else *oinking* at me. I clutch my books tighter against my chest and continue walking. I feel someone come up beside me and I reel back when I see it's Ezekiel.

"Keep walking and don't stop. I'm not interfering with your plans but I'm also not letting you walk out of here alone with these fucking vultures pawing at you." His words have me softening toward him. "Head up, Nova, you may wear his collar but you are not beneath him." Tears of gratitude prick the backs of my eyes. I do as he says and keep my head held high as we walk out of the school side by side.

CHAPTER TWENTY-SIX

Vox

I wait another five minutes for the lot to start emptying before I shove Nicole off me and ignore her pouting, I toss my keys to Archer, who frowns but says nothing when I shake my head. Hayze and Vivian climb in the back. We catch up to Ez and Nova in no time. When Archer pulls over beside them, she smiles at Ez and thanks him but before she takes another step I shove my door open and grab her.

"Vox!" she snaps as I pull her inside the car and lock my arm around her waist, securing her on my lap. "Jesus, let me go!"

"Shut the fuck up!" I snarl in her ear. Instantly she stills and clamps her mouth closed as Archer hits the gas. "Good girl," I whisper in her ear low enough for only her to hear. She tries to hide the shiver that runs through her by shifting but my chuckle has her growling and elbowing me in the ribs.

"Well, for someone who didn't know they were screwing

my brother you both seem cozy." Nova stiffens at my sister's declaration.

"Buzz kill, Vivi baby," Hayze says through his laughter. Nova huffs in annoyance when I wrap my other arm around her.

"I was joking," Vivian defends.

"Yeah, sure you were, pretty." Archer snorts out, earning a glare from me.

"Everyone needs to stop giving her fucking pet names!" I snap.

"Oh, but you can screw Nexus' sister?" Ezekiel calls out, the car descends into silence and the tension ramps up for a moment until Nova begins laughing. A few seconds later the rest of us join her, I have no idea what the fuck is so funny about that comment but the sound of her laughter is infectious and has me smiling like a lunatic.

"Can you pull over here for a sec?" Nova asks Archer. He obeys and pulls onto the shoulder of the road. She shifts on my lap and I growl when her ass keeps rubbing against my dick, and the second she feels what her wiggling has done she turns to me with wide eyes. I shoot her a deadpan look.

"What did you expect?" I ask her teasingly.

"Expect what?" Vivi pipes up and asks.

"Best to not know the answer to that one, Vivi baby."

"Call her that again, Hayze, and I'll break your fucking jaw." I sneer.

"Don't be so touchy," my sister scolds, earning an eye roll from me.

"Why did we stop?" I ask Nova redirecting the conversation back to her.

"Where's the letter I gave you?" My brows draw in and I shake my head.

She huffs. "She knows more than you think, dick bag." I dig

my fingers into her sides and she jolts and smacks my chest. "Stop being an ass, give me the letter."

"You gonna kiss Nexus again?" Her face reddens with anger but I'm fucking furious, the sight of her lips on his has been burning a hole in my mind all day.

"That wasn't my idea," she admits bitterly. "If I didn't do it he was going to hurt my mom. I told you, ignore me and pretend you don't know me."

"Unless you want me to feel your ass in front of everyone, little witch, you're going to have to grab it out of my pocket." The guys all snicker while my sister gags and huffs out her annoyance.

"So you can get laid but I can't?" In an instant Vivian has everyone's gaze on her.

"Who the fuck touched you?"

"I'll kill the cunt."

"He's dead!"

"The fuck?" My sister scrunches her face and crosses her arms over her chest. I look at each of my boys and narrow my eyes. The way they are looking at my sister is... not brotherly and that shit needs to stop!

"Got it!" Nova announces. I glower at her. "What? Did you really expect me to play with your dick after the stunt you pulled?" She doesn't give me a chance to answer and just scoffs. I'm more pissed she used my moment of distraction with Vivian to fish the letter out.

"What is it?" Ez asks.

"I told you I was getting letters from my long lost relative, last night he left this on my bed. When I ditched you guys and Nexus, it was in my room." She leans forward pressing her tits right in my face as she hands Ez the letter. I inhale her scent and fight back the groan that wants to break free. My mouth waters with the memory of how she tastes on my tongue and my cock twitches, drawing her attention back to me. I don't hide my lust from showing. She searches my gaze for a second and her mouth parts on a silent gasp when I lift my hips to show her what she has done to me, but the moment is shattered when Ez speaks.

"This is my family's seal..."

"What?" she questions.

"The seal, the T stands for Tempest." I can hear the shock and confusion in my best friend's voice.

"Read it," she encourages. Ez reads the letter aloud. Archer and I share a loaded look.

"He knows you met us?" Arch says.

Nova nods. "I think so."

"If he saw you with us then he knows who we are," Hayze mutters, looking shocked and slightly angered by this revelation.

"Can I see the other letters?" Ez asks, clearly shocking Nova.

"Yeah, I guess so. I need to get home or Nexus is going to lose his shit." I grit my teeth and say nothing as Archer drives. We stop at the end of the street and let her out but before she closes the door she says, "The proof you wanted, I wasn't lying, it's in your garden shed on the shelf at the back."

"With Thomas hunting your uncle and everything else going on, why would you give up your one bargaining chip?" I ask.

She rolls her eyes. "Because unlike you, Vox, I don't get off on hurting people. Plus, if you fuckers think I am paying you a debt for getting me into this shit, then you are sorely mistaken because I don't owe any of you a goddamn thing."

"Right on, sister," Vivian calls out as Nova closes the door and walks home. Archer spins the car around and does a few laps around the block so Nexus doesn't suspect us of giving her a lift home. When we finally pull into the driveway of my house I glare at the sight of Thomas' car. The five of us head inside. We find Mom in the kitchen, cooking with Olivia. We all say hi to mine and Ez's mom before we head to my room. I don't trust Thomas to not be watching us so we'll have to wait until after the meeting to get the proof.

I've been on edge all fucking afternoon. When it was finally time for us to leave for the meeting, I couldn't help but look at Nova's window, trying to catch a glimpse of her. Her room light was off but her balcony doors were open, almost as if she was inviting me inside.

The drive to the town hall is filled with tense silence. I park my car in the lot that is too full for this time of night but no one will ever question it. The town of Hollow Hills always turns a blind eye to shit like this, they never want to get on the wrong side of the big names in the community. Hayze leans forward and peers through the windscreen and frowns.

"Why the fuck is mine and Arch's dads here?" I follow his gaze to his father and Archer's standing there, staring right at us. Without delay the four of us climb out of my car and head toward them. Shane and Henry both look tired and unhappy about being here. Hayze cuts in front of me and steps closer to his father. "What are you doing here?" he asks his dad.

"When the lord summons *all* members to a meeting, we don't have the luxury of telling him to fuck off." The bite in Shane Draven's tone can't be missed, him and Henry haven't hidden their hatred for Thomas. We are not able to harm or kill a member but that doesn't mean Thomas hasn't made it difficult for them to work. He's brought in out-of-town construction companies, icing out Henry and Shane's construction company of the business. Ez and my family are just lucky we still have a steady income from our father's investments to keep us afloat.

"You boys need to have each other's backs. Thomas is up to something and I have this gut feeling his disgraceful son is included in this," Henry warns. Ever since mine and Ez's dad passed away these two have stepped up and raised us like their own sons. Shane taught me how to play football and took me and Hayze to every game. Henry is the one who taught Ez about fixing cars and how to change oil filters and everything else there is to know. They both took my sister to her first father-daughter dance at school. I remember standing back, holding my mom as she cried knowing it wasn't their place to do that but ever so grateful that my sister didn't have to miss out.

"We got this, Dad. We think we can finally take them down," Archer whispers. Both men jerk back with wide eyes.

"You found it?" Shane breathes out in awe.

"We need to go through it but I think so," I admit.

"How?" Henry asks.

"Let's just say, Vox's extracurricular activities with Thomas' new stepdaughter may have worked in our favor." I glare at the side of Ezekiel's head, the bastard just shoots me a wink.

"Fuck, play with someone else, Vox, if he catches you with her..." He lets his sentence trail off, we all know what he is implying. Thomas isn't above committing murder to get what he wants. "Just... keep us in the loop, okay?" Henry says as he places a hand on my shoulder. I nod. He darts his gaze between me and Ez looking sad. "They were your fathers but they were also our best friends, our brothers. We want in on what you have planned. None of us want to see your sister blooded in." I grit my teeth at the mention of Vivi. "Come on, if we're late he will make a scene about it and for now we all need to fly under the radar." We all nod and follow after Shane and Henry.

As we enter the main room where everyone is gathered for the meeting, I fight not to scoff at the sight of Thomas smiling and shaking hands with other high-ranking members. It still blows my mind that our own fucking principal is a member of the Saints—doctors, the mayor and even the police fucking chief is here as well. I spy Nexus standing beside his father, dressed to the nines in a suit looking the part of the perfect bastard son. When he spots us the smile slips before he quickly recovers and nudges his father, then flicks his head toward us. Thomas smiles politely and excuses himself before storming toward us. He isn't fooling anyone, I can see the hatred in his eyes as he looks to the four of us. He pays Henry and Shane no mind as he stops before me with a look of disdain etched into his features.

"I want an update," he grits out.

"There's nothing to update, we've tried tracking the fucker but there isn't a trace left behind," I answer with a cocky lilt to my voice. He knows for a fact we haven't lifted a finger or even really tried to find this fucker for him. If anything, we'd happily aid him in destroying the Saints.

"He's been in my house, toying with my daughter—"

"Stepdaughter," I correct.

"Don't fucking cut me off again, boy. I have been hospitable toward the four of you for long enough. I want this masked wearing fucker found, he knows too much."

Shock ripples through me, it takes everything inside me to

keep it from splaying on my face. I can feel the guys all staring at me but I say nothing. "Mask?" I query.

Thomas grinds his teeth and narrows his eyes. "He's broken into my home and my stupid stepdaughter has whored herself out to him, numerous times." My breathing grows erratic at the thought of this cunt seeing Nova like that. "Here." He lifts his hands and Nexus places four black envelopes into his hand, then Thomas passes them to me. I look over them and lock my jaw when I see he has clearly removed the seal from the back. "These should help, now get out of here. I don't want the likes of the four of you ruining my evening." Before Thomas can turn and flee, Nexus cuts in.

"You four need to stay the fuck away from Nova." All rational thought flees me as I take a step toward Nexus, but Archer grips the back of my shirt, halting me.

"Why? What does she have to do with any of this?"

Nexus' gaze darkens. "You fucking touch her—"

Thomas cuts his son off before he can continue spewing empty threats. "She is our family and is off limits, she has been promised to another." My brows raise in horror.

"What?" Hayze snaps, drawing their attention to him.

A devious smirk graces Nexus' face as he straightens his suit jacket and shoots Hayze a wink. "Nova isn't fair game. She may be a whore but she has a great pedigree and we will take great pleasure in teaching the pig how to behave."

"She isn't your fucking pet," I seethe.

Nexus just shrugs and smiles as he says, "She is nothing but a pig to the slaughter and the sooner she realizes that, the better things will be for her."

"The five of you have a reputation to uphold in the halls of your school, don't forget that," Thomas bites out before he turns and stalks away with his bitch of a son following after him. The six of us stand here staring after them.

"The four of you need to get out of here," Shane says, shooting us a pleading look. Begrudgingly we obey him, say our goodbyes and escape while we still can. With these letters and the evidence Nova found, we may just have enough to take Thomas down and finally put an end to the Saints once and for all.

CHAPTER TWENTY-SEVEN

Nova

I tossed and turned all night, unable to sleep more than a few minutes at a time. I was terrified to fall into a deep sleep in case Thomas or Nexus tried to come into my room. This morning I'm a jittery mess. Waylen has agreed to help search for my mom as well. He's been texting me but said it's probably safer if I don't Facetime him in case they overheard our conversations. I don't like the idea of not seeing his face but I get it, he doesn't want to put me in danger and I love him for that. I texted him this morning, asking for an update but he said he hasn't been able to find anything—he's been calling every hospital in the country trying to find her.

In my heart I know it's futile because they would never have admitted her under her real name and he's probably spent a good amount of money making sure no nurse discloses her whereabouts, but I can't stop searching for her. I feel useless and defeated every hour that passes, knowing that my mom is suffering. I push those thoughts away as I clasp the collar around my neck and make my way down the stairs.

My breathing is shallow and my hands are clammy as I make my way toward the kitchen, following the sound of Nexus and Thomas' voices. I give myself a minute to compose myself before finally making my presence known, Nexus shoots me a lust filled look that has my stomach plummeting. I wait for Thomas to scream, shout, threaten me or anything but what I don't expect is for him to just... ignore me.

When he turns back toward his breakfast and begins speaking to Nexus like I never interrupted them I balk. I stand here for another few minutes... waiting. For what? I have no fucking idea. I thought Thomas would be shouting and cussing me out. I heard them come home late last night and expected him to barge into my room but this... this is not what I expected.

Feeling utterly confused and wrung out from my emotional workout, I turn and tip toe my way out of there. The instant the front door clicks shut softly behind me, I sigh with gratefulness until I see the empty driveway. The car—*my* car—is gone. The rational side of me wants to say it was stolen but that dark twisted monster inside me knows this is Thomas' doing, he's teaching me a lesson. Truth be told, if this is the extent of his lesson I'm more than willing to take it. I never had a car until a couple of weeks ago so it's no bother to me to catch the bus again. I start walking down the street, getting lost in my own thoughts as I head toward the bus stop, only to be violently pulled from my thoughts when Vox's matte black Hellcat comes to a screeching halt beside me. The tinted windows are so dark I can't even see inside, but the instant the window rolls down and his angry glare pins me in place I begin to wonder who the fuck shit in his cereal this morning.

"Get in the fucking car, witch." I roll my eyes and turn away, managing a single step before he is out of the car and yanking me back by my arm. I slam into his chest and fight against his hold but he wraps an arm around my waist, anchoring me to him.

"Get the fuck off me!"

"Fuck you."

"Never again, dick bag!" I seethe.

"Where the fuck are the files, Nova?" I jerk in his hold.

"What files?" He darts his gaze around and then curses beneath his breath.

"Get in the fucking car, Nexus is coming." At the mention of the devil's name I don't argue, I push past him and climb into the passenger seat. I look back expecting to see the other three in the backseat but it's empty. Vox climbs behind the wheel and plants his foot, sending me back into my seat. "Where are the files about mine and Ezekiel's dads?"

I turn and stare at him, his jaw is locked and his hands white knuckle the steering wheel. "I told you, I put them in the garden shed out the back of your house."

He flicks his gaze to me for a second searching my gaze for any sign of deceit. "You're telling the truth." It's a statement not a question.

"Why would I lie, Vox?"

He sighs and scrubs a hand down his face, it's only now I notice how exhausted he looks. "No fucking idea, maybe the fact you hate me would be a reason."

I choke on my own spit as I gape at him. "Seriously?" I screech. The fact he actually looks perplexed just stokes the anger brewing inside me further.

"Yes!"

"You fucking asshole. You lied to me, stabbed me with a fucking pencil and had your asshole friends torment me, then fucked me every night while pretending to be someone else."

"It's not my fault you couldn't make the connection between the two."

My fists clench and I grit my teeth. "You made sure I couldn't make the distinction between the two of you," I force out.

"How?"

"You said, '*Vox isn't yours to fuck, I am*'. Remember that?"

He purses his lips and I can see he is fighting not to smile. "I mean, if I recall that night you admitted to thinking about me or should I say, *Your asshole neighbor*." I slouch back in my seat and cross my arms over my chest, utterly done with this conversation and his mind fuckery. A couple of minutes pass before he breaks the silence. "If you didn't move the files, then who did?"

I mull over his words for a minute and try to think back to who knew. I told Vox and the others, Waylen and I are the only other people who knew. I know for a fact none of us would have done anything to sabotage the information so how the fuck did it go missing?

I sigh as I run a hand through my hair, slightly frustrated. "I have no idea. Maybe I was caught on the cameras or something."

"You said there were none in your bedroom?"

"There were six but Waylen and I removed them." Vox's grip on the steering wheel turns white.

"Where were the cameras, Nova?" The anger that laces each of his words sends a shiver down my spine.

"Everywhere," I admit quietly. "They were in the bathroom, closet and throughout my bedroom—they have seen... everything." Shame washes over me as I hear the slight tremble in my own voice, I feel so violated that Thomas and Nexus have seen more than what either of them should. Before I realize what is happening, Vox pulls the car over. I turn to him to ask what he is doing but the rage etched into his features renders me speechless, so I drop my gaze to my lap. Vox reaches out and grips my chin, forcing me to meet his stare.

"What those cunts did isn't your fault." The venom in which he says that gives me pause. "You may not trust me or even like me but I swear, they will pay for what they did to all of us."

"And what about you?" I ask quietly.

"What about me?"

"Are you going to make me pay a debt even though I am helping with the favor?" He smirks but there is a dark edge to it that has me squirming. The way his eyes darken and when he darts his tongue out to moisten his lips makes me clench my thighs, trying to dull the ache that begins to pulse. This is all types of wrong but I can't lie, I am attracted to this arrogant asshole—even though he lied to me and used me in a way, I can't deny that I loved how he made me feel when he was inside me.

"A favor asked is a debt owed." I slam my eyes closed, hearing those words come from him but without the mask make them seem so ominous. "A debt won't be required from you, witch." I open my eyes and stare up at him.

"Why?"

"Because the *Filthy Few* was constructed to get us answers, there is more to us than what you know."

"Tell me," I implore.

"No. Not while you live under their roof. I will not risk my brothers or the ground we have made by them extracting the information from you. We are so fucking close. I have no idea what the fuck makes you so special to them but I am going to find out. The Haven Saints won't be around for long."

"Tell me about the Saints." He releases me and sighs as he slumps back in his seat.

"You get the cliff note version or we'll be late to meet your master." I shoot him a filthy look and ignore the dick's laughter as he pulls back onto the road and drives us to school while explaining everything about the Saints. By the time we pull into the school parking lot my mind is reeling with the information overload. Vox claims his parking spot and I dart my gaze around the lot to check and see if the coast is clear and relax when I don't spot Nexus' Audi.

"Thanks for the ride," I say as I push the door open and step out but the second I do, I wish I didn't. All eyes are on me, great. Before I can move, Vox rounds the car and stands before me. I crane my neck back and look up at him. He has his hood pulled over his head and hands in his pockets. He looks like a bad choice and fuck if it isn't a sight to behold.

"Thanks for the ride?"

I roll my eyes and push my lips to the side. "What did you expect me to say? Thanks for kidnapping me?"

He scoffs and the sound brings a half smile to my lips that I quickly snuff out. "Meet me after school."

My brows draw in, that was not what I expected him to say. "Why?"

"Thomas gave us some letters last night."

"What letters?"

"We think they are from your uncle but he removed the seal, you can clearly see on the envelope that he removed them. The handwriting looks the same as the ones you gave us." I nod my head at a loss for words. "We'll do as you asked. The guys and I won't step in or even try to help but if nothing comes of this meeting Saturday, then come Monday morning Nexus will learn real fast who's pet you really are." I balk at him as he turns and walks away. I watch him cross the lot and don't miss how every girl glares at me for arriving with Vox, then the instant they return their gaze to him they eye fuck him like he is a piece of meat!

The sight of Nicole and her cheer sluts chasing after him has me clenching my fists and my teeth aching from grinding them so fucking hard.

Oh fuck.

Am I jealous?

"Argh!" I groan. I am and that notion has me wanting to bang my fucking head against a wall.

CHAPTER TWENTY-EIGHT

Vox

By the time lunch rolls around, I'm already over the fucking day. Since the moment I arrived with Nova this morning, Nicole and her pack of THOTs have been up my ass. I stop by my locker and drop my shit off before catching up with Hayze and Archer.

"Where's Ez?" I ask them as we push through the doors of the cafeteria, everything inside me burns at the scene unfolding in front of my very eyes. Ezekiel has his arm wrapped around Vivian's waist, her feet are off the ground as she fights and screams to get free. Nova is on her knees with Nexus standing beside her with the dog leash in his hand. Nicole and all the others are jeering and have their phones out but it's the chant that rings out around the room that has me stiffening.

Slut. Slut. Slut.

"Fuck, he went too far," Archer mutters, then turns and hands me his phone. When I peer down at the screen my grip on the phone is so tight I fear I'll crush the fucking thing. The image is a still shot of Nova on her knees in her bedroom bathroom with *my* cock in her mouth. The image is cropped and zoomed in on her face, cutting everything about me out except for my dick in her mouth.

"What are you charging for blowjobs?" Jefferson our running back calls out, the rest of the team all cheer and laugh.

"You can suck my cock any time, piggy," another fucker calls out. Nexus stands beside Nova, who refuses to lift her head even as my sister continues to spew threats at him. Ezekiel is trying his best to pull Vivian back but she is fighting with everything she has to get free and help her friend.

"You just gonna let her take this?" I toss Archer his phone back and focus on Hayze. He stands there with a challenge in his gaze, I step into him.

"What the fuck would you have me do? She made her choice—"

Hayze cuts me off, shoving me back a step. I press forward but he doesn't back down getting right in my face. "You always were a weak bitch, weren't you, *Voxy*?" My jaw locks as I try to control the rage unfurling inside me, this motherfucker is going too far now. "She's good enough to suck your cock but not to defend?" He doesn't give me a chance to respond. "Maybe me and Arch might take a turn on the *slut* tonight."

A haze overcomes me, I see red. I lash out and clock him across the jaw. Hayze stumbles back a step and smiles before rushing me. He tackles me to the ground but refuses to throw a punch as we roll along the cafeteria floor. Unlike him, I do manage to get a few hits in before Ez and Archer are there pulling me off Hayze. Vivian darts past us and drops to her knees beside him and checks him for injuries, but the bastard just smiles and shakes his head.

"You still hit like a bitch," he says through his laughter. I frown down at him, not understanding what the fuck he is doing or why he would push me to this point but the moment I register the silence of the room I get it. My face slackens as I take in the sight of my best friend sitting on the floor with my sister fucking straddling his lap as she checks out the split on his lip. The sight of her that close to him has my blood boiling, but given what he just did to take the heat off Nova I keep my mouth shut.

"You fuckers want something to talk about, huh?" Archer calls out as he stares down the room of nosy fuckers. Each of them drop their heads and claim their seats to eat their lunch. None of them would dare question us—

"Oh my God, babe!" Ez groans as he takes a step back to allow Nicole past. She grips my face between her hands, acting concerned. Before I can tell her to fuck off, she is yanked back by her hair. A shrill scream tears from her as she falls to her ass in front of the whole school. "You fucking bitch!" she screams at my sister. Her friends rush forward to help her to feet. She tries to come at Vivian but Archer, Hayze and Ezekiel form a triangle of sorts around her.

"Try it and see what happens," Hayze warns in a deadly calm tone, but the threat that laces his words can't be missed.

"That crazy bitch just—"

Nicole is cut off. "Call her that again and I'll break both your fucking legs." All eyes snap to Nova as she stands there glaring at the bitch. The dumb whore doesn't know when to keep her mouth shut.

"Shut your mouth, piggy. Trash like you doesn't get to speak." Nicole flicks her hair over her shoulder like she just gave the best verbal lashing of her life. Her minions all jeer and start oinking but it's Nexus that garners my focus. When he grips the back of Nova's neck, I see her wince in pain as he forces her to her knees.

"For that outburst you will be punished tonight." Vivian pushes forward and bats away Archer's hand when he reaches for her. I watch in horror as my sister lowers to her knees in front of the witch. Vi reaches out and cups Nova's face between her hands and lifts her head to meet her gaze. The cafeteria has fallen silent and waits with bated breath to hear what my sister is about to say. Nexus' jaw is locked, he knows if he tries anything or says anything to my sister I will say fuck it to the rules of the Saints and lay his ass out right here in front of everyone.

"Fight!" That one whispered word from my sister has a fire swirling in Nova's gaze, I see the war inside her. Obeying that fucker goes against everything inside her but the threat of her mother's safety forces her to go against every instinct inside herself.

"Yeah, fight for the next cock you suck," Brandy says from beside Nicole. Everyone begins to laugh, snuffing the fire in Nova's eyes out as she shakes her head subtly and lowers her gaze to the floor, forcing Vivi to release her. Not wanting all of these fuckers to see my sister crumble, I stride forward, grip her arm and haul her to her feet. She turns and peers up at me with unshed tears in her eyes.

"Help her," she whispers low enough for only me to hear. I suck in a ragged breath.

"I am," I say as I grip her hand and drag her out of there before we blow this plan to shit and I break Nexus' jaw.

I missed chem today with Nova thanks to coach calling me and Hayze into his office and chewing our asses off for fighting. We all know he wasn't going to bench us, we're the best on the fucking team. We're waiting in the parking lot for Nova. I check the time on my phone and glare at it.

"She should have been out by now and we have practice in ten minutes," I grit out to the guys. The three of them scan the lot, Nexus' Audi is still parked so I know she didn't go home with him.

"Vox!" At the sound of Vivian's panicked voice I spin around to see her running toward us. When she reaches us the guys crowd her which pisses me off. I shove them out of the way.

"What happened?" I growl.

"Nova left after lunch, she was cornered in the bathroom. Jefferson, Neil and Justin tried to..." She clamps her mouth closed, unable to finish her sentence but she doesn't need to.

"I'll kill them," I vow as I try to step around my sister, but Ez stops me with a hand to my chest. I glare at him but the dark furious look in his eyes gives me pause.

"Go to practice, act normal and tonight the *Filthy Few* will dish out a just punishment for their crime." Excitement courses through me at the prospect of releasing my pent up rage on these wannabe rapists.

"I never thought I would ever be so excited to know my brother is going to fight." I cut my gaze to my sister.

"You don't breathe a word of this shit to anyone!" I snap.

She rolls her eyes. "Who am I going to tell? Unlike you, I only have one friend and she is currently the school's main target. So, if you could end this shit fast so I can have my friend back, that would be amazing." I shake my head and nod my head to Ez before Hayze and I make our way to practice. I look back over my shoulder and frown at the sight of both Archer and Ez with their hands on each of Vivian's arms.

"You fuckers need to lay off touching my sister," I snarl, Hayze shoots me a snide look.

"Yeah, sure thing, captain dick bag."

"Don't fucking call me that."

"Why, because that's Nova's pet name for you?" I bristle at the mirth in his tone and clamp my mouth shut. His laughter only serves to grate on my already frayed fucking nerves. I don't know why the witch is able to affect me the way she does but there is something about the she-devil that has drawn me in. Maybe it was the fact she saw me without really seeing me, while I was in the mask she admitted to liking me without knowing *two horns* was me. She's never hidden what she wants or been someone she isn't, she has just been herself and something about that shit is fucking alluring and sexy as hell.

When practice ends I am fucking wrecked. Coach made sure we knew we fucked up with our performance and we paid the price for it. Hayze and I slip inside my car and groan.

"You owe me after that shit," he grits out.

I screw my face up and look at him. "I don't owe you shit."

"The fuck you don't! I saved your girl's ass from being eaten alive today." I cringe when I see the split on his lip.

"That was my bad," I mutter as I start the car and peel out of the lot.

"Yeah, well, we all knew the great Vox Hatchett wasn't about to step in and do anything." The hint of bitterness in his tone pisses me off.

"She said she didn't want our help," I defend.

"Bullshit, you didn't help because you think showing you care is a weakness."

"My sister is my only weakness," I grit out.

"From where I'm sitting, it looks like you have a raven-haired-size weakness as well."

"Jefferson is going down tonight."

Hayze snorts. "Smooth subject change, asshole." I shoot him a grin. We spend the rest of the drive back to my house coming up with a plan for Jefferson and the others, and I hate to admit it but Hayze is right. We need to be smart and wait until Friday night. That way they will think they are in the clear and it won't draw too much suspicion to us. Our conversation is cut short when I pull into my driveway and step out, only to be met by the sound of arguing and shit smashing from next door. Without thinking about it, I dash across the lawn and kick the front door open just in time to see Nexus ducking when Nova throws a vase at his head.

"You ever touch me like that again and I'll break your neck!" she screams, neither of them are aware they now have an audience.

"Mommy's getting another round of shock treatment for that, piggy!" Nexus roars. Nova lets out a gut wrenching scream.

"Let her go and I'll do whatever you want!"

"You gonna suck my dick?" I inhale sharply and tense, I feel Hayze's gaze boring into the side of my head. Nova's shoulders droop as she drops her gaze to the floor and I see the fight drain out of her as she shakes her head. Unable to stand this shit any longer I storm toward them making my presence known. Nexus stares at me in shock but I know without a doubt Nova can feel me. The instant I step up behind her she sways into me. I grip her hips, steadying her but say nothing as I shoot Nexus a look that has him squirming.

"The fuck is going on here?" I ask playing my part.

"Nothing, bitch got handsy with me and didn't like being rejected." His answer has her stiffening but she doesn't rebuke his claim, I nod and purse my lips. "What the hell are you guys doing here anyway?"

I come up blank for a second but Hayze is quicker than me. "We came to get Nova, she missed chem today and they have a paper due. You know how shit Vox is at keeping up." I roll my eyes playing along but I can see from how Nexus darts his gaze between us that he isn't buying what we're selling. Before he can question us on it his phone pings, he pulls it out and curses beneath his breath.

"She stays here, I want you both gone by ten and I'll know if you stay longer." I nod. "Clean this shit up before Dad gets home, piggy," he barks before storming out of the room and out of the house, slamming the door closed behind him.

"Well, that was—" Before Hayze can finish speaking Nova whirls on him and opens her eyes wide in warning as she flicks them toward the corner of the room where a camera sits.

"Clean this shit up, I don't want to spend any more time than I have to with you," I spit out. Her jaw locks but she does as she is told and retrieves a broom, then cleans the shards of glass up and straightens the furniture in the living room. When she is finished, she motions for us to follow her up the stairs to her room, only when the door is closed and she presses play on the Bluetooth speaker does she finally relax. I never thought I would see the day she wasn't on edge in my presence but it appears I was wrong.

"What the fuck was that?" I snap as I get right in her face and force her back until she is flush against the wall. She places her hands flat on my chest and shoves me backward. I expect her to lash out but when she reaches for the hem of her shirt my eyes widen, it's torn in the middle slightly. She yanks it over her head and tosses it to the side leaving her standing there in a black lace bra with her stupid tattoo on display.

Waylen 4221.

"That was me showing that piece of shit that I may bow to him at school for the sake of my mom but not here, I won't let that cunt touch me..." Her bottom lip trembles and the anger drains from me as I watch her compose herself. "He can do what he likes and say what he likes but I draw the line at sexual favors."

My fists clench at my sides as I grind my teeth to the point they begin to ache. She brushes past me to head for her closet. Hayze keeps his back to her as she grabs a shirt and yanks it over her head, concealing those luscious fucking tits from me.

"Has he touched you?" I grit out through clenched teeth.

She huffs out her annoyance as she drops down onto the edge of her bed. "No, Vox, the only person who fooled me into bed with them was you."

"Don't recall ever fucking you in a bed, witch," I clap back, her eyes burn with outrage as she scowls at me.

"Okay, just so we're aware, I am still here, like standing right here and I don't need to know about you two doing the horizontal dance," Hayze says, earning a smirk from Nova.

"Come on, like he didn't brag about tricking me," she snidely replies.

Hayze's forehead creases as he looks down at her and shakes his head. "He never once bragged about banging you. Ez caught him sneaking out of here one night and that's how he found out but none of us knew, Nova." Her face slackens as she turns back to me.

"Is that true?"

I stuff my hands in my pockets and shrug my shoulders as I answer her. "I may be a bastard but I don't kiss and tell, witch. Fucking you was what I wanted, not the *Filthy Few*. I'll admit, I thought fucking you would force you to ask the favor but I realized really fast that I enjoyed it too much to care about the favor."

CHAPTER TWENTY-NINE

Nova

I stare at him with my mouth slightly open in shock, I truly thought him fucking me was his way of trying to convince me to ask a favor but... I was wrong.

"Where are the letters?" I ask, changing the subject, the slight hitch to his lips annoys me but I don't comment.

"My house," Vox answers.

My shoulders slump, "I can't leave the house," I grumble.

"No cameras in here, right?" Hayze asks.

I frown slightly confused, "Yeah?"

"Good. We'll walk out the front door making Nexus think we left, but then Vox can climb back in here and not get caught or have to leave." I gape at Hayze.

"I don't think—"

Vox cuts me off. "Be back soon, witch," he says, then stalks out of my room. Hayze shoots me a wink and wags his eyebrows as he follows his friend out. I groan, then jump to my feet and lock the door behind them, then shove my desk chair under the handle. I don't bother to unlock the balcony doors, knowing he can get in with or without them being locked. I decide to make the most of my time before he comes back. I head for the bathroom. It feels weird taking a shower without Waylen on Facetime but I get why he said it was too risky and safer to text.

I miss seeing his beautiful face.

I miss Mom as well.

I push those thoughts away as I strip off my clothes and dump them in the hamper, then step under the spray of the shower. I let the water wash over me, hoping it can wash away the pain I'm living with and the feeling of being lost. I hate that I don't know where my mom is or if she is okay. I hate that Waylen isn't with me when I need him. I gasp when the light shuts off. I try to calm my breathing as I turn the water off, but my heart is beating erratically inside my chest. I bite back the scream that wants to tear from me when I feel the cool draft of air on my naked back when the shower door is open.

"You look good, little witch." A whoosh of air escapes me at the familiar sound of the voice distorter. The instant his hands grip my waist and pull me back against his chest I melt into him. He trails his hand up my stomach and between the hollow of my breasts as he grips my throat and tilts my head back. The lack of lighting makes it hard to see anything but I can make out his mask in the darkness.

We stand here staring at each other for a long moment, I don't know when it happened but something has shifted between us. This isn't a masked stranger anymore, it's Vox. He knew who I was the whole time but I had no idea he was my masked man. He knows my desires and what gets me off. The second his free hand cups my pussy all rational thought flees.

"It appears I failed to satisfy all desires and wants of yours."

I gasp and push back into him as I rise onto my tip toes

when he slides a finger through my folds. "Huh?' I manage to gasp out.

"You want to be fucked in a bed." I shake my head not grasping what he's saying as he pushes a finger inside my greedy cunt.

"Fuck," I hiss when he hooks that finger inside me, stroking it against that sweet spot.

"I'll give you tonight, to demand what you want."

"If that's your apology, it sucks," I breathe out. When he leans down and the roughness of his mask scrapes against my cheek I shiver.

"Why would I apologize for taking what's mine?" The possessive edge to his voice and the way he touches me is what I've missed.

"I'm not yours, Vox." I gasp out when he inserts a second finger, his pace quickens and his grip on my throat tightens.

"Wrong. You are mine, witch, with or without the mask this pussy belongs to *me*." I cry out when he presses the pad of his thumb against my clit. "Tell me this is mine or I'll stop and make you suck my cock instead." A whimper escapes me, I want to deny him and tell him I belong to no one, but the cresting orgasm and the need to come has all rational thought taking a backseat.

"Okay!" I cry out, but the fucker yanks his fingers free and spins me around until my back is flush against the tiled wall. I hiss at the cold but his body keeps me in place. He grips the backs of my thighs and lifts, leaving me no other option but to lock my legs around his waist and wrap my arms around his neck. "Why'd you stop?"

"Because you need to be reminded who you belong to, witch." His words send a wave of heat coursing through me. He carries me out of the shower and into my bedroom—he has turned the lights out in here as well. He moves to the edge of the bed and releases his hold on me. I drop onto the comforter with the grace of a toddler. The moonlight streams through the open balcony doors, illuminating him. As usual he wears all black but it's the sight of his mask that has my breath hitching. Is it crazy that I see Vox daily but I miss two horns? I know they are the same person but it was different with two horns. I had no reservations. With Vox, I am always on edge and wondering what his next move is. "Your move, witch."

I push up onto my elbows and look up at him, I dart my tongue out to moisten my lips and decide to hell with inhibitions and everything else.

"I want to see you." He reaches for the mask but I stop him with my words. "Not the mask, just the clothes." He stands there for a moment unmoving, a small part of me thinks he will deny me this but I need it. I'm not ready for Vox, I need this moment to say goodbye to two horns and what I shared with him before I can think about Vox being the one to fuck me.

I don't miss the fact he isn't wearing gloves or a hoodie to hide his tattoos from me. He grips the back of his shirt and tugs it off, careful not to remove the mask. I drink in the sight of the ink covering his arms, hands, neck and chest. Fuck, Vox really is hot. When he pops the button on his jeans and tugs the zipper down, my breaths turn shallow and I'm nearly panting as he pushes them down his thick thighs. He stands before me naked except for the mask and Jesus have mercy on my pussy because it is pulsing with the need to feel him inside me.

I widen my legs in an invitation for him. He grips my ankles and runs his hands up my legs, slowly. When he reaches the apex of my thighs, he brushes his thumb over the top of my pussy, drawing a sharp intake of breath from me.

"What do you want, witch?"

I swallow and try to force the words out but then he ruins it by cupping my tits and a moan breaks free instead of words.

"I need..." I clamp my mouth closed when he climbs between my legs.

"For me to take control and show you that *I* am the one who knows what you need, what you crave?" He withdraws his touch and grips his shaft running it through my slick folds pulling a whimper from me. "Isn't that right, little witch?"

"Y-yes," I admit.

"Good girl." When he presses the head of his cock inside me I moan, dropping back against the bed. He grabs my legs and forces them back toward me as he slams inside me, drawing a sharp cry out of me. My legs rest on his shoulders as he pushes forward and places his hands on either side of my head.

"Vox," I whimper.

"You can't call me that with this on," he growls as he pulls back and slams into me with a punishing force. My back arches off the bed. He does this twice more before he bats my legs off his shoulders and flips us so I'm on top. I brace my hands on his chest and stare down at him in shock.

"What are you doing?" I ask.

"Take out whatever anger you have toward me on my dick because I'm not saying sorry for shit." I gape at him. "You want me to say I'm sorry? Not gonna happen, witch. I saw what I wanted and went after it, now it's time you take what you want." His words bolster my confidence. I peer down at him and grit my teeth as I reach out and grip his mask but his words have me pausing. "Be sure you're ready for that, witch, once it's gone there is no more fooling yourself. It will just be me with no more barriers between us, no more excuses of you blaming me for taking advantage of you." His words settle inside me like a boulder but I push on, tearing the mask off and tossing it to the side.

His blue eyes almost shine in the moonlight as he peers up at me without an ounce of remorse in his gaze. Whatever he sees in my eyes has him sitting forward and wrapping his arms around my waist. His minty breath fans across my face as we stare at each other. Before I can talk myself out of it, I wrap my arms around his neck and tangle my fingers in his hair, then mesh my lips to his.

His shock lasts mere seconds before he's kissing me back. This kiss isn't sweet, loving or clean. It's messy and a fight for power, our teeth clanging against each other's but needing the upper hand for even a moment. I grind against him, drawing a deep groan from him that I swallow. He breaks the kiss and stares into my eyes as I find my rhythm. His hold on my waist guides me but he doesn't take control of my movements even though I can see he wants to. He sucks my nipple into his hot mouth and I cry out as I feel my orgasm rising inside me and chase it. I try to reach for it, needing it more than my next breath.

"Vox... I need more," I whine as I quicken my pace, chasing my release.

"You want me to fuck you?"

I throw my head back and moan loudly as I continue to ride him. "Yes."

"Admit this pussy belongs to me and I'll make you come, baby." I want to deny his claim over my body but the need to come is high, I won't survive being denied another orgasm so I relent.

"Fine! It belongs to you, now fuck me," I scream. He hoists me off his lap and forces me face first into the mattress with his hand on the back of my neck. He knees my legs apart and slips up behind me.

"Head down, ass up, witch." I do as he says. When he pushes inside me this time a needy desperate moan tumbles from my lips. "Fuck this pussy is perfect," he praises me, I can't focus on his words though.

"Vox, please."

"Fuck, hearing you say my name while you beg is fucking beautiful," he growls as he pulls back and thrusts inside me.

"Yes, just like that." He rewards me with doing it again but each time his thrusts get harder hitting me right where I need him and within a minute my climax tears through me like a hurricane. "Vox!" I cry out as I clamp down on his cock and come, screams tear from me as he continues pounding inside me until he finds his own release.

"Nova!" he growls my name as he comes, and hearing that from his lips sends a delicious shiver down my spine. Vox pulls out of me and flops down beside me, panting. I do the same, trying to regain control of my ragged breathing but it's futile when he turns on his side and wraps an arm around my waist, drawing me back against his chest. His breath tickles the back of my neck but I don't move, we've never done the whole cuddle thing. Usually he fucks me then leaves, and that's it until he comes back the next night so this is uncharted territory for us. "You good?"

His gravelly tone has a smile etching its way onto my lips. "Yeah," I croak out but still when I feel his cum dripping out of me. I shove away from him, leap off the bed and race into the bathroom to clean up. I curse myself at least twenty times before I make my way back into my bedroom to find him sitting in the middle of my bed with his jeans on but the button and zipper undone. He flicks his gaze to me and the way his eyes travel the length of my body has my brain short circuiting and need thrumming inside me already. I spot his shirt on the ground and snatch it up and pull it over my head.

"No condom, seriously?" I snap as I turn and face him.

The fucker just shrugs his shoulders. "I don't like not being able to feel you." My jaw unhinges.

"And I don't want to be chained to you for eighteen years if

I push out a baby with your big ass head." The fucker scoffs and looks at me like I slapped him.

"My head is not big, witch." I roll my lips over my teeth to keep from laughing—the bad tattooed wolf doesn't like his ego being wounded.

"It kind of is." He narrows his eyes at me.

"Shut the fuck up and get your ass over here."

"No, you have to use a condom next time—"

"Next time?" I feel the heat in my cheeks and groan as I scrub a hand down my face, his laughter just serves to piss me off further. "Fine, next time I won't let carnal urges take control and I'll make sure to get you on the pill so I can keep fucking you bare."

"That is not what I meant!"

"Yeah well, too fucking bad. I like the idea of marking you and the sight of my cum dripping out of your cunt gets me off. Deal with it. Now get the fuck over here or I'm not showing you these letters." I balk at the fucker, he is seriously delusional. But the truth is, hearing that he likes marking me with his cum has me feeling giddy. "Nova?" I dart my gaze back to his. "I've never fucked any chick without a condom, only you and I don't want to stop doing it."

I bite the corner of my lip and nod. "Okay," I say quietly.

"Come here." How the fuck can I deny him when he looks better than God sitting there shirtless on my bed. Vox Hatchett is trouble with a capital T and I can't seem to stop myself, or even want to, from following his orders.

CHAPTER THIRTY

Vox

She settles in beside me and I can't stop myself from leaning into her and wrapping my arm around her to draw her in closer as I hand her the letters from my back pocket. She looks fucking perfect wearing nothing but my shirt, and knowing my cum is still inside has the beast inside me smashing his fists against his chest in triumph. Tonight, I hadn't planned to fuck her I just wanted her to admit it wasn't the mask she liked. I wanted her to admit that deep down she knew it was me the whole time. But then, I heard the shower and that plan flew out the window until I started fucking her and forced her to combine the versions of me she saw. When she finally let go it was amazing.

"He ripped the seals off so Ezekiel wouldn't know," she says quietly, pulling me out of my thoughts.

"We thought the same thing," I admit as I rub her thigh, loving the feeling of her skin.

"Why would he want to hide that from Ezekiel though?" she wonders aloud.

"Fuck knows," I mutter as she pulls the first letter and begins to read it aloud

Valerian,

You thought you won by killing my brother and his best friend.

Looks like you were wrong, your throne isn't safe.

She lives and I'll make sure she takes her rightful place.

Your reign is coming to an end.

Nova looks at me with a weird look on her face. "What?" I ask.

"Is he talking about me?"

A whoosh of air escapes me. "We think he is."

"This town is so fucked," she mutters.

"Watch it," I warn. "I live in this town."

She snorts. "Exactly. Ever since I got here, you've had it out for me and so have your friends. My stepfather and brother want to kill me, and I have a long lost relative that is stalking me. I had a group of masked guys chasing me and I wound up fucking one of them—how is any of that normal?" I raise my brows and shoot her a look.

"You never asked that question when you thought you were *seeing someone* and kissing me." Her eyes darken.

"You're a real dick, you know that, right?" I can't help the laughter that breaks free. She elbows me in the ribs as she pulls the next letter out.

Valerian,

You thought you were close.
Did it burn you up inside when your contract with the law firm was denied?
What about having your two companies shut down by the IRS?
That was just the beginning. Confess to your crimes and it will all stop.

"He's doing what the *Filthy Few* are. He's trying to take down Thomas," she says aloud as she goes for the next letter.

Valerian,
I know you have her.
Hurt a single fucking hair on her head and I'll slit your son's throat.
Release her and my niece and no harm will befall your heir.
I'll burn that fucking place down to free Kelly if I have to.
Keep playing and I'll kill you all.

She snaps her gaze to me, her eyes are wide with fright. "He knew about my mom. He was watching them the whole time they were out of town. He knows where she is, Vox!"

"We don't know that—"

"I know he does," she says, cutting me off as she reaches for the last letter—this one is going to be hard for her to read.

Valerian,
This is the last warning.

I have her, release my niece and we'll end this.
Keep holding her hostage and you'll force my hand.
You have two weeks before I expose the Saints and
come for what is mine.
She will never marry your bastard, her blood is too
pure for that mutt.
Fall back or you'll be burned.

The letter drops from her hold, she sits beside me stiff and unmoving. I grab her and lift her so she is straddling my lap. I run my hands up and down her bare legs waiting for her to process everything she has just read. When I read that letter I knew who the *she* was he was referring to and so does Nova.

"Why would he give those to you?" she whispers.

"He has no idea we know about your mom, he thinks we don't know anything. Whatever this guy is doing is making Thomas careless and he isn't thinking clearly. He's making mistakes and the Saints are starting to notice it."

"Why can't you just go to the police or the FBI?"

"Half of the cops are with the Saints and the director of the FBI has been a long time member himself. You need to understand that the Haven Saints reach is further than what you can comprehend. Speaking a word about them or trying to expose them means certain death."

"Death?" The horror in her tone is clear.

"Yeah."

"Why the fuck are you, Ezekiel, Hayze and Archer doing this then?" I debate telling her the truth. "Don't lie to me, I have a right to know." She reaches out and rests her forearms on my shoulders. I narrow my eyes in warning.

"If you plan to try and fuck the answer out of me, then you better be prepared to be fucking all night, witch."

She rolls her eyes. "Who said I was planning on using sex as a way to get the answer you want to tell me anyway?"

"Good try," I say as I grip her waist and press forward so we are chest to chest. "The fact your pussy is wet for me gave it away." Her jaw unhinges.

"How the hell could you possibly know that?"

I smirk. "It was a guess until you confirmed it."

"Vox, that—" I cut her off by sealing my lips to hers. I can see she was getting lost in her own head about what those letters said. All that knowledge would do is drive her mad, so I decided to distract her the only way I know how, with my cock. Nova doesn't complain or even resist when I strip her and slam inside her tight, wet cunt. All thoughts and reservations about condoms and her mother vanish from her mind as she loses herself in me. I hate to admit it, but as I spend the night fucking her like a savage, everything else in my life seems to become nothing but white noise.

CHAPTER THIRTY-ONE

I wake early the next morning with a smile on my face, last night was... Shit, I have no words for how fucking amazing it was. Being able to touch him freely, look into his eyes and even kiss him brought things to a new level for me. I can now finally merge the two men I had feelings for into one and knowing I don't have to give one of them up is a welcome relief. Vox wasn't able to keep his hands off me all night. We heard Thomas and Nexus come in late last night. I thought Vox would take that as his cue to leave but instead he made it his mission to fuck me harder and see if I was able to remain silent or not. I lost the bet. I had a pillow stuffed in my face and his hand over the top with the music playing in the background just to drown out my cries.

I roll over and sigh, his side of the bed is empty.

I lay on my back and stare up at the ceiling, smiling. Those letters have given me a new sense of determination. I told Vox about the files and what they said last night, unfortunately they don't prove Thomas was the one who killed their fathers, it just proves they didn't die the way they were told. No longer will I have to wear that fucking collar! I climb out of bed and wince, I can still feel the ghost of him inside me and that has a smile tugging at my lips as I make my way to the bathroom and shower before getting ready for another day of hell at Haven Prep. I take one last glance at my reflection in the mirror and smile. I'm not stupid enough to think this thing with Vox will go anywhere but I'm gonna enjoy it while it lasts.

I wish I could pack my shit and leave this place behind, but knowing what I do about the Saints, I know without a doubt that Thomas and Nexus would do something to have me arrested or locked up in a mental ward if I tried to flee.

"Move your ass, piggy!" I hear Nexus call from outside my door. I close my eyes and pray for patience before snagging my bag off the ground by the door and leaving the safety of my room. I find Nexus and Thomas in the kitchen. I stand in the doorway glaring at the back of Thomas' head. "Where's your collar?" I flick my gaze to Nexus and harden my resolve as I hold his stare.

"Fuck you." Thomas swings around to face me at my outburst.

"Choose your next words carefully. I will not tolerate disrespect, Nova."

I balk at Thomas. "But your son can force me to wear a fucking collar and treat me like a dog?" I snap back.

"Not a dog, a pig," the bastard in question adds.

"Nexus was just exercising his rights as a future king, you would be wise to learn to submit now or the rest of your life won't be so much fun." Fear begins to ripple through me, I fight to keep my composure. "Need I remind you what is at stake if you disobey?"

I blanch and clench my fists at my sides. "You don't have my mother."

An evil glint enters Thomas' eyes. "Don't I?"

The smug look on his face gives me pause but I put my trust into my long lost uncle and believe that he wouldn't have sent that letter if he was lying. "Catch ya later," I mutter as I turn to leave.

"Nova?" I keep my back to them as I answer Thomas.

"Yeah?"

"No more late night visitors, I don't like the idea of my step-daughter being seen as a whore who opens her legs to every-one." My jaw unhinges and my breathing turns erratic, I force my feet to move and ignore the sound of Nexus' laughter as I race out the front door. Vox wore his mask so I know even if they saw him on the cameras, or whatever, that his identity is safe for now but he can't come back any more, it's too risky.

I come to a sudden stop at the sight of Vox's Challenger idling at the curb. I stand here stumped for a minute wondering why the hell he is here until he climbs out of the car and rests his forearms on the roof of his car, his sunglasses shielding his eyes from me so I can't get read on what he's thinking.

"Get in the car, witch," he calls out. I fight back my smile and shake my head as I make my way toward him. I stop a few feet away from the car and eye him warily.

"Why?"

"Because you figured out there is nothing to worry about now and the fact you don't have his fucking chain around your neck means you're back to being mine to do with as I please." His words shouldn't send a delicious shiver down my spine but they do. I relent and climb in, this time when I check the back-seat I find the three guys glaring at me but it's the sight of Vivian sitting on Hayze's lap with the widest smile that has my heart swelling.

"Thank you," I say to her, the kindness she has shown me means so much fucking more than she will ever know.

Her features soften. "You don't have to thank me, Nova. I'm sure you would have done the same for me."

I nod. "Never doubt that," I say as I turn and face Vox who is staring at his sister, his jaw is locked and I can see the sight of her on his best friend's lap is not something he is okay with. I reach over and place my hand on his thigh drawing his gaze to me. "I can switch with her if you want?" I offer.

He lifts his glasses and the dark look in his eyes has my breath hitching. "You want me to kill them?"

I balk. "What?" I breathe out.

"You sit on one of their laps and I'm gonna kill them." The guys just laugh but I can tell Vox is dead serious which just pisses me off.

"Oh, but it was okay for those assholes to torment me?"

He shrugs. "I wasn't fucking you then." My jaw unhinges as he winks, pulls his glasses down, then drives while I continue to sit here stewing.

"So, to be clear," I look back to Vivian who is looking between me and Vox with a weird look on her face, "you're still sleeping with my brother even though you know he is the guy in the mask?" I choke on my spit while Vox just shakes his head.

"Stop telling her shit!" Vox snaps from beside me.

"Dude, you didn't come home last night. When she called us and figured out you weren't with any of us we didn't have a choice!" Archer defends. Vox stabs a hand through his hair and mutters about his boys being fucking dicks.

Seeing Vox so wound up is funny so I decide to push his buttons a little bit more. "So, Viv, you know that he spent the night with me, does that piss you off?" Vivian ponders my words for a second before she answers.

"Surprisingly, no. Most girls just want to be my friend so they can bone my brother or one of these three, but you never used me or even had to try to get Vox's attention."

"Vivian!" Vox warns but she ignores him.

"From the moment you arrived at the bonfire with Nexus, Vox couldn't stop staring at you. The four of us knew it was game over for you from that moment." I can see from the corner of my eye that Vivi's admission is making Vox uncomfortable. It brings a smile to my face, knowing he was just as affected by me as I was by him. I mean, the guy is a tattooed fucking God and fucks like the Devil.

"So, since you're okay with him sleeping with one of your friends, I totally think he should return the favor and let you fuck—" I don't get to finish that sentence. Vox pulls the car to the side of the road, then has his hand around my throat and my head pressed against the window as he gets right in my face. I can't stop the smile from breaking free. I pull the glasses from his face and toss them to the side, the dark look in his eyes has me wanting to squeeze my thighs closed to dull the ache pulsing there.

"Fuck with me all you want, witch, but don't play games with my sister," he warns.

"Vox!" Vivian tries to intervene but she doesn't need to.

"Aww, Voxy baby, was that a weak spot for you, babe? Did I strike a nerve talking about your sister screwing your friends?" His grip around my neck loosens so I press forward until my lips ghost over his but I never break eye contact. "It's not nice when you get picked on by someone you're fucking, is it?" The four in the backseat break out into fits of laughter. Voxy tries to remain stoic but the dark look in his eyes fades. He releases me and slumps back in his seat with a huff before pulling back onto the road as I laugh along with the others.

As we pull into the school parking lot I pull my phone out and shoot Waylen a text.

ME

I miss you *4221*

Ever since we were little 4221 became our thing, it's our code word of sorts and I guess we never grew out of it. His reply comes through as Vox parks in his normal spot.

WAYLEN

Miss you too.

I frown down at the screen, he didn't say it back.

ME

4221 *Eyes emoji*

WAYLEN

Yeah....

ME

You good?

WAYLEN

Yeah, why?

ME

Nothing, forget it I'll fill you in later.

WAYLEN

Is it about the letters?

ME

No, I told you all I know but at least we know Mom is safe.

I told Waylen about the letters this morning after my shower. He was ecstatic but now suddenly he seems... I don't know. He always says it back but this time he didn't, and something in the pit of my gut says something is wrong. I climb out of the car and stand beside Vox's car staring down at my phone until a shadow falls over me. I look up to see Vox standing there with a look of concern in his eyes.

"What's wrong?" I nibble on my lip debating if I should tell him. "Is it about that pussy friend of yours?"

I glare at the asshole. "Waylen isn't a pussy, you dick bag! But, yes," I admit.

He grips my waist and forces me flush against his car as he crowds me. "What is it?"

"You know the tattoo I have?"

He rolls his eyes. "How could I forget seeing the bastard's name every time you're naked."

I fight back my smirk at the hint of jealousy I hear in his tone. "Whenever one of us texts the other or says 4221, the answer is *Always together*."

He scrunches his face up. "And?"

"He never said it back."

"Has this happened before?"

I shake my head. "Never. I feel like I got my mom back but somehow I've lost Waylen and I hate that I can't call him."

"Why not?"

"He said it isn't safe to Facetime in case someone overhears."

"How much does he know?"

"Everything. I never hide anything from him." I can see he isn't happy with my answer but I won't keep anything from Waylen.

"Incoming," Ez calls out, both Vox and I turn our heads to see Nicole, Pamela and the rest of the cheer sluts heading toward us. I take a deep breath and push Vox back a step. He tries to hold me back but I shake my head.

"I got this." He searches my gaze for a second before releasing me. The sinister look on Nicole's face tells me she isn't going to leave this alone and wants to continue to try and tear me down.

"You really are a slut!" she sneers. Hayze and Archer form a wall to keep her away but they don't need to do that.

"Fuck off, Nicole," Vivian hisses.

"No one asked you, bitch." I feel Vox at my back and know he is about to let loose on this bitch but it's time I handled my business.

"I warned you," I sneer as I push through Archer and Hayze. Nicole opens her mouth but I don't give her a chance to utter a word, I cock my arm back and punch her right in her nose. She screams and falls back on her ass. Her sidekicks scream and shout but when Brandy tries to step toward me I let loose. I kick her right in the stomach she hunches over but I'm not done, I grip the back of hair and yank her head up to deliver a hit to her nose, loving the sound of her bones breaking beneath my fist.

Before I can do more, Vox is there ripping me off the bitch. "Witch!" he scolds as he throws me over his shoulder, then keeps his arm locked on the back of my thighs as he storms across the lot toward the gym.

"They had it coming!" I scream as I pound my fists on his back. I lift my head to see Archer, Ezekiel, Hayze and Vivian running after us with huge ass smiles on their faces.

"Shut up, witch," he snaps, then smacks my ass causing me to yelp.

"The fuck, Vox?" I seethe.

"Her father is the fucking principal, you idiot." I still in his hold, fuck. Vox shoves through the doors of the gym and heads straight for the locker room. Once inside, he drags me down his body then shoves me against the lockers. I expect him to fight more but to my surprise he grabs my face and then smashes his lips to mine, robbing me of air. I clutch his shirt in my hands and press up on to my tiptoes to get better access to his mouth. He grabs my leg and lifts it so it locks around his waist. I moan into his mouth when he grinds against me. I can feel how hard he is for me and I want nothing more than for him to sink his cock inside me.

A throat clearing has us pulling apart. I look toward the door to see the three guys and Vivian standing there. I shoot my friend a sheepish smile.

"Does me punching those bitches make up for you catching me making out with your brother?" The four guys laugh while Vivian blows out an exasperated breath and smiles. Vox steps away from me, keeping his back to the others as he tries to discreetly arrange himself to hide his boner.

"Yeah, it kind of does." I beam at my friend and wag my brows.

"How the hell did you learn how to do that?" Archer asks.

I shrug. "Waylen taught me, he said every girl should know how to defend themselves," I answer.

"Did he also teach you how not to get expelled from school?" I cringe and shake my head.

"I think he forgot about that one," I mumble in answer to Vox's question.

"We need a plan, if she gets expelled then Thomas is going to lose it," Hayze says, but it's too late the doors open behind us and there stands Nicole's father—our principal.

"Miss Quinlin, my office, now!" I cringe.

"Yes, sir," I mutter as I tuck tail and follow after the asshole. If I had known he was her father, I probably wouldn't have done that—no, that's a lie. I would definitely still have smacked the bitch.

CHAPTER THIRTY-TWO

Vox

If someone had asked me what I saw myself doing Wednesday morning, I would never have pictured this. We all know Nova isn't getting out of this one, so I sent the others to class while I wait in the parking lot for her to walk out because there is no doubt she is getting expelled. Haven Prep doesn't allow fighting unless you have a certain last name, I know Thomas won't fight for her to remain a student here.

When the doors slam open I smirk at the sight of her storming out muttering to herself. She comes to a stop when she sees me leaning against my car, then huffs in annoyance before making her way toward me. "What are you doing here?" she asks.

"Giving you a ride home, little witch." The fight drains out of her and her shoulders slump.

"Thanks," she mutters as she heads to the other side of the car to climb in. I follow her lead and drive us out of there. She keeps her gaze focused out the window but I can tell something more is bothering her. I know this shit with her mom, the Saints and even the shit I put her through with the *Filthy Few* is weighing on her, so I decide she needs a day off from everything. I head to my house and park in the driveway. She tries to climb out but I lock her door. She snaps her head toward me with a frown. "What are you doing?"

"Do you trust me?" She stares at me for a minute debating and I guess in the grand scheme of things I haven't exactly given her a reason to really trust me.

"In a sense, I guess so," she admits. Her answer grates on my nerves but I don't call her on it.

"Good. Get a bathing suit and some warm clothes for later."

She reels back. "What for?"

I pull my phone out of my pocket and fire off a message in the group chat to the guys to ditch school and Uber home to get their shit and to take my sister with them and meet us at the beach.

"We're having a bonfire tonight and you're coming with me to the beach. Get your shit, witch, and meet me back here in five." I unlock the doors and climb out, not checking to see if she follows or not because I know she will.

I sit on the sand with my boys and watch my sister and Nova splash around in the water as we drink our beers. I don't think I have seen Nova smile like this, she seems like a weight has been lifted off her shoulders. We spent the day at the beach swimming, playing volleyball and just hanging.

"So, is she expelled?" Archer asks.

I shake my head. "Nah, she got a two week suspension. That fucker knows expelling her will piss Thomas off and he doesn't want to fuck the lord off," I sneer.

"What are we doing about all of this, Vox?" Ez asks me.

I sigh. "Dude, I have no idea. I thought Nova was the key to getting us everything we needed to take down Thomas. Those files only hold the coroner's report, none of it leads back to Thomas. The *Filthy Few* gathered us the intel to know our fathers were murdered but that's it. The best shot we have is her uncle."

"What about the Tempest seal on the envelopes?" Hayze questions.

"That one stumps me, I have no idea who this guy is or why he is using Ez's family seal. None of it makes sense or why he saved her mom." I hate not knowing everything and it's starting to weigh on me.

"Maybe I should ask Mom about this," Ez says. I want to say no but the truth is we don't have any other option, we're at a dead end except for her uncle. All of this shit is riding on the meeting with him on Saturday.

"I think that is a good idea but don't say too much." Ez pins me with a dry look and rolls his eyes.

"I know, Vox, I'm not stupid."

"That's debatable," Hayze snarks as he leaps to his feet and takes off toward the girls, Ezekiel chasing after him. Archer and I sit here, laughing at the idiots.

"You're really into her, aren't you?" I mull over his words for a minute, not sure how to answer him. "You never allow a girl to hang with us or even get close to you, let's not forget you spent the *whole* night with her and you've never done that before."

"I don't know man, she's just... different."

He chuckles. "Why? Because she doesn't drop to her knees

and worship the ground you walk on like the other girls?" I bump him with my shoulder, causing him to laugh.

"Something like that. What about you three, I haven't seen any of you fucking someone for a hot minute." I see him tense out of the corner of my eye. Before I can call him on it, he points toward the beach and I see red.

"You gonna handle that?" The sight of Ez with my sister wrapped around him and running toward the water isn't what has me wanting to commit murder, it's seeing Hayze with Nova wrapped around him as he follows Ezekiel. I launch to my feet and stalk toward them, it's time these fuckers learned that the same rules for Vivian apply to Nova, no one touches her but *me*. The guys toss the girls in the water as I make it to the edge. All of them are laughing but when Nova sees me standing there her laughter dies out, then she makes her way toward me looking like a wet dream.

The barely there red two-piece suit she wears has me wanting to strangle her when she stripped off earlier. The bottoms are a G-string and display the perfect swell of her ass. Her tits look edible in those little triangles. But it's the way the water cascades down her body that has me getting hard. She doesn't stop until she is flush against me and cranes her neck back to meet my gaze with a devilish smirk on her lips. I don't use words. I bend at the knees and grip the backs of her thighs. She locks her arms and legs around me as I stalk into the water, ignoring the others as they hoot and holler at us. All that matters to me right now is her and reminding the little witch who the fuck she belongs to. I stop walking when we are far enough away from my sister and the guys so they can't overhear.

"Did you just have a pissing contest with your friends?" she sasses. I don't bother answering as I shift my hand from her ass and push it between our bodies to cup her pussy. Her eyes widen and her mouth pops open to form a perfect O. I push the thin material to the side and slide a finger inside her. Her nails dig into my shoulders and her eyes turn hazy as I begin to pump in and out of her.

"No more touching my friends," I growl as I press the pad of my thumb against her clit, loving the way she jerks and bites down on her lip to keep from crying out and alerting the others to what we are doing. "No more pet names for them," I grit out as I lean down and bite down on the soft flesh between her shoulder and neck, drawing a needy moan from her. Her hips buck as she pushes down onto my finger. I insert another and apply more pressure to her clit, loving the sound of the pained moan that breaks free from her. "Next time, I'll break their jaws to teach you a lesson."

"Vox..." There's a tremble to her voice. I lick a trail up her neck and nibble on her lobe.

"You want to come, baby?" I whisper in her ear.

"God, you have to stop," she pleads as I feel her pussy starting to clamp down on my fingers.

"Never," I vow.

"I won't be able to stay quiet." I seal my lips to hers and dunk us under the water. She clings to me as we breathe life into each other through this kiss as I finger fuck her. I know the second she is about to explode, her pussy clamps down on my fingers and she breaks the kiss screaming out her release into the water. I slowly stand and the second we break the surface she is gasping for air and clinging to me as I ease her down from her high. She buries her face in the crook of my neck as I withdraw my fingers and fix her suit.

"Next time, I'll fuck you in front of them so they know you are mine," I declare as I turn and wade through the water back toward the shore—I keep my hands on the globes of her ass the entire way. As we pass by my sister and the guys, Vivian shoots me a glare. "What?"

She scoffs and shakes her head, shooting me a disgusted look. "You disgust me. Next time you need to make my friend come, at least do it miles the fuck away from me." Nova burrows her face in closer to me while I shake with laughter. The guys all make jokes but I ignore them as I head back toward where we set up earlier. I lay Nova down on a towel but she doesn't release her hold on me, so I brace my hands on either side of her head and settle myself between her legs—only then does she come out of her hiding place with a huge smile on her face.

"I can never look your sister in the eyes again."

I scoff. "Witch, Vivian is my twin and we have the same eyes, looking at me is like looking at her."

"But she has better boobs than you do." I dig my fingers into her side, tickling her. She screams and begins to laugh as she thrashes beneath me. "I'm sorry!" she shouts, only then do I relent and switch our positions so she is sitting between my legs with her back to my chest. I wrap my arms around her waist and rest my chin on her shoulder.

"Oh my gosh, stay there." I dart my gaze toward my sister and watch as she pulls her phone out and snaps a picture of me and Nova. "Don't worry, I will totally send that to you." Nova ducks her head at Vivian's words. My sister shoots me a wink, then grabs the volleyball and runs back toward the water where the guys are waiting for her. My eyebrows raise when I see the look on all their faces.

"Motherfuckers," I snarl. Nova lifts her head and the second she sees what I see she begins to shake with silent laughter. I reach around and grip her chin, forcing her head to the side to meet my gaze. "What?" I snap.

She smiles coyly and says, "How have you not been able to see—"

"What up, dude?" Nova clamps her mouth closed when I snap my gaze up to see Jefferson and the rest of the senior year barreling toward us. The sight of him has my anger rising and Nova stiffening in my hold. Friday night after the game he, Neil and Justin are going down for touching my girl. When he stands in front of me with his hand outstretched I don't make a move to shake it. He frowns but shrugs it off and continues to set up near us. I force Nova's gaze back to me and I hate the sight of fear in her green eyes.

"No one will ever touch you again, little witch," I decree.

"You just touched me in the water."

I smirk down at her. "Your body is off limits to everyone else *but* me." Try as she might, she can't mask the shiver that rolls through her at my declaration. Her pussy is mine. The sooner she grasps that, the easier things will be for her.

I can tell Nova doesn't feel comfortable with everyone staring at her. She tucks her knees against her chest and wraps her arms around them, shielding her body. I reach behind me and grab her jeans, then hand them to her. She smiles her thanks and tries to discreetly pull them on. I shoot every fucker looking at her a death glare.

"New rule, anyone who touches or even looks at Nova Quinlin wrong has to deal with us!" I snap my gaze to the side to see Ezekiel standing there with Vivian in front of him, Hayze and Archer flanking him on either side. Ez darts his gaze around the large group, daring any of them to fight him on this but none of them will, they don't have the balls. Nova shoots Ez a grateful smile as she pulls out of my hold and stands, buttoning her jeans. I almost want to pout like a toddler who lost his favorite toy but I'd rather her ass be hidden than have any of these fuckers checking out her ass.

"Can you hand me my shirt?" I quirk a brow at her.

"What do I look like?" I say as I recline back on my elbows.

When an evil glint enters her eyes I fight not to tense. "A guy who isn't getting a blow job while he drives us home tonight." I glare at the witch when she starts laughing, I look around for her shirt but can't find the fucker. I growl when she takes off toward my sister and the guys in her jeans and itty bitty, triangle death trap.

CHAPTER THIRTY-THREE

Nova

Even with the other's turning up and making our small hangout a party, it's been the best day ever. Knowing my mom isn't being hurt and that I will be reunited with her in a couple of days has made everything bearable. But there is one thing that has been eating at me, when I do get her back, what then?

Would we leave?

The thought of leaving my new friends and...Vox doesn't sit well with me.

"You look like you ate a lemon." I turn away from the water's edge to see Vivian standing beside me with a concerned look on her face.

"Do not."

She giggles. "Yeah, you do and I am woman enough to know that a face like that can only mean you are thinking about a boy and that boy better be my brother." I smile.

"You gonna kick my ass if I was thinking about someone else?"

"Of course and then I would make the three idiots help me hide your body." I marvel at the bond her and Vox share. There is only one person I have been close to aside from my mom and that's Waylen.

"When I get my mom back, I don't know if we will be able to stay here and I guess... I kind of don't want to leave this place," I answer honestly.

"This place or a certain person?" I exhale and nod. She smiles and bumps her shoulder against mine. "You like my brother don't you?"

No use in lying so I tell her the truth. "Is it weird if I tell you that I liked him before I even knew him?"

"How so?"

"Vox hasn't been my biggest fan since I arrived. Him and the guys gave me hell but when he came to me as *two horns*, I don't know how or even when it happened, I started developing feelings for him. I guess, I never admitted it to myself but I think a part of me always knew two horns was Vox but I was too scared to allow myself to see the truth."

"I get it." Her tone holds an icy edge to it. "People can be someone totally different in the light of day but behind closed doors, a guy can be someone you have always wanted them to be and show you the world through their eyes, but when the sun rises they return to being elusive and acting like you are nothing to them."

"Are we still talking about me?" I ask. She shakes her head as if clearing away those thoughts and loops her arm through mine and drags me back toward the party. I can feel everyone's gaze on me and it's unnerving.

"Relax, they are all staring because you're wearing Vox's hoodie." I frown at her.

"How do they know it's Vox's?" It's just a plain black hoodie, nothing special.

"It says *Hatchett* across the back ." I groan as I lean into her and nuzzle into the side of her neck as she laughs and pats the back of my head. "I guess my brother forgot to mention that, didn't he?" The laughter in her tone is clear.

"Ya think?" I mumble into her shoulder, then pull back to look around at the crowd of students who are all mostly drunk and dancing around the bonfire. When I feel *his* gaze boring into the side of me, I fight back my grin.

"My brother not only declared you off limits with that hoodie but he hasn't been able to stop staring at you, Nova." The lilt of worry in her tone has me forgetting about Vox and focusing solely on Vivian.

"What's wrong?" I press.

"Vox doesn't let anyone get close to him, Nova. All he has is me, Mom, Ez, Hayze and Archer. It's been that way since our dad died, he's scared to care and open up to anyone in case they hurt him. Don't fucking hurt him because I don't want to hate you, but I will if you break my brother's heart." Her eyes are filled with unshed tears and I suddenly feel like the weight of an elephant has been dropped onto my shoulders.

"I..." I clamp my mouth closed trying to formulate words but coming up blank. I have no idea what to say to that. When an arm wraps around my waist from behind I instantly know it's him and melt into his embrace without thought.

"Why do you look like you're gonna cry?" Vox asks Vivian. She waves her hand and smiles at her brother, but this time the smile is filled with love and happiness for her brother. "You're acting weird, Vi."

"Shut up." They begin to bicker and poke fun at each other, I pull my phone out of my pocket and check my messages and feel a pang of sadness when I don't see a message from Waylen.

He has been acting so weird since he left and missing our nightly phone calls and not responding to my 4221 message earlier.

"Come on, time to go home." I deflate in his embrace. He spins me around and cups my face between his hands. He searches my gaze for a second before bending down and kissing me. I stand here shocked for a second. Not because of the kiss but because he is doing it in front of everyone. The kiss is over before I can give in to it, he rests his forehead against mine. "You're staying at our place, witch." I don't argue when he interlocks his fingers with mine and leads me away from the fire. We gather our things and head to his car with Ez, Hayze, Vivi and Archer following behind us.

The entire drive back I spend lost in my own thoughts, I keep thinking about Saturday night and what it entails. When we arrive back at Vox's I look across the lawn to see Nexus and Thomas' cars parked in the driveway. A part of me knows me not going home will just enrage them but the fact they can't hold my mom's safety over my head any longer means they can't do shit. I smile at the sight of Archer's car pulling in behind us and climb out of Vox's car.

"Do they ever go home?" I ask Vox when he comes to stand beside me.

"Sometimes, but mostly they crash here. Vivian doesn't like leaving our mom alone and I don't like leaving them either so we choose to stay here."

"What about Ezekiel's mom?" I ask.

Vox sighs and wraps an arm around my shoulder as he leads me inside his house. "She only comes here or stays home. When they lost his little sister she changed, losing his dad I think was the final straw." Sadness rushes through me for the woman with the kind eyes that I met briefly.

Vox leads me into the living room and pulls me down onto

the sofa beside him. I lean into him and sigh in contentment. The others join us moments later and then the guys begin fighting over the PS5 controllers and who gets to play first. Vivian rolls her eyes and shoots me a nod to follow her, I try to stand but Vox won't let me go.

"Where do you think you are going?"

"With your sister, now let me go." Much like his sister just did, he rolls his eyes and then reluctantly releases me. I smile down at him and shake my head.

"She's my friend."

He scoffs. "And I never thought I would see the day a chick ditched me for my twin."

I laugh at the big idiot. "You do know she is hotter than you, right?" I say teasingly, the mirth in his eyes dies instantly.

"Agreed."

"Yeap."

"Say it again for the ones in the back." The three guys call out in agreement. When Vox snaps his angry glare toward them, I take that as my cue and rush out of the room to find Vivi in the kitchen, smiling like an idiot.

"I knew you were going to shake things up around here, and I love it." I shake my head and help her carry some sodas and chips into the living room for everyone, then reclaim my seat next to Vox, who doesn't waste any time wrapping his arm around me and pulling me onto his lap. Vivian and I chat as the guys continue to play their racing car game that has them all shouting and fighting.

Jane came down earlier and ordered us all pizza and told us not to be up late. I felt awkward when she caught me sitting on her son's lap but all she did was smile fondly. I expected her to be pissed that Vox brought a girl home but she seemed almost happy about it.

The feeling of being jostled wakes me. I crack my eyes open and look up at Vox only to realize he's carrying me.

"Go back to sleep, witch." The husky tone of his voice has me snuggling into his chest. I know the second we enter his room because the scent of cedarwood and pine is strongest. Vox places me gently down onto his bed and moves across the room to his drawers. He pulls out a shirt and tosses it to me.

"What's this?"

"Sleeping in that has to be more comfortable than jeans." I mutter my thanks and suddenly feel nervous when I stand and peel his hoodie off. I can feel his gaze on me the entire time. The second I lose my shirt and push my jeans down my legs I feel his heat at my back and still. "Do you have any idea what seeing you in this fucking bathing suit all day did to me." To drive his point home he grabs my waist and pulls me into him so I can feel his hard length pressed against my back.

"Vox." I don't know why I say his name or what I even wanted to ask him but the instant he skims his lips along my neck I'm putty in his hands.

"What do you want, witch?" I tilt my head to the side giving him better access to nip at my neck.

"You." One simple word is all it takes for him to lose control, he spins me around and captures my lips in a kiss that robs me of air. He tugs at the strings on my top and the material falls away, pooling between our bodies. Next, he pulls at the strings on either side of my bottoms. The moment they fall away he pushes me back onto the bed.

Vox rids himself of his clothing and climbs on top of me, licking a trail from my belly button to my lips. The feeling of his heated skin pressed against mine feels amazing. He's right, having no barriers between us makes this real and different on so many levels. We're both exposed now and there is no more hiding who we really are. He nudges my legs open wider to accommodate his size, something about this moment feels different.

He stares into my eyes as he slowly pushes inside me. I can't bring myself to look away from him as he begins to move, his thrusts controlled and measured, hitting the right spot each time. I reach up and grip the back of his head, pulling his lips to mine and showing him without words that I care about him. I moan into his mouth when his thrust hits deeper and forces me to arch my back off the bed. He bends his arms and presses his elbows into the mattress either side of my head, bringing him closer to me. I lock my legs around his waist needing to feel him deeper.

"Oh shit," I moan, a devilish smirk graces his stupidly gorgeous face.

"You like that, little witch?"

"Yes," I grit out through clenched teeth, trying to keep quiet and not wanting his mom or any of the others to hear me.

"Good, now fuck me." He wraps his arms around my waist and lifts me as he rests back on his haunches. Without an ounce of hesitation I do as he demanded, resting my hands on the tops of his shoulders for leverage. I start bouncing up and down loving the strangled sounds that escape him each time I slam down onto his waiting cock. I bite down on my lip to keep myself from crying out when he meets my thrust. God, he feels so deep and I can't decipher where he begins and where I end.

"I'm so close," I cry out. He smacks his hand over my mouth, tightens his other arm around my waist, then sucks my nipple into his mouth and thrusts up inside me. I scream into his hand which doesn't do much to muffle the sound. The illusion he painted of me being the one in control is shattered—he may be on the bottom but we both know he has always been in control the whole time. I can do nothing except hold on to him as he fucks me into oblivion, the orgasm that rips through me has me spent and limp in his hold. Spots dance in the corner of my eyes but I refuse to give into the exhaustion as I watch him cum.

The face he makes as he empties everything inside me is a sight of pure beauty. Vox Hatchett is a God amongst men and rugged as fuck, but oh so sexy and knowing I am the one who put that blissed out look on his face is empowering. I know with certainty that seeing that look in his eyes is going to become an addiction which scares the fuck out of me because Vox isn't the type of guy to settle down and put a ring on it, he is a fleeting moment and I am terrified when he decides he's done with me that I won't be able to put the pieces of my heart back together.

CHAPTER THIRTY-FOUR

Vox

I wake to the sound of my phone ringing but when I see it's Thomas, I choose to ignore it. I know he would have heard about me skipping yesterday and the fact it's now after ten in the morning I know for a fact Principal Daniels would have alerted him to another of my absences but they can suck my dick and so can the Saints' rules. I have no plans for the day except to spend it buried balls deep inside of Nova. Who is now currently naked beside me and sound asleep.

I'm just about to reach for her and begin my sexcapade, but then my phone rings again but this time it's Hayze calling. I slump back against my pillow and fight back my groan as I answer the call and bring the phone to my ear.

"This better be good," I growl into the phone as I fling my other arm over my eyes.

"Dude, Nexus is here making threats and we don't think he

is just flexing this time." The hint of worry in his tone has me sitting up.

"What's he saying?"

"He knows you're with Nova and he said if she doesn't get her ass home within the hour, the loss she is about to feel is on her."

Fucking bastard!

"He doesn't have her mom, the little fuck can't do shit to her." My raised voice has Nova stirring beside me. I peer down at her and fight back my smirk at the sight of all the bite marks that line her body. I may have gone a little overboard marking her last night but she didn't seem to mind. My back can attest to the fact her claws marked me just as well.

"I don't know, man, he's always been an unhinged fucker but something about this just feels... off. I can feel it in my gut." Hayze doesn't do serious or feelings, so hearing him speak like this makes me feel uneasy. Nexus must have taken shit to the next level if my boys are concerned.

"Keep an eye on him, she isn't going back there," I declare as Nova clutches the blanket to her chest and looks up at me with wide eyes.

"Vox, your sister is attached to that girl and if you plan on hitting it and quitting it then you need to cut her loose now. We'll find another way to deal with the Saints and taking Thomas down—"

"Keep an eye on him and Jefferson." Nova's eyes widen at the mention of Jefferson's name. "Make sure Ez lays the trap and they are exactly where we want them tomorrow night." I end the call without waiting for a reply.

"Is everything okay?" Words aren't my strong suit so I toss my phone to the side and climb on top of her. Instantly her pupils dilate and her legs widen to accommodate my size.

"I want to hear you scream my name," is all I say before my

lips are on hers and I'm sliding my cock inside her perfect little pussy. This may not last and only be something for a fleeting moment. I'll be damned if I let a single moment pass where I don't enjoy her and all she is willing to give me.

Yesterday is history and tomorrow is a mystery.

Nothing is promised so why not take what I want while I have it?

I may have been able to cut school but there is no way I could cut practice, so I made Nova come with me. Coach was pissed and made me pay for ditching but he and I both know since Ez and Archer are no longer on the team, Hayze and I are his best chance at winning the championship. It fucking grated on my nerves having to train with Jefferson, Neil and Justin but just knowing that tomorrow night after the game they will get what is coming to them makes the anticipation sweeter.

Hayze and I stalk out of the locker room and head toward the parking lot where I know Arch, Ezekiel and Nova are waiting for us. The sight of her sitting on the hood of my car laughing at something one of the guys said to her has me feeling lighter, it's fucking weird feeling like this over a chick laughing.

"Dude, you have that pussy whipped look on your face," Hayze mutters. I shove him away from me and quicken my pace to get to her. When she spots me a broad smile spreads across her face. I grip her waist and lift her off the hood, she locks her legs around my waist and beams down at me.

"That is nasty." I snap my head to the side and frown at the sight of my sister, she never waits for me when I have practice which only means...

"Vivian wanted to keep me company," Nova says in

defense of her friend. Rather than wait for me to answer, she kisses me without an ounce of hesitation and I do nothing to stop her.

"Looks like the pig is still a whore." I break the kiss and place Nova on her feet as I turn to face Nicole, Pamela and Brandy. They stand there with some of the team behind them, but unlike these dumb bitches they are smart enough to realize that I don't do public make out sessions, which means they know Nova is... important to me and to keep their mouths sealed. "You are a real thirsty bitch, aren't ya?" Pamela pushes. I attempt to step forward but Nova grips my arm, holding me back and cuts in front, leaving me and my boys standing behind. The sight of my sister coming to stand beside Nova has pride swelling inside me, it's been a long time since I have seen her fight for herself or anything really and I guess that is all thanks to the raven-haired devil standing in front of me.

"What pisses you off more, Pammy? The fact I'm fucking Vox or the fact I could fuck him and his sister?" The guys all sputter beside me while I glare at the back of her head. I expected her to throw out that she could nail the team if she wanted to, but I never expected my sister to be a part of the equation!

The cheer bitches all gape at her while the team just shakes with silent laughter. "You nasty bitch, everyone knows his twin is..." Nicole rakes her gaze over my sister in disgust which has me clenching my fists at my sides. "Trash."

Nova doesn't skip a beat, she grabs my sister's arm and turns Vivi. The look in my sister's eyes kills me, the uncertainty and the fact she is always compared to me destroys her. She's never felt like she is my equal when in truth, she is the better twin. Nova grips Vivian's face and pulls her in, the moment their lips connect, every single persons' jaws hit the fucking floor, including mine. I can't move, I know I should stop this but in doing so would paint Vivian as weak.

Nova is going to pay for this fucking stunt, sister or not I don't share!

The kiss lasts longer than I care to admit. When Nova pulls back and winks at Vivian I grind my teeth. The little minx turns to me and her eyes implore me to go along with this so I do. When she yanks my shirt, I bend down so she can mesh her lips to mine but unlike my sister, I wrap my arms around her and pull her flush against me. I attempt to deepen the kiss so the witch knows she belongs to me, but she pulls back and whirls around to face the three bitches who all look like they swallowed a lemon.

"Yeah, so I think you're gonna have to rethink the pedestal you put Vox on because I can say with a thousand percent certainty that Vivian is the better kisser and speaking from first-hand knowledge, she has a way better rack than her brother." Nicole turns beat red while Brandi and Pamela look like they want to run because they know for a fact they lost this round.

"You think because he fucked you that your special? Newsflash, bitch, he's fucked half the school and so have they!" Nicole screams trying to salvage some of her dignity. I show no emotion on my face, hoping that Nova doesn't back down or this bitch will never let her forget it.

"Yeah probably, but the difference between me and you, Nicky." Nova steps into Nicole and you can feel the bad bitch energy wafting off her in waves. "I didn't spread my legs for all of them, only *him*. I didn't let him into my bed because I wanted to bag the school's king and the star QB, I let him inside me because I wanted *him*, not the title." Nicole's face is a picture of rage and I know for a fact that she won't let this go, she's a spiteful bitch. Nova spins around and her long hair smacks Nicole across the face. I expect her to come to me but she veers off and grabs my sister's hand leading them across the lot to Vivian's car.

The guys and I all jump into my car and peel out of the lot, following the girls. The three of them are shouting and laughing and I can't stop myself from smiling.

"Dude, that was fucking hot!" Hayze roars out, then laughs.

"Nova handed Nicole her ass without even trying and did you see Vivi's face?" Archer asks, I shake my head and meet his stare in the rearview mirror.

"Dude, she said none of us could defend her but watching Nova choose her and tell them she was better than you had this spark shining in her eyes," Ez says, his descriptive answer has me pursing my lips in distaste.

"Oh, shit. Nova legit just made out with the twins and is the first person in all of Hollow Hills to do that," Hayze says with sarcasm thick in his tone.

"She just hit legend status," Archer tacks on.

"Why the fuck would she be a legend?" I grit out.

"Because, no one has ever been able to kiss the both of you, dumbass. Name one person who has done that shit?" I clamp my mouth closed which just causes Hayze to laugh, the dumbass may be right.

"I think I might have a crush," Archer says jokingly but I snap.

"Try and touch Nova and I'll break your fucking jaw." All traces of laughter die out and the car falls silent at my declaration.

"You like her, don't you?" Ez asks after a tense minute of silence. I tighten my hold on the steering wheel, refusing to answer. I can feel all of their gazes on me but I ignore them and crack my neck side to side, choosing not to answer the question.

"Dude, you skipped school two days in a row to hang out

with her, you even kissed her at the bonfire in front of every-one," Archer adds.

"You also made out with her in front of the team tonight and didn't break any bones when she kissed your sister who has been off limits to everyone in this fucking town," Hayze tacks on.

"Will all of you shut the fuck up and mind your business?" It's a weak comeback and we all know it but the truth is, I don't know how I feel about her because I've never felt anything like this before and it... unnerves me. The guys don't push me for more, which I am grateful for because I don't want to have to break any of their jaws tonight.

Rather than heading home, my sister heads for the diner. The guys don't protest and neither do I. When I climb out of the car, Nova makes her way to me, telling everyone to go ahead and we'll meet them inside shortly. I lean against my car and cross my arms over my chest as I peer down at her, she stands there nibbling her bottom lip looking nervous but I don't try to ease her nerves.

"Look, I know I probably didn't handle things back there how I should have—"

"What gave it away?" I say in a hard tone that has her eyes narrowing and her resolve hardening.

"Vox, you can be pissed off and angry but I won't allow those bitches to come for my friend, okay?" She doesn't give me a chance to reply. "I like you, I really do but if you try to throw around your big dick energy and tell me I can't back my friend—"

"It has nothing to do with you sticking up for Vivian," I snap.

Her brows draw in. "Then why are you mad?"

I pin her with a blank stare. "Some guys get off on seeing their girl kissing another girl but I don't." Her brows hit her hairline and her mouth parts on a silent gasp. "You want to play mind games and go fuck around with chicks then go do that, but I won't be here waiting. I shouldn't even be here now."

"Then why are you?" Her anger is clear in her tone but her body contradicts her when she steps into me and grips the front of my shirt.

"It seems I can't seem to stay away and that choice will likely get us both killed."

"I have no interest in your sister, Vox," she mutters quietly.

"Then why kiss her?"

"Because... I don't know. I guess I knew it would piss them off and stop them thinking that you are better than your sister. I hate that she is seen as beneath you. Vivian is fucking amazing and I honestly didn't expect to care about her as much as I do but now that I do care, I can't help but want to protect her." Hearing the raw honesty in her voice floors me, I've never had a girl tell me that they would gladly dog me if it meant helping my sister. I grip her waist and pull her flush against me, relishing in the way her breathing changes and how her body softens at my touch.

"I get why you did it and I respect you wanting to protect my twin, but if you ever kiss another person or touch anyone else, I'll kill them and snap your fucking neck." I release her and brush past her as I make my way inside the diner, leaving her standing in the parking lot.

CHAPTER THIRTY-FIVE

Nova

Last night was awkward to say the least!

Vox wouldn't speak to me. When we arrived back at his house I expected him to send me home, but the second I took a step toward my house, he gripped my hand and dragged me inside. He was ravenous and couldn't keep his hands off me all night but he still refused to speak to me. This morning I expected to wake up with him beside me but he wasn't. I finally gathered the courage to make my way downstairs and ready to brave returning home but Vivian was waiting for me in the living room.

"Vivi?" I ask as I meander into the room. She smiles up at me and drops her phone to her lap.

"Come sit down, we need to chat." Her ominous tone has me stiffening.

"Is everything okay?" I ask without moving a step.

She sighs and nods. "Yes and no. Can I trust you, Nova?"

Her question has me reeling back. "Of course!"

She eyes me warily for a beat before nodding. "What I am about to tell you stays between us, you can never tell Vox" I push my lips to the side debating how to answer. "I mean it, Nova, if you can't agree to my terms then I can't tell you."

A whoosh of air escapes me as I nod and claim the seat beside her. "You have my word, I won't tell Vox."

"Good because if he ever found out about this he would not only kill me but his best friends. In case you haven't noticed, my brother has bad trust issues." I snort.

"Ya think?"

"Look, I know a lot more than Vox thinks. He always assumes because I sit here scrolling through my phone that I don't listen to what he and the others are talking about, but I'm nosy so I can't help it."

"What do you think you know, Vi?" I ask. She rolls her lips a couple of times, clearly unsure about disclosing this information to me.

"Nova, the Saints can't be stopped like Vox thinks they can."

I flinch, that was not what I was expecting her to say. "How do you know this?"

"Edmund ruled that the next lord would be a female but he died before that could happen, plus his own daughter died when she was like one or something. None of the boys were of age to take over. Thomas tried to lead but because my dad was Edmund's right hand he was made the new lord. I remember my dad acting sketchy and always worrying about us, more so me than Vox, but he would always tell us, *a union between the two families is the only way to stop it.* I didn't understand why he would always say this until recently. The night before he died he told me, when the time comes for Vox or the other's to lead they can never become the lord of the Saints."

"Why?"

She smiles sadly. "Because I am the only female of this generation, Nova. My brother has tried to protect me for years and so have the guys, but they had no idea that I have known about the Saints since we were kids."

"I'm not following, Vivian," I admit.

Her eyes fill with tears. "My brother can't lead because of Edmund's decree, none of them will be the new lord because I am the future of the Saints. I believe my father was trying to warn us that a marriage between me and Nexus was predicated." I gape at her in horror.

"No." I dart forward and grip her hands in mine. "I won't let you marry that piece of shit."

A watery smile crests on her beautiful face. "If it means Thomas won't hurt my family, then I will marry him. I don't see another way out for any of us."

"There has to be something we can do," I implore her.

"Vox, Ez, Arch and Hayze started the *Filthy Few* to garner information from members and even years later they are still no closer to finding a solution. I hate that they had to become killers because they thought it was the only way to save me from my fate. They were wrong."

"But why does it have to be you?"

"This is the part they haven't figured out." Something in her tone has dread pooling in my gut, knowing that this is the part I'm meant to keep from Vox. "In order to overturn the decree of a previous lord you must be from their bloodline. If Ezekiel's sister lived, she would have the power to do that but she died, so therefore there is only one Tempest left and he isn't in line to lead. I can't change the ruling—"

"But you could," I rush to add as the idea hits me.

Her brows furrow. "How?"

"You are a Hatchett, so you don't have that power but *if* you married Ez you would be a Tempest." Her eyes widen to the size of dinner plates. "Maybe that was the union your father was talking about, not Nexus."

"What took you minutes to piece together took us years." I scrunch my face in confusion for a minute. She stares at me as if waiting for me to piece together everything she is saying, but our moment is shattered when her front door opens and the four guys walk in. They all look at us with varying looks of worry.

"What happened?" Archer asks with concern thick in his tone.

Vivi waves him off. "Nothing, just nerves about what you have planned tonight and tomorrow," she says casually.

Vox looks at me expectantly, I inhale and plaster a smile on my face. "What she said." The way his eyes crinkle in the corners tells me that he knows I'm full of shit but won't call me out on it in front of everyone.

"Stay in tonight, don't leave the house. I mean it," Vox says to his sister before they all head upstairs. I deflate a little knowing he's still pissed at me. The second they disappear Vi turns to me.

"Is he still mad about the kiss?"

The air whooshes from my lungs as I slouch back into the sofa. "Yeah, I think I really pissed him off." Her answering laughter has me lulling my head to the side and glaring at her. "Seriously? Why the hell are you laughing?" I glare at her when she snorts and hunches forward, wrapping her arms around her stomach as her laughter grows loud enough to draw the guys back down here. They all stare at her like I do waiting to see what has set her off.

"Are you high?" Hayze asks with a shrug.

Vivian shakes her head and sits up, swiping away her tears, then looks to her brother still fighting back her laughter as she says. "You bullied her and did some fucked up shit to Nova but one little kiss with me has you going all ape shit?" Laughter breaks free from her again, I gape at her.

"What the fuck are you going on about?" Vox snaps.

She points at her twin then looks at me with tears of laughter rolling down her cheeks. "He can't stand being on the receiving end, Vox is a control freak and you stole the control."

I reel back. "What?" I croak out. When Hayze, Archer and Ezekiel all begin to laugh along with Vivian I start to worry if they have all lost the fucking plot until Ezekiel speaks.

"You're mad because she one upped you and you don't like being the one who isn't calling the shots."

"Oh, you fucked up now, Nova baby, you went and wounded his ego," Hayze chokes out through his laughter. Vox smacks both guys on the back of the head, forcing them to laugh harder.

"You went and did something only I can do," Vivian says.

"What did I do?" I ask seriously.

"You got under the monster's skin," Archer answers, earning a glare from Vox.

"Shut the fuck up! We got shit to do and three cunts to kill." At the mention of murder all laughter dies out and an eerie feeling overcomes us—worry for their safety gnaws at me.

Since when did I become involved with people who commit murder? Oh, that's right, probably around the time I allowed a masked stranger to start fucking me.

Vivi and I tried to stay awake, waiting for the guys. Mrs Hatchett cooked us dinner but neither of us could stomach it. I don't know if Jane is fully aware of what her son is up to or what he has done, but she doesn't seem the least bit worried. I wish I could be like that, instead we've sat here with our phones in our hands and the TV playing in the background as we lay on Vivian's bed, neither of us speaking as we get lost in our own thoughts.

I've checked my phone at least fifty times since the guys left a few hours ago. I know Vivian is worried and has kept checking her phone as well. Her and I did discuss how it felt good this time for her not having to hide and pretend like she didn't know what the guys were up to and could openly worry. It's well past midnight when both Vivian and I decide to try and sleep. I didn't think either of us would catch a wink of it but I guess I was wrong because the next thing I know I'm being lifted from the bed and startle awake. I open my mouth to scream but words silence me.

"It's just me, little witch." My sleep-muddled mind finally catches up with me and I wrap my arms around Vox's neck as he carries me out of Vivian's room and down the hall to his. Once inside, he gently places me on the bed and steps back. I blindly reach for the bedside lamp and flick it on only to wish I hadn't.

Even though he wears black I can make out the dried up blood that mars his clothing, his wooden mask hangs off his hip and the malicious look on his face has me gnawing on my bottom lip.

"Now you see that the *Filthy Few* doesn't play games." He leers down at me.

"But you did with me, why?" I press.

"Because I wanted you, simple as that." He turns his back and stalks across the room to the bathroom. Not done with this conversation by a long shot, I bolt out of bed and chase after him. I know he can feel me standing in the doorway but he still keeps his back to me as he undresses and tosses his clothes to the side, for a second my mind wonders as I take in the perfect shape of his ass and the coiled muscles of his back, heat begins to unfurl inside me knowing what those muscles feel like beneath my touch. "Go to bed, witch, I'm tired and we have a long night ahead of us tomorrow." He steps into the shower and doesn't even wait for it to heat before he stands under the spray. For a minute I just stand here watching him through the glass but my gaze slowly lowers to his thick cock and my mouth waters.

I know why he went after Jefferson, Neil and Justin and a sick depraved part of me loves the fact he did what he did tonight in my honor. I yank my shirt off—the one I stole earlier from his closet—over my head, then push my panties down my legs before stepping inside the stall with him. He doesn't open his eyes or even react when I stand before him.

"Tonight isn't the night to fucking play games with me, Nova." He leans forward and blinks his eyes open, the darkness that swirls in the depths of those blue eyes has me trembling. I choose not to answer him, instead I hold his dark gaze as I lower to my knees before him.

"Let me make you feel good." His nostrils flare and instantly I watch as his cock grows hard. I dart my tongue out to moisten my lips, needing to taste him and feel him in the back of my throat. I want him to take control and dominate me, force me to surrender to him and allow him to take the burden from my shoulders.

"Hands behind your back." I do as he says and lock my arms behind my back. "Mouth open." I obey his demand. "Tongue out." I eagerly do as he says. He grips his thick shaft in his hand and pumps it twice, groaning. I glare at his hand, wanting it to be my mouth that pulls those sounds from him. Pre-cum dances on the head of his cock making me salivate at the sight. "You want to taste it?"

"Mmmmhmmmm."

"Then lick it." I lean forward and dart my tongue across the head of his cock catching every drop of his pre-cum and swallow, a sultry moan escapes me. "Suck it, *hard.*" I wrap my lips around the head of his cock and take him as deep as I can but I can't take all of him. Not one to be deterred, Vox tangles his hand in my hair and forces me forward until I'm choking on his dick and unable to stop gagging. "Fuck, baby, breathe through your nose." I try do as he says and inhale through my nose and relax my gag reflex but it futile, he's too fucking big. He releases his hold on my head and I take over. I ignore his order from earlier to keep my hands behind my back and grip his shaft, a hiss escapes him. I pump him and bob up and down on his length, loving the sounds he makes and how the taste of him coating the back of my throat has me growing wetter by the second.

I never thought I would be the type of girl who loved to give blow jobs but ever since meeting Vox, I have become an addict. It's like I always need to feel his cock in one of my holes at all times and I love it when I swallow his cum. Knowing that he is swirling inside me has a sick sense of ownership coursing through me.

"Fuck, you suck dick like a perfect little whore, witch." His filthy words have me moaning, bobbing faster. "Fuck yes, play with your pussy baby." I slip my free hand between my thighs and cry out the instant I circle my clit. I'm so sensitive and turned on I know I won't last long. Vox begins to thrust his hips and fucks my face as I play with my greedy little cunt. "That's it, baby, swallow my cock and come on your fingers." My moans are muffled by his dick and because I know he loves the vibrations, I hold nothing back as I work myself up, knowing this orgasm is something we both need.

"Ahhhh," I cry out when the rising orgasm builds at rapid

speed like a wildfire inside me. I want to drag it out and deny myself a few more times, not wanting this to end, but I can't. I need to come with him, I need this connection like an addict needs their next high.

"Fuck yes, witch. Swallow every last fucking drop of my cum." Vox explodes inside my mouth and shoots streams of cum down my throat. I swallow greedily, wanting every ounce of him inside me. Before I can work him down he tears out of my mouth, kneels before me and slaps my hand out of the way. His mouth covers mine as his fingers delve inside my tight wet cunt. I scream into his mouth when the pad of his thumb presses against my clit, as he finger fucks my pussy like he wants my come more than his next breath. "Give me what I want," he snarls before smashing his lips to mine and swallowing the cry of pleasure that rips through me when I detonate on his fingers, coating them in my own release. Vox breaks the kiss and stares me dead in the eyes, we're both panting and trying to catch our breaths. "I'll fucking kill you if you ever pull another stunt like you did last night. You're mine, witch, and I don't fucking share."

"Does that mean you're mine?" I blurt without thought.

"Was me breaking into your house and fucking you behind my best friends' backs not indication enough that you owned me before I owned you?"

Well shit, that was not what I expected to come out of his filthy mouth.

CHAPTER THIRTY-SIX

Vox

Saturday...

The day is finally here.

We can put a face to the writer of the secret letters and find out what we need to take down these cunts. I can tell Nova is nervous, she has been quiet all morning and keeps gazing out the living room windows at her house with a pained look on her face. Ez has been quiet since he and the guys arrived this morning. I know that he's been going out of his mind wondering why his family seal has been used for all the letters.

"Vox, can I have a word?" I turn away from Nova and face my mom who is standing in the kitchen looking... frightened. I step in front of her and grip her arms.

"Mom, what's wrong?"

She inhales sharply and blinks a couple of times as if she is trying not to cry. "Whatever you are planning to do tonight with your friends, don't... please." I release and take a step back eyeing her cautiously.

"Why?" I ask.

Her eyes harden as she stares up at me. "After Edmund died, your father thought he could take down the Saints and grant your sister freedom but he couldn't. He died trying to accomplish a goal that was unreachable."

Anger unfurls inside me. "No, he died trying to protect his family." Her face slackens at the bite in my tone. "If my fate is to join him then so be it, because I would rather fucking die than ever see my sister blooded in!" I roar. When I hear a gasp behind, I spin around to see Vivian standing there with my boys standing protectively around her. "Fuck!" I grit out as I scrub a hand down my face.

"Take a walk, you need to calm the fuck down," Ez snarls. I eye him for a second but the harsh look in his eyes tells me if I don't fuck off and calm down, he and I will go a couple of a rounds and right now, I don't need that shit.

"Fuck this," I snarl as I storm out of the house and glare at Thomas' place as I pass by. I nearly make it to the end of the street before I hear footsteps pounding the ground behind me. I peer over my shoulder to see Vivian coming toward me. "What are you doing here?" I ask when she falls into step beside me.

"You want to risk your life for me and I understand that, but you need to realize that I will do the same for you, Vox."

"Like fuck you will—"

"Shut up and listen to me!" I snap my mouth closed and turn to face her, sometimes I forget we are twins until moments like this. Her and I are similar in many ways but then in some we are polar opposites. "You have spent your whole life trying to protect me and I love you so much for that... but somewhere along the way you stopped being my brother and became a father to me when I didn't want that."

"I never tried to replace Dad." I am horrified that she feels like I would ever try to do that to him.

She shakes her head and smiles timidly. "You never actively tried, it just kind of happened. I need you to be my brother right now and hear what I am about to say." I nod curtly. "I will never be blooded in because I have a plan and if it does fall through, I know you, Ez, Arch and Hayze will be there to protect me. I'm not scared to die if it means you get to be free."

"There is no way out from the Saints, Vivi, unless you are banished for crimes against The Brotherhood. No one has been banished since..." I try to think over everything I have learned about the Saints and I can't recall when the last person was banished. "I don't know if anyone has ever been banished before."

"We'll find a way out of this." I move forward and cup her face between my hands. She grips my wrists in her hands and gazes up at me with hope in her eyes.

"Your optimism is admirable, sister, but this isn't a movie. For years I couldn't understand why Mom didn't just pack us in the car and run, I was so mad at her. It wasn't until I was inducted that I understood why she stayed."

"Why?" she whispers.

"If she had run, the Saints would have hunted us down and not just killed me but you and her as well."

A gasp tears from her. "We were kids."

I nod. "I know but to them it doesn't matter. We are minions that they mold into soldiers and force us into places of power so we can better line their pockets. This is nothing but a way for these fuckers to gain power and wealth. If we were caught trying to do what we are, they have grounds to kill us, Vivian."

Tears cloud her eyes, her bottom lip trembles and she shakes her head. "I can't lose you too," she chokes out. I growl and wrap my arms around her, holding her close. Her arms lock around me in a vice-like hold. "Don't leave me."

"Never. I will never leave you, Vivian. I swear on Dad's grave I will always be here for you."

I stand in my bedroom changing my clothes as we get ready to head to the cemetery. All afternoon Nova has kept quiet and not uttered a single word. Vivian has been gnawing on her nails like they are fucking chocolate. She wanted to come with us but I flat out refused, she may know about us and what we do and have done but I won't allow her to get herself into harm's way. My sister is pissed but I have no time for antics, I'd rather her focus her wrath on me and be safe then put herself in danger trying to help us.

"Hey." I turn around to find Nova standing in the doorway, she looks like she hasn't slept. The jeans she wears clings to her perfectly but she hides her curves beneath one of my hoodies. I won't lie, the sight of her in my clothes makes me hard.

"You good?" I ask.

She rolls her lips over her teeth and shrugs. "No... Yes..." Her shoulders deflate.

"Come here." She stalks across the room and comes to a halt before me. I reach out and grip her face, tilting her head back until she meets my gaze. Those green eyes look tortured and full of fear—I wish I could keep her out of this. From the first moment I learned she was coming here and who she was to Nexus, I had planned to torture her, break her until there was nothing left, but somehow... things changed. "Say the word and we call this thing off."

Surprise ripples across her face. "You'd do that?"

I inhale sharply and nod. "Yeah, I guess I would."

"Why?" she whispers.

I bend at the knees so we are eye level. "Because getting what I want doesn't seem so important anymore if it means breaking you in the process." I see my words have shocked her but I don't take them back. She presses forward and seals her lips to mine. I don't pull away or stop, instead I shift my hold on her face and grip the back of her head, deepening the kiss. I slide my tongue across hers and groan into her mouth, fuck, a simple kiss from her has me wanting to say fuck it to the world, locking her in my room and getting lost inside her until I can figure out what spell this witch has cast on me.

"It's time." Nova and I break apart. I pull her against me, holding her close as I flick my gaze to Archer and nod. He looks from me to Nova and sighs, he can tell shit is hitting her hard and I know just like me the guys don't want her to come tonight either, but if she doesn't, we lose the only lead we have on this uncle of hers.

"Vox?" I step back and peer down at her, the sight of unshed tears in her eyes has me frowning.

"What's wrong?"

"I have this feeling in the pit of my gut and it feels like whatever is gonna happen tonight is going to turn our worlds upside down."

"Nothing will happen to you." I growl.

"So much has already changed."

"Like what?" I push.

"Waylen doesn't even answer my calls, he won't say the words back. My mom is gone and the man she married is the leader of a crazy secret society. My stepbrother keeps blowing up my phone and I'm too much of a coward to check his messages or listen to the voicemails. Since moving here, I've changed—"

"Hey, hey, hey, calm down," I say, trying to ease some of her stress. "We get your mom back tonight. We find the intel we need on Thomas and take him and Nexus down, then we work on that Waylen fucker." She glares at me.

"He's important to me," she defends.

"So, killing him isn't an option?"

She balks at me. "Touch him and I'll murder you." The fire in her eyes has me smiling.

"There she is," I murmur as I place another kiss to her lips, then snatch my mask off the dresser.

"Do I get a mask?" her question has laughter bursting out of me.

"Never." I grab her hand and lead her out of the room. We meet the guys in the garage as they begin loading both cars. We're taking my Challenger Demon and Hayze's 350Z. Nova pulls free and begins helping Archer load shit into my trunk, my mom hates that we all own guns, but I'm not going to this meet unarmed.

We plan to arrive earlier and scout the area out to make sure that this isn't an ambush and we have the best vantage point. All the shit we are taking are for traps in case shit goes sideways and he tries to run.

I didn't say it before because I didn't want to worry Nova, but I have the same feeling she does—something feels off and I'm not sure what it is, but I've always been taught to follow my instincts and tonight, I hope like fuck for the first time that they are wrong.

CHAPTER THIRTY-SEVEN

Nova

I've been standing next to Vox's car for nearly an hour as he and the guys went off to lay traps. I'm nervous and scared out of my mind. My throat is dry so I make my way to the trunk and search through the mess to find the water. I push the shovels aside and shake my head at the sight of them. If he thinks I will help him bury a body, he is out of his fucking mind. I find the bottle of water, pop the cap and guzzle the liquid. I screw the cap back on and pull out my phone to check the time.

11:37pm

I exhale and toss the bottle back in the trunk and roll my shoulders just as the four guys emerge from the woods to my left, all of them are dressed head to toe in black and wear their masks. The sight of Vox in that mask has a shiver rolling through me. I knew there was something about him, a darkness that clung to him when I first met him. His aura was pitch black but now it's grayish.

"We need to move, the meet point is through there," Ezekiel says, the voice distorter would confuse anyone to who is speaking but it's the masks that make it easy for me to tell them apart.

Two horns has flecks of blue in his mask.

Right horn has gray through his mask.

No horns masks has darker brown coloring through his.

Left horn has green on his mask.

It's only now that I realize that the colors running through each of their masks match their eye colors. Vox interlocks his fingers with mine and leads us through the woods so we enter the cemetery through the back. When we break through the brush my gaze automatically looks to the headstone with the head where I found out who the *Filthy Few* really was. I never expected to return here with them or even be... dating their leader?

Am I dating, Vox?

"Stay here, we'll go look around," Vox says to me, then he and the other's take off. Suddenly I feel utterly alone, though the dim lighting of the moon allows me to see their silhouettes in the darkness. I dart my gaze around and feel trickles of fear thrumming through me, who the fuck thought meeting in a cemetery was a good idea?

I hear a noise behind me and whirl around, I squint my eyes trying to see better in the darkness but all I can see is the headstones. I move toward a wooden sign and pull my phone out, turning the flashlight on, my eyes widen as I read it.

Children.

Oh my God!

I look up again and see a figure standing in the middle. My breath lodges in my throat and I begin to shake when I feel the shadows eyes on me. I'm motionless, unable to move or utter a sound as the shadow makes its way toward me. I open my mouth to scream but no words come out. The closer the figure gets to me the more I begin to panic, feeling a cold sweat working its way down my spine.

My phone begins to ring in my hand and that's all it takes to snap me out of my inner turmoil, I spin around and dart across the grass toward the lanterns where the guys are.

"Help!" The sound of my scream has the four of them whirling around. Vox rushes toward me and I leap into him. He catches me and wraps his arms around me protectively as the other three move in front of us, forming a blockade of sorts.

"I got you," Vox growls in my ear, the voice distorter can't mask the rage in his tone. Vox walks us backward and I chance a glance over my shoulder to see the three guys doing the same but it's the sight of the lone figure making its way toward us that has me burrowing my face in his neck. I know this is irrational but seeing a shadow in a cemetery isn't exactly something any normal person would be okay with. Vox releases his hold on me and places me on my feet, then shields me with his body as he pulls a remote out of his pocket and flicks a switch. Instantly I'm blinded by the lights that they had set up earlier around here and I slam my eyes closed. I blink a couple of times to clear my vision, then dart my gaze around Vox to see the figure standing there with his hood up, covering his face.

"Who are you?" Hayze growls.

"The one person that can keep the five of you and Vivian alive." His deep baritone has me shivering behind Vox who tenses at the mentions of his sister.

"I'll ask you again, who the fuck are you?" Ezekiel snaps, he reaches behind him and grips the hilt of his gun that is tucked into his waistband. I gasp silently and pray that this doesn't end in a shootout because I am not prepared for that.

The man stands tall and cocks his head to the side. "If I

reveal who I am, all your lives will change. Are you ready for that, Ezekiel?" This time I do gasp out loud, he knows who they are! The man tilts his head toward Hayze and Archer. "Archer Malik, Hayze Draven." He then stares directly at Vox as he continues. "Vox Hatchett." Vox doesn't flinch or even show an ounce of surprise, I move out from behind him and stand by his side. "Ah, my niece."

"Who the fuck are you?" Ezekiel roars. I get the strange sense that this guy is worried about revealing who he is, not for himself but for... us.

"I warned you," is all he says, then reaches up and pushes his hood back. A pained sound escapes Ez as he stumbles back a step and catches himself on one of the tombstones before he can fall to his ass.

"You know him?" Archer asks. Ezekiel says nothing as he turns to face me. His gaze bores into mine and I fight not to fidget under the intensity of it.

"*Taylor?*" Ez murmurs, I jerk back into Vox's side shaking my head.

"I told you my identity would change everything," the man says but his tone is filled with regret.

Vox shifts and pulls a gun from his waistband and points it at the man. "No more bullshit, who the fuck are you?" Vox snarls. I still can't tear my gaze from Ezekiel, he reaches up and pulls his mask off. The guys protest and scream at him to put it back on but he ignores them as he stumbles toward me. Vox stiffens at my side and doesn't move until Ez drops his mask at my feet and cups my face between his hands. Instantly Vox is there, shoving him back and using his body to block me from Ezekiel's view.

"Get out of my way," Ez screams as he pushes right into Vox.

"You stay the fuck away from her," Vox seethes. "I told all of you she's mine, none of you are touching her!" Vox's declaration and the power in which he says that has heat unfurling inside me. Ezekiel snakes his arm out and smacks Vox's mask off, drawing a shocked shriek from me. Ez gets right in Vox's face, not even bothered by the gun in his friend's hand.

"I need to know if it is her!" Ezekiel shouts, the pain that laces his words has me taking a step back and turning to the man who has gaze focused on me.

"Who does he think I am?" I ask. The man smiles sadly and takes two steps toward me, but pauses when Vox whirls around and points the gun at him again. Hayze and Archer move to stand at my back.

"My name is Nikoa... Tempest." My eyes widen.

"You're a *Tempest?*" I breathe out.

He nods. "Yes," he answers. Vox turns his head toward me and the utter shock and devastation on his face floors me. He shakes his head.

"No, not you," he murmurs. I stare at Vox as worry churns inside me. He's never looked at me like this before, the pitying look in his eyes tears me to shreds. "I can't save you both," he mutters as he drops his arm back to his side.

"You can't but I can," Nikoa says, drawing all our attention back to him.

"How?" Archer presses. My mind begins to shut down as I process everything, the letters said he was my uncle, he told me my father died and that I had a... *brother.*

Oh, no!

I stumble backward and land on my ass. Vox still has a guilt stricken gaze on the ground in front of him but not Ezekiel, he stares at me with a broken look in his gray blue eyes.

This can't be happening.

"I had you meet me here because neither of you would

believe the truth separately. You needed to see the other's reaction and process everything I have told you." Nikoa's voice sounds so far away as I continue to stare up at Ezekiel. So many emotions are running through me.

Confusion,

Fear,

Confusion,

Anger,

Confusion.

"This is why I couldn't—"

Ez cuts Nikoa off before he can continue. "Shut the fuck up... *uncle.*" A choked sob escapes me. Ezekiel drops to his knees in front of me. I flinch when he lifts his arm toward me, he instantly drops in and sighs. "How are you alive?" he whispers with regret in his tone.

I shake my head, Nikoa answers for me. "After your father made his decree, he never thought he would have children. When you were born, Ezekiel, he was elated and relieved that you were a boy but mere weeks after your birth your mother got pregnant again." Nikoa looks at me as he continues to speak. "You were born premature, which is why there isn't even a year between both of your births—"

"No!" I rasp put as I stare up at the man with tears clouding my vision. "My mother is Kelly—"

"Your mother is Olivia Tempest, Nova-Scotia," he injects.

"Stop calling me that," I scream as the first tear trails down my cheek. "My name is Nova Quinlin, my mother is Kelly Quinlin-Valerian. I was born in Washington DC—"

"You were born in Hollow Hills as Taylor Tempest to Olivia and Edmund Tempest on the eighteenth of December 2006. You are the younger sister of Ezekiel Nikoa Tempest." My bottom lip begins to tremble and I shake my head.

"No," I choke out as I bury my face in my hands. When Ez

reaches for me, I bat his hands away and climb to my feet. "Don't touch me!"

"I thought you died, I fucking watched you die, Taylor!" he shouts. He scrubs a hand down his face and pushes to his feet. "You were my best friend, how is she alive?" he grits out as he slowly turns to face Nikoa. "And how are *you* alive?" I flinch in surprise.

Nikoa stabs a hand through his black hair and sighs. "Thomas and the others were coming for your father, they were elated that he had a daughter because it finally meant that the title of lord would be passed to another family. He tried to over-rule his decree but the board wouldn't allow him to change it. A lord's decree cannot be overruled for twenty years. The only way to save his only daughter from certain death and having her forced into a marriage of convenience was to make her... disappear." I gasp.

"I saw her body, I fucking held her!" Ezekiel screams as he pounds a fist against his chest.

"You saw *a* body," Nikoa says with an edge. "Her death had to look real, if Thomas and the others caught wind she was alive they would have come for her. Your father made sure she was protected."

"How?" I snap.

Nikoa smiles and his eyes soften as he gazes at me. "Nikoa Tempest died three days after his niece, his car was run off the road by a drunk driver."

"Why?" Ez breathes out.

"Your father trusted no one with his daughter so I vowed to watch over her, find her a family that would love, cherish and raise her right. Kelly had struggled for years to conceive a child of her own, I watched her for months before I finally approached her and made a deal."

"What fucking deal?" I scream.

"I hand you over and she sends me updates. I have watched you grow up from a distance all your life Nova-Scotia."

"Why do you call me that?" I hiss.

"That was also a part of the agreement, she had to name you Nova. Our family originated from Nova Scotia and I thought it fitting that the future queen of our family be named after our homeland."

"Does Thomas know about her?" Hayze asks. Nikoa's shoulders hunch.

"I believe so. Kelly had no ties to this place or anyone in it. I have no idea who ratted us out. My informant has been trying to figure that out for me."

"You have a rat in the Saints?" Archer hisses.

"I will neither confirm nor deny that," Nikoa cockily answers.

"If she is a Tempest then that means she is the rightful lordess of the Saints," Vox says, speaking for the first time since my world imploded.

"No," Nikoa says.

"She's a fucking Tempest!" Vox spits.

"Yes, she is, but that doesn't mean anything. Your father was the lord after Edmund. The one with the stronger claim to the throne is *your* sister," Nikoa answers.

"If that was true, why the fuck would Thomas be going after her?" Archer bites out.

"Because he wants the decree overturned and the only one who can do that is a Tempest. He wants Nexus and Nova to be married. She didn't need to know the truth of her origins, Nexus just had to supply her birth records to the board and they would have ruled in his favor. If they succeed in doing this, they will banish all of you."

"Good!" Archer spits.

"No, you fucking fool, if you are banished it doesn't mean you walk free. The lord has the right to execute your entire family and tell me, Archer, do you think Nexus Valerian would spare any of you and your families?"

CHAPTER THIRTY-EIGHT

Vox

I can't wrap my head around this shit!

Nova Quinlin is actually Taylor Tempest, Ezekiel's kid sister who we all thought had died years ago.

Nexus and Thomas know who she is and want her to marry Nexus so they can overturn her father's decree and make a new ruling so no woman can ever lead the Saints. How the fuck did we not piece all of this together?

Was I so blinded by her that I didn't see what was staring me right in the face?

"What happens now?" Hayze asks.

"Now, I will take Nova away from here—"

I cut Nikoa off before he could continue. "You do that and you subject my sister to the vile shit they will put her through."

"And you would rather I go through with it?" Her voice has me slamming my eyes closed, I can't look at her. Knowing who she is and what her taking over would mean for my sister makes this situation ten times fucking harder. She scoffs when I don't answer. "Of fucking course, stupid me for thinking that you actually gave a fuck about me. My bad. I forgot two horns." I don't defend myself.

"I won't let them touch her!" Ezekiel vows.

"Oh, now you fucking care?" Nova screams.

"I didn't know!" Ez defends.

"And that makes it okay? You put me through fucking hell, Ezekiel. You all did. I thought we had moved past all of that but I guess I was wrong."

"I would never let them hurt you, *Taylor*," Ez grits out.

"Stop calling me that! My name is Nova and I am not a Tempest, I'm a fucking Quinlin. My mother is Kelly and I don't care what the fuck he is telling you, I am not your sister or some pawn you can use to save Vivian." Nova whirls around and flees. The instant she does I chase after her. She nearly makes it past the headstone where she first met us here before I tackle her to the ground. Hayze and Archer hold Ezekiel back when she begins to fight. I roll her over and pin her arms beside her head and trap her legs between mine. "Get the fuck off me."

"Calm the hell down, witch!"

"Fuck you, Vox, fuck all of you!" she chokes out, then begins to cry—guilt gnaws at me. I handled this whole thing wrong. "I want my mom," she rasps out through her tears. I turn and peer over my shoulder to look at Nikoa, he shakes his head.

"Where is she?" I snarl.

"I don't know." Nova screams beneath me at his answer.

"Get off me!" The utter devastation in her tone is the only reason I release her and drop back onto my ass. She crawls away and turns her back to me, but then suddenly the sounds of her cries die out and her body turns rigid. Worry begins to gnaw at me when she pulls her phone from the pocket of the hoodie she wears, she frantically unlocks it and then dials a number bringing it to her ear.

"Pick up, pick up, please, Waylen," she pleads.

Anger soars inside me. "Why the fuck are you calling that bitch?" I snarl. She ignores me and she continues chanting for him to answer his phone. She tosses her phone to the side and begins digging, I frown and look down to see the grave has a fresh mound of dirt. I look over my shoulder at my boys, Hayze and Archer have their masks off now and I can see they are all confused by the sight of the fresh dirt as well. This grave is one of the oldest in this place and looks the most daunting which is why we chose it.

"God, please... no... no," Nova cries out as she continues to dig. I shift and try to reach for her but she shoves me away. "Fuck off," she screams as tears trek down her face. "I will kill you if something happened to him," she spits out.

"Who?" I snap.

"Waylen." I recoil at her reply, I haven't seen that bitch since Homecoming.

"Nova, what the fuck are you talking about?" She snaps her head to the side to glare up at Nikoa.

"That!" she hisses as she points toward the headstone. I look to where she is pointing and my brows hit my hairline. Carved into the headstone is four numbers.

4221

The same numbers she has tattooed on her and the same numbers I know mean everything to her and best friend.

"Get the shovels out of my trunk!" I snap at my boys, then I turn around and help her dig, praying to God that this is just a sick joke.

The loss she is about to feel is on her.

That's what he said to Hayze. Tingles of unease work their way up my back as Archer, Nova, Nikoa and I continue to dig with our hands until Ez and Hayze get back with the shovels. We move out of their way but Nova doesn't. Without thinking I wrap my arms around her waist and drag her back, ignoring her threats. She kicks and tries to hit me but I don't relent.

"Let them dig, it will be faster," Nikoa says from beside me.

"Where is my mom?" she snaps.

"I don't know," he answers.

"You said you had her in your letter." He reels back and shakes his head.

"Thomas gave me the letters you sent," I add.

Nikoa's face slackens. "I meant I had *her* as in, I had Nova in my sights *not* Kelly."

"Oh God, Mom!" Nova screams as the boys continue to dig as fast they can.

"This was a trap," Nikoa breathes out as he spins around in a circle. Suddenly the hairs on the back of my neck stand on end and I get the sense we are being watched. I remain stoic and unmoving, knowing that she can't handle more than what has already happened tonight. Ez and Hayze switch out with Archer and Nikoa and keep digging. Nikoa keeps looking around and pulls his hood over his head, if we are being watched they would have already seen him and heard what we discussed.

When we hear a thud everyone stops moving, Nova tears free of my hold and jumps into the shallow grave. I dart forward and look down, watching as she swipes away the dirt. Nikoa and Archer climb out of the hole and stand on either side. Whoever did this, wanted us to find this and made it easy enough that we didn't have to dig more than a few feet. When Nova clears the dirt from the head of the casket a strangle sound escapes her. The top is ajar and I see four fingers poking out. She shifts to the side and flips the lid off.

The second she does, everything turns cold around us. Her

broken screams rent the air and we can all feel her pain. She brushes the dirt from his face and tries to pull him up but rigor mortis has set in and he is stiff. Waylen's eyes are a cloudy white and his mouth is open, filled with dirt. He wasn't only buried alive, he was clearly beaten, then suffocated and choked on the dirt when he pried the lid open.

"Come on, just wake up. This isn't our plan, we still have to go to Rome," she sobs out. A hollowness settles inside me as I watch her claw at her best friend's lifeless body. I run my gaze over Waylen and cringe. His clothes are torn and look like they are the same ones he was wearing the night she sent him packing. I'm guessing he never made it on that flight. The smell is intense and suffocating, he's clearly been dead for a few days but Nova doesn't seem to register that as she keeps screaming for him to wake up.

"Vox," Ez hisses. I turn to him. He flicks his gaze toward the lid of the coffin, I follow it and my features slacken. There, scratched into the pine wood lid of the coffin.

4221 RUN.

Waylen knew what was coming and rather than blame Nova for what was happening to him, he sent her one last message. He was telling her that he loved her and to run.

"Please, don't leave me. You're all I have. I need you and I need Mom, Way, please," she begs as she flops forward onto his body. I slam my eyes closed, unable to deal with the sight of her breaking. I can only imagine the pain that is coursing through her right now, losing Ez, Arch or Hayze would break me.

They aren't just my best friends, they are my brothers.

The sound of sirens wailing in the distance has all of us snapping out of it. I leap into the hole and try to pry Nova off Waylen but she continues to cling to him.

"We have to go," I snap.

"I'm not leaving him!" she screams.

"Vox, they're getting closer," Archer hisses. I try to pull her again but she won't budge.

"We have to go, man," Hayze snaps.

"I'm not leaving my sister," Ezekiel sneers.

"All of you go, I will get Nova out of here," Nikoa says. I look up at him and the resolute look in his eyes has something inside me trusting him to do as he says. "Get home to your families, they have all lost enough." I war with myself for a few more seconds before I release Nova.

"This isn't over, witch."

When she peers back at me I see nothing but hatred and loathing in her eyes. "I'm burning it all to the ground and I will take all of you down for what you did."

"I never touched him, I swear."

"You didn't have to. If you had stayed away from me then Waylen would be here. I hate you and everything you stand for. I'll kill Thomas and Nexus, then I'm coming for the *Filthy Few*. Your deaths will all be by my hands and I will be *Forever Filthy*." The promise in her tone has me steeling my spine and walling off my emotions, we not only have the war against the Saints to fight but it appears we have another contender.

Taylor Tempest is coming after all of us.

CHAPTER THIRTY-NINE

Nova

Secrets and Lies…

They bind you and rule over you until eventually. You have no choice but to give in and live in the reality that your bullshit created.

Like I am.

Sitting here and gazing out at the creek that runs through the back part of Nikoa's property, I can't stop my mind from replaying the events of that night. I had a gut feeling all day, I could just feel that something was wrong—all day I felt off. I never said anything to *him* or the others until before we left.

Learning the truth about who I am rocked me to my core but that wasn't what broke me. It was seeing that headstone with *our* numbers carved into it.

4221.

Forever together to love one another.

That was what we had lived by since we were kids. We

didn't need a large group of friends or ever felt left out when we didn't get invited to parties because we didn't need anyone, we had each other. Tears prick the backs of my eyes, I haven't been able to stop crying or get the picture of his face out of my head. The forever frozen terrified look in his eyes will haunt me for the rest of my life. I bury my face in my hands and cry.

Waylen is gone!

My Waylen!

I left him there.

I should have stayed but Nikoa made me a promise, he vowed to help me end the Saints and enact my revenge against those who hurt my best friend and he promised to help me find my mom. I thought he had her, if I had known otherwise I would never have defied Nexus. I would have worn that fucking stupid collar and knelt in the cafeteria until my knees bled. I would have done whatever he wanted. Instead, I chose to be selfish. I let my feelings for Vox Hatchett cloud my judgment.

I knew the texts from Waylen sounded weird. I should have known when he didn't reply to my 4221 message that it wasn't him, but I was too wrapped up in Vox and his evil dick to notice my best friend was kidnapped.

The numerous calls from him the night he left make sense, he was calling me for help and I was too self-absorbed and throwing myself a pity fucking party, so I ignored the calls. If only I had answered...

"You need to eat, Nova-Scotia." At the sound of Nikoa's voice, I turn rigid. I keep my face buried in my hands not wanting to look at him, every time I do all I see is Ezekiel. The knowledge that he is my biological brother still tastes bitter.

"Not hungry," I force out.

"You haven't eaten in nearly five days, enough is enough—" I lurch to my feet, feeling dizzy, and spin around to glare up at the fucker who stands on the porch, holding a plate. I try not to sway on my feet.

"It will never be enough!" I scream.

Nikoa's eyes shine with pity and I fucking hate that we have the same color hair and eyes. Unlike Ezekiel, who looks nothing like me with his blond hair and blue eyes, Nikoa does look like me and I fucking loathe it!

"I know but starving yourself and sitting out here all day, every day until you finally fall asleep isn't going to get you your revenge. If you want to slaughter those bastards that robbed your friend of decades worth of his life, then you need to woman the fuck up and get strong." His words may be crass and blunt but they resonate with the darkness that has been festering inside me since that night.

"I want them all to pay," I force out through clenched teeth.

"Then start by eating, showering and acting like you are actually living instead of walking around like a shell of a person."

"Fuck you," I snap.

"That fire, the one I see burning in your eyes, is what will give you the strength to carry yourself through all of this. Use it." He bends down and places the plate with a sandwich on it on the steps, then stands and looks at me. "Until you can show me that you are ready for this fight, I will not lift a finger to help you."

"You promised to help my mom—"

"And I intend on keeping that promise. I have people searching for her and my informant is looking into it as we speak. Everything else is on hold until you prove you are ready. I will not bury another fucking member of my family, understand?" When I don't acknowledge his questions he just shakes his head and stalks back inside the house, leaving me alone to wallow in the turmoil of my thoughts.

I know he's right. I'm not in the right headspace to go up against the Saints let alone the *Filthy Few*. I know Nikoa doesn't support my thirst for his nephew or his friends' blood but I don't care. If they had all just left me the fuck alone Waylen would never have been... I can't even think about what they did to him before they eventually... did what they fucking did to him.

I force myself to think about something else, anything aside from my dead friend and missing Mom. I slump back on the stairs and stare at the sandwich, my stomach rumbles for the food but just the thought of eating it makes me feel ill. My cell begins to vibrate beside me and I look down to see it's Vivian calling, again. She calls me at least a dozen times a day and texts me nonstop but I never open them or reply. I know she wasn't the one who killed Waylen, but I can't stop myself from placing some of the blame on her.

My phone begins to ring again and this time it isn't Vivian, it's Nexus. Red-hot anger soars inside me at the sight of his name. I still haven't listened to his voice messages or read the texts he sent, too afraid of what I will hear. I allow the anger riding me to take control and hit answer bringing the phone to my ear.

"I'm going to destroy you," I vow.

His laughter grates on my nerves and has me grinding my teeth. "Stop it, you sound like a spoiled little girl who lost her favorite toy."

"And you sound like a dead man on borrowed time," I grit out through clenched teeth. A range of emotions are warring inside me, pain and hatred are the strongest but there is also deep seated guilt. Nexus warned me not to cross him and I didn't listen. I chose to believe that I had somehow outsmarted him and I was untouchable because I had Vox and the *Filthy Few* at my side.

"That's funny, I think your friend ran out of time before I did." A choked sob rips out of me without consent.

"Fuck you!" I sneer.

"You want your mother back?" I gasp at the mention of my mom and snap my mouth closed, biting down on my tongue to keep from lashing out at him. His condescending chuckle has me grinding my teeth so hard that my jaw begins to ache. "I assume you have learned from your last mistake?"

It takes every ounce of self-control I have to keep my tone even. "*Yes.*"

"Well, that is good to hear, piggy. Now, there are a few rules for you to follow." I inhale to try to calm myself and remember that I need to play by his rules or my mom will suffer. "You are going to come out of hiding and return home. You will do as you are told and not step a single fucking foot out of line." The threat in his tone is clear. "You disobey me and your mother will start losing fingers. The collar is to be worn at all times and you will stay the fuck away from Vox and those other assholes."

I don't say it but he has no need to worry about Vox coming near me, he knows I want him dead. "Fine."

"You have three days to get your ass back here, your *masked man* won't be able to save you both." My eyes widen, he ends the call and I am left standing here staring out at the creek, wishing the current could wash me away with it. I have three days to formulate a plan and try to find my mom or I am left with no other choice but to return to that house of horrors and endure whatever that little snake puts me through.

"Nova?" I turn to see Nikoa standing in the doorway with a stern look.

"What?" He doesn't say anything about my tone.

"You need to come inside." The look in his eyes gives me pause and I stiffen.

"Why?" I grit out.

"Because if we make a plan I'm sure that phone call can be forgotten and you won't have to do something stupid like go back to living with those murdering sons of bitches." I can't keep the shock from splaying over my face. The bastard just grins and flicks his head for me to follow him. I begrudgingly do as instructed and follow him into the small living room where I freeze in the threshold. I have no idea who the two men are but the sight of the woman has my hackles rising and my anger spiking.

"You have no fucking right to be here," I seethe. Nikoa shoots me a look of warning but I ignore him. Her bottom lip begins to tremble and her eyes fill with tears. I scoff at the sight of them and harden my features, she doesn't deserve any fucking pity from me.

"I had no choice." Her voice trembles as she tries to fight back tears but it's pathetic if you ask me. Olivia Tempest is standing here in front of me looking like a lost little puppy.

"But you knew though, didn't you?" I ask as I force my legs to move and walk toward her. The two men shoot Nikoa a look but neither of them backs away from her. I stop a foot away and look at her. She has the same gray-blue eyes as her son but unlike Ezekiel, his mother's hair is a lighter shade of blonde. Judging from Nikoa's raven hair and green eyes, I would assume I take after Edmund's side of the family. "The night of Homecoming, you knew who I was, didn't you, Olivia?" A lone tear trek trails down her cheek but I feel nothing aside from a deep-seated loathing for this woman.

"Y-yes, I knew the moment I laid eyes on you that you are my—"

I cut her off before she can finish. "Don't even think about saying what you were about to say. Kelly is my mother." A pained look crosses her face but I am well past caring about her or her feelings. She bites down on her lip as more tears fall down her cheeks and she nods. "I don't know why you are here or what you want but I can tell you now, I want *nothing* from you." A whimper escapes her and the man on her right wraps an arm around her shoulders and draws her into his side.

"Nova." I snap my gaze to the man on her left and narrow my eyes, he looks oddly familiar. "My name is Shane Draven—"

"You're Hayze's father?" I say. The man smiles tightly and nods.

"Yes. But, I am also a member of the Haven Saints and so is Henry." I look at the other man, who nods his head. I study his features for a moment.

"You're Archer's dad?" Henry nods. "Why are you here?"

It isn't the men who answer my question, it's Nikoa. "They are here to help us get your mother back." I spring around and face him, his eyes are hard as he stares at me.

"What's the catch?" I push knowing there has to be something in this for them.

"Once we have Kelly back, we'll take the Saints down," Nikoa vows.

I scoff earning a hard look from my dear old uncle. "Your plan is futile," I answer.

"How so?" Shane asks.

"I'm not stupid, it may be true that I am a Tempest by blood, but I don't have the highest claim to the lordess spot, that honor belongs to *Vivian*."

CHAPTER FORTY

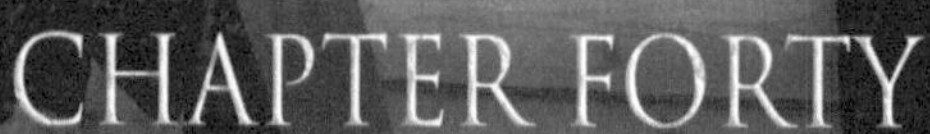

Vox

"If you had stayed away from me, then Waylen would be here. I hate you and everything you stand for. I'll kill Thomas and Nexus, then I'm coming for the Filthy Few. Your deaths will all be by my hands and I will be Forever Filthy."

Her words have haunted me for days. I can't stop them from replaying over and over again in my head. The look on her face that night shredded something inside me. I thought her taking off with Nikoa would be the worst of it but I was dead fucking wrong. Our problems are only beginning, we had no choice but to pack what we could and run. Nexus and Thomas knew what we were planning and I couldn't risk them or the Saints coming after my mom and Vivian, so we left. The guys alerted their families and all of them ran with us.

Vivian is refusing to speak to anyone, my mom is a mess. Hayze and Archer's moms are scared out of their minds because unlike their fathers and mine and Ez's moms, they have no idea about the Saints. I can tell keeping their mothers in the dark is weighing on Arch and Hayze, but with the shit storm we created it's safer if they don't know.

"My dad, Shane and Olivia are gone." I turn from the fire pit and peer over my shoulder at Archer, he looks like shit. None of us have slept much. We've given ourselves time to sort through our own shit and come to terms with the fact that our lives are forever changed. I feel responsible for all of this. Arch makes his way over to me, drops down on the log beside me and stares into the flames.

We may have had to flee our homes but it's not like we didn't run away to a fucking mansion that is big enough to house all of us and our families. This place has been in Hayze's family for generations and is secluded from everyone and everything. The only way to get here is by boat and there is no chance of anyone sneaking onto this little island paradise with all the security measures his father has put in place.

"Where did they go?" I ask him, breaking the silence. Archer shakes his head as if clearing it of his thoughts and sighs. The way his shoulders hunch and how he hangs his head makes me feel apprehensive and I start to tense, knowing that his answer is going to set me off.

"They went to see Nikoa and... Nova." Instantly I spring to my feet and glare down at him.

"The fuck do you mean they went to see her?" I snarl.

Archer releases a whoosh of air and lifts his head, the defeated look in his eyes has guilt gnawing inside me. "What other choice did they have? We need her to step up and take her place, Vox. Without Nova claiming her birthright we have no chance in hell of ever going home."

"That isn't our home!" I roar.

"It is to us!" he shouts as he climbs to his feet and gets right in my face. "Hollow Hills is our home. None of us can return until she takes over and removes the deserter tag from our names. Nova is our only hope right now. If she hates you enough to not remove the bounty on our heads, then we will spend the rest of our lives on the run from the Saints, always looking over our shoulders. I don't want that life for our parents and I know you sure as fuck don't want that for Vivian."

The mention of my sister has my anger fleeing and my fists unclenching. Vivian has hidden out in her room since we arrived here that night. She took one look at me and when she didn't see Nova in the car her eyes blazed with anger and I couldn't blame her. The one friend she had and I went and fucked it all up for her.

"I'm not trying to be a dick, Vox." I nod, knowing he's right, he's just saying what everyone else is thinking. "Hayze isn't liking being locked on this island but Ezekiel is the one I'm most worried about."

My brows furrow. "What's up with, Ez?"

Arch shoots me a deadpan look and shakes his head, motioning for me to take a seat so I do. He follows my lead and stares at the flames of the fire. "He won't speak to his mom and I can tell learning that Taylor—Nova is alive and has been this whole fucking time is fucking with his head."

"I forgot all about her being his sister," I admit.

"Yeah, well, that must be nice for you because that shit has been plaguing him and I can tell he is beating himself up badly. Taylor was his fucking world, he cherished her. I mean her room is still like a fucking shrine in their house, man."

I know what he is refusing to say so I say it for him. "And then Nova turned up and I declared her fair game for the *Filthy Few* making him do some fucked up shit to her, only for her to be his sister."

Archer grunts. "Yeah and the fact he knew you were fucking her like an animal isn't helping him not wanting to kill you." I cringe. Everyone knows that my sister is off limits and anyone who has dared tried to touch her or even ask her out has wound up with broken bones, and here I was fucking his sister hard and rough like she meant nothing to me. "You need to give him time, Vox."

I scrub a hand down my face. "He is never going to get over this or forgive me." I can hear the regret in my own tone.

"Answer me this, if you knew who she was would you still have gone after her?" I open my mouth to answer but my denial doesn't come out, instead I find the words stuck in my throat. Archer faces me and pins me with a look, urging me not to lie to him.

I grind my teeth and tug on the strands of my hair. "What the fuck do you want me to say, Arch?"

"That you would never have touched her and stayed the fuck away like everyone else has Vivian." My jaw locks as I stare at him.

"What the fuck do you mean everyone else?" I snarl in a cold tone. Archer's eyes widen and his mouth pops open but it's too fucking late, I see it in his eyes.

"You both need to come inside now!" Archer and I both turn at the sound of Hayze's panicked voice, our impending fight is put on hold as we both dart across the lawn and race after Hayze into the house.

"Touch me again and I'll kill you," Vivian snarls at Ez who is standing in front of her. I spot the suitcase on the ground beside Vi and narrow my eyes. The front door behind her opens and Shane and Henry enter the house, standing behind my sister. I spot our moms out of the corner of my eye, standing off to the side. The tears trailing down my mom's cheeks as Olivia and Mary hold her back has warning bells ringing in my head.

"I won't let you go," Ezekiel grits out.

"I'm not your problem," Vivian snaps back.

"Are you sure about that?" The cocky tone of Ezekiel's voice has me tensing, there is something going on here and I'm starting to get really fucking pissed off at not knowing every detail these bastards are hiding from me.

"What the fuck is going on?" Hayze asks, interrupting their little dispute. Vivian turns her head toward us while Ez keeps his hardened glare pointed at my sister.

"I'm leaving." Her words have me stumbling back a step.

"What the fuck do you mean, *you're leaving?*" I grit out through clenched teeth.

My sister's eyes narrow but I see the fire swirling in her eyes. "Because I refuse to stay here and hide out, away from my friend who was put in danger all because you wanted her to ask a fucking favor so she owed you a debt." The way she is looking at me and the venom in her tone shows me how angry she really is right now. I had no idea she was harboring this much anger toward me for what happened with Nova.

"You know why I had to do it, Vivian. I was trying to save you—-"

"From what, Vox?" she screams. "You never gave me the courtesy of asking what I wanted, you just assumed you knew like you always do!" The bite in her tone tells me she is raging and whenever Vivian gets like this it never ends well for her opponent. A part of me is happy to see this side of her again after so long, but another part is pissed the fuck off that her rage is directed toward me!

"What the fuck would you have wanted, Vi?" I don't give her a chance to answer as I stalk toward her. "Did you want to walk the fucking line like our father and Ezekiel's who were beaten within an inch of their life?" I stop beside Ez and don't miss the way he tenses having me this close to him. "Or, how about the new rule those cocksuckers implemented, where the new lordess must be *tested* out by the former lord?"

Disgust splays across her features as my meaning sinks in. "Thomas can try to fuck me," she snarls with venom in her tone.

"I'd kill the cunt before he ever had a chance." I peer over my shoulder at Hayze, his gaze is focused on my sister.

"I'm not your concern, Hayze," Vivian grits out.

"You are and will always be our concern, Vivian, which is why your ass is staying here with us!" Archer declares as he comes forward to stand on my other side just as Henry and Shane enter the room again, looking at each of us.

"Vivian, the boat is ready," Shane says quietly.

"She isn't going anywhere, Dad, her ass is staying right fucking here," Hayze says with a hint of dominance in his tone that rubs me the wrong fucking way, especially when its directed at my sister.

"Hayze, that isn't your call to make, Son," Shane defends.

"Technically, she is the superior, I'm afraid, and as members of the Saints, we are bound by law to obey the orders of the superior." Henry's declaration has my eyes widening and my fists clenching at my sides, I bare my teeth at both of them.

"She is not the fucking lordess and never will be!" I roar. When Shane and Henry both cut their gazes to Vivian briefly, I pause. I'm not fucking stupid and can read a room and I sure as fuck know when people are hiding shit from me, like they are now. "What the fuck did you do, Vi?"

She lifts her gaze but doesn't look at me, instead she turns to Ez with a smug look on her face. "I'm gonna let you answer that question while I go help my best friend save her mother. When you all finish killing each other, then call me." Vivian doesn't wait for an answer, she grabs her bags and heads for the door but pauses to glance at our mom once more. "I'm sorry. If there was another way I would do it but I will not let you bury another loved one." My mom chokes out a sob, her knees give out but Olivia and Mary are there to hold her before she can hit the ground. Vivian turns to leave with Shane and Henry, but Archer and Ez both step forward. Archer grabs her arm, halting her escape.

"Please, I am begging you," Arch says barely above a whisper but the weight of his words hang in the air between them.

Vi's face softens slightly but the instant Ez reaches for her she yanks free of Archer's hold and glares at Ezekiel. "You've done enough," she forces out before turning back to Archer. "Years. Fucking years have passed and you choose now to finally speak up? It's too late, Archer." My best friend stumbles back a step and drops his chin to his chest. Ezekiel looks furious as he stands there but it's Hayze who tries to save the day and cuts in between the two of them. When he grabs my sister's face between his hands, I move forward ready to rip him off her but Ez smacks a hand against my chest, forcing me to a stop.

"Vivi, baby, if you leave and do what I think you are about to, we won't be able to save you or Nova. We can't save the both of you," Hayze pleads.

Vivian reaches up and grips his arms. "I was never any of yours to save. This is my destiny and I will lead the Haven Saints and finally bring all those corrupt fuckers to justice and restore that town to the glory it once was. If there is a choice, Hayze, you save Nova, not me."

"Like fuck!" I shout.

"And his pigheadedness is what is going to get us both killed," she mutters before pulling free and walking out the door and away from me. The second Shane closes the door behind them, my mom breaks down and the three guys all turn to me, the looks on each of their faces actually gives me pause.

"If anything happens to her because of you, I will kill you!" Archer snarls as he shoulders past me and escapes out the back.

"She may be your sister but she is... more to us." Hayze's cryptic words have me studying him for a beat before he follows after Archer, leaving me here to face off against Ezekiel.

"Come on then, let me have it," I taunt him.

Ez shakes his head and scoffs in disgust. "*A favor is a debt owed.*" I jerk in surprise at his words. "You owe me a favor, you son of a bitch."

"And what favor is that?" I growl.

"You're going to help me save my sister and bring Vivian back."

"And why the fuck would I help you?" I snarl as I step into him, bringing us chest to chest.

"Because I'm the reason Vivian has the power to rule the Saints and overturn my father's decree."

CHAPTER FORTY-ONE

Nova

This is my last night before I need to get back to Nexus and save my mom. The thought of being around him again has a sickening feeling stirring in my gut. Just thinking about him has my skin crawling, he is the epitome of revulsion.

"Nova?" I roll my eyes at the sound of Nikoa's voice and ignore him. I refuse to go inside. I'm quite happy sitting out here on the back porch, staring out at the creek that is illuminated by the soft glow of the moon and thinking about the memories I shared with my best friend. I hear the back door open behind me, but don't bother to look. I hear him come closer and drop down onto the step beside me. I peer out of the corner of my eye and the sight has me turning fully and staring with an open mouth.

"Hey, girl," Vivian says quietly with a sad smile on her face.

"What are you doing here?" I breathe out.

She shrugs. "I'm here to help, Nova."

My anger surges and I narrow my eyes before turning back to the creek and ignoring her. "I don't need your help," I snap.

I hear her exhale beside me. "I know you think that—"

"I don't need or want your fucking help, Vivian. You and your family have done enough." She flinches but doesn't say anything. "Just go home."

"We can't."

I turn my head and study her for a moment, she doesn't cower or recoil from the pressure of my gaze. "Why?"

"The night that everything... happened. We all had to flee. The Saints are hunting us. I'm here to help you and help my family at the same time."

I scoff. "What? Your brother too much of a bitch to fight his own battles?" I sneer with hatred dripping from my words.

I expect her to defend Vox and have a go at me but what I didn't expect was for her to laugh. "No one and I mean no one has ever accused Vox of being a bitch before."

I shrug. "Guess they don't know him well enough then because he is for sure a bitch." Vivian shoots me a wink and I can't help the smile that stretches across my face. When I realize what I'm doing, I snuff the smile out and face the creek again.

"Nova—"

"Don't, Vivian, I don't want to hear it." I rest my arms across the tops of my thighs and drop my gaze to my lap.

"Tough, because I need to say it." I grind my teeth and interlock my fingers, digging my nails into the tops of my hands to use the pain as a distraction.

"Say whatever the fuck it is you need to, then go."

"Nova, I'm not going anywhere and I plan to be by your side when you return to Hollow Hills."

"Why the fuck would you do that?" I ask.

"Because they can't touch me until I'm twenty-four. Unlike

my brother and the others, I am not a member of the Saints, therefore there is nothing they can do to me until I am inducted into their bullshit secret society."

"How the fuck can you be so sure?"

She smiles and waggles her brows. "I have a backup plan. If they try to make a move against me, I will turn their world upside down in a heartbeat." I scrunch my face in confusion, she waves me off and continues on. "Look, I know you have to return back to your house tomorrow and I am here today to help you."

"How exactly are you going to do that?" I push.

"I'm going back to school with you and I am going to help you get your mom out of that house and taken to safety with my mom and the others." I instantly stiffen.

"I won't send my mom to the same place Ezekiel's mother is."

Vivian reaches out and places her hand on mine but I pull away from her touch. A flicker of anguish shines in her eyes before she masks it. "I can only imagine how you must be feeling right now. I can't understand it because I have never been through something like this but I need you to know something."

"What?"

"That the safest place for Kelly to be is on the island with the rest of our moms. She will be used against you. With us all fleeing, we have painted a target on our families backs and they will be the first people they use to ambush us like they did with..." She lets her sentence trail off and I appreciate her not saying his name. If she did, I would have lost my shit because right now isn't the time or place for her to say his name, not with how my anger is stewing inside me over his death.

"I'll take that into consideration," I bite out, but we both know I'm full of shit and never going to think about it. The truth, it's still too fucking hard for me to wrap my head around everything!

"Can I ask you something?"

A whoosh of air escapes me. "Yeah, why not," I snark.

"Bitch, that tone is as sour as your face." Without consent, laughter bursts out of me, I can't stop it now that it's started. Before long, Vivian joins me and then suddenly my laughter changes to sobs. Tears trek down my cheeks and I'm wrapping my arms around myself as if hoping to hold the broken pieces inside me together. "Ohh, Nova." Vivian wraps her arms around me and pulls me in close as I break down. All the pain I have pushed down inside me has finally broken free and I can't stop it from pouring out. The pain is unbearable, I can't breathe properly because it's consuming me whole and I don't know how to pull myself out of this rut.

"Move." I hear someone say before Vivian tries to extract herself from my hold. I refuse to release her until my hands are pried free from another. I snap my gaze to the right and the sight of that fucking mask sends my rage toppling over. I scream out as I shove him down the stairs. I run purely on instinct as I jump on top of him and begin wailing on him, my hands scream in protest as I punch his fucking stupid mask and chest but he never once raises a hand to stop me.

"Fuck you!" I land another hit to the side of the mask and cry out when my knuckles split, only then does he lift his hands to grip my wrists. "I fucking hate you!" I try to fight to free myself of his hold but he doesn't budge. "You ruined every-thing! You should have left me the fuck alone, you piece of shit, then none of them would be gone!" When I fall back and land between his legs he releases my arms and sits up, staring at me. We look like a tangled mess but I don't care.

I hate him!

This is all his fault.

"Nova—"

"Get the fuck out of here, two-horns, and don't ever come back or next time, I'll kill you," I snarl. I may not be able to see his face but I can see his eyes and the pain etched into them does nothing to thaw my anger or hatred toward him. I push to my feet and glance down at him once more before I turn on my heel, only to freeze at the sight of the other three masked fucks standing on my back porch. "All of you need to get the fuck out of here now and stay the fuck away from me."

Right horn lifts his masks and the sight of Ezekiel's gray-blue eyes that are filled with anger, confusion and familiarity has pain exploding inside me again and robbing me of air.

"You want us gone for good, then help us and I swear to you I'll help you bury Taylor Tempest for good, so you can carry on being Nova Quinlin as if Taylor never existed or came back from the dead." My eyes widen at Ezekiel's declaration. I can feel the others staring but I ignore them as I focus on him.

"Taylor Tempest *never* existed, she was someone you conjured up in your mind."

His lips purse at my answer and I can see he wants to fight me on this, but he chooses to go with another option. "Fine."

"Good," I clap back, earning a glare from him.

"You want to know the plan or you gonna keep being a stubborn bitch?" Ezekiel's words have me ready to fight but the instant I feel Vox at my back, I shutdown.

"Call her a bitch again," The fucker behind me growls.

"That's what she was to you though, wasn't she? When you were fucking her like a whore just so you could get what you wanted?" Ezekiel volleys back, earning a gasp from Vivian. I choke on my own spit. Vox tries to cut around to go at him, but Nikoa chooses that moment to join us and forces everyone to stay where they are.

"I just got word that Kelly has been moved." The mention

of my mother has me darting forward and up the stairs to stand in front of Nikoa who looks... worried.

"Where have they taken my mother?" I ask.

"My guess is they are moving her to keep you in line, so they can continue to dangle her safety over your head," he answers.

"Did your informant follow the car?" It grates on my fucking nerves that Vox asked the question I was about to. I can hear him and the guys behind me, pushing and shoving and a part of me loves that he is on the outs with his friends because if his ass had just stayed in his own lane none of this shit would have happened!

"He lost them on the interstate," Nikoa grits out.

"How?" I ask.

"There were four other cars of the same make and model waiting and they played musical fucking cars, my guy followed the wrong one. I'm sorry, Nova."

"Fuck!" I snap as I stab a hand through my hair and tug on the fucking roots. "Fuck, they knew we were watching them like they are probably watching us now and this dumb fuck had to blow it all," I snarl as I turn and glare at Vox.

"You got something to say to me then fucking say it, little girl, because I'm done with your fucking mood swings." The dirty fuck has the nerve to snap at me like that! When I turn to fully face him I see Hayze and Archer holding Ezekiel back. Vivian is smart enough to take a step back and not try to defend her asshole of a brother.

"You think you have the fucking right to show up here and act like you are a knight in shining fucking armor after what you did?" I scream.

"Tell me exactly what it is that I did, witch, because from where I'm standing you're the one who knew exactly what you were doing. You spread those fucking legs and let the monster come inside that pretty little cunt of yours." Chaos erupts around us. Ezekiel is trying to fight against the others to get to Vox but the instant Vivian steps before him he stops fighting instantly—interesting.

I smile darkly up at Vox. "You think throwing around the fact that I let you fuck me any way you wanted and however you wanted would embarrass me? Aww, that's a bit cute, Voxy, considering never once was I the one at your mercy, you were at mine from the first fucking moment. You had a job to do and failed not only me but everyone else. Instead of doing what a leader should and thinking about his people, you thought with your mediocre cock and that is the reason my life is fucked and my best friend is dead, because you're a selfish piece of shit who cares for no one but himself." One minute he stands before me as two horns and then in the next he removes his mask and is the Vox I know and hate. His face is etched in hard lines and his eyes burn with disdain as he stares down at me.

"Touch her and I'll fucking kill you, Vox, I swear it," Ezekiel vows but we both ignore him as Vox steps into me. The heat radiating off him seeps into me and I fight my body's reaction to having him this close. I hate that he can still bring this reaction out of me without even trying, even after everything he has done.

"I told you when you figured all of this shit out to be sure, you knew once you took the mask off that there would be no more blaming me for shit." I balk up at him.

"That was before... before..." I can't get the fucking words out and it's pissing me off.

"Use your fucking words, witch. You want to argue and throw around your hate, then you need to speak." His manipulation works and my vocal cords begin to work again.

"You got my best friend killed!" I scream. I hear the pain

and anguish in my voice, I can't find it within myself to care that they all have a front-row seat to my pain.

A shudder rolls through his eyes before he masks it. "I never meant for him to get hurt, Nova. I swear." The truth in his words has my chest splitting open. I refuse to let go of my anger, it's the only thing getting me through this and if I let it go, I'll be forced to face the pain head on and I'm not strong enough for that right now.

"Even if that was true, your actions still have consequences and Waylen paid the price for them. I can't do this shit with you, Vox. Playing with my emotions before was different, I had no idea who you were and I let myself fall for a guy with a mask. I won't make that mistake again." His eyes widen at my declaration but I'm not done. "You and your friends need to go, you can't be seen around me anymore. I'm going back to Nexus and Thomas and I won't let the four of you fuck up my chances of getting my mom back."

Before he can answer Nikoa speaks, "Actually, with what I have planned I am going to need them and they are going to need to play a part."

I turn to my uncle and study him for a second, but the asshole is like a vault and gives nothing away. "What part?" I push.

Nikoa flicks his gaze to Vox as he answers. "The part where you keep your feelings for *her* in line and don't fuck this up for all of us."

"How am I going to do that?" Vox demands.

"You are returning to school and the four of you are going to get close to Nexus and help him make her life a living hell."

CHAPTER FORTY-TWO

Vox

He has lost his goddamn mind! He has seriously gone crazy!

"If you think for a second I am going to let that little cunt touch my sister, you're out of your fucking mind!" Ezekiel snaps as he shoves Archer and Hayze away from him.

"I'm not your—"

Ez cuts Nova off before she can continue. "Deny it all you want but the truth is in our fucking DNA. I was a bastard to you and I am sorry for what I did Tay—Nova, I know my apology means nothing to you, but I swear I will make it up to you. If you want Taylor to die then so be it, but I won't let Nova cut me out of her life. I lost you once and I can't fucking do it again so don't ask me to... please." I stare at my best friend in shock, I've never heard him sound so vulnerable before.

"I can't," she murmurs. "My best friend died because of all of you and this bullshit brotherhood. He spent his last moments scratching *4221 RUN* into that coffin lid." The watery tone of her voice has guilt churning inside me for the loss she has suffered.

"We never meant for him to get hurt, I swear that to you, Nova," Ez pleads.

"His last words, his last fucking moments were spent warning *me* to run and telling me we would always be together to love one another. Don't you get that? If I let you all back in, then his death was for fucking nothing! Those bastards took him from me. Waylen was innocent and his only crime was fucking loving me." A strangled sob tears out of her. I step forward but she shoves me away. "Don't." That one word has me staying in place. It kills me that she won't let me near her—I need to start learning how to wall my emotions off and not allow my feelings for her to cloud my judgment.

"They may know that you have helped her and turned against them but they still don't know that it was me that you helped," Nikoa says.

"How does that help us?" Archer asks.

"It means that they cannot outright go against you or even banish you or your families from The Brotherhood without alerting them to the fact they have killed an innocent and used their positions inside the Saints to boost their own wealth and power. Thomas is getting sloppy and I just need a bit more time to get my hands on the information we will need to take them down."

"What information is that?" Hayze pushes.

"I need to find the eye witness that saw him run your father's car off the road and put the bullet between his eyes." A choked grunt escapes me at his words and I shoot a look at Ez who looks just as perplexed as I feel.

"The fuck do you mean a gunshot?" Ez snarls.

Nikoa looks between me and Ezekiel with a frown on his face. "Both of your fathers were shot after the accident."

I shake my head trying to deny his claim, then drop my gaze to the ground and force myself to think back. I saw my father and I know for a fact there was not a fucking hole in the middle of his head.

"You're wrong," I whisper. I can feel everyone looking at me but I turn to my sister and the pitying look in her eyes that are mirrors of my own robs me of air. "Vivian?"

Her features soften. "Even as young as we were, I know makeup, Vox. I questioned Mom about why Dad's face had makeup on it and she brushed me off. I always knew there was a reason behind the makeup, but it wasn't until I found out that dad was murdered that I knew why."

"And you never thought to say anything?" I shout. Nova whirls around and pins me with a hard look.

"You get to be upset but you don't get to take out your anger on her!" she seethes.

"You don't get to tell me to stay the fuck away from you and then decide to speak to me when it suits you, witch. Know your fucking place." Her brows raise in surprise.

"You don't get to fucking speak to her like that!" Ezekiel roars but I ignore the fucker, he can fuck off and so can *his* sister.

"You and I have never hidden things from each other—"

Vi cuts me off before I can finish. "Don't you dare pull that shit on me! You hid the truth about the Saints from me and let's not forget about the *Filthy Few*." The snark in her tone fuels my anger.

"I did all of that for *you!*" I defend.

"Bullshit. You did that for you! You wanted to feel like you were the one in control and that you hold the power. Look at where we are now, Vox, because you tried to hide everything." Her words hit me like a sledgehammer. I look around at everyone and fuck me if it doesn't sting to see the look of blame in each of their gazes.

"Fine. You want me out and to deal with this shit on your own, go for it. I'm out." I don't wait for a reply as I stalk away from them and head for the woods. They want someone to blame for all their pain and their losses, I'll be the bad guy so they can sleep better at night, but they better not fucking forget that they are the ones that made me turn my humanity off. If Nova thought I was a cunt before, she is in for a rude fucking shock when she turns up to school and sees who I really am.

When I pull up out front of his house I debate my choice for a moment until the front door opens and he steps out. I climb out of my car and cross my arms over my chest and eye him with hatred.

"Why are you here, Vox?"

"Because I want to watch them all fucking burn, I want in on whatever you have planned."

He scoffs. "And I'm just supposed to trust you after everything you fucking did?" he snarls.

"Considering I'm the one who got rid of the evidence of your son's murder spree, yeah I think you are."

His eyes widen for a split second before he schools his features and tightens his lips. "You have my attention, boy."

"I pledge my allegiance to the Haven Saints and hereby vow to serve the lord in *all* his endeavors."

A dark smile tugs at the corners of his lips. "You know what this means right?"

"Yes," I grit out.

"Your sister will never take over, am I clear?"

My nostrils flare at the mention of my twin but I force my emotions down and remind myself about how they all betrayed me.

"Agreed."

"Your feelings for the girl will do you no good, she is promised to my son, Vox."

A wicked smirk crosses my face. "I want nothing more than to see her suffer and be forced to marry Nexus. She deserves every fucking thing that is coming her way."

"I never thought I would see the day where you actually fell into line and realized the good I can do for all of us." I keep my face blank of the hatred I feel for him, he has done no fucking good for anyone in this town. He's lied, cheated and stolen from everyone just to further line his own pockets.

"I want in on everything, Thomas. I want to see Nova and those other traitors fucking burn."

"I always knew you were the smart one." I snort. "You need to prove to me that you can be trusted."

"How exactly do I do that?"

A dark look overtakes his features. "You start by killing Ezekiel Tempest, I can't risk that fucking fool marrying your sister and overturning the decree before my son can marry Nova."

"Consider it done."

"You make it look like an accident, The Brotherhood can never know about this. We are beholden to our laws and if they find out you killed another member, they will kill you and your family. Am I clear?"

"How long do I have to plan this?"

"You have one week to make the fucker disappear, prove to me you can do this and you will be welcomed into my fold and then and only then would you have earned my trust."

"Consider the traitor dead," I say with a grin.

"I want evidence, Vox."

"I'll record it all for you," I promise.

"You stay out of Nexus' way at school, those other three cunts and your sister are permitted to return. Once you take care of Tempest, I'll give you the next order."

"Fine," I grit out, then climb inside my car and peel out of the drive.

CHAPTER FORTY-THREE

Nova

Just being back down this street has chills rippling through my entire body. I talked a big game to Nikoa and told him I had this under control and knew exactly what I was doing. Truth is, I just wanted to get the fuck out of there and get this interaction over with. I didn't expect to be driven back to this prison by Ezekiel, Hayze, Archer and Vivian, though. I only relented because they said Vivian needed a ride back to her place and they would be staying there with her until Vox got over himself.

I hate to admit it but I'm angry with myself for worrying about him. The look in his eyes tore me up inside. I have never seen him look at his sister the way he did earlier. Vivian may not realize it but she is the center of Vox's world and he would do anything to make sure she is safe. Ezekiel pulls into Vivian's driveway and kills the engine, but none of us make a move to get out. I peer out the window and stare at the house that is going to be my glorified cage for the foreseeable future until Nikoa can get the intel he needs.

"Nova?" I turn to look at Vivian who sits in the middle of me and Hayze. "Nikoa has a month to come up with the information and witness, if he can't do it by then we will get you out and overthrow Thomas."

I open my mouth to ask how, but Archer beats me to it. "How are you going to do that, Vi?"

Vivian shoots him a cold look before turning back to me. "I have a plan. The Saints hold a gathering once a year where you can challenge the lord and that is in a month. I have a plan and I promise it will work but I really hope Nikoa can beat me to it." Her ominous words rub me the wrong way but I don't push her, I have too much on my mind right now to decipher that shit.

"You all good with the plan for school Monday?" I ask changing the subject. The four of them nod.

"Are you sure Nexus and Thomas will get your suspension overturned?" Hayze asks me.

"Yeah. Nexus texted me and told me that my collar was waiting for me and that his dad smoothed everything over with Nicole's dad." I don't regret smacking that bitch around, she had it coming and so did her sidekick. I know Pam, Brandy and that slut are going to love every minute of my hell that Nexus is going to put me through until I turn eighteen.

"Here, take this," Ez says as he hands me a phone. I stare at it for a second before flicking my gaze back to him.

"Why?" I ask.

"Because it's a fucking burner with our numbers programmed into it. I guarantee you he is going to take your phone from you the second you step through those doors and I need to know I can reach you when I need to. I put the charger in your backpack." I purse my lips and take the phone, stuffing it inside my bra and opening my door. Vi hands me my bag and shoots me a sad smile.

"I'm so sorry, Nova," she whispers.

"Don't be, just don't get involved okay?" She sucks in a sharp breath. Hayze wraps his arm around her shoulders and shoots me a nod. "Look after her until I can finish this, yeah?"

"On my life," Hayze vows.

"You watch your back. You stay as far away from that cunt as you can," Ezekiel says through his open window. I shut the back door and face him. I take in the sight of him and sigh.

"I've grown up without you, I know what I'm doing."

Pain flashes in his eyes at my words before he quickly masks it. "He touches you and all fucking bets are off." I open my mouth to argue but he pushes on. "You may not like me, Nova, but I'll be watching your back. I won't let anyone hurt you, I swear." I have no idea what to say to that or how to respond so I just nod and drag my sorry ass across the lawn. I stand in front of the front door, debating if I should knock or just walk in, but the decision is made for me when the front door swings open to reveal Nexus standing there with a smug smirk on his hideous face. His black hair is slicked back against his head, his green eyes are filled with malice. Unlike Vox and his friends, Nexus has no ink on his skin and always tries to act like he is superior but the reality of the situation is, Vox and the others don't have to try, they are just superior.

"Welcome home, *piggy*." I bite the inside of my cheek to keep from lashing out. He runs his gaze over me and I shiver in disgust. I hate Nexus with a passion so great that I can feel the blood heating inside me with the need for vengeance. He steps aside to allow me pass. I try to keep as much space between us, but the fucker presses forward so I brush against him. I wait in the entryway for him to lead the way. A part of me wants to escape out that door and run. "Let's go, Dad wants to see you."

I follow him through the house to Thomas' office. When I enter I can't stop my gaze from straying to the file cabinet. Memories of the night two horns found me in here and fucked me against it assaulted me, sending a shiver of delight straight to my core.

"Hello, Nova." I tear my gaze from the cabinet and look at Thomas. He sits behind his large desk with an evil glint in his eyes and a sadistic smile on his weathered face. I remain silent not wanting to say anything to this fucking monster. "After your little late graveyard meet up, I can assume that you now know the truth about who you really are?"

My nostrils flare as I inhale sharply. "Yes," I force out.

"Good." He motions for me to claim one of the seats in front of his desk. I want to refuse and tell him to go fuck himself, but I also know Thomas and his bastard son don't make idle threats. I reluctantly do as I'm told. When Nexus claims the seat beside me, I shift as far away from him as I can. "You are going to have to get over your reluctance to be near my son."

Before I can stop myself the words spew out of me. "That cocksucker killed my best friend!"

Thomas launches out of his chair and rounds the desk to stand before me. I ignore Nexus' laughter from beside me, too wrapped up in the dark look in his father's eyes. I expect Thomas to yell and throw around his big words of reprimand but what I don't expect is for him to lash out and slap me so hard I topple off my chair. My ear rings from the force and my eyes fill with tears as I reach up and cover my cheek with my hand and stare up at the coward with hatred in my eyes.

"You'll learn to keep that fucking mouth of yours shut or I will be forced to close it for you." I bite my lip to keep from shouting at him. "My son let you get away with too much. My future daughter-in-law will learn that her place is to be seen and not heard. Learn that fast or Mother will pay the price for your fuck ups, am I clear?"

I swallow past the lump in my throat. "Y-yes," I choke out.

The psychotic fuck smiles down at me and nods. "Good. Now I have spoken to Principal Daniels and he has graciously agreed to overturn your idiotic suspension on the terms you apologize to his daughter and agree to stay after school every day to help clean up." Anger unfurls inside me. "Of course I told him you would be more than happy to help." When I remain silent his eyes narrow to slits. "Speak up!"

I flinch backward and nod. "Yes, I'll do it." I hate that one hit is all it has taken for me to turn into this meek little creature sitting on the floor in front of him.

"Perfect, you will travel to school every morning with Nexus. You are to obey everything he says—"

"What if I don't?" I ask before I can think better of it.

Thomas' face contorts and I brace myself for him to lash out at me again but he doesn't. Instead he reaches into his pocket and pulls his phone out and clicks a few buttons then turns the screen toward me. All the blood drains from my face and I turn ice cold at the sight of my mom in a white padded room, her hair is a mess of knots and tangles, the hospital gown she wears is filthy. When she lifts her head and stares up at the camera I die inside. The petrified look in her eyes destroys any humanity I have left inside me. Thomas locks the phone and tosses it on his desk.

"Now you know what is at stake if you try anything or those fucking idiots next door try to play heroes," he snarls.

"I'll do whatever you want," I whisper brokenly as the first tear falls down my cheek. "I won't step out of line. I'll do as I'm told just don't... hurt her, please," I beg as more tears trail down my cheeks.

Thomas bends down in front of me. He reaches out and I

flinch away from his touch, only to cry out when he grabs my hair and yanks me forward. The stench of his breath fans across my face, forcing me to breathe through my mouth or risk gagging in his face.

"Your whorish ways are over. The only person you are spreading those legs for is my son. Defy me once, just one fucking time, and you will never see your mother again. Am I clear?"

"Yes," I breathe out.

"Yes, what?" he pushes.

"Yes, *sir*," I grit out through clenched teeth.

Thomas' grip on my hair tightens and a whimper escapes me. "Get the fuck out of my sight," he snarls and releases me with a hard shove. I scramble to my feet, ready to flee to my room but Nexus' words have me halting in the doorway with my back to them.

"You stay in *my* room." I take a deep breath and try to compose myself, before peering over my shoulder at him.

"I have to share with you?"

The smug look on his face has bile rushing up my throat. "Until we figure out who the fuck your masked fuck buddy is, we can't trust you to stop being the town slut, so yes, you will sleep where I can keep an eye on you." The anger brewing inside me is only held at bay by the knowledge that he doesn't know who the *Filthy Few* members are. I keep the shock from splaying across my face, if this is true then they can still work behind the scenes and help me get my mom back.

"It's not like we can trust you to be honest with who the masked man was. We did contemplate torturing your mother until you admitted it but..." Thomas lets his sentence trail off while I stand here gaping at him, wondering how a human being could be so cruel.

"Just in case it wasn't clear before, whatever that shit was between you and Vox-fucking-Hatchett, it's over now," Nexus spits.

"That fucker is dead to me," I snap.

"Good, he can be dead and in your past like Waylen." My jaw unhinges as Nexus laughs. "Too soon?"

"I hate you," I bite back as I fight to keep my tears at bay.

"Too fucking bad. You breathe a word about what happened to that fucker to anyone and your mother will be buried with him." I didn't think it was possible for me to hate Nexus more than I already do. but clearly I was wrong.

I need to warn Ezekiel and Nikoa about what I have just learned. If we play this right, we all might just get out of this alive.

CHAPTER FORTY-FOUR

Vox

Fall is here and the gloomy fucking weather matches my sour mood. This time of year is my favorite—Halloween. It's the one night of the year where we could all go out and wear the masks and never have to hide in the shadows. We could walk out in the open without anyone suspecting something was amiss, but this year, the excitement isn't there. Instead, I sit here in the parking lot of Haven Prep alone, staring out the windshield at the fuckers that betrayed me. My three so-called best friends and my sister all stand around Ezekiel's car, shooting side glances toward me but none of them make a move to come over. Good, because I don't need them or my twin.

I have until Friday to fulfill my promise to Thomas. I have no plans to back out on my deal. If Ezekiel has to die to prove I am loyal to the Saints, then so fucking be it. The sight of Nexus' emerald-green Audi pulling into the lot draws my attention. He parks next to my car. I don't bother to even look at him or his pig of a passenger as I climb out and slam my sunglasses down to shield my eyes. Only then do I turn to face Nexus. He stands there with a broad grin on his face. When he pulls me in for a bro hug, I meet Nova's gaze over the roof of the car, the sight of betrayal on her face has me smiling as I pull back.

"You back for real?" Nexus eyes me carefully as he waits for my reply.

"Yeah, man. I'm over fucking with your pig and those fuckers," I answer as a devilish glint enters his eyes.

"Piggy!" he calls out. Nova rounds the car and stands beside him. "Like the collar I got her?" I take a quick glance at the black studded collar around her neck and smirk at the bright pink name embroidered on the collar, *Bitch*.

"The name fits." Nexus laughs and smacks me on the arm, but it only takes a second for his laughter to die out and his face to take on a serious edge.

"She's mine, Vox. You want to torment the fuck out of her, then go for it but you don't touch her, understand?" The dominance he is trying to exert over me is fucking comical. The cunt thinks respect is bought and not earned, and that has been and will always be his biggest downfall.

"Been there, had that, fucked that and done with that," I answer. Nova clenches her fists at her sides, showing me that my words affect her but she is too fucking stubborn to admit that I got under her skin. We're in this position right now because she chose to blame me for the death of her bitch ass friend, but then turns around and goes and shacks up with the cunt that buried the fucker alive!

"Babe!" I fight not to growl at the sound of her nasally voice. I turn my head to the side in time to see Nicole, Pam and

Brandy coming toward us. I spy my sister and the other's glaring at me, good because I want their anger. I need it to fuel me. When Nicole comes to stand before me, I shoot her a cocky smirk that has the dumbass swooning and huddling into my side. Nova cuts a glance to me and the look of hurt in her eyes has me smiling. I want the bitch writhing in pain so I grip Nicole's chin and force her head back, then angle my lips over hers. Nicole being the A-class actress she is, grips the front of my shirt and lets out a heady moan.

"I got class." I hear Nova say. The moment she leaves, I release Nicole and brush past, calling out to Nexus that I'll see him at lunch. I have a bitch to torment first period and I can't wait. Hayze tries to call out to me as I pass by, but I ignore them as I zero in my sights on Nova's retreating back.

By the time she makes it to first period, I'm already sitting in my usual seat, her eyes widen at the sight of me. "What the fuck are you doing here?" she grits out as she slowly makes her way toward me.

I don't respond until she claims the seat beside me. "Getting to class early, that a problem, *witch*?"

She scoffs and glances out the corner of her eye at me. "You never get to class early. Shouldn't you be out there sucking face with your whore?"

I fight to keep the smile from my face at her jealousy. "And here I was thinking you wouldn't give a fuck about who is sucking my cock since I ruined your life. If I recall, you are the one who promised to kill me and become *Forever Filthy*."

She sucks in a ragged breath and her eyes burn with fire, but the bell rings and students begin entering the classroom, forcing our exchange to come to a stop. She can't wipe the look of rage from her face even as the teacher begins speaking, I lean back in my seat and hum low enough for only her to hear. I can see her trying to fight against snapping at me but I know it's only a matter of time before she finally breaks, so I decide to hurry her along. I grip my pencil and stab it into the side of her thigh. She lets out a loud shriek, garnering the attention of everyone in the room.

"Miss Quinlin, I don't tolerate interruptions in my classroom, is that clear?" Nova is grinding her teeth so hard I can almost hear it.

"Yes, Ma'am." She tries to sound apologetic but fails miserably.

"One more outburst like that and you will be out of my class." Nova is as stiff as a board as she nods her agreement. The remainder of the lesson is spent with me jabbing my pencil into her side, thigh and forearm. When she stops giving me the reaction I want, I get pissed off and decide to up my game. When my hand grips the top of her thigh, she sucks in a ragged breath and tries to shove my hand away but I don't budge.

"Get the fuck away from me, Vox," she growls under her breath.

"Are you wet, witch?" I purr.

She snaps her head toward me and narrows her eyes to slits. "No."

I smirk, I can see it in her eyes that she's full of shit. I trail my hand up higher until my fingers skim the lace of her panties, causing her to jerk in her seat. "Even if you hate me, your pussy doesn't."

"Every single part of me loathes you," she spits.

"I told you before, little witch, I always get what I want. I'll be fucking you whenever and wherever the fuck I want and you are going to take it like a good *bitch*, or I'll slit your brother's throat." She searches my gaze for a second, wanting to call me on my bluff but she can see it in my eyes and hear in my words that I mean what I say.

"My mom or my brother, are those my only options these days?" She doesn't give me a chance to answer. "I fuck you, I save Ezekiel. I get caught fucking you and my mother dies. Seems like either way I lose, so I will take the chance and save my mom because there is no way you are sneaking into my room anymore."

"Want a bet, witch?" I sneer.

A cocky glint enters her eyes just as the bell rings. "Yeah, I do, considering I sleep beside Nexus every night in *his* room, I don't like your chances, two horns." Her words are laced with so much hatred, then she smacks my hand away and stands, gathering all her things and practically running out of the room to get as far away from me as she can.

I sleep beside Nexus every night in his room.

Those words play over and over in my head as I head for my next class. She could be lying but I know Nova is a lot of things and a liar isn't one of them. I can read her. She used that shit to get under my skin but I heard the hint of hatred in her tone when she said it. She hates Nexus so that means he is forcing her to obey his rules.

"You seem lost." I slam to a halt and roll my eyes at the sight of Ezekiel leaning against the lockers. I frown when I notice the hallway is deserted, am I late? Did I miss the next bell? "Your class is on the other side, dumbass."

Fuck!

I was too caught up in thinking about Nova to register that I had gone the wrong fucking way, I have English this period and that's across the other side of the fucking school!

"What the fuck do you want?"

Ezekiel pushes forward and comes to stand a foot away from me. "Pull your head out of your ass, Vox. You're angry because Vivian—"

"This has nothing to do with my sister."

"Then why the fuck are you acting like a bitch who got her feelings hurt?"

I chuckle but there is no humor to it. "Because, unlike you dumb fucks, I have a way out and I'm taking it."

Ezekiel's face drops. "What the fuck did you do?" The disbelief in his tone is crystal clear and that brings a smirk to my face.

"I chose the winning side." I reach out and pat his cheek a couple of times until he shoves me back. "I'll be seeing you real soon, *brother*." I turn and head back toward my English class. Just as I round the corner, I bump into Nicole who looks like she was just caught in the act. Rather than call her on listening into my conversation, I sling my arm over her shoulders and continue walking. She says nothing and melts into my side.

By the time I reach the cafeteria, it's already packed with students hooting and hollering, I scan the area to see what the cause of everyone acting like this is a fucking circus. As I walk in further, everyone parts for me, they all know not to get in my fucking way. I spy Hayze and Archer out of the corner of my eye, dragging Ezekiel from the room who is fighting against them but the instant my sister reaches them and says something to him, he quits fighting and stalks out of here with his head down.

Fucking pussy.

When I break through the crowd I see what all the noise is about, Nexus has Nova on her knees beside him but that isn't what has everyone riled up. It's Nicole placing a dog bowl in front of Nova that is piled with wet dog food. When Nexus spots me, I blank my face of all surprise and plaster a bored look in its place and cross my arms over my chest.

"Make the pig eat the fucking food or get rid of it, the sight of the mutt disgusts me," I snap. Everyone begins laughing and cheering, Emmet even claps me on the shoulder, but the instant I shoot him a glare his face falls and he melts back into the crowd.

"Babe, a good show takes time and you are just in time for the main event," Nicole coos. I roll my eyes in response. "Daddy said she has to say sorry for being a bitch to me. I don't want her words. I want her to prove to me that she means her apology and the only way to do that is to eat what I made for her." Nova's chin is against her chest and her long raven hair is acting as a curtain, shielding her face from everyone.

"Eat the fucking food, piggy," Nexus says in a cold tone that causes Nova to cringe. I inhale sharply as she slowly lowers her head toward the bowl.

"*Piggy, Piggy, Piggy,*" everyone begins to chant. This is fucking pathetic and designed as nothing more than a tactic by Nicole to try to break Nova. Nexus doesn't give a fuck either way, he's just punishing Nova for fucking me... My brow furrows as a thought hits me.

Nexus isn't just punishing her for hooking up with me, he's punishing her for fucking *two horns* which means, he has no fucking idea who the members of the *Filthy Few* are.

I'm yanked from my thoughts when the fire alarm sounds out through the room. I look back to Nova to see her face an inch from the food. Nicole screams in frustration and shoves Nova's face into the bowl, screaming out how she is a fucking bitch and this isn't over. I dart forward. Nexus shoots me a look of warning that I ignore as I bend at the knees and lift Nicole, slinging her over my shoulder.

"Vox!" she tries to sound angry but we both know she is loving that everyone is going to see her with me like this. I ignore her offers of sexual favors as I carry her ass outside, my gaze instantly locking with my twin, who is shooting balls of fire at me with her eyes. We all know there is no fucking fire, those four pulled the alarm to save Nova's ass.

CHAPTER FORTY-FIVE

Nova

The pain of Waylen's death coupled with the fact I am forced to serve and obey my fucked-up stepbrother's demands daily is becoming too much. I have no escape from him. Every day after school I am forced to stay behind and clean until five. The torment doesn't end there, by the time I leave the school there are no buses so I have to walk home, but my shame doesn't end there. The football team finishes practice around the same time and every single one of them follows their captain's lead and hurls insults at me or boxes me in, grabbing their junk and telling me to suck their cocks. The first two times Hayze tried to stop it and help me, but when I ignored him and refused to take his offer of a ride home he got the hint.

It's Friday and the school is buzzing with the weekend mere minutes away. Everyone is counting down the time for last period to end so they can race home and glam themselves up for the bonfire at the beach. Vox and Nexus organized it, saying since the team had a bye this week they were going to celebrate. I hate Vox, I hate him so fucking much and I can see his best friends are starting to dislike him as well.

He has treated his friends like shit and joined in on making my life hell, he even helped Nexus come up with ways to torture me. I was forced to kneel next to their lunch table as they joked about throwing a Halloween party and making the main attraction of their party a coffin with a body in it.

"We could even have the lid askew and make it look like the fucker was clawing his way out." Vox's cruel words pierced me right in the heart and I couldn't hold the tears back as I knelt crying silently as he and Nexus made cruel jokes about my best friend. When the bell sounds, everyone cheers and rushes from the room but I can't find the excitement inside me. I'll be forced to spend two whole days at home with Nexus. The bastard won't even let me close the door when I shower. This morning he had the audacity to climb in the shower with me. I tried to shove him out but all that earned me was a back hand and a split lip.

Tonight I plan to ask Thomas to allow me to see my mom or at least speak to her so I know the video feed isn't looped and she is *actually* alive. I ignore everyone around me as I head toward my locker to drop my books off before going to the office to collect the supplies I need to scrub gum from under the desks.

As I open my locker, my eyes widen at the sight of a black envelope. I dart my gaze around to make sure no one is watching as I grab it and quickly stuff it in my pocket. I shove my bag inside and turn to head toward the office, but smack straight into a rock-hard chest. I stumble backward but the collar around my neck is gripped and keeps me from falling to my ass. I flick my gaze up to see it's Vox. I smack his hand away and quickly right myself.

"Huh, I guess that collar did come in handy for something," he taunts. Rather than engage with this fucker like he wants me to, I try to step around him but he blocks my path. "Where are you off to, piggy?" Hearing that name from Nexus and everyone else means nothing to me, they mean nothing to me, but hearing Vox use the vile fucking name always cuts me deep.

"I got shit to do, let me pass," I snap as I keep my head down, not wanting to even look at him. I feel him creep in closer and I still, my breaths turning ragged when he leans down and I feel his hot breath against my ear.

"Stay away from that party, witch."

I snort. "Like I could even fucking go if I wanted to."

"What's coming is going to test you, push and potentially break you. Don't let it, little witch."

"Don't play games with me, Vox," I grit out.

"That's all I got left, witch. I'll see you later but just remember I always chose the winning side from the start." He pulls and stalks off down the corridor. I glare at his retreating back, hating that the tattooed bastard can still turn my own body against me. I'm pulled from my inner turmoil when I'm shoved into the lockers by a group of assholes who all laugh and point at me. I hang my head in shame as I walk away.

By the time I hand the supplies back into the office I am bone tired and just want to go home, curl up into a ball and cry. Every day bleeds into nightfall and along with it a part of me disintegrates, my will to fight lessens daily as Nexus continues to strip away pieces of my self-respect and dignity. I am forced to eat and drink from dog bowls here and at home. *Home* isn't the word I want to use for the place I am forced to sleep at each night. I stop by my locker to grab my bag and it's then that I remember the letter in my pocket. I look around to make sure I am alone before pulling it out. The sight of the *T* for the Tempest seal has a knot inside my chest loosening.

Nikoa hasn't forgotten about me.

I tear it open and pull the letter out.

Nova Scotia

I'm aware of the troubles you face daily and it sickens me!

I am pushing my informant for the information I need so I can get you out of there.

I have a team searching for your mother.

Things are going to take a turn for the worst, I need you to trust me when I tell you that nothing is as it seems and everything has been planned out.

I can't risk saying more in case this letter is discovered.

N x

I slam my eyes closed and want my emotions to remain in check. I thought I could do this alone but it turns out knowing I have Nikoa trying to help me, and my friends as well as their parents, seems to be the only thing keeping me going. I return the letter to the envelope and shove it inside one of my books that I leave in my locker. I can't risk carrying that letter with me and Nexus or worse, Thomas discovering it. The sooner Nikoa can get my mom the sooner I can kill both of them. Thomas warned me if I tried to kill him, he has a failsafe in place and the people holding my mom would kill her if they didn't hear from him at a certain time every day.

I push through the doors of the school and come to a stop at the sight of Vivian standing beside Archer's car. If this was any other day I would ignore her and walk home but the devastated look on her face is what has me moving toward her.

"He's gone," she whispers when I stand before her.

My brows draw in. "Who?"

"Ezekiel. He was supposed to meet us at the diner after school yesterday but he never showed up. We went looking for him today. Arch tracked his car's GPS and it led us to the cemetery." I suck in a sharp breath as panic begins to bloom inside me.

"What did you find?" My tone is firm.

Tears cloud her eyes as she stares at me. "A note." She reaches into her pocket and hands me the letter.

4221 sister...

My breaths turn ragged and I begin to sway on my feet as a haze of grief slams into me. I reach out and place my hand on the hood of the car to stop myself from toppling over. Vivian is speaking but I can't hear a word she says over the blood rushing in my ears. I start to feel faint and then before I know what is happening, my whole world tilts on its axis and I black out.

I gasp and snap my eyes open in a panic. I look around and furrow my brow when I realize I'm in a car. No, not just any car, I'm in *his* fucking car and in my driveway! Alarm bells blare inside me, if he brought me back here then Nexus is going to lose his mind. A whimper escapes me as I shove the door open and dart out of the car. I race through the front door and race around the house looking for Nexus so I can explain but I come up short when I hear the sound of Ezekiel's voice.

I creep down the hallway toward Thomas' office, the door is open and Thomas stands there with... Vox. Both their backs are to me as they stare up at the flat screen TV on the wall. I cover my mouth with my hand to keep the horrid sounds from escaping at the sight of the video playing.

"You don't have to do this, brother," Ez pleads on the screen and tears build in my eyes at the sight of him on his knees in the cemetery, with his hands bound behind his back. The look of betrayal and fear in his eyes will haunt me. His face is battered and bruised, I can see a cut above his brow and his cheek is split, blood trickling down the side of his mouth. I don't under-stand why Vox is here with Thomas and not out looking for whoever the fuck did this with his friends... unless, did Thomas do this to Ez? Was Nexus a part of this?

"You chose the wrong side." My jaw unhinges and my eyes widen at the sound of Vox's voice on the TV. I shake my head, wanting to deny what I heard but I can feel it in the pit of my stomach.

"No, you chose wrong by forgetting who you are and where you came from." Ezekiel's tone drips with venom but I hear the hint of fear and see it in his eyes. Tears trek silently down my cheeks as I stare into the eyes of the brother I never knew I had or even wanted. The resignation I see in those gray-blue eyes shreds me internally—Ez knows his best friend is about to kill him and still won't yield and plead for his life.

"I always win, I will always get what I want," Vox says as he comes into view of the camera. I expect to see him wearing his mask but he isn't. I want to announce myself and scream that Vox is the leader of the *Filthy Few* and blow Vox's world apart, but if I do that I risk Hayze and Archer being discovered and I can't do that.

Ez spits on the ground by Vox's feet and glares up at him. "That son of a bitch murdered our fathers and forced our sisters to live lives they never should have, and yet you choose to help him, why?"

"Because that little witch you call sister needs to be taken down a peg and shown she is beneath us." Before Ezekiel can respond, Vox pulls a gun from his waistband. The sight alone has me frozen in time and my breath hitching as I pray to anyone who is listening to let this be a trick but then Vox's finger squeezes the trigger and Ezekiel is sent falling backward to the hard earth. "4221, motherfucker," Vox snarls. It's the sound of those numbers coming out of his mouth that breaks through my haze and has me falling to my knees as sobs claw their way out of me. I bury my face in my hands and allow all the guilt and shame I feel wash over me. I pushed Ezekiel away and told him I never wanted anything to do with him because I was angry and hurt.

He died thinking I hated him!

My own fucking brother died and the last thing he did was leave a note for me using the code Waylen and I shared to tell each other that we would always be together to love one another. I sense more than seeing him crouch down in front of me, I don't even have the energy to lift my head. The grief is swallowing me whole and I am beyond fighting against it so I give in and allow the pain to consume me.

"You shouldn't have seen that, witch," Vox whispers low enough for only me to hear. "Let me get rid of her then we can talk," he says to Thomas, then gathers me in his arms and lifts me off the ground. I don't even fight against him as he strolls away from the office. I allow his warmth to soak into me and nuzzle in closer to him. I fool myself into believing that this is my two horns, the guy who took what he wanted but always made sure I was safe. I let my weakness take control and wrap my arms around his neck and burrow my face into his shoulder as sobs rock my body.

Before I can get too lost in the comfort his hard body and presence affords me, he places me on my feet. I keep my head down and refuse to untangle my arms from him. I expect him to push me away and be cruel but in a move so bold it robs me of air he wraps his arms around my waist and pulls me flush against his hard chest. This boy just killed my brother and was the cause of my best friend's death and yet here I am finding comfort in the wrong place, not being strong enough to push him away or even let go because somehow two horns became my safe haven and then Vox came along and ruined everything.

"I told you not to let it break you and I meant it. I chose the winning side from the start and I stand by my vow, witch," he murmurs into my hair.

"Why did you have to ruin everything by being you, why couldn't you just be *him*," I choke out. Vox untangles himself from me and shifts back, but cups my face between his hands.

"I've always been both those people, little witch, you just never wanted to see the truth."

"Then show me," I plead as tears continue to trek down my cheeks.

"Too little too late, witch. The game has begun and there is nothing you can do to stop it." He releases me and stalks out of the room, leaving me standing here in confusion. I frown when I realize he didn't bring me to Nexus' room, he brought me back to my room. I drop down onto the edge of the bed and pull my knees up to my chest, burying my face in the top of them. I feel like a fraud sitting here mourning the loss of my brother.

My brother.

Just thinking about Ezekiel Tempest as my brother and not the guy who was mean to me is strange, but then I think back to the day in the cafeteria when he was the one who told Vox he wouldn't stand by and watch Nexus bully me. Or the day when he told me to keep my head up and walked out of school with me. He had no idea I was his sister then and yet he still showed me kindness when he didn't have to. I shift and reach into the drawer of my side table and pull out the phone Ezekiel gave me. I stashed it in here the other night. I scroll through the contact list, there are four numbers: Vox, Ezekiel, Hayze and Archer.

I click on Archer's name and bring the phone to my ear. I wait for him to answer and try to remind myself that they need to know the truth. When he finally answers after the sixth ring I begin to clam up.

"Who is this?" The deep gravelly tone of his voice does nothing to ease my anxiety over being the one to share this horrible news with him.

"It's Nova," I whisper.

"Are you okay?" The fact that is his first question has the vice squeezing my chest loosening and my apprehension about calling him dwindles slightly.

"Archer, I have to tell you something."

"Why do you sound like you're crying?"

I close my eyes and try not to let his concern for my safety sway me from sharing this news. "Are you with Hayze and Vivi?" I ask instead of answering.

"Yeah, why?"

"Can you put me on speakerphone?"

He's silent for a second, then Vivian's voice comes through the phone. "We're here Nova."

"What I have to tell you is going to—-"

Vivian cuts me off before I can finish. "You know what happened to Ez don't you?" I remain silent trying to think of how to tell them. But I don't get a chance to say more when a shadow appears in my doorway. I end the call quickly and try to act like I wasn't just on the phone but when he steps inside my room a part of me is glad to see it's Vox and not Thomas or Nexus, but another part of me is disgusted by the sight of him.

"I'm assuming Ezekiel made sure you had a burner before you walked your ass back in here?" he says as he closes my door then locks it. My breathing turns ragged, I can feel the phone in my hand vibrating but I ignore it as I continue to watch Vox stalk toward me. When he stands before me, he reaches out and pries the phone from my hand and tosses it inside the drawer. "You won't be needing that." I swallow audibly, as fear slowly unfurls inside me.

"You shouldn't be here," I mutter. I dart my gaze toward the door expecting Thomas to break through it any second.

"No one is coming to save you, witch, it's just you and me." I dart my gaze back to him and gape up at him. "Nexus is going to be out all night and Thomas has a meeting with the Saints so he can announce the death of a member." The mention of death has me springing to my feet and shoving Vox out of the way so I can escape. He doesn't try to stop me as I unlock the door and run. His laughter follows me down the hallway. I race down the stairs and just as I hit the landing the lights cut out and I'm bathed in darkness. My fear amps up and I dart my gaze around to see enough in the dark so I don't bump into anything and give away my position. "You wanted *him* to come back and now he has, run as fast as you can, witch, because two horns is hunting and there is nothing you can do to escape us. The cameras are looped and all the locks on the doors have been fitted with a fingerprint scanner so you are locked in here with me." The fact his voice is distorted tells me he is wearing his mask.

My fear turns to anger. "Come get me, bitch," I snarl into

the darkness as I take off and pray I don't fucking smack into a wall or something.

I'm sick in the head. He killed my brother and is part of the reason my best friend is dead, but my body is excited and getting turned on by the fact I am being hunted by two horns.

CHAPTER FORTY-SIX

Vox

Getting Thomas out of the house was easy, I just had to make him think I left after taking Nova to her room. My car is hidden down the street. Nexus' biggest flaw is that he loves to brag and the dumb fuck bragged about how his new security system works, so it was easy enough to figure out how to hack into it without them knowing and loop the feed.

They will never know I was here hunting the witch.

I know she's angry and wants to kill me but that won't be happening tonight because she hates Vox and blames him, but the dirty little witch craves *two horns* and it's for that reason alone why I am wearing my mask and hunting her through the house. Unlike her, I know how to walk without being heard, she's easy to track. I stand in the living room and strain my hearing, when I hear the sound of a foot hitting something toward my right I take off in that direction and pivot around the corner into the laundry room. I stop in the entryway and watch as she tries to pry the sliding door open that leads to the back-yard but after a moment stops, and I see her back tense.

She knows I'm here.

Her arms drop back to her sides as she stands tall, keeping her back to me. "You found me, now what." I say nothing as I stalk into the room and don't stop until my chest is flush against her back. A shiver works its way through her and she does nothing to hide it. I reach around her front and grip her throat in my hand, tilting her head back until she stares up at me. She darts her tongue out to moisten her lips. I force back the groan that wants to break free, knowing what that tongue feels like sliding up and down my shaft as she sucks me all the way into the back of her throat.

"Now, I take what is *mine* and remind you who the fuck you belong to."

"I belong to no one and especially not you... two horns." I smile beneath my mask, she called me two horns not Vox, which means she wants this as much as I do and I plan to give her everything her dirty tainted heart desires. I shift my hold on her throat and unclasp the collar around her neck and toss it to the side.

"You only wear that when I'm not around," I growl.

"I'm around you every day," she fires back.

"Correction, you're around Vox every day, not *me*."

"You told me that the moment I removed the mask that I had to make peace with you and him being the same and I couldn't hide from the truth. So, are you a liar as well as a murderer?"

Her defiance should anger me, but it doesn't. All she is doing is making me rock fucking hard.

"You knew I killed before and never once turned me away." I spin her around and force her back until she is flush against the wall. I pin her in place with my hips, which draws a sharp gasp from her when she feels my hard length pressed against her stomach. "You love that I am Filthy, it turns you on and the fact you can hate Vox but want me makes you disgusted with yourself." She turns her face to the side, refusing to look at me. I lean down and run my mask along her neck knowing she loves the feeling of it against her skin.

She slowly turns her head toward me. I rest my forehead against her and stare into the fiery depths of her eyes. Her hatred burns deep for me but I can also see the need in those green eyes. I skim my hand down her side and watch her as her eyes twitch. She's trying to fight the feelings I am eliciting inside her but she and I both know it's a losing battle. The moment I force my hand between our bodies and cup her pussy she moans.

"So filthy," I purr as I shift my hand and push inside her pants. She widens her legs, giving me better access to stroke her through the material of her panties. I can see how wet she is and it has my cock twitching in my pants. I push the lacy material to the side and stroke a single finger through her folds. She cranes her neck back and moans while thrusting her hips forward, urging me to stroke her clit, I oblige willingly.

"How did I end up in your car and not Vivian's?" she pants. I refuse to give her what she wants by being distracted by her question. She wants me to falter and pull away so she can feel good about herself and not have to deal with the fallout of fucking me.

"I was there watching. I didn't give her a choice like I'm not giving you one now," I growl as I push her pants down her legs. She steps out of them and kicks them to the side. I can see the war on her face, part of her wants to stab me right in the heart but the other part of her that is craving the release her body *needs* refuses to allow her feelings to take control. "Take my cock out." Her breath hitches at my order and she hesitates for a moment until I wrap my hand around her throat and squeeze, leaving her no choice but to obey my demand.

She pops the button on my jeans and yanks the zipper down, all while keeping her eyes locked on mine. The defiance I see in her has a smirk ghosting across my lips. She pushes my jeans and boxers down, allowing my cock to spring free. I hiss when she wraps her dainty hand around my shaft and pumps. I brace my hand beside her head on the wall and lean in but keep an inch of space between our faces.

"I hate you," she grits out through clenched teeth as she continues to stroke me.

"The feeling is mutual." I fight to keep my eyes from closing when she uses her free hand to cup my balls. A groan slips from me and the satisfied look on her face snaps me out of it. I force her hands away, grip her thigh and lock it around my waist as I line my cock up with her entrance. Her mouth parts, forming a perfect O when I press the tip of my cock inside her tight wet cunt. I push inside her and relish the sight of her eyes rolling back and the way she arches forward, pressing her tits against me. I grips her other thigh and lift her, she locks her arms around my neck and stares down at me with a wistful look on her face. "Ride me."

Without argument she braces her hands on my shoulders, locks her ankles around my waist and begins bouncing up and down on my cock. This isn't about caring or liking each other, this is our way of showing the other that we are still in control of our own prospective lives and loathe each other, but when it comes to needing to be fucked and ravaged we know that the other is the only person who can give us the release we both crave. I grip the globes of her ass and guide her up and down when her movements turn choppy, her filthy cunt is trying to milk my cock for all it's worth.

"I need... more," she snaps. Gripping her waist, I lift her off my lap and place her on her feet. She stares up at me with an open mouth.

"Turn around, hands on the wall, legs apart." Desire pulses off her as she spins around and obeys my command. I run my hands over her perfect ass and love the sounds she makes when I smack that edible peach. Fuck, I want to sink my teeth into it and listen to her cry out but I know the instant I remove this mask she will put a stop to this and my balls are way too fucking blue right now to risk her saying *no*.

I grip my cock and line it up with her pussy. I slam inside her, not giving her any warning until I'm balls deep inside her tight wet hole. She screams out and the sound is like music to my fucking ears. I don't allow her time to recover as I pull almost all the way out, then slam back inside her, the sounds she makes has the beast inside me purring and taking control. My grip on her is punishing and bruising but I don't care, I want Nexus to see my fingerprints on her and know it was me that was fucking his fiancée senseless while he was out at his pathetic party.

"Oh, fuck, I'm going to come!" she screams out. I want to deny her the release she craves and keep her teetering on the edge but my own release is screaming at me to give into her demands and allow us both this bliss, so I do. "Two horns!" she screams as she clamps down on my cock and explodes. I bite down on my lip to keep her name from tearing out of me. This moment of weakness was nothing more than me needing to be balls deep inside her and that's it.

The only sounds that can be heard is our labored breathing. I ease out of her and don't miss the way she flinches and quickly turns away from me, trying to hurriedly find her pants. We both dress without a saying word. The second I'm done, I move past her and nearly escape without having to speak to her but her words have me freezing on the spot.

"That will never happen again, you have helped them take everything from me and I will *never* forgive you for that."

"The fact you doubt my intentions says more about you than me, little witch."

"They killed my best friend, took my mom and are now holding her hostage. But you... you killed my brother." I spin around and glare at the witch.

"If I recall you wanted nothing to do with him and now that he is gone you think you have the right to call him *brother?*" I don't give her a chance to answer. "Play the game, witch, and you may just make it out of this alive and with your mother."

"How the fuck am I supposed to do that when you are risking everything by coming here and..." She clamps her mouth closed, unable to finish.

"I came to you like this because you seem to see me as two people. You want to hate me as Vox, so it makes you feel better about what has happened, but you latch onto the idea of me as *two horns* because you think this mask makes me your savior or some shit. I told you, witch, I chose the winning side and I meant it."

"What the fuck does that even mean?" she screams.

"It means, I won't fucking lose. Keep playing the game Nexus wants you to—"

"So I should let him keep showering with me and trying to fuck me every night?" Her revelation has a red haze overcoming me and my fists clenching at my sides. I force my anger to reside or I risk blowing this all up.

"If he touches you, I'll kill him and it will ruin everything. Don't let that happen because everyone's lives and freedom are resting on your shoulders." I've already said too much, so I turn and get the fuck out of there before I ruin everything by telling her.

CHAPTER FORTY-SEVEN

Nova

"Get the fuck out of here, Nexus!" I scream as I plaster myself against the shower wall. The fucker just smirks down at me and wags his brows. Last night was the first time I actually slept soundly because he didn't come home after the party, not that I gave a fuck but he just had to go and come home this morning, didn't he?

"You think your pussy is so special?" He scoffs and moves beneath the spray of the shower while I stand huddled in the corner of the stall, using my arms to shield my nakedness. In a move I don't expect, Nexus grips my waist and presses in so his body is flush against mine. I fight the bile rushing up my throat when I feel he's hard. I turn my head to the side, unable to look at the sick fuck. "It's nearly Halloween and guess what? You have one more month of freedom before you turn eighteen and become my wife. You will fulfill *all* the duties that are expected of a wife."

I scoff and slowly turn to face him so he can see the hatred in my eyes. "I would rather be buried alive next to my best friend than ever let you between my legs," I spit out.

"You had no trouble opening them for Vox though."

"That was a mistake and I don't plan on making another mistake like that again."

"Good, considering he showed up late to the party last night and then left with Nicole, I suspect you don't stand a chance anyway, piggy." His words shouldn't have pain spearing me but it does. How the fuck could he come here and chase me down then fuck me only to leave and take that whore home.

I feel sick!

"Oh, you thought he was pining after you?" he says in a stupid mocking voice. "Nah, piggy, you were nothing but a shiny new toy for him to fuck and he always gets bored, so I know your pussy won't keep me satisfied. But not to worry, the minute I knock you up, I'll find someone else to satisfy me."

I balk up at him. "What?" I screech.

The smug look on his face has me wanting to slap him. "The only way to ensure my family remains on top inside the Saints is to produce an heir and guess what?" I don't answer because I know he wasn't expecting me to. "No one would be able to fight us for the top spot because a Valerian and Tempest mixed into one would be a true born leader."

"Your father was never meant to lead the Saints, the rightful heir to The Brotherhood would be a Tempest and a *Hatchett.*" Nexus' gaze darkens. He shoves away from me and I sigh in relief, until he cocks his arm back and punches me in the stomach. I drop to my knees, gagging and gasping for air. He yanks my head back by my hair and smiles when he sees the tears trailing down my cheeks.

"Don't ever speak out of turn again, piggy, and put the fucking collar back on before Mommy gets another shock treatment. I would hate to have to tell Martha to refuse to let her out in the valley." I keep my face blank of emotion. He releases his hold on me and steps back. I hunch forward on my hands and knees, trying to breathe through the pain but then I feel something warm hitting my side and turn my head to the side and shriek, the fucker is *pissing* on me. His laughter is manic as I try to scramble away from him but I can't escape. I'm forced to huddle into a ball until he's finished. His laughter follows him out of the shower and bathroom. I sit here curled up and just cry.

I tried to ask Thomas this morning if I could speak to my mom or just see a picture of her, but the evil bastard just laughed and told me to fuck off and never to ask again or she would pay for my disobedience.

I've been sitting out back all afternoon by the pool with one of the photo albums my mom had made me. Seeing pictures of her hurts so much, I just want her to be here so she can hold me and tell me everything is going to be okay. I can only imagine the pain and fear she is going through right now. I'm past the point of caring now what happens to me as long as she is okay. I can't lose another person, I won't fucking survive it.

"Here." I snap my head to the side in time to see Nexus tossing my phone to me that he had taken when I arrived here. I catch it and stare up at him with a raised brow. "Try anything and we'll know."

"Then why give it back?" I ask.

"Because I want to give you enough rope to hang yourself with, so please, piggy, fuck up and ask for help."

I scoff. "I'm not stupid. You gave this back to me in the hopes I would reach out to my masked friends."

His face hardens. "You try to hook up with that masked fuck again and I'll slit your mother's throat myself. I don't give a fuck who those bitches are, no one does because I'm untouchable, piggy, and it's about time you learned that." I roll my eyes at his retreating back. He and Thomas think I am stupid enough to reach out to the *Filthy Few* and Nikoa so I can help them figure out who was with me that night. Vox spun a story saying he was following me and got rid of the evidence of Nexus' crimes and from what Thomas has said, he wasn't lying.

This list of things to hate about Vox is growing and the fact he did something to Waylen's body is at the top of my list. I power my phone on and input my pin, then just stare at the screen. My wallpaper is the picture that Vivian took of me and Vox at the beach. I'm smiling up at the camera but Vox is just staring at me with... I slam my eyes closed and shake my head. I fooled myself thinking it was love I saw in his eyes but clearly that was bullshit. You don't treat the person you love the way he has treated me.

"Nova?" I bolt upright in my lounger and throw my legs over the side at the sound of Vivian's voice. She forces her way through the bushes separating our properties and comes toward me, I dart my gaze to the house waiting for Thomas or Nexus to barge out here any minute. "They just left," she says in answer to my unasked question. She drops down onto the lounger in front of me, her eyes are red and puffy, clearly she has been crying.

"You can't be here!" I hiss.

The pleading look in her eyes has me swallowing my protests for her to leave. "Where is he, Nova?" The broken tone of her voice has all the air rushing out of me. I place the album and my phone beside me as I lean forward and grip her cold hands in mine and squeeze them.

"With Waylen." Vivian's eyes shoot wide and she yanks her hands free and shakes her head.

"No, you're lying. Ezekiel wouldn't leave me not after—he wouldn't leave me!" she shouts and stands. I follow her lead and try to reach for her but she stumbles away from me.

"Vivian, I saw the video proof last night. I watched him... I saw him..." I can't force the words out past the lump in my throat. Vivian's bottom lip begins to tremble as tears flow faster down her cheeks.

"No. He promised me he wouldn't leave me, they all did and now they've all left," she cries and my brows raise.

"What do you mean? Where's Hayze and Archer?"

"They were gone by the time I woke up this morning. They left me a fucking note!" she screams. Before I ask what it said, she pulls it out of her pocket and tosses it to me, then turns and runs back to her house. I watch until she disappears through the back door of her house, then bend down and pluck the folded piece of paper off the ground.

Vi, baby,

We know you are going to be mad and we are sorry.

We wanted to tell you but he made us swear to keep you in the dark.

Stay safe, baby.

We love you.

A + H

My jaw is unhinged as I reread the note at least four times before the words finally sink in. Archer and Hayze have left but that isn't the most shocking part, it's the words in the fucking note. They *both* love her but from her reaction to losing Ezekiel, a huge part of me seems to think Vivian is in love with my brother!

But does she love Hayze and Archer as well?

Those thoughts plague me until late that night as I climb into the bathtub in my bedroom. After Nexus' stunt this morning, he can get fucked if he thinks I will be showering in his room. The memory of him laughing at me while he pissed on me has my anger and disgust warring inside me. I vowed to myself this morning, I would no longer cry over any of this shit. When all of this is over, I will mourn the loss of my best friend and Ezekiel, then deal with the trauma of this whole situation but not before. If I let it consume me I won't be able to get myself out of bed every day and deal with the horrors that await me at school.

My thoughts are muted when the lights cut out. I lean forward and wrap my arms around my knees. "If you try to get in this bath with me, Nexus, I will fucking kill you!" I shout into the darkness. When no reply comes, I begin to shiver in fear and panic starts to flare inside me. I stand quietly, reach for my towel and wrap it around me, then climb out and quietly pad out of the bathroom and freeze as I enter my bedroom.

I swallow audibly and stare at the three masked men standing by the open balcony door, two horns, no horns and left horn stand there but it's the sight of right horn missing that has my emotions choking.

Right horn was Ezekiel.

Right horn is gone and never coming back.

"What the fuck do the three of you want? I thought you all hated each other now?" I snarl. Left horn—aka Hayze Draven

—reaches into his hoodie pocket and pulls out a card, then tosses it onto my bed but I make no move to grab it.

"*A favor asked is a debt owed,*" no horns—aka Archer Malik —says, earning a glare from me.

"The last favor I asked cost me the life of someone I loved so I'll pass and you can fuck off."

"A favor asked is a debt owed, witch," two horns says as if his voice alone can sway me.

"I'll never ask anything of the three of you again, your fucking game got Waylen killed and now my brother is dead—"

"Ask the favor and a debt will be owed," left horn pushes.

"You fuckers don't know shit, you want me to ask a favor yet you couldn't even deliver on the first one I asked."

"This favor isn't for you, witch." I furrow my brow and stare at two horns, trying to decipher his meaning but then my bedroom door slams open behind me and I scream in fright until I see it's Nexus, and then my fear turns to panic as I slice my gaze back to two horns.

"I fucking knew the second I gave her that phone back that she would fuck up," my stepbrother spits out smugly.

"I didn't—" Nexus cuts me off with an icy look, he's illuminated by the light pouring in from the hallway.

"A favor asked is a debt owed," two horns says.

Nexus scoffs. "You have nothing I want—"

"Eleanor Denver," says no horns. I see Nexus pale out of the corner of my eye.

"She's dead," he grits out through clenched teeth. I've seen Nexus angry, smug, aroused and even furious but I've never seen him scared until now.

"Is she?" two horns taunts.

"What the fuck are you trying to do?" Nexus snarls.

"A favor asked is a debt owed," left horn says, then the three of them turn and race out onto the balcony, leaping over the side. I would have thought Nexus would chase after them but instead he stands there staring at the open doorway, like he's seen a ghost. I attempt to slink back into the bathroom to get away from him but halt when he snaps his head toward me.

"Who the fuck were those cunts?" he forces out through gritted teeth.

I gulp. "That was the *Filthy Few*," I whisper.

"Get them back here, now!" he roars. I stumble back a step in fear. I begin to shake my head but stop when he moves toward me.

"I can't," I shout. He stops advancing and searches my eyes.

"How do you find them?"

My eyes dart to the note on the bed, he follows my gaze, then darts over to it and plucks it off the comforter. I flick the lights on and sigh in relief that I'm not stuck here in the dark with Nexus. I look at the postcard in his hand and shake my head, it's the same one two horns gave me when he first came to me.

Where they rest for eternal life is where a favor is asked.

The stone with the head is where you will be led.

Be certain of the favor you ask, we will not offer a second.

The debt will be collected when the favor is complete.

A favor asked is a debt owed.

I can remember the words on that fucking without even trying, they will be forever ingrained in my memory until I die.

"Where the fuck is this place?" he demands.

"The favor isn't worth the debt," I find myself saying.

"Tell me where the fuck to find these cunts or I'll be burying my cock in your ass willing or not." Hatred and disgust roll through me.

"You should know the fucking place well, dick, you buried my best friend there."

CHAPTER FORTY-EIGHT

Vox

The fear in his eyes is everything I hoped it would be.

When Nexus and Nova arrived at school I could see he was rattled, his usual cocky grin and holier than thou attitude was nowhere to be seen. I kept playing my part and was a bastard to Nova all day long, Nexus didn't even seem interested in her at this point. She wasn't forced to kneel or eat out of the dog bowl Nicole gave her.

When Nicole tried to shove Nova's face in the food, Nova fought back and Nexus didn't even bat an eye, he just stood up and walked out. The rest of the week played out the same, Nova had returned to her own room and Thomas was growing irritated with his son and kept calling on me for favors that should have been carried out by his heir. The fear of his past catching up to him is unraveling him, which is why I find myself standing inside Thomas' home Friday night.

"I need this done, the Saints are being seen as weak because of this fucking mole and we need to find out who it is. Calvin, Russell and Bert are doing their best but even they can only do so fucking much."

"What has the mole done?" I ask.

"The funds for the community account have vanished!" Thomas roars, that admission captures my attention. The Saints have an account that they pile all their money into to fund their businesses like the new hotel they are opening in town, which is just a cover for the brothel they will run inside it. They also have plans for a casino to be built but without the funds they're at a standstill. I have no idea when the Saints changed and became a mafia-like brotherhood where we dealt in illegal shit and killed people for stepping out of line.

"How much money are we talking?"

A vein bulges in the middle of Thomas' forehead. "Eighty Million." I just manage to keep my mouth from popping open, these bastard have foreclosed on houses and upped the interest rates on properties in town to fund these projects and give zero fucks about the people they are robbing to get richer.

"What do you want me to do?"

"I want you to find out who the fuck this mole is and bring me the head of the cunt!" he roars and slams his fist down on his desk.

"Can't the bank just get your money back?" I push.

"Are you fucking stupid boy? The money is gone and there is no fucking way of getting it back, I have made deals with very powerful people and made promises that need to be kept." A smug sense of satisfaction washes over me, I know who the mole is and Nikoa is making sure to hit Thomas where it fucking hurts. I have no doubt this idiot has gone and made deals with the wrong types of people and I'm sure it goes without saying that if he doesn't deliver they will collect compensation in the form of his or his son's flesh.

"You want me to take Nexus with me to shake down some fuckers?" I go for a casual tone. Thomas grinds his teeth and tugs at the strands of his hair.

"No. I don't want my son involved in this, he's got a bitch to keep in line and train." I keep the anger from splaying across my face as I nod and turn to leave. I make it out front and unlock my car, only to have searing pain explode in the back of my head. I whirl around ready to fight but then I see the rock on the ground and dart my gaze up to see my sister standing a foot away from me, with a look of rage plastered across her face. It isn't just rage I see etched in my twin's features though, I see so much pain and sorrow in her eyes that my chest splinters open for her and the immense grief she must be feeling.

"What the fuck, Vivian?" I snap.

"Where are they?" she screams.

"Who?"

She scoffs. "You want to abandon me, then fine, but you give me Archer, Hayze and Ezekiel back now."

Fire burns through my veins and my jaw locks as I scowl at my sister. I spy Nova out of the corner of my eye, walking up her driveway clearly just getting home from her cleaning duties. She pauses at the sight of me and my sister and stares.

"Archer and Hayze took off after Ezekiel's body was found. You're on your own, Vivian." Pain explodes inside my chest at the devastated look on my twin's face. Unable to stomach the sight of her tears. I climb in my car and start the engine, but before I can peel out of there, the passenger door is yanked open and Nova slides inside, glaring at me. I say nothing as I plant my foot and get the fuck out of there. Neither of us says a word until we are two blocks away then she finally speaks.

"Why did you lie?"

"Want to be more specific? Shouldn't you be at home blowing Nexus?" I bite out.

"One, fuck you. Two, you're a pig."

"You never seemed to mind sucking my dick." She scoffs and crosses her arms over her chest, then slouches back in her seat.

"Dick," she mumbles beneath her breath.

"Why the fuck are you here, witch?" I clip out.

"You're up to something and I want to know what it is."

I laugh but there's no humor to it. "You think I would tell you? I thought you hated me and blamed me for killing your *bestie*?" I taunt.

A strangled sound escapes her and I fight to not feel guilty for throwing that shit in her face. I don't know what she expected from me today, after that fight with my sister she should have known I wouldn't be in the mood for her bullshit.

"I know you're up to something."

I growl in annoyance. "Yeah, I have shit to do for my lord. Now, unless you are here to suck my cock or give that pussy up, then I suggest you get the fuck out now because I don't have time for your—"

"I fuck you and you tell me who the hell Elenor Denver is!" I pull over onto the shoulder of the road and slam the car park, then turn to her. I run my gaze over her body and instantly my cock is growing hard at the sight of her, unlike every other girl I have had in the past, Nova Quinlin doesn't even have to try to turn me on, just the thought of her alone has my dick twitching. I open my mouth but the words die in my throat when she shifts and straddles my lap. Instinctively my hands grip her waist.

"The fuck do you think you are doing, witch?" I try to

sound unaffected but the second she pushes down and feels how hard I am for her already, a sinister smirk graces her full lips.

"A favor is a debt owed, right?"

I frown up at her. "Your point?"

"I'm doing us both a favor by fucking you and forgetting the fact that you took Nicole home after the party—"

"I didn't touch that clap infected bitch and I didn't go to the bonfire." She jerks back and searches my gaze for any sign of deceit, which she won't find.

"You didn't fuck her?" she whispers.

I press forward until our noses touch and stare directly into her eyes. "I haven't touched anyone since I first fucked you, happy now?"

"But Nexus—"

"Wanted to make you jealous in the hopes you would revenge fuck him and destroy me."

Her eyes widen and I curse myself for letting that shit slip. Instead of voicing the question I can see swirling in her eyes, she leans forward and meshes her lips to mine. I remain still and unmoving, thinking she will pull away at any minute when she remembers I'm not wearing the mask but then her arms wrap around my neck and her tongue prods my lips. Powerless to fucking stop or even void of the will to push her away I open, allowing her the access she demands. The kiss quickly turns heated, then our hands are all over each other and pieces of clothing are being shredded as we race to get undressed quicker just so we can lose ourselves in the other.

Is this healthy?

Probably not.

Do I give a fuck?

Hell to the fucking no, I don't.

She breaks the kiss and stares down at me, my shirt somewhere in the back seat and my jeans are open, my cock is out. So if she is thinking about stopping this, she is out of her ever fucking loving mind if she thinks I am not going to be balls deep inside her. But the realization of what she is seeing hits me, I scramble to come up with a plan.

"Turn around and ride me reverse cowgirl." I can see the refusal on the tip of her tongue so I narrow my eyes. "Now!" I grit out. I help her turn and it's fucking awkward given the limited space but we manage. I pull her panties to the side and line my dick up. "Hold the steering wheel." She does as she's told and then slowly lowers herself onto my waiting cock—fuck me if this doesn't feel like the best feeling in the world, having her pussy swallow me until I am balls deep inside this perfect little cunt.

"Fuck!" she cries out. I reach around and yank the cups of her bra down and pinch her nipples, drawing another cry from her.

"Bounce on my cock, baby." She uses her hold on the steering wheel as leverage to help as she begins to glide up and down on my shaft. I can feel the juices of her pussy coating me and the sound it makes each time I slide in and out of her is music to my fucking ears. I twirl her nipples between my fingers and relish in the sounds she makes. They're like a fucking drug that I crave to hear daily.

When her movements begin to grow frantic, I wrap an arm around her waist and force her back, resting her head on my shoulder as I seize control and thrust up inside her.

"Oh, yes," she purrs, but then her gaze collides with mine and I can see the hesitation there so I kiss her. She closes her eyes and gets lost in the feelings I evoke inside her. I use my other hand to rub her clit, she jolts in my hold, then moans into my mouth as I continue to fuck her. She rolls her hips and I groan, then bite down on her lip forcing a whimper from her. I release it then lick it, her eyes meet mine and this time all I see is need. I keep my gaze locked on hers as I pinch her clit and thrust inside her harder.

Our breaths mingle and suddenly shit changes, this isn't just fucking anymore this is... us. Tears shine in her eyes and it fucking kills me that she is looking at me this way. I can deal with the hate and the anger but this... the way she looks right now, like I blew her whole fucking world up, is going to kill me.

"Vox..." she whispers my name as if she's afraid that if she says it any louder this will all be a dream.

"Come for me, witch." Her features grow taut, then her eyes turn glazy as she arches forward and comes all over my cock. I use this moment of ecstasy and her distraction to quicken my thrust until I find my own release, this time I don't stop her name from tumbling from my lips.

Minutes pass as we try to control our breathing, the car windows are all fogged up and neither of us has made a move to separate from the other. The truth is, I don't want to let her go and that is the worst part because I know I have to. If anyone or anything is going to blow this whole plan to shit, it's going to be me because I can't seem to stay away from her.

"Vox?"

I close my eyes and inhale sharply. "Yeah?"

"Promise me that I didn't fall for the wrong person and all of this... is just a ruse?" I want to give her the answer she seeks but I can't risk it, so I remain silent. A minute goes by before she withdraws from me. She leans forward and fixes her bra and shirt before slowly easing off me and climbs back to her seat. I tuck myself back into my pants and just sit here. "Here," she says as she reaches into her bag and pulls out a black hoodie and hands it to me. I look from it to her and frown. "It's... yours." That has my brows raising and her ducking her head.

"You kept it?"

She drops the hoodie to her lap and turns to stare out her window. I see the name *Hatchett* across the shoulders of it and realize it's the hoodie I gave her the day we went to the beach. It was my way of declaring her off limits to any fucker who thought they could fuck with what is *mine*.

CHAPTER FORTY-NINE

I'm appalled at myself for allowing him to get under my skin and having sex with him. Last week I could play it off as him being two horns and not Vox but today, I can't. Shame washes over me, he may not have killed Waylen but I know for a fact that he did kill my brother and here I am whoring myself out for answers.

"It was the only thing I had left of you when my world fell apart," I admit quietly.

Vox remains silent a while digesting my words. "I need you to hate me, Nova."

Nova.

Not witch.

I slowly turn back to face him and find his gaze already focused on me. I search his gaze and when all I see is resolution I sigh. "Then you need to stay away from me."

"I'm trying," he admits.

"Even at school, I need you to stay away from me."

He scrunches his face. "I'm a cunt to you at school."

"You don't get it, do you?"

"Get what, witch?"

I shake my head and will my tears to remain at bay. "No matter how badly you treat me, it doesn't erase the fact that I have your attention on me. I want to hate you more than anything, I want to blame you for everything, but I can't!" I shout the last part as tears begin to flow down my cheeks. "Any attention you give me is better than not having you. You want me to hate you, then I need you to act like I don't exist and stay as far away from me as you can. I won't come to any games with Nexus, I see you and I'll go the other way but I need you to do the same."

He's grinding his teeth so hard I swear he's going to break some. In a move that surprises me, he snaps his arm out, grips the back of my head and yanks me forward until our foreheads touch. Having him this close confuses me and has my heart beating so fast I fear it may leap out of my chest and land in his.

"When I was little, I wished that I would find a way to save my sister from taking over the Saints. I swore I would never let anyone come between me and that goal." I take a shuddering breath and nod.

"I understand—"

"No, you don't, because you have come between me and that goal." My eyes widen in shock. "I can't save you both and here I am trying to find the will to sacrifice you for her and I can't do it ,so I am going against everything I believe to save you both."

My mouth pops open. "What?"

He releases me and slumps back in his seat. "Everything is a ploy, nothing you think you know is real. Everything is a plan and I am so fucking close. So close. I just need some more time and I have until Halloween to get it done or I fail."

"What are you doing, Vox?"

He lulls his head to the side and stares at me with a distraught look on his face. "Trying not to lose my twin or the witch who cast a fucking spell on me I can't seem to break."

His words fill me with warmth, they're like a balm to my battered heart. "I didn't tell her that it was... you... in the video," I admit.

A whoosh of air escapes him. "I know."

"How?" I push.

He keeps his gaze focused ahead but I can see that what he is about to say is angering him. "Vivian thinks I have no idea that she has feelings for Ezekiel..." I gasp. He faces me and the burning embers in his eyes have my breath hitching. "*And* Archer and Hayze. If she knew what I did, she wouldn't have spoken to me."

She has feelings for all *three* of them!

"You knew how she felt and you still..." I let my sentence trail off, unable to finish.

"The anger you feel for me right now, hold onto that, witch, because that is what is going to keep you alive." He ends the conversation by starting the car and pulling back onto the deserted road, while I sit here reeling. I feel more confused now than I did before I climbed into his car. I expect him to continue on his mission he was sent on but instead he drives me home. He doesn't pull into the driveway, which I am grateful for because I don't have the energy to deal with Thomas right now. I reach for the handle but his words stop me. "What's the debt I owe, witch?"

I peer over my shoulder at him. "Huh?"

"You said a favor asked is a debt owed. You fuck me and I give you something in return, what do you want?"

You.

I don't say that aloud, instead I force my feelings for him back into the box I have been hiding them in and ask, "Who is Elenor Denver ?"

"The girl Nexus raped and killed when he was sixteen." My face slackens.

"What?" I squawk.

"Nexus has an asphyxiation kink. He went too far with her and killed the wrong girl."

"Was there a right one?" I snap back.

His eyes narrow in warning. "Anyone would have been better than Alexander Denver's sister." The name rings a bell and I rack my brain trying to put the name to a face. "You probably know him better as *The Butcher.*" A shiver of dread rushes down my spine.

"The serial killer?" I shout.

"*Alleged* serial killer."

"How do you know that and how do you know Nexus killed his sister?"

"Nikoa." My uncle unearthed a secret so huge that it's sent Nexus into a tailspin since the night the *Filthy Few* came to my bedroom.

"Why did you offer him a favor?"

"When he comes to ask for the proof of how we found out, he will owe us a favor and that favor will be him helping us destroy his father or we turn him over to Alexander."

"Do you even know Alexander?"

"No, but he doesn't know that."

"Has Nexus come to you?"

A cocky glint enters his eyes. "He's tried every night since we left the card."

It hits me then. "You didn't come to *me* that night, you

knew he would be watching and come in. You were there for him."

Vox nods. "Yes, now you need to stay away from me, witch. Nikoa digging up the information he did on Elenor has attracted the attention of Alexander himself."

"What does that have to do with Thomas and the Saints though?"

"We believe Thomas and the Saints helped Nexus hide the truth of her death and if we can prove it, Thomas is out. I have his trust now and I can get closer to him because of that. I just need him to slip up once and then we have him."

Bitterness sours my mood as I push the door open. "It just took you slaying your best friend to earn that trust," I spit as I slam the door and march toward the house. I can feel his gaze on me the entire way until I slam the front door closed behind me and sigh.

Home sweet prison.

I trudge up the stairs to my room, ready to shower and then climb into bed and call it a night, but the sight of Nexus standing in my room blows those plans to hell. I don't close the door behind me, I drop my bag by the dresser and move further into the room but keeping enough space between us as I run my gaze over him. He looks like shit, black circles rim his soulless eyes. He looks pale and like he has lost weight.

"You will take me to them tonight." I scoff.

"That's not going to—" The words die on my tongue when he raises a gun. Fear holds me in a chokehold as I stare down the barrel of that gun.

"Take me to them and I'll tell you where your mother is."

I suck in a sharp inhale. "Don't fuck with me—"

"Take me to those masked freaks and you get the whore back, fuck me over and I'll kill both of you."

"Kill me and you will never be the lord," I snap back.

"We'll find another way, I mean there is always the trashy twin next door—"

"Stay the fuck away from Vivian!"

"Do as you're told and I'll consider leaving the frigid bitch alone." I grind my teeth to keep from lashing out at him and nod.

Nexus pulls his car into the parking lot of the cemetery and instantly I begin shivering as memories of the last time I was here assault me. I close my eyes and try taking some calming breaths but it does nothing to calm the sorrow inside me. Pain lances my chest as an image of Waylen's terrified face flashes through my mind, making a choked whimper escape me.

"Why the fuck are you crying?" I snap my head to the side and shoot the son of a bitch a frosty fucking glare that I hope chills him right to the fucking bone.

"How the fuck could you forget what *you* did here?" I snap.

His features contort for a second before a smile graces his hideous face. "Yeah, I forgot about that. Lucky Vox cleaned that mess up for me, huh?" I gape at the fucker in shock as he climbs out of the car and smacks the roof twice, telling me to hurry my ass up.

"I fucking hate you," I snarl as I climb out and stare at him over the roof of the car.

"Yeah, yeah, whatever, just find these fuckers so I can bury this shit."

"I pray to anyone who fucking listens that your past comes back to *butcher* you." Nexus' jaw unhinges but I stalk off toward the grave that is illuminated by the lanterns. The closer I get the slower my steps become. I feel like I am literally spitting on Waylen's grave by bringing the son of bitch who ended his beautiful life here. Just as I reach the first lantern, I freeze, my feet remain rooted to the spot, unable to move as I stare at the headstone where Waylen is buried beneath. "Move, piggy," Nexus grits out and then shoves me forward. I stumble and catch myself before I can fall.

"Touch her again and you join the rest of the souls here." I snap my head to see the *Filthy Few* walking toward us, the darkness that surrounds them adds an eerie quality to their appearance. It still stings to see only three of them and not four.

"She isn't important, I want the information you have and I'm not fucking leaving until you give me what I want!" Nexus is a fucking fool. I look at each of the guys and notice they have gone all out and Vox is back to wearing his gloves and hoodie that covers his neck tattoos.

"*She* is the only reason we are here," no horns says, earning a snort from Nexus who clearly believes that I am nothing but a piece of shit under his boot. I remain silent with my gaze fixed on the headstone with the numbers carved into it.

4221...

Those numbers used to hold so much love and meant everything to me but now they are tainted with a horrible memory. The tattoo on my ribs pulses, reminding me of the loss I have suffered and how I am now braided with the memory of him not only in my heart and mind but on my skin.

Forever together to love another...

We will never be together again.

I feel sick.

I'm a fraud for being here and feeling so broken when I stand beside the man who murdered my best friend and standing across from me is the man who unintentionally helped kill not only him, but he definitely killed my brother. I ignore all of them as I head over to the mound of dirt and kneel down beside it. I place my hand atop the dirt and bow my head, I can feel all their gazes on me but I don't pay them any mind as I speak.

"You were my first friend, the first boy I ever loved and you always had my back. You never wanted anything from me or expected anything in return when you did something for me. You kept me safe and never made me wonder what it was like to be loved by you. I always knew you loved me from the moment we met and I will *always* love you for that, Waylen." I feel the tears building and try to blink them away but they fall regardless and I do nothing to stop them. "We will always be together forever, to love one another no matter how much time or space is between us because without you there is no me."

"But there is a *you* without him now." I lift my head and shock ripples through me at the sight of two horns kneeling before me. I may not be able to see his face but his eyes, they shine with remorse and this time instead of anger flaring to life inside me all I feel is this crushing pain in my chest that robs me of air.

"How touching, now can we get back to business now, the piggy will get over it." The emotion in Vox's eyes vanishes and is replaced by unfiltered rage. He pushes off the ground and stands tall as he turns to face Nexus. I look at my stepbrother and fight not to growl. The dumbass stands there looking smug, like the world owes him a debt but in a few minutes he will learn that the favor he is asking will incur a debt from him.

CHAPTER FIFTY

Vox

This motherfucker still thinks he is superior.

I move forward and stand between Hayze and Archer, the three of us remain silent with our gazes fixed on Nexus, knowing that the silence will make him crack and offer information he wouldn't be willing to give without being prompted.

Eleanor Denver was sixteen when he spiked her drink and raped her. The bastard didn't stop there, he suffocated her. That girl's last minutes alive were filled with terror. I don't think Nexus knew who her brother was when he chose her as his next victim. Alexander is locked up, serving three life sentences but everyone knows he is still calling the shots from the inside. Nikoa hasn't come through with more information, I'm told his informant has been tight lipped as well.

"I want that information you have!" Nexus grits out through clenched teeth.

"A favor asked is a debt owed," Hayze replies.

Nexus throws his hands in the air. "I'll pay whatever fucking price you want, now give me the fucking intel!" The unhinged look in his eyes brings a smile to my mask-covered face.

"Ask the favor and a debt shall be owed," Archer says.

"I just fucking did!" I reach into my back pocket and pull out the stack of rolled up papers. "Give that to me now," he snarls as he steps forward. Archer reaches over his shoulder and unsheathes his machete, bringing Nexus to a screeching halt. The pussy flicks his gaze to Nova like she is going to save him.

"Make more threats and this bit of information will be sent to every news station in the country and I will *personally* send this file to the Butcher myself," I snap.

"What the fuck do you freaks want?" I dart my gaze to either side of me and smirk, Archer and Hayze hate being called freaks and I know for certain that these two are going to make his end painful and taunt the fucker until he breaks.

"Your life," Hayze says in answer. Nexus' eyes snap wide as he takes a step back.

"Fuck you! Nova, get your ass over here now." The fact Nexus referred to her as Nova and not *piggy* shows how scared he is and I relish in that. Archer takes a step forward, making sure to scrape his blade along the ground. Nexus' gaze is fixed on it.

"You reek of fear," Archer taunts as Hayze breaks away from me and circles Nexus, blocking his escape. Nexus shifts, trying to keep the three of us in his sights.

"He is unworthy of the favor we offer," Hayze says.

"The price of the debt just went up," I add.

"What price?" Nexus' voice is tinged with terror and that's how I know we have him right where we want him.

"You will give us the information we seek on the Haven

Saints and in return we will erase every copy we have made of your disgusting act," I snarl.

His eyes pop wide and the color drains from his face. "I do that and I am as good as dead! The Saints don't—"

Archer cuts him off before he can continue rambling. "You are dead either way, with your father as the lord you have a chance of survival."

Sweat begins to bead his brow and I study him, trying to decipher why he is so nervous but then it fucking hits me. "Your father is unaware of the crime you committed." Nexus' gaze snaps to me and his eyes narrow.

"She was willing, she knew what was happening." I toss the papers at his feet, pictures of her corpse scatter around him.

"The coroner's report shows she had drugs in her system. You spiked that girls drink, then raped her and allowed your sick fucking kink to kill her because it makes you feel like a man, doesn't it, Nexus Valerian?" Archer taunts as he closes in on him.

He shakes his head but his focus is on the pictures at his feet. "I didn't mean to," he mumbles, earning a scoff from Nova. All our attention snaps to her as she climbs to her feet and makes her way over to us stopping beside me.

"Ask them to help you erase the fucking crime you committed and they will make it happen. All you have to do in return is give them the information they need to take down your father and you get to remain breathing," she bites out.

A dark look shadows his face as he looks at Nova. Without being prompted I shift and block her. "Nah, I have a better idea." The cocky lilt to his voice has me darting my gaze to Hayze and Archer who look just on edge as I do with his sudden change of attitude. "You give me the copies you have and I agree to let the pig live." Anger washes over me.

"Fuck you!" Nova screams.

"She isn't part of the deal," I snarl.

"You made her part of it the moment you tried to protect her from me. Give me what I want or I will kill her," he claps back.

"Kill her and you lose every and any chance you had of leading the Saints." I snap my head to the side to see Nikoa stalking toward us, he has his hood up which obscures his face. The gasp that slips free from Nova is filled with pain and I know she thought it was Ezekiel for a second.

"Who the fuck are you?" Nexus snaps.

"I'm the guy who just sent pictures of you with the *Filthy Few* to your father."

Nexus scoffs. "My father won't care." The cocky cunt says, but snaps his mouth closed when Archer raises the machete to his throat. Hayze closes in behind him, blocking his escape.

"Oh, but he will since I have sent him ransom demands." Realization crashes into him. "You should have incurred the debt and taken the favor they offered but now, things will be much worse for you." Nikoa tsks at him and nods to Hayze and Archer. My boys grip each of his arms and yank them behind his back, securing his wrists with cable ties.

"The Saints will slaughter all of you for this!" he screams, then swings his gaze to Nova. "Help me or your mother dies," he roars.

"That won't be necessary since the price for your freedom is the safe return of Kelly," I answer. Nova grips the back of my hoodie as we watch my boys drag Nexus away. When they are out of sight, I whirl around on her. She stares up at me with tears in her eyes. I reach out and grip the back of her neck. "I'm bringing her home, I couldn't save Waylen but I can save her."

She searches my gaze for a moment before she answers, "Why?"

"Because it was the plan from the start, witch."

She flicks her gaze to Nikoa for a moment before turning back to me. "He knew, didn't he?" I nod. "Did Hayze and Archer?"

"Not at the start, I needed Thomas to trust me and the only way I could do that was to make them all think I had switched sides. I told you so many times I chose the winning side and I meant it."

"You meant you picked our side, not theirs." I nod. "Ezekiel?" she whispers his name as she is afraid to dare hope. I suck in a shuddering breath then push my mask up, her gaze roams the planes of my face greedily.

"He's my best friend, witch, I may have a twin but he knows me better than her. I may have been able to fool Hayze and Archer and have them and even you believing the worst of me, but not Ez. He saw right through my act and I had no choice."

She tears out of my hold and shakes her head, the sad look that graced her face a minute ago is replaced by loathing as she scowls up at me. "You always have a fucking choice, you were a coward!" My face slackens and my resolve hardens as I stare down at her shaking my head.

"A coward, huh?"

"Yes! What was this, a fucking game?" She doesn't give me a chance to answer. "Waylen is dead, he's fucking dead, Vox, and so is Ezekiel! You are selfish and self-centered and only care about yourself. Vivian is better off without you and so is my brother." Her words knock the fucking wind right out of me. I dart forward and grip the back of her neck in a bruising hold and she flinches but I don't loosen my hold.

"You think everything is about you, witch, newsflash, you were nothing but a toy in the middle of a war that was to be used and guess what? I fucking enjoyed every minute of using your holes," I sneer, then release her with a shove. She stumbles backward but doesn't fall to her ass because of the fucker standing behind her. "The next time you feel lonely and think the fucking worst of me, just remember it was because of me that you got your mother back."

"That's enough." At the sound of his voice she spins around and at the sight of him her knees give out, but I do nothing to help her. Instead he snaps an arm around her waist as a choked sob burst free of the witch.

"Ezekiel," she breathes his name out like it's a fucking prayer, my best friend smiles down at her and nods. She shakily reaches out and brushes her fingers along his jaw as if checking to make sure he is real. "Oh my God," she cries out, then wraps her arms around him and tugs him close. The sight of him holding his sister stirs emotions inside me that make me want to break shit. Unlike him, the reunion I have with my sister won't be like this. Vivian won't forgive me for what I have done, no matter how good my intentions were, she will hold this against me.

My sister is many things but forgiving isn't one of them. She not only thinks I took Ezekiel from her, but she knows I am the reason Archer and Hayze left her. I may hate admitting it but I know the three of them leaving her has broken her spirit but I had to do it, I couldn't risk her.

"How are you alive?" the little witch asks as she draws back from Ez.

He flicks his gaze to me briefly before returning it to her. "It was a dummy round, hurt like a bitch, but it made Thomas believe Vox followed his order and gained his trust." When the witch looks at me, I keep my face blank of everything except anger and disgust. She flinches but says nothing even as Nikoa comes to stand by them.

"You knew Vox didn't kill Ezekiel?" she asks their uncle.

He nods. "I did, we needed to get someone on the inside as my informant has gone silent and the only way to do that was to get Vox inside with Thomas."

"The night at your house, was that staged?" she asks.

Nikoa shakes his head. "No. The fact you all fought made it easier. You were all pissed at him and that anger was real and sold Vox's lie of switching sides and fooling Thomas." Her shoulders bunch but she doesn't look at me, good because I want her to feel shame for all the bullshit she put me through.

"Was Vivian in on this as well?" she asks but her voice is tinged with hurt. I fight not to scoff. She is more worried that my sister betrayed her than she is that she fucking shit on me.

Ezekiel shakes his head. "No, we made a choice to keep her in the dark for her own safety," he says.

"She thinks you're dead."

"You can't tell her, Nova," Ezekiel implores her. "You can't tell anyone the truth. Thomas has to believe I'm dead in order for our plan to work. If he finds out Vox was lying, then he will shut us all out. Please, I know you don't like Mom but this is the only way to keep our families safe until we take down the Saints."

"How are you going to do that, Ezekiel?" She backs away from him and clenches her fists. "Are you going to make me do it?" Horror flashes through my best friend's eyes.

He darts forward and grips her shoulders. "No! I would never sacrifice you. I swear we are finding another way to do this. If there is no other way then we run, do you hear me?"

"You're not going to make me do it?" she asks again.

"I would never ask you to do that, we all want out of this Tay—Nova. Me, Vox, Hayze and Archer want to go to college and play ball. None of us want our futures mapped out for us, we want our freedom and we can't have that while we are a part of the Saints. I would never allow you to be subjected to that shit."

Before she can answer Nikoa cuts in. "We all need to go, Thomas has just replied."

CHAPTER FIFTY-ONE

Nova

"Go where?" I ask Nikoa.

His eyes shine with remorse. "You have to return to Thomas—"

"No. You have Nexus," I interject.

"We do, but until we can guarantee he will fulfill his bargain, then we need you to return and play along for a while longer. The sooner we have Kelly back the quicker we get you out." Dread unfurls inside me. I drop my gaze to my feet and try to calm my racing heart.

"Hey?" Ez cups my face between his hands and forces my head up. "I swear the second we get your mom we'll get you out."

"Okay," I whisper.

Ez wraps his arms around me and crushes me against his chest. "Vox is going to take you back." I stiffen in his hold.

"Why?" I grit out.

"Because he is the one who came and picked you up when Nexus was kidnapped, Thomas trusts him to a degree now and he will lean on Vox to help him, which keeps us two steps ahead of him. He is going to mobilize the Saints to help him track down his son and we need to know when this is taking place." Wanting to get this over with, I hug Ezekiel bye and promise not to tell anyone he's alive. In return, he promises me that when this is all over we'll sit down and *talk*. When Nikoa and him leave, shit turns awkward real fast. Vox stalks toward the woods, leaving me no choice but to follow him. I keep a couple feet between us.

When we reach his car, he goes to the trunk and begins stripping off his clothing. I'm like a moth to a flame, unable to tear my gaze off him especially when he yanks his shirt off and exposes all that tanned, inked skin. My mouth waters at the sight of him and I curse myself for being so fucking attracted to him!

As if sensing my gaze on him, he flicks his eyes to mine and glares. "If you didn't just accuse me of being a selfish murderer I might actually be tempted to fuck you right now." My breath hitches. "But, I'm a coward, right?" I flinch at his cold harsh tone and avert my gaze from his, gnawing on the corner of my lip.

I really fucked up, I shouldn't have said what I did but all his lies and secrets made it hard to see through the mask he wore and see the good inside him. He was cruel and mean to me and yet I still fucking let him inside me. I cross my arms over my chest and turn my back to him. Ever since I moved here things have changed so fast I have barely had a chance to catch my breath.

"Get in," he clips out. I do as he says and climb inside the car, trying to shrink as far into the seat as I can, the last time I was in here I wound up riding him.

That won't be happening tonight!

The tension radiating between us is making it hard for me to breath. I know he has every right to be mad at me but I'm also fucking furious with him! Neither of us says a word the entire drive back to Thomas'. When Vox parks the car out front, I can't help my eyes from straying next door where I see Vivian's bedroom light on. A pang of guilt hits me in the gut. I wish more than anything I could run over there and tell her the truth, but I also don't want to put her in danger or worse, have my mom hurt because I couldn't keep my mouth shut.

I reach for the handle but Vox's words stop me. "You saw three masked men try to extort money out of Nexus. They abducted him and told you to deliver Thomas a message." I peer over my shoulder at him.

"What message?"

"The life of your mother for the life of his son."

I balk at him. "He's going to know I had something to do with Nexus being taken!" I screech.

"He can't do shit, if he tries anything Hayze and Archer will send videos and believe me, witch, Nexus doesn't have a high pain threshold. Now take this." He pulls a manilla envelope from the glove compartment and hands it to me.

"What is it?"

"Just give it to him," he snaps before tossing the pack at me and climbing out of the car. I follow his lead. Vox doesn't stop to knock, he just pushes the door open and walks in like he owns the place. He changed into a pair of Converse sneakers, dark blue jeans and a white shirt. It's a stark contrast from the black clothing he was wearing earlier but I get it, Thomas saw a picture of them in all black but given what he is wearing he is exposing all his tattoos. "Thomas?"

The sound of thudding footsteps has me staying put in the living room. Vox stays where he is and leans against the wall crossing his arms over his chest. He keeps all traces of what he's thinking and feeling from showing on his face as Thomas barges into the room with Principal Daniels and two men I haven't seen before. Thomas looks from Vox to me and the look in his eyes as he stares me down sends a shiver of fear skating down my spine.

"What the fuck happened tonight?" he shouts. I reel back and clutch the envelope in my hand tighter. "Answer me, you little bitch!"

"I-I..." I become tongue tied, unable to get the words out. I shoot a pleading look to Vox to help me but the bastard just glares back at me. I swallow and remind myself that my mom is counting on me right now. "Nexus told me to go with him."

"Why?" Thomas screams, spit flying out of his mouth and a crazed look can be seen in his soulless eyes.

"Because he said they would come if I was there," I answer. Thomas comes toward me and I force myself not to back away. I know he is trying to scare me and the reality is, he is but I refuse to let it show. I won't give him the satisfaction of seeing me crumble before him.

"And they just so happened to take my son and not you?"

"I didn't know—" He back hands me across my cheek and I lose my balance, falling to the ground, tears instantly pricking the backs of my eyes.

"You lying whore, my son had no reason to—"

"Eleanor Denver," Vox says, drawing Thomas' attention to him. I look up to find Vox has pushed off the wall and stands there with his fists clenched at his sides. To everyone else he looks calm and indifferent but I can tell from the way his eyes have darkened and his jaw is locked that he's mad.

"Who the fuck is that?" Thomas snaps. Vox finally flicks his gaze to me and there is nothing but deep rooted hatred in those eyes.

"Give it to him," he barks. I tentatively reach out and hold the envelope out to Thomas who snatches it out of my hand. While he is distracted tearing it open, Vox comes to me and offers me his hand. I take it and allow him to help me to my feet. He pushes me behind him and uses his body to shield me from Thomas and the others. "Where the fuck did you get this?" Thomas asks as Vox shifts slightly so Thomas can see me.

"They gave it to me," I answer and hate that my voice trembles.

Thomas turns to the other three men and orders them to get out and tells them he will meet them in an hour. He doesn't utter another word until the front door closes behind the three men. "Did you know about this?" he asks Vox.

"No. I had no idea about this until Nova texted me to come pick her up," he answers without skipping a beat.

Thomas looks... worried. I've never seen that look on his face before and I would be lying if I said I wasn't enjoying his torment.

"If this gets out..." Thomas doesn't finish his sentence.

"I know. Which is why we need to put an end to this before it gets out," Vox says, faking concern.

"Are we sure this information is accurate?"

"I thought it was best to bring it to you so you could have Fern validate it." I have no idea who this Fern person is but Thomas seems to know exactly who he is referring to.

"Good thinking," Thomas says.

"Have they made any demands?" Vox asks. Thomas cuts a glance to me and narrows his eyes.

"Get upstairs, you're not to come out of that room until I say." I nod and drop my gaze to the floor as I scurry out of the room and race up the stairs to my room. I lock the door behind me even though I know it won't stop Thomas from getting in here if he wanted to. I try to keep my mind off everything and take a quick shower, then change into my sleep shorts, crop top and pull my hoodie on and climb onto my bed. I tuck my legs under myself just as my phone rings. When I see who is calling, I swipe to answer the call and bring it to my ear.

"Hey," I say.

"Why is my brother's car in your driveway?" Vivian asks.

"He's here to speak to Thomas," I answer quietly.

"Nexus sent me a video a couple of hours ago," she chokes out, her muffled cries spear me right in the chest.

"What video, Vi?" I ask just as I hear the lock turning on my door. I stiffen in anticipation until the door opens. Vox strolls in, carrying something that looks like a pair of tweezers in his hand.

"It's a video of Ezekiel, Vox killed him, Nova!" My eyes widen and Vox's eyes narrow.

"Vivian." At the mention of his sister's name his entire body turns rigid. "I don't think—"

"I know what I saw! He killed him and then forced Archer and Hayze to leave me."

"Do you want me to come over?" Vox shakes his head but I ignore him.

"No. I have a plan and I'm going to make the three of those bastards pay for breaking my heart. Mark my words, Nova, I will make them pay!" Before I can try and talk her out of it she ends the call. The air whooshes out of me and I slump forward, hating that I can't tell her the truth.

"Block her number."

I snap my head up and shoot him a scathing look. "Fuck you."

"Don't push me, witch. Block her number and stay the fuck away from her."

"You can kiss my ass," I snap as I climb off my bed and storm into my closet to change my pants so I can go next door.

Vox, of course, follows after me and slams the door closed behind us. I whirl around ready to hurl insults at him but the fucker shoves me forward and uses his body to pin me in place against the wall. I turn my face to the side so I don't crush my nose.

"The next time you offer me your ass, I'll fuck it."

"You pig! I never offered you shit—"

"The only piggy around here is you, witch." I cringe. "You stay the fuck away from my sister or I tell Thomas this was all your idea." I glare at him from the corner of my eye.

"He would never believe you!" I spit.

"He saw you fucking the very masked man that kidnapped his only child tonight, you really think he would take your word over mine?"

"Get the fuck off me, Vox," I grit out through clenched teeth. He pushes off me but doesn't step back. I turn around hating that I have to brush up against him to do so and have no choice but to crane my neck back to meet his gaze. "Why are you even here?"

"Because Thomas wants you watched in case your *friends* decide to come back."

I snort. "If only he knew who my *friends* really were, huh?" Vox cages me in and places his hands on either side of my head, he's so close I can feel his breath fanning my lips. His pine and cedarwood scent surrounds me and drives me crazy.

"You are the most frustrating fucking person I have ever met."

"Ditto, dick bag."

"I thought I was a coward?" He leans in until his lips ghost over mine. I suck in a ragged breath, hating how my body reacts with need whenever he's near.

"I thought you were a killer as well," I admit.

"And?"

I allow the fight to drain out of me as I stare up at him. I don't hide my feelings from him and allow him to see everything. I'm so sick of playing games and always feeling like I'm being pulled in two different directions, so I decide to risk my pride and my... heart.

CHAPTER FIFTY-TWO

Vox

I wait for her to answer my question, I refuse to give in. I showed her my fucking cards earlier today and still she doubts me!

"I blamed you for Waylen dying." I tense at the mention of that fucker. "I thought you killed Ezekiel. You were horrible to me at school, you flirted with Nicole right in front of me and made me believe I was nothing but some toy you could pull out and play with whenever the urge struck, yet... I still willingly went to you whenever you called." A lone tear streaks down her cheek, drawing a frown to my face.

"What are you saying, witch?"

She reaches out and grips my shirt between her hands. "I'm saying that even though I thought you were pure evil, I still fell for you."

"Sometimes falling is the only way to know where you stand."

"And look where that got me, Vox? I'm a mess, my life is a mess and here we are hating each other because we're both so hurt from the losses we have had to endure. I don't want to fight you, I don't want to watch you with Nicole. Nexus' stupid torture was easier to stomach than seeing that bitch with her hands all over you."

"You sound like a jealous girlfriend, witch, and you're not my girlfriend."

"No, I'm not but I want to be." I suck in a sharp intake of air at her admission. "You can't tell me you don't feel anything for me—"

"For fuck's sake, Nova, you really are stupid, aren't you?" She recoils at my harsh words.

"Vox, please—"

"No!" I snap as I shove away from her and scrub a hand down my face.

"So what? This is it? You just come to me when you want your dick wet and then fuck off and treat me like shit?"

I glare at the little shit. "You are fucking dumb."

"Stop calling me that!"

"Then open your fucking eyes!" I roar. "I've never brought a girl home, taken her to the fucking beach, allowed them near my friends or declared them off limits to anyone! If you were anyone else I would have cut your ass loose and never looked back. Open your fucking eyes, witch."

"They are!" she screams.

"Do you see me standing here?"

Confusion clouds her features. "Yes?"

"Then you should know that I'm here because even though you drive me crazy and I want to strangle you ninety fucking percent of the time, I can't seem to stay the fuck away from your annoying ass. I did all of this for you! I shut my best friends out and broke my sister's heart for *you*!" She gasps and covers her mouth with her hand as tears continue to fall but I'm not done. She forced me to open this can of worms and now she is going to deal with the fall out. "All my life all I have wanted is to make Thomas pay for taking my father from me and Vivian, but then you came along and begged for my help to save your mom. I could have used Nexus' abduction to get Thomas to admit to killing mine and Ez's father but instead I'm using him to get *your* mother back!" She stares up at me with wide eyes and shock splayed across her face. "Now tell me, witch, who is playing games with who because from where I'm standing, the only one who seems to be getting fucked over here is me."

She drops her hand back to her side and just looks at me with an awed look on her face. My chest is rising and falling fast as fuck, I've never said shit like this to anyone before and I don't like it. I fucking hate it, actually, and I hate the fact that this little black-haired witch has power over me, which I never willingly gave her yet she still has the power to fucking destroy everything we have worked for.

She takes a step forward and I turn to stone, part of me wants to brace for her lashing out but another part refuses to give her the satisfaction of knowing she gets under my skin. When she reaches out and grabs my hand, I allow it. She places my palm flat against her chest and covers it with hers.

"Do you feel that?" she asks quietly.

I furrow my brow and nod when I feel her heartbeat against my palm. "Yes."

"I've never allowed anyone inside my heart aside from my mom and Waylen." I bite the inside of my cheek to keep from lashing out about her mentioning that fucker. "Moving here I never expected to find anything aside from misery." She huffs out a breath. "I guess I found that as well but that isn't the point. I never meant to let you in or even wanted it to be truthful with you, but I never stood a chance against you, Vox. Even when I didn't know it was you, a part of me always hoped that you were two horns."

"Why?"

She shrugs and shoots me a small smile. "I was too scared to admit it to myself but I was scared to want you because I was afraid to lose you. I don't trust easily and I sure as hell don't go around screwing random guys with masks."

I smirk. "Then why'd you let *two horns* do it?" I feel like an idiot talking about myself in third person but I get it, she doesn't see me and the mask as the same right now but someday she will.

"He reminded me of *you*."

"That's fucked up, you know that, right?"

A watery laugh escapes her. "So is making me kneel and watching me eat out of a dog bowl but that didn't stop you." I exhale loudly and grip the back of her neck with my free hand, drawing a breathy moan from her when I lean down and rest my forehead against hers.

"If you expect me to say sorry, then you will be waiting a long ass time because I'm not. Everything I did led us to this moment and I wouldn't change shit about how we got here because we are *here*."

"I would change losing my best friend," she says with an edge to her tone.

"But *he* wouldn't have."

Her features contort. "How do you know that?"

"Because if he could change what happened, then that would mean you would have been in that grave. Deny it all you want, witch, but that fucker was in love with you." She begins to shake her head so I push on. "He was, Nova. He loved you more than a friend and you were just too blind to see it. I saw it the night he came to Homecoming and the way he looked at you when I had my arm around you. He hated me instantly because he knew I had what he wanted." Tears pool in her eyes. "He didn't spend his last moments angry, take solace in the fact his last moments were filled with good memories of you and him." Fuck, that shit tastes bitter on my tongue. When tears escape her eyes, I swipe them away with my thumbs.

"How could you know that, Vox?"

"He scratched 4221 RUN into the lid. He chose to warn the love of his life and remind her that he would always love her forever. In my book, that makes him... alright." A sob forces its way out of her. I pull her against me, lock my arms around her and hold her close as cries for the fucker—I mean the guy who she loved as a friend and meant a lot to her.

"I want them to pay for what they have taken from me," she hiccups out into my chest.

"And they will, I'll make sure of it." When her knees give out, I scoop her up and carry her out of the closet and place her on the bed. Her eyes fill with worry when I step back. The panic ebbs when I kick my shoes off and climb in beside her. Fuck the cameras and fuck Thomas, he told me to watch, he never said I couldn't fuck her. I lay on my back and she scoots over to rest her face in the crook of my neck. She wraps an arm around my middle and holds on tight, almost like she is afraid I'll vanish, stupid girl. Was my admission of not being able to stay the fuck away from her not enough?

"Vox?"

"Hmmm?"

"I can't lead the Saints," she whispers.

"I know, you won't have to."

"Vivian wants to lead them." I tense beneath her. "She hasn't outright said it, but... but..."

"Spit it the fuck out, witch!"

"Vox, I think your sister is Nikoa's informant."

Two point five seconds, that's all it takes for me to leap out of her bed and start pulling my shoes on. Nova lunges for me but I step back and shoot her a warning look to back the fuck off.

"Vox—"

"Shut the fuck up, witch!" I snap, then rush out of her room. I can hear the fucking demon chasing after me. It takes me no time to reach my house. I attempt to shove the door open but it's locked. I pull my keys from my pocket and try to unlock it as Nova comes up beside me but the key... doesn't work. "She changed the locks," I mutter, then race around the back of the house. I try the back door but it's locked.

"Vox!" I turn to see Nova climbing through the window. I rush over and help her by gripping her waist and hoisting her through it. I grind my teeth as I wait for her to open the fucking door. The second she does I shove past her and head for Vivian's room, taking the stairs two at a time. I don't knock, I shove her door open ready to lose my fucking shit at her but her room's empty. I look around and find her drawers are open but empty. I check her closet and find the same thing. "Vox?" I turn and find Nova standing by my sister's bed, clutching a piece of paper.

"What?"

"She knew," she whispers. I stalk toward her and snatch the paper from her hands.

Vox,

If you found this then I guess you figured it all out.

I warned you that I would do whatever I had to in order to ensure you and Mom are safe.

I thought I could do that with you and the guys by my side but I was wrong.

They proved their loyalty to you by leaving me. You didn't have to kill Ezekiel though, that was something I didn't see coming.

Nexus won't give up his father, Thomas won't give Kelly up either.

You don't need either of them though, Kelly is at the Botanical Garden rehab center in Michigan. She is under the name Isla Farrow.

I wish we didn't end up here but I guess everyone always expects twins to remain close since they were womb mates, but not us.

You ripped my heart out in order to save your own.

For that, I will never forgive you!

Take her mother and run. The Saints will be dealt with and won't come after you.

Care for Mom and make sure she is safe.

There is no place for any of you here in Hollow Hills anymore, go to college and build a life somewhere else.

The Saints are mine.

The Lordess,
Vivian Tempest.

I stare at the fucking name on the letter for so long my vision turns hazy. It has to be a lie, there is no fucking way...

When would they have had the time?

She's lying, she has to be!

My own best friend wouldn't have stabbed me in the back like this, there is no fucking way unless... was this his way of getting back at me for fucking his sister?

"Are you okay?" I fold the letter and tuck it into the back pocket of my jeans. I keep my gaze focused ahead as I answer her.

"Go home, witch, I got shit to do."

"Vox, don't push me away... not after everything we just shared."

I whirl around on her, the look on my face has her taking a step back. "My fucking sister is gone, Nova!" I roar.

"I know," she mutters.

I narrow my eyes at her. "What did she say to you on the phone?"

"Don't make me betray my friend—"

"You already did by fucking her brother so spill, witch." She flinches at my cold harsh tone.

"She said she has a plan and that she is going to make the three of you pay," she spits out. Before I can press her more, she shoulders past me and rushes out of the room.

My mind is still reeling long after Nova is gone—everything is fucked.

I pull my phone out of my pocket and dial Nikoa's number. He answers on the second ring.

"Vox, I was—"

"Is my sister your informant?" I snap, cutting him off.

I hear him sigh on the other end of the phone. "Yes."

"You are going to pay for this, you son of a bitch," I roar.

CHAPTER FIFTY-THREE

Nova

It's been two weeks since the night Nexus was taken, Vox admitted his feelings for me and Vivian fled.

Since that night I haven't seen or heard from Vox or any of the guys. I've even tried reaching out to Nikoa but my calls are going straight to voicemail. For the first few days I tried to hide out in my room but on the third day Thomas broke down my door and dragged me out of bed by my hair and threatened to dress me himself if I didn't get my ass to school.

School...

Yeah this place fucking sucks.

Without Vox, Ezekiel, Hayze, Archer, Vivian and even Nexus to keep everyone in line, it has been hell. Nicole, Brandy and Pamela have ramped up their torture and I am forced to endure it. Thomas warned me not to step out of line. While I am at school, I have one of his guys following me around everywhere but he never steps in when the others toss things at me or even call out horrible things. When I'm home the guard changes out and a fresh one shows up to remain with me at all times. Thomas is hardly ever home which I am grateful for.

"Nova!" Thomas shouts my name as soon as I enter the house after another fucking dreadful day at Haven Prep. I sigh and head toward his office, even with the door open I still wait and don't enter, I knock. He cuts me a frosty glare. "Get the fuck in here." I do as I'm told and stand before his desk, not assuming that I can sit down.

Nerves begin to get the better of me when he crosses his arms over his chest, leans back in his chair and studies me. It takes everything inside me not to fidget under the pressure of his gaze.

"I'm going to ask you some questions, you answer them truthfully and I will allow you to attend the Saints ball tonight." My eyes widen a fraction before I quickly school my features. Going to that ball means I would get a look inside their operation and finally be able to see the threat in person without having to be told about it.

"Okay."

A devilish smirk touches his thin lips. "Where is Vox Hatchett?"

His question stuns me for a second and the pause in my reply doesn't go unnoticed. His eyes hone in on me, daring me to lie but I have a horrible feeling that if I lie it won't bode well for me.

"I think he left town."

"Why?"

"The night he was last here we went to his house and found a note from his sister. She told him to take their friends and run and never come back." It's not a direct lie, more of a lie by omission.

"Are you lying?" he says in a sickly sweet voice that sends a tremble through me.

I shake my head. "No, Vox has the note with him."

"Why didn't you run?"

I clench my teeth and fight not to show my anger. "You have my mom," I force out.

Thomas laughs but there is no humor to it. "You fucking idiot." I suck in a sharp inhale. "If I had your mother do you think I would need you tailed?"

I draw back in confusion. "I don't follow?"

"That's because you're fucking thick. Your mother is no longer in my possession." My mouth parts on a gasp. "Oh, you didn't know?" he taunts. "You have a guard with you in case you get the bright idea to run. Your mother was the easy choice to keep you in line, but now she is gone I needed to make other arrangements."

"Why are you doing this? I thought you cared about my mom."

He scoffs and waves his hand. "She was a good fuck but nothing more."

'Don't speak about my mom like that!" I snap.

"Watch your fucking tone, bitch." I take some deep breaths to try squash the mounting anger inside me. "Do you know where my son is?"

I shake my head. "No."

"Who are the cunts that took him?"

"The *Filthy Few*," I answer without missing a beat. Just saying their name has courage spurring to life inside me, almost like their name alone could inspire fear in my enemy.

"Who are they?" he growls.

"A favor asked is a debt owed." Thomas' eyes narrow to slits.

"What?"

"They grant a person a favor but a debt is always acquired."

"What was your favor?"

"What makes you think I had one?" I toss back at him.

"We saw you with them and so did my son."

"My favor wasn't granted."

"Why not?"

"Because you're still alive." The words spew out of me before I could stop them. Thomas stands slowly and I know without an ounce of a doubt that I'm going to be in a world of pain if I don't fix this fast. "They wouldn't grant the favor because they know you are the lord of the Saints."

"What do those fucks know about the Haven Saints?"

"Only that the members are untouchable," I lie.

"Yet, they have taken my son."

"He asked a favor of them the night we met with them."

"What was his favor?" he snarls as he places his hands flat on the desk and leans forward.

"He asked them for all the evidence they had of his crime."

"Did he get it?"

"Get what?" I rasp out.

"The fucking proof, you stupid cunt!" he roars, I flinch back a step, only to gasp when I smack into something. I turn and realize it wasn't a something, it was a *someone*. My guard stands there with a sinister look in his eyes. "Answer me!" he bellows. I shriek in fright and quickly turn to face Thomas.

"I don't know," I quickly answer.

"Something isn't adding up here and I can't wait any longer. My plan is now moving forward. Take her to her room and have her ready, she gives you any problems. beat her," Thomas orders his man who grabs my arm in a bruising hold and drags me out of the room. Once inside my room, I'm instructed to shower and dress in the gown hanging on the back of my closet door. I don't even check out the gown before rushing to my bathroom, I have an hour to be ready and look my best before the beating begins so I waste no time.

It doesn't escape my notice that my guard has chosen to remain stationed inside my room, having to pass him in my robe as I enter my closet after my shower while he leers at me. The guy is a fucking creep but I keep quiet and do as I'm told. The silk dress is a dark ruby red, it reminds of the color of blood. The plunging neckline will leave nothing to the imagination, the back is cut lower and stops just above my ass. There's a slit in the front that runs from the top of my thigh to my ankle. One wrong move in this thing and everyone will see Vox's playground peeking out and that doesn't sound like a good time.

I berate myself for thinking about him!

I've done everything I can to keep all thoughts of him from playing out in my mind. It hurts too much. The first week sucked I missed him so much. I thought we were past hurting each other after confessing how we felt for the other, but I was wrong.

I straighten my hair and leave it loose, then choose to go with a two tone smokey eye to make my green eyes pop, my lips painted a deep red. I grab the heels that were left with the dress and begin strapping them on. They wrap around my calves and with the height of the heel and the dress matched with it, I appear taller than I am. I take in the sight of my reflection in the mirror on the back of the door and suck in a sharp intake of air.

I don't look like Nova Quinlin.

No, tonight I am embodying Taylor Tempest and channeling all her feelings because if I channel Nova's, I'll crumble. I lock out all thoughts of my mom, Vox, the guys and Vivian. Tonight, I need to put my game face on and end this shit once and for all. Or, I need to at least try because it's clear I'm on my own now and I need to save myself from this fucking nightmare.

"Watch over me, Way, I need you with me tonight," I whisper as I open the closet door and step out, ready to walk straight into hell if I have to in order to be free of these fuckers.

Sitting next to Thomas in the back of a limo is not how I thought my first ride in one would go. Unlike me who is fighting not to tremble and crumble under the worry of what tonight holds, he sits there nursing a tumbler of Scotch. He's been on the phone most of the drive which I am grateful for, it means he isn't focused on me. I expect to head to the town hall where Vox told me they hold all their meetings, but we drive straight past. I want to ask where we are going but I don't want to rouse suspicion from him so I remain silent and stare out the window.

When we finally pull up out front of a luxurious hotel in the city, I sit up straight and stare out in wonder at all the paparazzi and the many limos lined up to drop off their patrons who are led inside by a maître d. My face is practically pressed against the glass when I see the Governor exit a limo ahead of us.

"You keep your fucking mouth shut when we get in there. You try anything or say anything and I will make sure your friend's death was a fairytale compared to what I will do to you." The mention of Waylen has steel infusing in my veins. I shoot Thomas my best look of indifference.

I plaster a smile on my face and nod my head like a fucking idiot. "Of course. So, do I not mention the fact I am being forced to marry my stepbrother in just over a month?" His reply comes in the form of his hand wrapped around my throat. He's crushing my windpipe, I claw at his suit-covered arm but he doesn't release his hold until black spots start dancing in the corners of my eyes.

When he drops his hold, I drag in lungfuls of air and cough, trying not to choke. "If anything happens to my son, you will be marrying me, you little cunt."

CHAPTER FIFTY-FOUR

Nova

Thomas steps out of the limo when the door is opened for him by one of the valets. I try to control my breathing when he reaches his fat snubby hand back inside for me. I glare at the fucking thing but when my guard grunts at me, I place my hand in his and allow him to drag me out of the car. Cameras flash and I try to shield my face but Thomas hisses at me to drop my arm and smile. I do as I'm told like a good little puppy and plaster a fake as fuck smile on my face, then allow him to lead me through the crowd of reporters and enter the hotel.

The pure opulence of this place is astounding. I have never been inside a hotel reeking of wealth on this magnitude. Chandeliers line the ceilings and servers walk around with silver trays balancing on one hand with flutes of champagne. Thomas snags one for himself and when I reach for one for myself he shoots me a scathing look, so I drop my hand back to my side and plaster my fake ass smile back on my face and allow him to drag me around the room. We stop numerous times so Thomas can speak to people. The men don't take notice of me and that grates on my nerves, clearly they deem women to be beneath them. When Thomas is finally finished having his ass kissed by half the people here, he takes us into a ballroom of sorts.

The place is lined with red velvet chairs that are trimmed with gold, a stage with a raised dais sits at the front of the room. It doesn't escape my notice that this room has no windows and only two points of entry.

"Tonight, you will be announced to the Saints as the future lordess and my son's future bride," he says when he releases me and stalks down the aisle in the middle of the chairs. I look around and take note that we are alone.

"Why?" I ask.

"Because tonight is the only night of the year where I can be challenged for my roll as lord. I have taken every precaution to make sure your masked freaks can't come and ruin everything."

"Why is tonight the only night?"

"It has been this way since The Brotherhood first began. On the thirtieth day of October each year on all Hallows Eve, but as we like to call it the Night Of The Saints, the lord will be subjected to the votes of his peers. I've worked too fucking hard to forge alliances with everyone and gathered enough blackmail material on each of these cunts for some schmuck to ruin it by throwing up red tape on my deals and my son being kidnapped."

"You aren't going to give into their demands are you?" I press. Thomas purses his lips and narrows his eyes. "That's why Nexus hasn't been returned, isn't it?" He says nothing but I know I'm right. "They offered the safe return of your son in exchange for you stepping down, your role as the Lord of the

Haven Saint's means more to you than the life of your only child."

"What makes you think he is my only child?" I reel back in shock.

"You have more children?" Thomas ignores my question as he steps onto the stage and stands behind the gold podium.

"My son made his choice, he chose to be ignorant and refused to grow up and fall into line. He was more concerned about burying his head in any pussy than he was about leading. I thought that would be obvious to you of all people."

"What, why?" I ask incredulously.

"Because, you rejecting him and turning down every advance he made only to fuck his friend sent him over the edge and forced him to make a stupid error. That fucking error put me in the debt of Vox Hatchett."

"You owe Vox?"

Anger clouds his features. "The bastard is the one who disposed of the body of your friend." Hatred coils inside me at the way he speaks about Waylen like he was nothing.

"Why am I here tonight, Thomas? You say you want them to know I am your son's future wife but you have no intention of ever getting your son back."

"Oh, but I know he will come back because I made sure everyone knew I had an announcement they didn't want to miss tonight. I also know those masked freaks have infiltrated my brotherhood and will show themselves tonight to save you."

"Save me?" I repeat.

"Yes, there will be a wedding tonight and when my son doesn't show, I will have your hand." I gasp and step back.

"No!"

"Yes!" he snaps.

"You're still married to my mom!"

"We were divorced three weeks ago. The joys of having

lawyers in The Brotherhood and it's even greater when you have a judge in your pocket to fast track things. You will be the new Mrs. Valerian before the night is out." Horror washes over me as people fill the room. I try to calm myself but it's futile. My whole fucking world is turning on its axis, I can't do this. If I am to marry this son of bitch, then he will have the power to lock me away like he did my mom or worse, he'll be fucking me. I stumble forward and nearly lose my footing when someone knocks into me but an arm snakes out and grips my own, stopping me from falling face first into the carpeted floor.

I snap my head to the side and instantly the chatter around us becomes white noise as I drink in the sight of him wearing a tux. The tattoos on his neck peek out from the collar of his shirt enhancing the dark aura that naturally clings to him. His eyes are hard and his features are pinched but underneath the hard front he is putting on, I can see tension lining his eyes.

"Vox," I breathe his name like my prayer has been answered and this evening's events suddenly feel bearable with him being here. The past two weeks of unanswered calls and messages seem to fade away as I breathe in his intoxicating scent.

"Be ready, witch," he says low enough for only me to hear. He releases my arm and tries to step away but I grip the lapel of his jacket forcing him to stay where he is.

"He's going to make me marry him, I can't marry him, Vox." I watch the mask he wears slip for a moment as he reaches out and cups my cheek. I nuzzle into his touch, pleading with my eyes for him to rescue me from this nightmare.

"I told you, witch, you're mine and I'll never let anyone take you from me no matter what it costs me." The instant he pulls away from me I feel cold and terrified, but there is a slight bubble of hope inside me now that he is here. I look around and scan the growing crowd. I spot Hayze and Archer's dads, each of them give me a slight nod. When Archer and Hayze themselves walk through the grand double doors, the noose I have felt around my neck for the past two weeks begins to loosen. If they are all here then that must mean they have a plan, or at least I hope they have one because I can't go through with marrying that sleezy fuck.

"Brothers, claim a seat so we may begin." I face the podium to see a red-haired man standing there, with two men carrying a throne-looking seat onto the dais and it comes as no surprise when Thomas parks his entitled ass on it. I look around for a spare seat but then Thomas calls my name and beckons me to join him. I can feel the numerous eyes of all the members on me as I make my way toward him, but there is one set of eyes I feel burning into the side of my head and I know without a doubt that it's Vox.

As I lift my leg to climb onto the stage a shadow falls over me. I look up to see it's Hayze. He shoots me a wink and I thank him, his body shielded me from unintentionally flashing the men in the room. I don't miss the way Thomas glares at my friend when I stand beside him.

"Welcome to the Night Of The Saints, my brothers." The red-haired man calls out. I look out at the faces in the crowd and it shocks me to see how many of these faces I have seen in town but it's not just that, it's the many faces of influential men I see that stumps me. "On this night we are here to celebrate the leadership of our lord Thomas Valerian." Everyone begins clapping and it takes all my willpower not to roll my eyes. "As you are aware, this is just a formality before the party can begin, so let us put this old tradition to bed." I frown, not following what is happening. "I doubt there will be any complaints but as the law states, I must ask as the keeper of the rules if there are any grievances against our lord?" I can tell from the tone of his voice that he suspects everyone will remain silent like they clearly have for years.

A smile so full of self-satisfaction stretches across Thomas' face as he says. "I think we can move on, David."

"Of course—"

The man is cut off when Vox stands. All heads snap toward him and gape at him until Hayze, who is three rows behind Vox, follows his lead. Archer follows his friend's lead and stands but he is seated across the room. His and Hayze's dads are the next to stand. Murmurs break out and begin to grow in volume as the red-haired guy looks at Thomas for guidance.

Thomas reaches out and grips my wrist. I wince in pain and bite down on my lip to keep from crying out when he yanks me down to hiss in my ear. "You better not have had anything to do with this, bitch."

"I have no idea what's going on, I swear," I grit out through clenched teeth.

"Well... this is unexpected." Red hair man sounds exasperated and at a loss for words, considering it's his job you would think he would be better equipped for something like this.

"As stated by the code of conduct by The Brotherhood of the Haven Saints, any member with a grievance is given a chance to speak freely and openly in front of The Brotherhood on this night." Shane speaks clearly and firmly causing more murmurs to break out around the room. I scan some of the faces and see varying ranges of outrage, shock, awe and confusion on members' faces.

"Speak your terms," Thomas snaps, his grip on my wrist doesn't lessen and I know for sure that I will have bruises. Shane flicks his gaze to Vox and nods for him to take over. Thomas follows his line of sight and instantly turns rigid. I watch Vox in a sort of trance as he steps forward, without uttering a word or doing a single thing aside from taking a step he has garnered the attention of everyone in the room, his presence alone has a hush falling over the room. It's almost like they can sense they are in the presence of royalty.

"I hereby vote against the accession of Thomas Valerian." Shocked gasps and scoffs of outrage break out but Vox ignores them as he pushes on. "I hereby move to have the lord stripped of his title and exiled from The Brotherhood and Hollow Hills."

Thomas opens his mouth but the keeper of rules beats him to it. "State your terms, brother Hatchett."

"Thomas broke the code of The Brotherhood when he had Ezekiel Tempest's father and my own murdered." Men jump to their feet and begin shouting, while others remain seated with clear shock plastered on their faces. Thomas releases my wrists and pushes to his feet, then stalks toward the edge of the stage.

"You vile bastard—"

Thomas is cut off again by the keeper of rules. "Lord, you know the rules!" he admonishes in a tone that brokers no wiggle room. Thomas' face turns crimson as he tries to mask his disgruntlement but he is failing. I can see the hatred he feels toward Vox. "Everyone, quiet!" Surprise washes over me, I thought the keeper of rules was some soft pushover but clearly I was wrong, the guy takes his job seriously and is definitely a stickler for the rules. All the members slowly claim their seats except for Vox, Hayze, Archer, Shane and Henry, who remain standing but now all converge in the center of the room in front of the stage. Vox's gaze cuts to mine and I see it, the past two weeks he hasn't been around wasn't because he wanted to leave me, he needed this time to gather the proof he needed to end this bullshit with Thomas and set me free.

"I will not stand here and be accused of murder without being able to defend myself, David," Thomas shouts.

"Your title holds no power now that the court has been

brought into session, in these matters I am the one deemed with the highest ranking. Be seated now... please," David the rule keeper snaps back. Thomas purses his lips and marches back to his chair but not before grabbing my arm and forcing me back with him. As if appearing out of nowhere, my guard materializes beside me and grabs my other arm just as Thomas let's go. "State your proof," David asks Vox.

"The coroner's reports were destroyed by Thomas himself."

"Then you have no proof, Vox," David states.

Archer reaches into his tux pocket and pulls out a folded sheet of paper and hands it to Vox. "I said the reports were destroyed but I never said I didn't have another form of proof," Vox states in a cocky tone. "We have an eye witness who is willing to attest to the fact that Thomas paid them to cover up the evidence that their deaths were not caused by a car accident and that they were in fact murdered." I can feel the tension wafting off Thomas in waves, it's clear to me he had thought he was in the clear when Nexus destroyed the files I hid in Vox's garden shed.

"Rule Keeper," Thomas grits out drawing David's attention to him.

"Yes, lord?"

"As per the rule of Saints, now that he has confessed they have a witness I am able to speak." David purses his lips but nods his agreement. Thomas stands with a wicked smirk on his face and looks directly at Vox as he begins to speak. "I vote to have Vox Hatchett removed from the Saints for the murder of Ezekiel Tempest." Members begin to shout and call out at the admission. Thomas stands there smugly thinking he has clearly won this argument but the second a smile touches Vox's face, his bravado begins to falter.

This fucking fool was three steps behind them this time.

CHAPTER FIFTY-FIVE

Vox

The smug cunt's smirk starts to slip as he stares at me, he can see from the look on my face that I have a fucking trump card and I'm about to play it. For the past two weeks the guys and I have done nothing but plot, hunt and try to find everything we needed to take this fucker down. We finally found the witness.

Turns out, Nova was right, Vivian was Nikoa's informant and I have no idea how she managed to find the information she did about the Saints and Nikoa refused to disclose that information as well. The tension between him and I has been stifling but I refused to forgive the fucker for involving my sister in this shit!

"Brothers, quiet down now!" David shouts, it takes a minute for the others to shut the fuck up and sit their asses down before he finally looks at me. "You have been accused of murder—"

"Pretty hard to murder someone when they are still alive, Rule Keeper," I clap back.

"He lies!" Thomas roars. "He showed me a video of the murder he committed."

"And you did not report it, lord?" David is clearly pissed off from the way his jaw is locked and his eyes are blazing with fury.

"I was scared for my life. When a killer walks into your home and shows you proof of a killing, what would you have done? My young daughter was in the house and given that she and that boy had *history*, I worried he would harm her." Thomas is trying to play the role of caring stepfather but it doesn't suit his lying ass.

"Was that before or after you locked my mother up in a rehab center to get me to fall into line?" Thomas whirls around and sends Nova a scathing look that promises pain if she doesn't shut the fuck up.

"You committed your wife?" David asks.

"She was depressed and wanted to harm herself, I had no choice but to intervene, brother, my wife is not well." Thomas tries to act like the decision he made pains him but he is full of shit. David on the other hand seems to eat up the compassion he is faking.

"Rule keeper?" All eyes swing back to Nova.

"Yes?" David asks just as the guard on her side tightens his hold on her arm. forcing her to wince.

"Vox didn't murder my brother—" Nova snaps her mouth shut when people begin talking.

"Your brother?" David pushes.

She nods. "Ezekiel Tempest is my brother." At her admission everyone begins to speak louder, the surprise in all their tones is understandable.

"How is that possible, Nova?" David urges her to speak the truth.

"My name..." She flicks her gaze to me as if searching for strength, I nod telling her to carry on and that I have her back no matter fucking what. "My real name is Taylor Tempest and I am the daughter of Edmund and Olivia. You all believed I died years ago but I didn't. My father sent me away with my Uncle Nikoa, who also faked his death to stay off Thomas' radar. Ezekiel isn't dead, my brother is alive and well."

The doors behind me bang open and someone speaks. "Someone won't be alive for long if they don't get their fucking hands off my sister, though." I shoot Thomas a smile, he's turned pale at the sight of Ezekiel. I can see the cogs in his mind turning over as he tries to piece together everything but he won't. We have been two steps ahead of him this entire time. The guard doesn't release Nova as Ez comes to a stop beside me.

"Brother Tempest, I see you are in fact *not* dead," David grits out and shoots Thomas a glare.

"Of course not, I just had to go away and help gather the proof we needed to take down our murdering lord and have the targets removed from our backs so The Brotherhood would stop hunting us."

"Hunting you?" David asks.

"Yes, ever since Thomas learned that Vox and his step-daughter were dating he has been sending brothers after all of us to get us to flee town. He even used his own son to torment Nova at home and at school, to try and get Vox to break the code of The Brotherhood," Hayze says, earning a look of death from Thomas himself.

"This is all hearsay, if they cannot provide the proof they speak of then let us move on. I will not have my reputation sullied by these ingrates because I refused to allow my daughter to date the likes of him," Thomas snaps.

David mulls over his words for a moment then nods. "Very well, bring your witness forward, brother Vox." I look over my shoulder at Henry and nod, he scurries from the room to retrieve our witness while we all wait. I look at Nova and hate the fear I see in her eyes.

"When this is over, no more running or hiding, I promise, witch." Her brows slant as my words sink in, unshed tears fill her eyes and I have to force myself to remain where I am and not go to her. When gasps sound out around the room, I know Henry has returned with our witness. My ego soars to new heights inside me when Alinta Cash is brought to a halt beside Ez. "I'm sure you all remember brother Alinta, our former medical examiner—" The words have barely left my mouth before a shot rings out and everyone ducks for cover, but not me. I rush the fucking stage and tackle the fucker holding my girl. He manages to punch the right side of my face but I land two quick hits to his ribs. I jump off him and get to Nova. She falls into my arms and clings to me like her life depends on it.

"Detain him!" I hear David roar, then follow his sight across the room to where Principal Daniels stands with his gun outstretched and a deadly smile on his face. I dart my gaze to my boys who are being held back by Henry and Shane. I look at the body lying limp on the floor and everything inside me turns to ice. Alinta was the medical examiner for both mine and Ez's dads. He was the witness to the fucking crimes Thomas committed and now that he is gone... we have nothing.

It's all ruined.

"I am within my rights, he was a deserter!" Daniels argues. The four men who were holding him stop moving and turn to look at David for clarification, but the latter looks uncertain. David waves over the two bookkeepers and then begins speaking in hushed tones, their conversation is animated and their hands are slicing through the air. Nova pulls back and looks up at me. I cup her face between my hands and say fuck it to everyone including my best friend who is watching me with his sister. I kiss her, pouring everything I feel for her into this kiss, telling her without words that I will always come for her and never turn my back.

She's my witch.

"We've reached a decision." I break the kiss and dart my gaze to David, he doesn't look happy which doesn't bode well for us. Thomas is grinding his teeth so hard I pray he breaks them. "I do not agree with the methods used in a public setting such as the one we are in now." He shoots Daniels a withering look. "Cleaning this up is going to be hard!"

"He just murdered a brother in front of all of us," Archer snaps.

"A deserter!" Daniels shouts.

David sighs and runs a hand through his thinning copper hair. "He's right. No matter what purpose he was here to serve, Alinta was in fact a deserter and betrayed The Brotherhood." I look around the room and fight not to scoff at the sight of the high-profiled members on their phones, trying to do damage control. No doubt the reporters outside would have heard the shot, security will be holding them all back but the rumor mill will be circulating.

"What happens to us now?" Nova whispers, drawing my attention back to her.

"Now, you stay the fuck beside me and do exactly as I say. I won't let that cunt get his hands on you again, witch."

"Vox?"

"Yeah?" I answer as I dart my gaze around the room, looking for an exit, I need to get her the fuck out of here.

"Do you have my mom?" The hope in her voice pulls my eyes back to her.

I place a kiss on her forehead and smile. "Yeah, baby, we got her." Relief washes over her and she sags against me.

"He was our witness!" Shane shouts.

"I understand but I cannot change what has been done, if you have no further proof I have no choice..." David lets his sentence trail off and I know for sure we're all fucked. Everything we had was riding on Alinta and his admission. He told us that he was there when Thomas put the bullet in Edmund's head and he was the one to perform the autopsy on both bodies. He may not have seen Thomas kill my father, but the fucker admitted to doing it when he called Alinta.

"Well, now that we have that resolved, brother's, detain these traitors," Thomas bellows. Nova is ripped out of my arms. I fight against the bastards who dare to take my girl from me but the sheer amount of them overpower me and drag me off the stage. It takes two of them to cuff my wrists behind my back and force me to my knees. Archer, Hayze, Ez, Shane and Henry are in the same position as I am before the stage. I dart my head around trying to find Nova and the instant my eyes lock on hers, my chest cracks. Tears stream down her cheeks as two cunts hold her back. Thomas smiles down at us like he won a war. When I feel my pant leg grow wet I look down and growl at the sight of Alinta's blood pooling around me.

"Please, don't hurt them! They are telling the truth—" Nova is silenced when Thomas whirls around and backhands her. All of us fight to get to our feet but can't thanks to the cock suckers holding us down.

"You touch her again and I will slit your son's fucking throat," Ezekiel vows. Thomas whirls around and studies the four of us, running his gaze slowly over our faces as if looking for a clue and that's when it hits me.

He just figured out that we are the *Filthy Few*.

"You lying little cunts!" he roars, then attempts to step toward us but David places a hand on his chest, halting his movements.

"They are to stand trial like the rules state, we are not above our own laws," he snaps.

Thomas ignores the Rule Keeper. "Where is my son?" he roars.

"In hell with his mother," Hayze replies. Ez and Arch chuckle but there is no humor to it, they are just winding Thomas up, hoping to break him.

"They kidnapped my son," he shouts.

"But, do you have proof?" I volley back.

"I never kidnapped my dear friend," Ez says.

"Me either, pretty hard to take the lord's kid when we have been keeping our heads down and staying out of trouble as we were ordered to do," Archer tacks on.

"Vox?" Hayze calls out.

"Yeah?" I answer.

"You don't happen to have the fuckers kid, do ya?" I smirk at the smartass and shake my head.

"Nah, H, I do have the affection of his stepdaughter he was trying to force to marry his son so he could take over as the new lord. And then to force my girl to overturn the decree of Edmund though." At my admission another round of shouts sound out around the room.

"I had no idea who she was!" Thomas snaps. "I want these six taken out of here, we will finish our celebration and then they will be dealt with later—"

The doors behind us bang open again, forcing Thomas to snap his fat mouth closed. I try to look to see who it is but I can't see past the fuckers behind us. I turn to Nova and the wide eyed look on her face has me tensing. Thomas even looks surprised and that doesn't bode well for me.

CHAPTER FIFTY-SIX

Nova

I can't believe my eyes!

She stalks toward us with a swagger only her brother can match—the way she looks is breathtaking. Her hair is tied into a high ponytail, the lady suit she wears hugs her curves perfectly and the fact she doesn't wear a shirt beneath her jacket allows the swell of her breasts to be seen. Men part and allow her past as if they are in a trance. I can see Vox and the other's trying to get a look at who has entered but they don't get a chance to see her until she steps around them. Their wide eyes and unhinged jaws tell me this wasn't part of the plan.

Vivian steps onto the stage and comes to stand beside Thomas, who just stares at her in confusion. She smiles but it's dark and deadly. She reaches into her jacket pocket and pulls out a piece of paper, then leans around Thomas and hands it to David. He unfolds the paper and reads the contents before looking back at Vivian with a stumped expression on his face.

My friend places her index finger against her lips and winks at him before turning back toward the guys. The moment her eyes land on Ezekiel, her features pull taut and I see her stiffen.

"This is not the time for your childish antics, if you have come to say goodbye to your brother then so be it." Thomas sounds like an entitled prick but Vivian doesn't react, she just tsks him and shakes her head.

"For years I lived in fear because I knew what you and your crooked son were capable of." Thomas opens his mouth to argue as members try to flee the room, clearly worried that their privacy is at risk with Vivian being here but she speaks, forcing them all to a halt. "I wouldn't open those doors if I were you!" she taunts, heads snap toward her.

"Why?" a man with a bald head says who I recognize, he's the district attorney!

"Because my security team has orders to stop anyone from leaving this room until I say so."

"Your team?" Thomas scoffs and some men begin to laugh along with their lord but Vivian doesn't take the bait.

"Vivian, get the hell out of here now!" Vox forces out but his twin just shoots him a cold look. Hayze and Archer stare at her with longing in their eyes but not Ezekiel, he hasn't lifted his head to look at her once.

"Yes, my team. Isn't that right, David?" The red-haired man just opens and closes his mouth without being able to utter a single word. "He's clearly in shock given the new information he was given."

"What information? This isn't the time or place for games, little girl—"

"Shut the fuck up, Thomas," Vivian says in a tone I have never heard her use before. "You have had your time and now, you murdering son of a bitch, it's time you paid for your crimes. Thomas Valerian is to be stripped of his title—"

"You have no right to speak here!" Daniels, the stupid asshole, calls out. A few *yeah's* and *that's right* follow his speech.

"Well, it appears we have a few members to remove, David." The man just gapes at Vivian.

Thomas reaches for Vi but she sidesteps him. "Touch her and I'll fucking slaughter you!" Ezekiel roars. Vox darts his gaze between his sister and best friend a few times, a deep groove appears on his face as he tries to piece together what I already knows.

"She is not a member, remove these traitors so we may deal with this security breach," Thomas says, but before the men can touch Vox and the others, Vivian cuts in.

"You are ordered to release them and stand the fuck down," she shouts. Laughter breaks out but my girl doesn't falter.

"Silence!" David screams, finally finding his tongue. "Release them," he barks.

"What?" Thomas shrieks.

"Oh, was it not clear?" Vivian taunts. "You are no longer the lord."

Thomas' eyes narrow to slits. "Those cunts couldn't prove shit, you little bitch."

"Oh, I know that, silly, but you see..." She leans in closer to Thomas and stage whispers. "I can."

"You... what?" Vivi ignores Thomas as she addresses the room.

"My name is Vivian Tempest..." At the mention of her last name shock ripples through the room. "I am the daughter of your former lord and the daughter-in-law of Edmund Tempest." I watch as Vox turns to Ez, who has his shoulders hunched and head down. Archer and Hayze can't take their eyes off Vivian but the range of emotions on their faces spears me, the dominant one is pain. All the noise around us begins to fade to nothing as I stare at Vox, his features are etched in betrayal as he stares up at his sister.

"Why?" his quietly whispered word holds so much weight to it.

"Because, Brother, you tried to play dad when I begged you not to. I told you I needed my brother to trust me and you didn't. You chose to keep me in the dark and left me with no choice but to take matters into my own hands."

"By marrying my best-fucking-friend, Vivian?" he roars.

"Yes, Vox! I married Ezekiel because *I* am the one with a greater claim to be lordess than your girlfriend. I am the one who is willing to sacrifice what I need to in order to rule over this brotherhood and grant you the freedom you never granted me!" my friend screams.

"There is no proof of this—"

David cuts Thomas off. "I have the proof right here," he says and holds up the marriage license for all to see. Hayze and Archer both turn away, refusing to see the proof. My heart aches for them. Vox may not want to admit it to himself, but his three best friends are in love with his sister and this stunt she pulled to save us all will put a huge divide between the four of them.

Thomas snatches the paper from David and reads it over, and the moment it sinks in you see it. His face pales and he darts his gaze around the room, looking for the support of his peers but they seem to find their shoes more interesting. "She hasn't even been blooded in." He's grasping now.

"And she won't be," Ezekiel snarls as he pushes to his feet, this time no one stops him. He lifts his head and looks right at Thomas. "As the laws of the Saints state, since the new laws were bound into the old by Virgil Hatchett, the husband of the lordess may take any and all punishment *or* being blooded in for the wife." Thomas' features pull taut, he knows he's losing and he can't stomach it. "I choose to walk the line for my *wife*." Hearing him call her that has me sucking in a ragged breath, when Vivian and I discussed her marrying Ez as a way out I never thought they would actually do it.

"As the lordess, I hereby agree to my *husband's* terms," Vivian says but doesn't even look at Ezekiel. "I know the rules of The Brotherhood better than most of you. I am no tyrant like Thomas Valerian."

"They kidnapped my son!"

Vivian faces Thomas and stares at him with such hatred it robs me of air. "No, your son was set free right after I wrote a letter to Alexander Denver himself, letting him know what your son had done. Nexus' days are numbered. But don't worry, you will have plenty of time to find him and try to save his ass." Vivian flicks her gaze to David. "I declare Thomas Valerian as a traitor to The Brotherhood and hereby banish him." Thomas gasps and stumbles back a step.

"You can't do that," the former lord shouts.

"Actually, she can!" David says in a firm tone. "As the law states, you have twenty-four hours to leave town, in seventy-two hours The Brotherhood will begin to hunt you, should the lordess sanction it."

Thomas looks around the room but no one comes to his aide. "Don't worry Thomas, you won't be on your own. Alec Daniels, you are now banished." Principal Daniels gapes up at Vivian. Before he can even protest she swings her gaze back to her brother and the other three. "As the new lordess of the Haven Saints, I, Vivian Tempest, banish Archer Malik, Hayze Draven, Vox Hatchett and Ezekiel Tempest." All the guys are on their feet now and shouting at Vivian to rescind her decree, but she ignores them and slowly turns to face me. "Unhand her." The two guards release me and I rub my arms, trying to regain circulation in them as I stare into the eyes of my friend I once thought I knew.

"You can't send them away," I say quietly.

Her eyes soften as she comes closer to me. "Believe it or not, Nova. I'm doing this for them, this way they are free of the burden of the Saints. I'm not the monster you and them are thinking me to be, you can't leave the Saints once you are in."

My brows raise as it dawns on me. "You took over so you could have access to everything to end the Saints because they couldn't find the proof, you knew by taking over you had the power to set them free." A sad smile touches her lips but she doesn't confirm or deny my claim.

She reaches out and pulls me into a hug. "They broke my heart, Nova. A woman's scorn is worse than the depths of hell." She then pulls back and turns to face David. "They are to be gone within twenty-fours, if they return to Hollow Hills they will be met with a traitor's death."

"You gonna walk the line then *wife* since I am now banished?" Ezekiel sneers, Vivian still won't look at him.

Instead she keeps her eyes on David as she speaks. "My husband will be blooded in tonight, if his injuries are life threatening then he will be airlifted to a Washington DC hospital where he can recover and be far, *far* away from here." David nods his understanding as Vi turns to Vox. "Don't ever come back here, you are no longer welcome in my town or my brotherhood." Anger and pain war in his eyes but he keeps his mouth shut as she addresses the room. "Thomas and Alec are free to be hunted. Vox, Ezekiel, Hayze and Archer are not. Any member caught hunting them outside of Hollow Hills will be met with swift punishment. Uncuff them and set them free."

I dart forward and grip Vivian's arm. "Please, don't do this, it will kill them all to leave you behind," I beg.

"They all left me, Nova, they made their choice. I understood Vox wanting to protect you because he loves you." I gasp but she pushes on. "The others had a chance to prove to me that I was their first choice, they chose wrong and they will live with that."

"Vivian, they love you. I know they do but Vox is their best friend—"

"If Waylen forced you to choose between him or Vox, who would you have chosen?" I drop my hand back to my side and snap my mouth closed. "Exactly. You love my brother and would have chosen him over Waylen. I'm not choosing any of them because for the first time in my life, I am choosing me and I am going to make the most of this situation. I'm not weak like they think I am. I'm smart and I have been playing this game behind their backs for years but they were too ignorant to see that."

"Vivian." She and I both turn toward Vox as he steps toward us. David and the two guards who held me back close in on her, the shock ripples across his face. For the first time ever his little sister no longer needs his protection and that shit is going to wage a war inside him.

"Go, brother. I won't offer you a second chance," she says firmly.

He may not be wearing his mask but I see how a shadow falls over him and he turns into the monster I first fell for. "This isn't over," is all he says before turning to me and holding out his hand. I hesitate looking between him and his sister.

"You loving him is what gave him the courage to break free of the prison he put himself in, don't turn your back on him now when it counts the most," Vivi says low enough for only me and three guys around her to hear.

"I won't turn my back on you," I promise.

She smiles and nods. "I'm counting on that." I walk to Vox

and place my hand in his. I expect him to wait for the others before leaving but I was wrong. As we walk out of the grand hall with Thomas' pleas for the members to reconsider following us, I breathe and for the first time in months I feel like everything is going to be okay.

CHAPTER FIFTY-SEVEN

Vox

It's been five weeks since my sister turned my world upside down. I've been struggling to come to terms with it but Nova has been by my side the entire time. When we walked out of that fucking hotel, I told her to pick anywhere in the world she wanted to go but of course, she fucking chose Washington DC, knowing her brother would end up here. Unlike her, I haven't gone to see him once since he was flown here. They put him in a coma to help reduce the swelling on his brain but still, I never visited him.

I can't.

"Vox, can you come down here?" Kelly calls out. I push back from my desk and decide to finish my college applications later. I know she has been trying to organize a surprise birthday for Nova and no matter how many times she tells her mother she doesn't want anything big she refuses to listen. I enter the kitchen of our new home and freeze. Nova, Kelly, my mom and

I all got a house together. Our moms thought it best to keep us close. My mom has flown back once to see Vivian, but my sister kicked her out and refused to allow her to stay. That shit has been hard for my mom to deal with but it's not the sight of them that has me stumped.

"Nova is going to kill you both," I say. My mom waves me off while Kelly snorts. For someone who was drugged and locked away in a padded room she seems to be recovering well, her resilience reminds me of her daughter.

"Hello, Vox," Olivia says and I shoot her a loaded look and shake my head before turning back to my mom.

"If you think I have a bad fucking temper then you clearly haven't seen my girlfriend go the fuck off." The three of them all smile as if Nova's temper is something to be proud of, it fucking isn't! She is a crazy fuck that likes to punch me in the balls if I snap at her. I fight to keep the smirk from splaying across my face, my little witch has a wild side and I fucking love it when she loses her shit because that's when we fuck hard and I get to wear the mask. She loves it when I fuck her with my mask on.

"Ezekiel is being released from the hospital today," Olivia says. I grit my teeth.

"Vox, Olivia has purchased the house next door," my mom admits.

"Good, Nova and I are moving out," I snarl, then turn to leave but Kelly rushes forward and grips my arm, halting my escape.

"Vox?" I reluctantly meet her gaze and the sliver of fear I see etched into her eyes gives me pause. "I know this is hard for you, it's hard for me too. Nunu has no idea Olivia is moving in next door."

"You haven't told her?" I hiss.

She shakes her head. "She spends so much time at the

hospital getting to know her brother and avoiding me." I sigh, Nova has been avoiding Kelly but it isn't because she is angry at her for not telling her she was adopted, it's because she feels like shit about what happened to Kelly because of her.

"She doesn't hate you."

"I know my daughter, Vox, she has a quick temper and doesn't trust often or even love easily. The fact you have been given more chances than any proves she may one day forgive me." I spy Olivia out of the corner of my eye, dropping her gaze to the floor.

"Kelly, she isn't mad at you she's mad at herself."

She reels back. "Why the hell is she mad at herself?"

I smile sadly down at her and place my hands on her shoulders. "She blames herself for what happened to you. She thinks all of this is her fault, you being taken and Waylen dying." She shakes her head, trying to deny my words but she knows deep inside what I say is the truth. "She is still recovering from *his* death." It still grates on my nerves that she pines after that little fuck but I get it, he was her best friend.

The night Nikoa took her, I went back and exhumed his body, paid off the right people and had him cremated. I gave her the urn the night we fled. She broke down in tears and clutched that thing for hours until I pried it out of her grasp and took her mind off things by making her ride my face until she came screaming my name.

The tattoo of his name and the numbers don't bother me much anymore since she has a VH tattooed behind her ear. Seeing my initials inked on her forever always gets my pulse racing, knowing she is branded as mine forever.

"What do we do, son?" my mom asks.

"That should be a question you ask me, not him." We all swing around to see my witch standing in the entryway, clearly she came in through the back door. I step away from her mom and raise my hands.

"I had nothing to do with this." She rolls her eyes, I've learned the less I piss her off the more access I get to that pussy and fuck me, living with her and being able to fuck her whenever I want is drug I'll never give up.

"Nunu, this isn't what you think." Her mom tries to calm her but it's useless.

"Mom, stop." Olvia flinches but still won't lift her gaze. "I know you think that by bringing her here it will help me but it won't." Kelly deflates. "I love you for trying but right now, all I want to focus on is getting Ez out of the hospital, getting into college with Vox, and then figuring out how to help Vivian."

Olivia finally lifts her tear-filled gaze and looks at Nova. "Will you ever have time in your life for me?" she asks brokenly. The second her shoulders droop, I cross the room and wrap my arm around her. I won't let her face this shit on her own, we have already worked out that trying to do things on our own only hurts us more, so we promised to always stay together no matter what. Nova looks up at me. I nod encouragingly, telling her without words that I'll always support her like she has done with me even before we fled.

"I won't lie to you, a part of me wants to know you." Mom grips Olivia's hand when she sobs. "But, another part is still so angry and confused." Tears flow down Liv's cheeks as she nods.

"I understand," she chokes out, Nova sighs and pulls out of my hold and makes her way toward Olivia then grabs her free hand.

"I'd like it if you could just... I don't know, maybe hang around more and let me wrap my head around *this*."

Hope fills Liv's eyes as she nods. "I'd really like that," she whispers.

"I know you gave birth to me but I need you to respect the

fact that Kelly is my mother and always will be, can you do that?" I'm so fucking proud of my girl. Kelly places her hand over her heart and fights back tears of her own. I know she has been scared that Nova would leave her for her birth mom and my girl just put those worries to bed for her.

Liv pulls her hand free of my moms and tentatively reaches out to cup my girls cheek. "Kelly is your mother in every sense of that word, all I want is a chance to know *you*. I swear I will never pressure you for more or want more than you are willing to give me, just please don't shut me out," she cries. Nova smacks her hands away and pulls her in for a hug. Liv breaks down in her arms, my mom and Kelly both begin to cry at the sight. The sight brings a smile to my face but pain starts to bloom in my chest.

I'm happy for Nova getting everything she deserves, but a huge part of me mourns for the loss of my twin. I'm used to being the one to save her and protect her from anyone and everything, but this time she took control from me and sent us packing. I haven't spoken to Ez, Hayze or Arch since that night. Henry and Shane are still members so they go between Hollow Hills and wherever the hell they have decided to live. I stopped keeping tabs on Archer and Hayze, they broke my trust that night. Their masks fell and showed me everything I was too blind to see, my three best friends have been in love with my sister for years.

"Hey." I shake my head to clear my thoughts and focus on my witch who stands here smiling up at me while our moms go back to planning her birthday.

"You caved, didn't you?"

She huffs and nods. "Your mom pulled the whole my daughter got married without me, this would make me happy." I laugh which earns a growl from my girl.

"She is going to keep using that line against you, witch."

"I know!" she snaps. "You have to talk to her because she even mentioned me wearing a dress and heels and I am not okay with that." My pulse quickens as I remember the dress she wore weeks ago.

"You look fucking sexy in dresses. Do you still have that one from the Night Of The Saints?" Her brows furrow until she takes in the look on my face.

"Vox, no," she hisses. "Our moms are home and they'll hear us," she whisper shouts.

"Sick of biting pillows, huh?" She snorts out a laugh and smacks me on the chest.

"Ya think?" I wrap my arms around her and pull her against me, loving how she melts into me.

"I love you, witch."

"I love you too."

"Do you love me enough to blow me while I drive us to a hotel?" Her answering laughter has a smile tugging at my lips when she pulls back and nods.

"Pack the mask, I want two horns fucking me tonight." She rushes out of the room to go pack while I stand here staring after her.

When I met her at the bonfire that first night, I never expected to fall in love with the witch who cast a spell over me. I never thought I would ever choose anyone over my sister or my brothers, but here I am, crazily in love with a witch.

I look down at my wrist and smile at my new ink.

4221 *Witch.*

I know this is something totally new for me and not my usual mafia but I have been dying to write Vox and the Filthy Few for so long that I just had to do it

I hope you love Vox and Nova as much as I do because they are fucking life and such a freaking dream to write.

Have no fear, book 2, ***FOREVER FILTHY*** will be in your kindles really soon!

ACKNOWLEDGMENTS

Marcus, it has been a pleasure being able to bully you and forcing you to submit to me so I could get into the mindset for Vox. You playing Nova in our role play helped me so much, baby, thank you!

My children, you both are my reason for existing, my strength and my backbone. I wouldn't be where I am or who I am without you both. Thank you for always being my biggest fans and loving me like you do.

Leah, you help me make all of this possible and work with my crazy ass schedule. I can't say thank you enough for being an amazing friend but also the world's best designer.

Jaye Pratt, I'm only putting you in here so you don't fuck up my formatting, ya mole.

My alpha's, Debbie, Sarah, Clare and Erin, you ladies have stood by me through so much shit and so many plan changes. I can't thank you enough for believing in me and always pushing me to strive for more. I love you!

My beta & ARC army girls, thank you beautiful souls so fucking much for always sticking by me and trusting me to mend those hearts that I break.

My dad, you are my rock and my whole fucking world. I love you more than you will ever know, old man, and the fact you support me through all of this crazy as fuck journey means more than you will know.

Lizz, my friend, here we go on another journey! I know I

must annoy the shit out of you with all these new genres and tropes but you are such a champ and never complain. Thank you so much for coming on another adventure with me.

My darling dark delicious readers, thank you again for following me and reading each of these books. I know I break your hearts and leave you mad when I end a book on a cliffy but I love that you trust me enough to heal those hearts and come back for more, I love you.

Sam xxx

ALSO BY SAMANTHA BARRETT

<u>Mafia Romance</u>

<u>Murdoch Mafia Series</u>

Played By The Bishop

Tormented By The King

Tortured By The Knight

Tempted By The Queen

Turned By The Pawn

Ruined By The Rook

<u>Murdoch Mafia Novella</u>

Stalemate

<u>Memento Mori Series</u>

Reign Of Royal

Broken By Sin

In Havoc Lays Chaos

<u>Godfathers of the night</u>

London has Fallen

<u>Damned By His Angel</u>

<u>Re Della Strada</u>

Shattered Soul

Fractured Heart

<u>Tainted Essence</u>

<u>**Fairytales With A Twist**</u>

Condemned Beast

Secret Society/ Bully

<u>Filthy Few</u>

Forever Filthy

Filthiest Of Them All

<u>**Sports Romance**</u>

Playing For Keeps

Offside

Touchdown

End Game

Hail Mary

Blindside

<u>**RH Sports**</u>

Hate Us Like You Mean It

Love Me Like You Mean It

<u>**Paranormal Romance**</u>

<u>**The Dream Series**</u>

A Beautiful Dream

A Twisted Fate

A Beautiful Nightmare

Redemption

Anarchy

Brutal Savages

Savage Lies

Brutal Truth

Savage Beast

Brutal Beauty

ABOUT THE AUTHOR

Samantha Barrett is originally from Auckland, New Zealand but now lives in Brisbane, Australia.

Sam writes all things dirty, dark and delicious with a side of twisted mind fuck.

She is a lover of all things red flags and an anti-hero is a must.